THE DISGRACED MARTYR TRILOGY

BOOK III

THE LADY'S CHAMPION

THE LADY'S CHAMPION

M. F. SULLIVAN

Come to me once more, and abate my torment;
Take the bitter care from my mind, and give me
All I long for; Lady, in all my battles
Fight as my comrade.

—Sappho, "Ode to Aphrodite"

I

The Flight of the Governor

Would Governor Theodore del Medico go down fighting? Probably not. Look at him there, his chestnut head sometimes bobbing with shrill laughter above the crowd. Oblivious to eyes on him outside of those he paid, befriended, or paid to befriend. Teddy had no more chance of escaping fate than he did of noticing that teashaded individual who studied him from across the bustling restaurant of eight hundred customers.

Also oblivious to this predatory focus, though it came from a member of his own table, the Franco-Japanese professor of English whose name was René Ichigawa overexplained to a dreadlocked woman called Gethsemane, "You can hardly find good dim sum in the United Front anymore. It's only going to get rarer if the military keeps rounding up humans on the West Coast! Lucky thing New Elsinore has a strong base of hardworking, hard-eating immigrants who've been here too long to throw out. That's true of the whole nation, though. We can thank all those second-generation migrants. Especially after the war with Mexico! The coastal regions lost a lot of families when the militias were called to account in the aftermath, and most of them had already sent their healthy young men south to die in the war against—" He coughed a little and cracked his neck in the direction of their silent friend, who spared him a resentful glance even as René carried on.

"What the Midwest doesn't understand is it's *all* immigrants now. West Coast, and East. They don't understand that when they let their government act this way, it's their neighbors being taken. And they always seem to forget that their families were immigrants, too!" The pedantic Berkley professor, caught up in his own rant, turned to the disguised individual—the only other UF expat at the table. "When was the last time you met an *actual* Native American?"

"Why doesn't the Hierophant have his men shut these places down, or use them to trap big quantities of humans? Especially if they're focused on Asian populations." This was asked by René's cousin Tenchi, who sat another small plate atop his growing pile. "Seems like an irresistible lure to me!"

Their disguised member studied the portly man, mustache quivering into a frown. The place was packed, and loud, and Governor Theodore, along with anybody who cared, was far across the ballroom-size restaurant—but did they need to reference the Holy Father? Any mention perked ears in a martyr hangout. In a human establishment? Bad idea.

Gethsemane sensed this displeasure and refilled the teacup of that most important, silent member as René explained, "I'm sure he does use a few of them as traps, but he has to leave *some* for the legitimate populace. People would be incensed if he just started shutting down Asian businesses. Overnight change hasn't been tried since the Black Night. There's a complicated licensing procedure— *Xièxiè.*" Sweet relief! The professor paused to show off another of his many languages by addressing the businesslike, hairnetted woman who swept up their plates. Her partner in crime, stopping her cart, interjected, "Pork *schaomai*? Chicken *schaomai*? Shrimp dumpling? Chicken feet?"

"Ooh," sang Tenchi, pointing at the cart, "chicken feet, please!"

"Can we hurry this up," the mustached member said with a sharp glance over the shades. Tenchi turned guilty doe eyes on their leader as the waitress, uncaring for any inter-table conflict, further stamped the well-marked card and thrust a small basket of fried chicken parts before her fellow human. Organic chicken, too—none of the lab-grown stuff. This place could have been raided on that ground alone if they didn't have all the proper licenses.

"There's no reason to rush," said René, reaching over for one of the greasy feet. This, he stuck into his mouth to suck tiny bones free of flesh even as he spoke. Gethsemane did not bother hiding her disgust as the professor continued through smacking lips, "Our—appointment's having a good time, so we'd ought to, too. I mean, look at him over there!"

Too true. Theodore's piercing laughter was audible beyond almost a thousand patrons chatting and laughing in a wider variety of languages than one could learn in a single human lifetime. Every time he laughed, so did his party of twelve, and so did a few of the guards hovering around him. Guards, hah. What kind of martyr needed a security detail?

One who had been warned what might happen to him. The mustached infiltrator sipped tea filled by Gethsemane and watched the Governor of the United Front yuck along with his cronies. Tenchi insisted, "See, dim sum is great because everyone can have fun! Chicken foot?" He offered the basket to their quietest member, for whom Gethsemane took on the burden of shaking her head.

"No: we're"—she waved a finger between herself and the mustached individual—"trying to be ready for action."

"We'll be ready to act, *Mom*," said René with a sigh and a roll of his eyes. "Anyway, we're serving good purpose. How weird would it be if it was just a couple of intense-looking *gweilos*, not eating and not having fun, staring at the Governor from across the room? Alarm bells."

"That's a racist thing to say, René," chided Tenchi.

"Oh, so you know that one! I was going to say 'a couple of intense-looking *gaijin*,' but you'd obviously know and complain about that one."

Gethsemane shared a withering glance with her shaded friend at the cousins' instant argument. She seemed just about to ask something of her martyr companion when Theodore, with a hand upon the shoulder of a friend, pushed himself up from his table. The disguised member of their party stood in the same instant, unnoticed in a packed room where people perpetually stood up and sat down while jabbering waitresses pushed fragrant carts to and fro. This near-invisible figure cut a calm, smooth path in the direction of the bathrooms where Theodore had gone with a guard.

René sucked a tooth. "Guess we'd ought to settle up."

The dimly lit men's room already seemed something out of a horror movie, with limitless stalls and too few people coming in and out to jive with the size of the restaurant. The guard who had accompanied Theodore like a parent taking his child to go potty stood daydreaming as five men urinated and left without washing their hands. More filtered in one by one. Teddy, naturally, had shut himself in the stall to pee, and yammered to his guard even as he did.

"Don't you just love how they know me here," the Governor prattled over the sound of his urine. Having tarried a second too long and drawn a glance from the guard, their observer hurried into a stall near Theodore's. The preening martyr continued. "The best thing we did this year was move my offices from San Valentino to New Elsinore. It's nice to be appreciated by the citizens—nice when people, even humans, can see reason. Those San Valentino people, it's just too close to home for them! I had a waitress actually thank me tonight for the work we've done in getting the riffraff out of our country. Would you believe that? Scrap the bit about 'this last year'—it was the best decision I've *ever* made, moving the capital from San Valentino to New Elsinore. And the people agree. The West Coast has gotten all the attention since Trimalchio had his paranoid little power trip before Dominia's control, while out East it's nothing but neglect! No more, I say."

With his toilet's flush, Theodore zipped his trousers. The hidden observer, pulse raising, prepared to be known. A second flush followed the Governor's and their doors swung open in time. "It's sort of like being a celebrity. *Really* a celebrity, instead of just being part of a famous Family. Like I've finally done something that I can be proud—"

This pair of flushes covered the sound of the electrodart gun's safety being released, but the guard was still quick to see the pistol and shout, "Sir," over the sound of Theodore's mindless blather. Sad to say, it didn't muffle Teddy's feminine shriek to see the drug-laced electric dart crumple his bull of a security man upon the bathroom floor. Always too bad to leave a fellow martyr in that condition, but it would be bloody chaos whatever happened. The General needed get the drop on the violence now, before the violence got the drop on her.

"Frederico," the Governor shrieked. The two unlucky humans in the bathroom reacted with shrill cries and swift departures while the single most useless member of the Holy Family reeled toward his assailant and recognized her with prompt horror.

"You! Oh, no—oh, no, no!"

"Just shut up, Teddy." Dominia jammed the pistol into his back and, with every shift of the toy in her hand, missed her relic .44 Magnum. Lost for over a year! Poor old friend. It would send a sterner message than the non-lethal weapon she held. "We're not going to hurt you, but I would appreciate it if you were compliant."

"You just shot a man in front of me, you're sticking a gun in my back, and you say you're not going to hurt me?" As voices rose outside the bathroom, tears formed in the corners of the Governor's eyes. "And I've told you a thousand times, my name is 'Theo'!"

She was going to throw up. "Will you please come along with me, 'Theo,' so I don't have to pistol-whip you unconscious and carry your sorry ass all the way to Jerusalem?"

"*Jerusalem!* I can't—" Eyes darting to the door, Teddy laughed in an unsteady pitch and said, "I can't go to *Jerusalem*, Dominia, please! It's a *war* zone! Father's been bombing it looking for *you!* Haven't his forces been actively clearing neighborhoods? I can't go there—not with you! He'll think I'm—*with* you, you know. What do you want from me? What good could I possibly be to you?"

"Are you in there, sir?" called a guard outside the door. "Are you alive?"

"Yes," the sweaty Governor responded, prompted by the jut of Dominia's gun in his back. "Yes, yes, I'm here! I'm alive, I'm fine. Frederico—"

"I am the General Dominia di Mephitoli, and I have incapacitated your man. If you do not relieve yourselves of your weapons and make way for me to exit with the Governor, I will kill him, and you will all be similarly disposed of." After a second of thought, she added some old-fashioned Bitch of Europa menace. "I don't wish to do that to your families."

The men outside were silent. Theodore gave a soppy exhalation, his hands held high on either side of his head. "She really means it. She means it, please, I can't die! Or—God, she could shoot me in the spine. I could be paralyzed! Please, believe her!"

For God's sake! The idiot didn't know the difference between a regular gun and an electrodart gun. It was as if he weren't a martyr—couldn't be healed from even a real shot in the spine with a little surgery and a month of physical therapy! Were these not dire circumstances, she might have given him a clout of annoyance, both for Theodore's nature (could one even damage the spine of a spineless man?) and his belief that Dominia would hurt him. Almost seventy years they'd known each other, and still he bought this. Perhaps that was her issue: why the world had listed her public enemy number one for a year. Her acting was just too good.

If not hers, certainly the Hierophant's, whom she was braced to see at any second. When would he appear, chiding and clucking like the old hen he was? She had to get this show on the road.

"I need my brother for a chat," Dominia said through the door. "Let us leave and no further harm will come to anyone."

Silence resounded until another scream rose from the dining room, and Dominia tried to stifle her annoyance. "What is it?" asked Theodore. Outside, shots were fired. "What's going on?"

"Just wait." She closed her eyes and tried to remember how many times this plan was discussed with her so-called assistants. How many times was René told to leave the building as soon as she got up? How many times had he said, "Sure, I'll take Tenchi right out"? How many times did she stress a minimal body count to Gethsemane? She didn't want any conflict, let alone bodies, whether dead or incapacitated.

Dominia glanced at Frederico. Not that she was one to criticize on that account.

After a few seconds' squabbling and more silence filled by the whimpering of Teddy, the bathroom door opened. She relaxed to see blood-spattered Gethsemane, calmer than the Dominia. "I apologize. Things did not go according to plan."

"So I heard." The General caught Theodore by the collar of his sports coat to drag him out of the bathroom. "The police will be here any minute, along with the military and special investigators."

The difference in the room was a startling one, because those eight hundred people had flooded for the exits and still pushed through. Fewer were left than one might anticipate. This ease of escape was largely due to the kind waitresses, who had parked their carts along the perimeter of the massive room before fishing weapons from their aprons. Only a handful of customers yet hovered near the escapee-crowded doors to film the proceedings from their phones, watches, or DIOX-Is. At this stage in her "career", Dominia felt the recordings were a good thing, and allowed them to proceed.

There was a lot to be shown. It was impossible to know who had made the first move—René, or one of the Red Market girls masquerading as waitresses, or maybe Gethsemane—but the end result was that the security detail hired to protect Theodore now amounted to a pile of corpses. The Lady's women did not abide by the General's new nonlethal preference. Theodore's personal friends had fled at the first sign of trouble, judging by the bodies, but the Governor still uttered a womanly shriek on seeing the remains of his staff.

"Please shut up." The picture of barely repressed impatience, the General thrust her little brother toward her human lieutenant as though holding a kitten. "The collar, now, quickly."

Before Theodore could ask, "What collar?" Gethsemane slapped the device around his neck. As Dominia tugged the fabric of his shirt to obscure the silver choker of the brand that once she'd worn, herself, her human companion bowed toward the nearest waitress.

"You've done good work tonight," said Gethsemane, and the General nodded her superficial agreement as the waitress put her gun back into her apron, then fixed the plastic of her gloves.

"Anything for the Lady," answered the woman, who waved her colleagues into the removal of the bodies. "And anything to get rid of that boneheaded bigot of a Governor."

"Weren't you the one who thanked me?" asked pathetic Theodore. He'd barely finished his question before the General and the earthbound nymph were dragging him through the vacated kitchen still so cluttered with utensils, in-progress dumplings, hanging ducks, and half-carved chickens that it was no less of a tahgmahr to navigate than were it full of chefs. Dominia filtered out her brother's whining tone of voice with a well-practiced ear and turned her attention toward Gethsemane.

"What's the ETA to the tarmac?"

"Twenty minutes."

"Followed by an easy, breezy three-hour flight into the middle of the Atlantic. Why aren't we just making the whole trip that way, again?"

"Flying?" asked queasy Theodore as the women continued speaking.

"It's true that the E4 is risky, but if we can make it to the extraction point, our journey will be cut in half."

"And if we can't, or if it fails, we might crash into the sea instead of flying straight across, which would have been the easiest and safest." The wonders of prototype technology developed by the labs of terrorist organizations! "It's not so much that we're hitting a moving target as it is that our target is an incredibly small and specific region of space-time. There's too much opportunity to be shot down between takeoff and extraction. I appreciate that they couldn't smuggle the components for a whole new teleporter into the Front, and that the jet is ultimately faster than walking the Void the whole way, but I still don't like using the E4 to maybe, possibly, show up in Tangiers just to take the teleporter to Jerusalem."

No talk of teleporters and interdimensional jets could transmute Teddy's terror to curiosity. "I can't go on a plane, Dominia, please."

"You have voiced this opinion many times, General, but it is nonetheless the option we have taken. Strictly speaking, your Father could dispatch drones anywhere across the globe to strike our plane. No flight route is truly safe."

"But some are safer than others. And some would keep us from risking you." She studied the beautiful human, who kept her gentle features turned ever forward, and resembled only in her boldness that nymph with which the Lady's servant was linked. "If the E4 doesn't fail, and doesn't crash, it could end up stuck in the Ergosphere."

"Then I will fight to remain myself, while knowing my sacrifice was a worthy one."

The Governor hadn't finished. "I understand you want to take me to Jerusalem, but can't we—take a ship, maybe, like a respectable—"

Theodore shrieked as the General zapped him into silence with the collar. A mild jolt, more effective than a slap in the head. Not as satisfying, though. "I want you to make sure," she continued to Gethsemane as they hauled the somewhat-subdued Governor up several flights of stairs, "that you have everything ready for an emergency situation. The last disaster I need is to lose you, René, Tenchi, or Farhad for a reason as stupid as Teddy."

"Now you're hurting my feelings."

Dominia at last addressed her brother as she hauled him out to the roof of the building, where Farhad landed their helicopter in the available space: a mere lifeboat to the greater E4-GL3 unit that would sweep them to a safer mass of land than the Americas. "I just mean to say that it's not like we're going to kill you, so losing my—friend's life in exchange for yours is out of the question." Even now, even here, she was hesitant to refer to Gethsemane as her "girlfriend," and this earned one long blink from the stoic woman who otherwise continued her visual sweep of the area.

"Aren't my men's lives worth as much as your friends'? Is that a helicopter? Oh, Father! Father, where are you! You said you'd always protect me."

Now he was crying. Dominia tried not to roll her eyes as the grown man (over a hundred years old, combining human and martyr years!) hyperventilated when the simple flying machine touched the ground with the delicate bounce of a ballerina. "Just give him the pill now," she urged.

As Gethsemane rooted through the handbag in her elbow, the red-eyed Governor gulped out the words, "What pill?"

"It's not a hard-core tranquilizer," Dominia insisted. Gethsemane lifted the little pink speck and said in her placid tone, "This will help you, Governor, to relax on the trip."

Even before his sister clarified, "Just one of DIOX's stupid benzos," Theodore had already snatched the pill from her fingers with a hilariously birdlike movement of his lips. He now swallowed it dry, eyes leaping between the faces of the two women and the open flanks of the helicopter to which he was again pulled.

"Please, let me sit between you."

"That is perhaps a good idea," agreed Gethsemane. Dominia watched from the corner of her expressionless eyes as the woman climbed into the helicopter, her kaleidoscopic dress shifting against her mocha thighs, and Theodore drew from both the General's line of sight and the human's tone all he needed to know.

"Oh, no, you two aren't— *Dominia*, didn't you learn your lesson last time? Humans and martyrs mingling only leads to trouble!"

"You were a human who mingled with martyrs," Dominia reminded him, climbing into the helicopter and shouting among the din of the propeller and distant scream of sirens, "*Asre'*," as though Farhad did not know to hurry up perfectly well, himself. As the women strapped themselves in and helped the fumbling Governor, the General continued, "Anyway, it's none of your business with whom I'm doing what."

"It's simply wrong," insisted the stuffy man. "I mean, meeting a girl in a club for a night is one thing! But somebody you *know*? Long-term? A human!" Dominia tried to stifle another eye roll and succeeded only because Gethsemane leaned forward as though to kiss her. The General presented her face as such, expecting an opportunity to horrify her younger brother, when in fact Gethsemane's aim was to whip the (surprisingly well-adhered) mustache from its place upon Dominia's upper lip. While the General first swore, then sneezed, both Theodore and Farhad laughed, and Gethsemane settled, smirking, back into her seat. With a resentful glance for her brother, the General drew the gun that was not, strictly speaking, hers, and swapped it for a more fatal model in the back of the pilot's seat.

"I didn't mean to laugh," the Governor whined, but Dominia glanced at the ceiling of the helicopter.

"It's not for you, dingus." From the breast pocket of her suit coat, the General removed the pocket scope and screwed it on; Gethsemane did the same, and Dominia tried to find some sanity in the girl now that she'd worked out her feelings. "Tenchi and René left as planned?"

"The second they could—they were the first ones out."

"What happened in the restaurant, then?"

"I did not see how it was possible for the engagement to end without you swarmed, General. I made a call."

Annoyed for her defiance as much as for the rapid-pace Spanish prayers uttered by her brother, Dominia gave in to her urge to clout Theodore. "Stop doing that. You'll draw the Lamb's attention, assuming it isn't here already."

"That's what I'm *hoping* for! Oh, God, don't let me die!"

"You've already died once," remarked Gethsemane.

"That was terrifying, too, but not like this. And I don't want to die again, forever! Dominia, please."

He clutched her sleeve at more or less the same instant Farhad said, "Drones," so yet again, his plea was ignored. Both women leaned from the helicopter, guns steadied upon their forearms and heads lowered to their scopes to fire into the well-illuminated night of the United Front's new capital. The police and military reaction had been quicker than Dominia had hoped, but the incessant glow of New Elsinore— Longacre Square, an exposed, neon heart—illuminated her targets better than even her abandoned DIOX-I could have. With but two natural eyes, her shot was phenomenal. Gethsemane, not so trained as her companion, still made quick work of a pair of drones while Theodore sobbed, "I barely even know what's going on."

There wasn't much to know. Wasn't it all self-evident? He was being kidnapped. The police and the military were trying to rescue him. The General might have explained it to him had they more time, but she was just as happy—or happier—to wait for the benzo to loosen him up. Until then, her focus was on meeting the automatic fire of the nearing drones with patient shots that sent them reeling into the miasma of lights. Every glance she took after them made Dominia sick—not for heights, but for memories of living in the Front. She had another home, now. Her own city. She had to remind herself.

Of course, what was that self she reminded? She had felt herself less and less over the past year. This would not have been so alarming had it not produced a physiological effect: a kind of numbness in her cheeks and hands, as though she was literally not feeling herself. It was hard, most nights, to admit the source of this oppression, but seeing New Elsinore with its black Hudson river and glittering lights reminded her of San Valentino, reminded her of happier times she dare not imagine, and dredged the feeling again.

This numb sensation reached its apex when the Lady suggested it was time to respond to the Hierophant's year-long campaign of bombing and pussyfooting troops into territories around the perimeter of Jerusalem by less cowardly, more direct action: the acquisition of Theodore, who, deserving of the position or not, was one of the most prominent martyrs in the world.

A few weeks back, in the center of war-torn Israel, the General had accepted an invitation to come to the Lady's chambers, to watch Her recline upon a chaise lounge and speak without moving Her lips in a sound that was the voice of each woman who had hosted the Lady. Each woman, including the present avatar, Miki Soto. The chambers rested within Jerusalem's library, ever growing to keep out the Hierophant in the tradition of the ill-fated statues from the Cairo gardens. He could not bear to bomb a collection of rare and beautiful books; therefore, the corner of Jerusalem with that vast library was the safest spot in town. The immediate increasing of the library's size had been Dominia's idea, and had become an overarching background task across the first several months of her leadership. The following year, as UF and Europa troops pressed into Jerusalem and began, block by block, building by building, to clear the city of Hunters, Dominia worked harder for the Lady than she ever had for the Hierophant. Yet when called to that silken, windowless palace room in the center of the library, it was not for praise of her efforts.

You have not been doing your work lately, the Lady observed when she arrived.

The boggling General tried to laugh, but the noise caught in her throat. "I built you a palace in one month and filled it with books to keep my Father away. I've disciplined the men who once abused your women and whipped both groups into a genuine army. My Father's troops have pressed into the city using my presence as an excuse but that same presence keeps our men and women fighting ferociously to push him back. We've begun to experiment with the Ergosphere teleporters, and I've trained men in the navigation of the Void—Farhad and three of his pilots, and Gethsemane, although she's a little…unstable."

That is not the work We mean.

It was only in intuition that she took the Lady's meaning. "You want me to drop the defense and move against my Father."

The time is coming that an aggressive move shall need to be made—and sooner, rather than later. Do you know, Dominia, what happens in the Front even now? Do you think those humans can withstand his tyranny any longer than Jerusalem can brace itself against his bombs?

Yes, she knew what was happening in the Front. A mass culling. Concentration camps. Deportation, and not back to the respective home countries of those immigrants detained: deportation to city centers across the UF and Europa, for fuss-free food. Not that Europa was any less inclined to violence than usual. Since Dominia had risen to control of the Hunters, Israel had voted to exit the union of the Middle States in a double-edged sword of a move that gave the General and the Lady control of the holy country, but that also left that same state without any official political allies. The Hierophant immediately massed troops in Turkey, increased military presence in Cyprus, and received permission from the Middle States to rid their region of his terrorist daughter. The rest of the world, terrified of being accused of terrorist collusion, strove to mind its own business. Therefore, outside of cells in Tangiers and Tunis, Jerusalem was alone, and so were the Front's immigrant humans.

Your Father must be shown that what is happening in the Front is not acceptable. The Lady sat up, feet tucked beneath Her body as Her Bearer hurried forward with a tea tray of fruits. As she fed the obligingly parting lips of the physical avatar and the Lady's voice carried on, Dominia thought of a ventriloquist routine she'd once been forced to endure for Lavinia's feast night. *A disruption must occur if we are to catch his attention without declaring outright war, and the largest and most vocal disruption would be the deposition of Theodore.*

Though at first she laughed to think of her idiot brother and the useless figurehead he was, her laughter faded, for the Lady hadn't sense of humor enough to make a joke. And besides, the General could see the reason in it.

There was, after all, something Dominia wanted to ask him.

You wish to ask why your Father really keeps Lavinia locked in her high tower? Always probing where She wasn't welcome. Dominia narrowed her eyes in the then familiar displeasure of having one's thoughts read without permission. *As if you do not know already.*

"The best reason to get Theodore is for his own good. He's a simp. There so a member of the Family can be present on the continent until the Hierophant finds a replacement child for me."

Or he wins you back.

"He's not going to win me back."

Are you so sure? What if he were to offer you Cassandra. Would you believe him?

Oh! The dashed hopes! The broken promises. The wound was not as fresh as it once was, but its grasping by the cruel hands of sadistic outsiders enflamed her pain worse than ever. "We've been through this," said the General. "He can't give her to me. You can't. Nobody can."

You can. When all of this is over, and you have crushed your Father—when martyrs are under control, and given the grace of God's forgiveness—then you will have Cassandra again.

After the travesty of the Lady's ascension ceremony, Dominia wasn't interested in raising her hopes. Time to focus on a more relevant topic. "I don't think this is a good idea. The liability here is extremely high."

But, as you said, you are doing Theodore a kindness. Extricating him from an evil life. He could serve much purpose in this place, were he to find the glamour in compassion that he finds in your Father's way. But there is something important you wish to know from him, as you have only just thought.

"Something you and Lazarus know," said Dominia darkly. The Lady's chewing lips smiled.

Something you already know, deep down inside. Deeper down than that secret you keep from even yourself.

The General listened to the antique clock upon the nearby writing desk, counting its ticks in time with her breath. At ten, she unclenched the jaw she had not realized to be clenched, and asked, "Are we finished here?"

You will call to order a meeting and suggest as We have. Lazarus is more inclined to agree with ideas from your mouth.

"Why is that?"

Because—the Lady had chuckled on Dominia's way out the door—*he knows it is not worth the trouble of arguing with you.*

Perhaps not. One could go so far as to say that the General was the sort of person to make up her mind before she'd gotten all the facts, but that was because it was a wandering mind that fell easily into the flow of her work—a flow only shattered by Gethsemane's high cry above Theodore's smug, "Serves you right," and Dominia's matching, "Are you all right?"

"My arm." The human grit her teeth, looking over the side of the helicopter. "And my gun."

"Stay back, Gethsemane. Theodore, shut up. I'm still thinking about shooting you."

Blessedly, he obeyed, and in the relative silence, Farhad was as slick a pilot as Dominia was a shot. Between those two factors, by the time the police copters were in reasonable pursuit, the path was almost entirely clear of drones. Good thing, too. With one foot wedged beneath her seat and the other crammed beneath that of the pilot, the General released her seat belt to clamber into the empty passenger's position in the cockpit. Theodore scoffed. "Are you insane?"

"Why don't you get useful by making your tie into a tourniquet." Dominia shifted the massive, emergency-only weapon Farhad had been forced to jam between the console and the headrest. As her hands wrapped around the cold metal of its grips, she frowned. Would it always come to this? Would she never be able to escape this awful cycle of blood? Once, she'd hoped to make the late dentist, Tobias Akachi, her final human kill. With the Hierophant's troops pressing upon her city and opening conflict with her soldiers, she had not taken long to dash her own hopes, like a former smoker who slipped back into the habit after a bad day at work. All smokers knew it was a whole lot harder to quit than it was to just keep lighting cigarettes.

As the weapon lifted into the Governor's view, he shrieked. "Is that a rocket launcher?"

"I thought it was a ridiculous suggestion, too." After checking the sights of the weapon, Dominia looped one arm through a strap mounted in the chopper's ceiling and leaned into the open air. "But after I thought about it for a while, well…it was sort of inevitable that this kind of scenario would emerge."

"But a *rocket* launcher?"

"Technically"—Gethsemane raised her voice over the aiming system's occasional beeps—"it is a rocket-propelled grenade launcher."

"Oh, *pardonnez-moi*. Sorry I don't know the difference." He seemed set to go on until a burst of laughter rose from him. He had noticed the necklace swinging around Gethsemane's neck and said while tying off the gunshot wound, "I know that diamond."

Dominia took her shot at that announcement, as a loudspeaker-augmented voice called, "Terrorist Dominia di Mephitoli, deliver the Governor to safety and stand down." This unfortunate timing made it seem like the police chopper's explosion into thunder and smoke and death was causal—a direct result of its attempts at hostage negotiation, rather than of her idiot brother's decision to bring up her dead wife at that very second. Good luck trying to get the government to empathize with family problems at a time like this.

Gethsemane repeated her only response. "It is my duty to bear Cassandra for the General."

Theodore looked between them, now sufficiently drugged to be more aghast at Dominia's relationship choices than at being in a helicopter—or the center of a very serious shoot-out. With a smug wave of hands before his arrogantly shut eyes, Teddy said, "Dominia, I hate to say it, but you've reached a new low. I mean, not just climbing right back into bed with humans, but making her wear your dead wife? Like a necklace! You weirdo. Was that an anniversary gift?"

"It is my duty," repeated the Bearer, who reached under her seat with her good arm to pass Dominia another grenade. Irritated, Theodore leaned forward to address the pilot.

"Do you speak?" he asked, and Gethsemane answered for him, "To you, Arabic." This elicited an eye roll from the Governor while the General, still half outside the chopper, ducked within to evade a spray of gunfire from a dedicated drone. This straggler was caught in the explosion that claimed the second police chopper, whose propellers burst in a brilliant marigold blaze before the machine wheeled into the sprawling park below.

"Do you speak Arabic?" the Governor deigned to ask the human beside him. When she nodded, he asked, "I don't suppose you'd tell him I'm rich, and that I'll give him a lot of money and immunity if he lands this thing and lets me out?"

"And why would I tell him that?"

"Because I'll give you money, too?"

"What good is money?" As the remaining police helicopters stood down, Gethsemane made no move to tear her eyes away. A wise choice. The General, like a dog guarding the lambs, remained stone-faced outside the helicopter until they were well away from the island and able to pull north: the shortest route out of the city's jurisdiction on the way to the landing strip. The Water Bearer continued to speak over the eerie whip of the copter through the wind. "What good is money to anyone? The world is ending soon. This one, anyway. It will be very different. Money as it is will not matter anymore. Not to your people. Not to me."

Poor Teddy looked as if he didn't quite know just what to make of that one, but of course, there was no one with time to explain it to him. For her part, the General was preoccupied. It wasn't the relative ease with which they had accomplished their goal that made Dominia suspicious. It was that they'd accomplished it at all. The Ichigawas would be checking in at the government's airport using false Halcyon accounts just a mere twenty minutes after she'd fed her younger brother that pill—only lightly tainted with Lazarus's blood, in case of emergency.

Because Dominia was almost certain that there would be an emergency.

So be it. She could handle it. Given danger came in the ideal circumstances, anyway—but it would have been nice to have a little foreknowledge. Then she really could have handled anything. That was the rub, wasn't it? Especially when all your enemies, and even some of your less helpful (read: absent) friends, had been through this great, sordid game before. Sure, Lazarus was on her side, but he was so old and dry about it, and so withdrawn about what information he actually knew, that it was impossible to count him as wholly trustworthy.

For instance: at no point in the past year had he once acknowledged the alarming frequency with which Dominia heard the voice of the Hierophant in her head. Worse, he had never addressed the external visitations. Like now, as her Father spoke unseen from the periphery of her restored right eye, approximately he would sit were he in the passenger's position beside Farhad:

"It is woefully difficult to know who to trust in a world such as this."

"Such as yours," she muttered, taking advantage of her position outside the vehicle, amid the relentless beating of the rotor, to address her pursuer aloud. It was an alarming habit in which she engaged with increasing frequency since the traumatic *hieros gamos* of the Lady and Lazarus, so far away in Cairo. A bad habit, talking to him out loud, but she couldn't shake it.

"At least you know to whom this world belongs." His innocent retort led her to look sharply into the seat and find it empty but for the assault rifle. Good. That couldn't always be said of the apparition that haunted her, almost nightly, since its first appearance in the *tanque* from Cairo to Jerusalem. Sometimes her Father's specter remained when she looked at it, staring her down in defiant mockery of her impotence to accomplish its dismissal.

Gethsemane, noting Dominia's eyes narrowed for something unseen, leaned past fretful Theodore. "Are you all right, General?"

"Fine," she lied, reaching into the helicopter for the sniper rifle as, from below, similar fire shattered the air. "Stay back, stay small, and keep the Governor from getting shot. You think what I did to your man in that bathroom was bad, Teddy?" With a glance for her terrified baby brother, Dominia leaned out once again and flicked on the high-powered scope. "Just imagine what Cicero would do to these guys for accidentally killing you."

II

In the Event of a Water Landing

After their escape from New Elsinore airspace, Dominia was almost looking forward to their second flight. How sad, what passed for pleasure these nights! It was only natural, though, that she would be grateful for even two or three hours of smooth sailing. For one agonizing year, the General had no rest.

Just over a year, truth be told. If she was counting the months, it was something in the order of fifteen. Maybe eighteen. It was certainly that if one counted Cassandra's death as the starting gun of her bloody, tiring race. And race she had, from San Valentino to the isle of Japan, and then aboard a train to Kabul, to Cairo—and finally, against her will, to the Israeli desert. She'd remained there since, her race contained to a constant cycle around Jerusalem's vast cityscape. Here to build goodwill among Abrahamian humans by making public appearances in Catholic Mass and allowing the global broadcast of her hasty confirmation as a nice big "fuck you" to the Holy Martyr Church; there to investigate the ruins of a drone bombing or to join a unit in pushing back UF troops; off to her labs for a chat with the researchers about her needs from them; and somehow in the course of that same day, she'd find time to throw on a suit and scrape and bow before the Knesset, the legislative body of the state of Israel, to beg that what meager legitimate funds the isolated nation had left be given to her army.

Yeah. She had her army. Her homophobic, misogynistic, trash heap of a terrorist cell had straightened out somewhat when forced by honor or religious principle to follow a lesbian and work with a cabal of prostitutes—but only somewhat. Some still forgot their rank when (in)convenient, and the seven-something-foot martyr had more than once resorted to screaming in their human faces until grown men wept like children at her feet or, in the harder examples, deserted the unit.

Such improvements gave no satisfaction. Praise the saints there were people like Farhad, reasonable men who assembled around her within a fortnight of her control. In a technical way, this de facto jurisdiction extended to Hunter-plagued Israeli cities such as Tel Aviv, which had clung to its glamorous atmosphere in the face of its country's violence so that it resembled a kind of coastal Vegas. So she'd heard, anyway. She hadn't seen it, herself. No time. If not for the doings of her few loyal men, she would have been awake day and night, falling ever more behind. Israel—yes, even Tel Aviv—had been bombed no fewer than thirty times since November of 1997 AL, with Jerusalem in particular facing a brutal thirteen drone strikes. And amid it all, there was the Lady, pouring money into the ad campaign that had encouraged Israeli voters to separate from their union and leave themselves undefended.

Dominia could understand why She'd done this. It made Israel really theirs—gave them license to do with it, its funds, and its military as was needed, once she discerned the depths of Tobias's tendrils through the Hunter network. The scientists were her best friends in this endeavor of sorting out the power structure, and the scientists revealed to her that even Tobias had suppressed certain avenues of research which the General was more than happy to encourage. The former leader's reasoning had been that plenty of research on transport, medicine, and other constructive avenues was done elsewhere. He wanted to focus on what he believed to be "military technology."

This was the problem when you let a dentist into a military profession. It took a soldier to understand that all technology was military technology. Take, for instance, a secret project stowed from even the dentist's prying eyes: the E4-GL3, or the Electromagnetic Glider.

Why everything had to resolve to an animal name with these people, Dominia was never sure, but by God she loved those eagles. Filled a woman with real patriotic vigor just to see its oblong shape beneath the tarp as their helicopter set upon the dirt of the abandoned Vermont farm they'd enlisted for the job. There had been a lot of trepidation about whether the thing would be able to make it into the Front at all, but the trans-dimensional vehicle was designed for discretion while flying above Earth. It was, first and foremost, a stealth plane. It just so happened that this stealth plane could, upon entering a safe range, rip through space-time to the point in the future where it would find itself on its associated landing pad, safe and sound. And a stealth plane that allowed its passengers to skip half their journey, well—that was military technology if ever she'd heard of it. It might not have been able to carry a hundred of Tobias's anti-martyr exoskeleton ALIF-8s, but it would get their asses out of Dodge, and that was all she wanted. Even Teddy, still clamoring on about this horror and that indignity, was silenced into a few seconds of astonishment when Farhad whipped the tarp from the cigar-shaped object.

"Is that a—is that a *UFO*, Dominia?"

"It can't be unidentified if it's ours," she said, masterfully refraining from tacking on an unnecessary (but deserved) "dipshit."

"But I mean—it *looks* like a spaceship, like something out of a video game or a—"

"Because it's a new model. It's just a plane like any other at the end of the day."

Easier to let him think as much, anyway. It was, in a way, just a plane; but it was a plane designed to navigate inner space, rather than outer space. The graphene-coated surface of the E4 was, strictly speaking, a series of two-dimensional objects stacked to resemble a three-dimensional object; this trans-dimensional quality of graphene was the only thing that helped Dominia grasp why the substance was so conductive to the teleporter technology developed from the blood of Lazarus, because the deeper she stumbled into the scientific explanations of what was happening when electrons and their little friends were introduced to the material, the thicker the dictionary she needed to grab. At certain moments, she wished she'd gone into engineering or medicine rather than the military, but the medical field wasn't exactly thriving with geniuses. Look at Teddy. Everybody had their own specialized knowledge, she supposed. She couldn't tell you just how it was the damn plane functioned; but she could tell you how to use that same device to annihilate a nation, or entertain her brother into passivity. Once in his cushy seat with another pill, a collar-free neck, and a book to ignore, his tune changed so much he didn't even notice Farhad's smooth takeoff.

"Well this isn't so *bad*," Teddy said—repeatedly said, because the drug dampened one's ability to form memories. "I don't know why I was in such a fuss over flying before. I mean, it's perfectly *normal* to most people. Isn't it, Dominia?"

Lifting her cheek from her hand and her gaze from the window, the General said, "I used to commute via plane almost every week during the height of our military involvement in the 3900s, going from war theater to the proper Front to Father's castle and then off again. Even later in the special forces, and then again during the South American Conflict, it seemed like I was always flying. I was glad when I was promoted to Governess—some time to rest. If you can find it, anyway."

"Tell me about it! I've never been busier in all my life. No wonder you ran off!" The lazy man waved his hands with his flippant mischaracterization of Dominia's motivations, distracted while she made sly eye contact with Gethsemane. "I admit, some days I've thought about doing…well, not the *same* thing, obviously, but—I just don't understand what's happened with you, Dominia." His stream of consciousness having become less a train than a car driven by a drunk weaving in and out traffic, Teddy crossed his arms and settled back into one of six seats in the tiny cabin. "Even if you can't take the pressure, that's no reason to run off and join terrorists."

"I'm leading the terrorist organization now. Or its splinter, anyway." Offense over his half-baked aspersions would be laughable as experiencing hurt feelings on the pitiless observations of a toddler. She squinted to study the night through her reflection against the window. "Terrorism, like terror, is a state of mind."

And it was one that sought, increasingly, to envelop her. As a sad result of her control and Israel's exit from their union, the Middle States were more chaotic than ever—and the same could be said not just of its official governing body but its unofficial one. With the former crux of the Hunters now led by one of the organization's avowed enemies, those many satellites and associate terrorist cells had refused to acknowledge her fealty and insisted on splitting off. As expected. There were now such groups as the New Hunters, the True Hunters, the Old Hunters…the list went on, and those were only the English tags the news channels gave them. If she got into the Arabic, Turkish, and even the Farsi variations, there seemed little point in even calling them a unified organization. The General had not given a name to her units, but she supposed it was no more proper to call them Hunters than it was for the world to call her a terrorist.

That was what she preferred to tell herself, at any rate. As the cabin lights stubbornly cast her ghostly reflection against the dark glass, she avoided eye contact with that phantom double as though in shame. She refused the title of "terrorist" and struggled to maintain her old identity, but the truth was that the person ready for Saint Valentinian in the McLintock farmhouse just over a year before was a very different woman from the one sitting in a plane flown by a Hunter with the kidnapped Governor beside her. That difference was clearer all the time, but there were plenty of similarities, too: there she was again in the restaurant bathroom, blistered to hear sounds of violence outside a mere fifteen minutes before she would blow up a helicopter with an RPG; the gunpowder smell of rotten eggs in her nose, and the abrupt end of thousands of screams in those thousand battles of hers; the abrupt end to the scream of Benedict, Cassandra's beloved husband, when he was just some kid sent to war. It was not a death like a military death, not even a death like the slaughtering of a human for food—although it had been in defense, in a way. Her mind could never escape it, never justify it. Could never justify its own care, either, since she knew she only cared because of his relation to Cassandra. This deepened the shame.

Nothing in her life was meant to be this way. To feel this way. Dominia could not help but think that she'd never been meant to experience that feeling of grief or guilt. A martyr should have been stronger. The General was supposed to be stronger than this—supposed to be a cold, dark child of the Lord with no pity in her heart for human cattle. She was supposed to be successful, clever, and well-liked by her people. She was supposed to be happy. Supposed to, supposed to… Dominia was increasingly far from the self she once expected to find within her body. Increasingly far from the person she had thought herself to be, who she now realized never existed. It was that self that she expected others to see, and that self that inspired constant surprise in its owner by its perpetual absence.

Should it have surprised her? She had given up everything she wanted. Everything. Her eyes skipped across to Gethsemane—more specifically, the diamond lying in the dark notch of the woman's clavicle—then away as she found the matter-bound naiad studied her with great eyes painted in colors like seawater that recalled those crashing waves, the cerulean sky, the taste of salt on sweet Cassandra's impossibly plush lips.

Sorrow! Yes, there was that pang of sorrow, that ache of shame, that terrific tragedy of the question that kept Dominia self-occupying night and day—working until she was so exhausted she could not but collapse into a sleep where she was still not wholly safe. For some reason, when the blood of Lazarus altered her body such that mere human food and a bit of sunshine left her healthier than the false protein ever had, she'd expected the swap she forced in her sleeping schedule to alter her dreams. If that couldn't cure her tahgmahrs—*nightmares*, she had to remember to call them now—nothing could.

And clearly, nothing could. Still, she once a week awoke with the crinkle of her wife's eye plastered across her mind. Then she would be forced to ask that question she so carefully avoided in waking: *Have I given you up?* In such moments, she was shamed by her own reluctance to think on her wife. Was that the real way in which Dominia gave her up—neglect of thought? Was it wrong to avoid thoughts of Cassandra? Was it wrong to *hate* thinking of her? Was it wrong to nonetheless pray every morning and every night that she would someday hold this world's, that world's, any world's, most beautiful soul again in her own arms?

Dosed though he was, Theodore must have noticed the brief direction of Dominia's melancholy gaze. "Why are you *wearing* that?" he pressed of Gethsemane again. "And don't give me this nonsense about some duty."

"But that is the reason, Governor." With her left hand primly in her lap and her wounded right arm elevated with a makeshift sling provided by Theo's torn coat, the human insisted, "I fear a matter like this is beyond your understanding."

Teddy laughed, too doped for offense. Dominia shrugged. "She's right. I don't pretend to understand it, either."

"Yes," agreed the girl, her tone still matter-of-fact. "Such issues are also beyond the General's understanding. At least, at this point in linear time."

"Why do you speak like a robot? 'At this point in linear time.'" He pronounced the words like an early text-to-speech computer program, stilted and artificial. "If you hadn't bled right in front of me, I'd have thought you were some kind of android."

"Sometimes," admitted the Gethsemane with a sad chuckle, "I feel like one. Perhaps it is all the time I've spent working in the Red Market." She glanced at Dominia, who had heard her story just once, in the dark, after the human thought the martyr wouldn't remember. A miserable story, about human trafficking, and how cruel people could be to kids. The General respected how hard it had been to talk about it by not talking about it, herself, and the human obviously appreciated it. For the sake of the present audience and her desire to leave her early history unspoken, Gethsemane summed it up in simple terms. "One does not require rescue from the Lady and Her formal organization of working women as early as I did, then go on to maintain much desire to experience emotion."

"Running around with prostitutes, terrorists, murderers, and thieves." The sighing Governor shook his holier-than-thou head in a habit learned from the Hierophant. "What kind of person does that?"

Unbuckling her seat belt, Gethsemane said, "In all fairness, sir, I have not worked in that capacity since I was twenty-one, when the Bearer awoke within me and I was promoted from the fold into my true role. However, this is another matter I would not expect you to understand. Forgive me, General." The tall woman stooped to move forward, but her dreads still brushed the weapon-stuffed overhead compartment. "I believe Farhad will require company to ensure he is fully awake."

"Now that's a horrible thought." Teddy giggled. As Gethsemane disappeared up the aisle of the plane and shut herself up with the pilot, the kidnapped Governor returned his attention to both his present sister, and his absent one. "Doesn't she remind you of Lavinia? I mean, not in looks, obviously. Maybe it's her devotion to you, her loyalty. I can't put my finger on it."

"I hadn't thought of it," lied Dominia, having noted the comparison on more than one occasion—interestingly, not to Gethsemane's earthly form, but to her nymph counterpart. Leave it to Teddy to see through the dreadlocks. "You should know better than anyone."

Not even drugs could keep the sour note from his voice. "What's that supposed to mean?"

Innocently, Dominia said, "Only that you've spent so much time with her," as though not referring to a notoriously un-secret romantic crush widely regarded as—for lack of a more exact term—kind of creepy, considering Theodore, as a human, had been the doctor assigned to monitor the welfare of the comatose Lavinia when she was roughly twelve. Nothing untoward had happened, of course. At the time, his feelings for her had been strictly those of a caregiver. But since Lavinia awoke into the spotlight, and Theodore was rewarded for his efforts with that oft-cherished "gift" of a late-life martyring, it had been impossible for the public to miss the puppyish mannerisms Teddy adopted in his closest sister's presence. Certainly, they had been impossible for Dominia to miss. But the crush was such a harmless and pathetic thing, and Lavinia was so oblivious to it, well—sad to say poor Theodore's unrequited love was more of an international running gag than the great romantic saga he envisioned.

"Of course I've spent time with her." His tone was as defensive as the hunch of his shoulders. "More time than you, anyway. Always too busy off in the Front to come home and visit your Family. We went four—no, five, years without seeing you that one time." Yes, a fine couple of years. Not as fine as the Canadian vacation, and not motivated by anger so much as apathy, but still very fine, very fine. She tuned back into his rant. "Poor Lavinia misses you, she looks up to you! Do you know how disappointed she's been?"

"When was the last time you visited Europa since taking the ship to America?"

"Don't try to make this about me." His voice mounted that womanly pitch that inspired, as always, Dominia's smirk. "I don't deserve any criticism. You're the one doing the kidnapping here!"

"That's right. And you're giving me a lot of lip for somebody who's been kidnapped."

"Well, I just don't see the point! You'll only succeed in getting Father all riled up. Cicero, at least. He cares more—well, not about *me*, but about normalcy."

"That's what I'm hoping. And I'm also hoping you're more valuable than you let on."

"Of course I'm *valuable*. But what's helped you see the light?"

"Other than the fact that our Father martyred you instead of killing you when Lavinia woke up, call it…the inspiration of a friend."

As much as Tobias Akachi could be called a friend. Of course, Teddy tried to point out, "You know everything that I do. More. This job is the first time Father's trusted me to so much as take out the garbage."

Gritting her teeth at the horrendous euphemism for genocide that she herself had been guilty of using many times over (then wondering if she overthought it and he really meant "take out the garbage," which was possible), Dominia inhaled. "But I think you *do* know something, Te—Theo. Something you're not telling. Why did he martyr you? Why not just kill you?"

"Well *that's* very kind of you, Dominia."

"That's how *he* thinks, not me. I'm trying to think like him. If I were him, and knew all the things he knew, I would only martyr you if you were of use to me. I would only martyr anyone if they were of use to me."

As she herself had been martyred for a strange and abstract destiny: for purposes of ending the modern world, and granting victory to one side or the other. She studied her brother and tried with caution to evoke the spirit of her Father without literally invoking it, as she had in Akachi's van when the Ergosphere was still so close and her mind, translucent with psychedelic drugs. She imagined the Hierophant's being, could smell in the center of her mind the distant edge of sandalwood and frankincense—a walking Mass, that man, their Father, who disguised pragmatism with joviality and could make anyone in the world feel as if he loved them most of all not seconds before seeing them put to death. Or, more rarely and always more brutally, killing them by his own hand. He did not martyr Theodore out of affection. Not out of generosity or kindness. If the man had secrets that the Holy Father did not want Dominia to someday learn, the most expedient thing would have been to kill him.

Instead, knowing through his admitted dry run of reality that this moment would come, the Hierophant had martyred Theodore and made him part of the most powerful, spiritually decadent *Famiglia* in the world. And if Dominia were the Hierophant, she would only do a thing like that if Theodore possessed information the Hierophant wanted her to have—if the kidnapping of the Governor served no use but to turn her around in circles. Then why had the Lady given her the task? Surely the divinity knew all her Father did, and more.

She was tired of being a pawn. Blindly wandering at the behest of those who knew the many histories of the many realities happening for eternity. Who was to say it was a matter of chronology? Perhaps Lazarus was placed arbitrarily in any one of an infinity of random, concurrent probabilities, and was therefore present in all his lives at once, as she had felt herself so physically in another world. That world of the Kingdom. The magician's world.

That son of a bitch, Valentinian. There was still not a trace of him: not after all this time. True, she hadn't looked hard for him. Her work in the world had kept her from finding time to try and visit the Kingdom within the event horizon of the black hole at the end of Earth's linear time. Many flesh-and-blood, living people needed her help, because they still experienced matter and time as normal people.

Dominia experienced it, too, of course. But, having been in that strange other place, that Void, that dark essence of the black hole, the General was numbed to the sordid reality that her Father considered his. She saw the strings. The whole social charade reminded her of the concerts in which her Father would employ Cassandra, who had by the end of her life moved from Noctisdomin school into a career as the music teacher in a very fine Holy School (one of roughly four hundred across the United Front, all exceptional academies where exceptional human children learned that they would, nonetheless, always be inferior to martyrs). Those concerts were but a handful of extensive interactions American Cassandra had with European Lavinia, who did everything with tooth-gritting perfection because pleasing their Father was the girl's sole reason to live.

For the first—oh, almost two hundred and fifty years she was alive, Dominia was able to enjoy concerts and theater as sheer entertainment. But when the Hierophant wanted Lavinia to be a star for his entertainment and felt he needed to drag Cassandra into it, the then Governess was exposed to all the dramatic minutiae that came with her wife's preparation for the show. Voices of background choristers going out, Lavinia being a spoiled drama queen about some costume… it was all such a tahgmahr. And it was all Cassandra would talk about for a while, there, too. The concert, her nerves, how grating Lavinia could be when given license to exercise her undeserved political powers—or, worse, her protein-given ones.

Yet, for all the stress and angst and nonsense those scattered nights of buildup brought to the General's life, she would gladly live them again if that was what it took to be with Cassandra. It was a heretical, human belief among the women of the Red Market that the universe unfolded in oscillations, existing again and again in alternating amplitudes of existence and nonexistence. Dominia had come to believe that, and not because Valentinian had told her so or Lazarus had proven it with many lifetimes' worth of foreknowledge. She had come to believe it because, with what was left of Cassandra relegated in this world to a shiny little stone around Gethsemane's neck, the hope that her miserable life would happen over again was all the hope Dominia managed.

She had to tell herself that this effort was worth something. This time wouldn't be like those last times that she couldn't remember, but that were implied by fairly convincing arguments for a cyclical timeline (or timesphere, perhaps). An infinity of failures, which demanded to know: What, precisely, had she failed? What were the incorrect variables in those iterations abandoned by Lazarus, the magician, and her (un)Holy Father? What was out there, out of her control, ready to get her—and what was within her control, only to serve as the means by which she might destroy herself? A year's worth of unanswered prayers and tahgmahrs and unceasing work had left the General more hardened than ever before, and more ready for anything to go wrong.

"Anything" happened sooner than she'd hoped, but it made her glad for their plane's speed: they were practically within extraction zone by the time the jets came into screaming distance. Through a window clarified by reduced cabin light, she caught the abrupt appearance of a trio of monstrous hypersonic planes that tore through the sound barrier at Mach 12, or about 2,747 kilometers per hour faster than most missiles developed by humanity early in the Hierophant's rise to power—a difference of about 1,707 miles per hour to those stubborn rural folk of the Front. Any chance they had of completing their journey to the landing pad in Tangiers dropped to zero as soon as those enemy aircrafts were on Farhad's radar screen. It was already too late to avoid projectiles that were comparably faster than the hyper-fast jets, and surely informed by exact knowledge of their location—probably from the Lamb, as much as any battle fought with his help in her once-lived life. Teddy, well hypnotized by his two sedatives, had begun dozing off around the time of the first impact. He awoke with a squeal while Farhad's tinny voice clicked over the cabin speakers.

"Mahdi, we are being targeted."

"No kidding," was her response, as Theodore cried, "But I'm *on* here, you idiots!"

"They know." Head low, Dominia ducked from her seat to the cockpit.

"So why are they shooting at us, then?"

"Because they're trying to shoot us out of the sky, of course." She smirked, feeling a responsibility to find humor in the situation while avoiding the obvious fact that the Hierophant didn't care if Theodore lived or died. As she reached the door, it slid open to leave Dominia face-to-face with Gethsemane.

"There are more missiles coming, and the fighters will wheel back around, but it will take some time. We have countermeasures available at our disposal, General."

"Not enough countermeasures to handle all they're going to throw at us," Farhad said without so much as blinking, lest the precious microseconds mean the difference between another direct impact and a near miss. "Already, that one strike— We are looking at very serious damage and will not be able to fly much farther."

"I thought you couldn't speak English," said Theodore sourly from behind Dominia's shoulder, rendered brave enough by the drug to leave his seat in the chaos of an emerging dogfight—the exact time he ought to have stayed sitting.

"As we tried to tell you the first time, he just doesn't want to speak it with you. Not that anyone does." Dominia turned her attention back to Gethsemane. "All right, listen. We're going to—"

"General." Gethsemane's expression was tight as another screaming missile rocked the plane. An alarm had begun to go off, and the martyr grit her teeth while her closest adviser took her hand. "We must evacuate reality early."

"This is why I told you that you shouldn't have come."

The naiad offered a thin smile. "Then I would have lost my life in some Jerusalem bombing while you were out of town. This is how misfortune likes to play its cruelest games. I'd rather risk staying in the Ergosphere forever than failing you, General."

"It's dangerous for you," Dominia repeated.

"I do think I come out a little less myself, and replaced by nothing… but I do not think anyone—even you—can safely do this forever." The General could already smell her Father's cologne, the pressure of his presence creeping through the plane as the human gently said, "I see in your eyes you agree. Well: you are very strong. Frighteningly strong! And you have only one woman to be. I am two women; that makes me as strong as you." A playful edge danced along the woman's tired smile. "Perhaps stronger, if I could but dream as much."

No kidding. Certainly stronger. Gethsemane made a selfless decision with such knee-jerk ease that it was almost implicit she had thought of it before the moment. Dominia always struggled with such things, herself. She'd lost Miki and Kahlil within fifteen minutes; she was pained at the thought of losing another friend, if not to death, then to a kind of subsumption of the soul. Was that the true nature of madness? A frightening notion.

But would the General rather lose her friend, or see her entire party blown to smithereens? To parachute to their arrests? A thousand paintings whose violence was illustrated to an outlandish, sometimes lurid degree flickered through her memory like a series of martyr trading cards. She could not speak. There was never any good in speaking of the tortures, the war crimes, her Father had committed. Never any good in inspiring fear. Hope was the way, and the generous sacrifice of her human friend was the source of a sliver of optimism. She squeezed Gethsemane's hand, then released it. "We have to go soon, before the electronics go down, or before the battery blows and we lose the BLP."

"A blip," said Theodore, pale, now, no matter how many pills he'd taken. He glanced up to the lights as he repeated the common nickname of the Blue Light Projector, then asked, "This jet is equipped with a blip? What do we need that for? Dominia? You know blue light will *kill* us, don't you? That much blue light? That's why it was *invented*, you understand, it's the same technology as those damn fences, those thresholds!"

Yes, she understood why the idea made him upset. The BLP was a device humans commonly installed in all sorts of solar-powered vehicles, personal and public. In fact, the Light Rail was only lacking a BLP in every car because its construction had been partially sponsored by the DIOX corporation, which Dominia now understood to be controlled by the Hierophant. The use of Blue Light Projectors was simple, though highly illegal in the United Front and other martyr-controlled territories if not in the form of a DIOX-approved threshold kit. Otherwise, if one found oneself trapped in one's home with a martyr as one's uninvited guest, and negotiations (for lack of a better word) took a southern turn, one could flip a switch to flood the room with sunlight-approximating beams. These, hyper-concentrated, were far more brutal than actual rays. BLP units vomited a room so full of light that even humans could only bear exposure for a few seconds without welder's goggles. Though true that, in the case of a unit such as the one on the plane, extended use would drain the associated battery to nothing with alarming efficiency, even a twenty-second exposure would blind and wound a martyr long enough for a human to find means of escape.

And, in the case of the unit on the plane, it was only intended for a single use before requiring recharge. The threshold technology employed on the E4 was not intended as a defense against martyrs but as the means by which the aircraft could raise its electromagnetic frequency and pierce into the Ergosphere. Like Akachi's teleporter, the whole plane was an artificial solar plexus in that the entire craft was able to exit physical spacetime. But it had to be tied to a future/present destination point by way of entry at any one of several carefully decided past/present positions in space-time, calculated to a narrow window of extraction space for any given potential exit. In ideal settings, the E4 had made it to the landing pad but once. The other three wasted planes now qualified as cosmic junk sitting where they'd crashed in the Ergosphere, because nobody could figure how to get them out. At the start of the experimental project, she'd been presented with four inter-dimensional jets, and three had predictable failures of timing for one reason or another, usually due to imprecision of location. Planes weren't sentient, so they couldn't look up at the "black sun," aka Earth at the edge of time; the BLP and all other electromagnetic devices of the crashed jets were rendered nonfunctional; and most people were uncomfortable about spending a lot of time in the Void, so very little follow-up had been engaged, and there was precious time to ruminate on failure, anyway. Better to focus on the one success and see if it could repeat itself in the field—that had been the aim. The reality was success had no chance of repeating itself, and they would have to crash the plane into the Ergosphere's interpretation of the Atlantic Ocean.

Good thing those pills she'd given Theodore were laced with Lazarus's blood, containing the real sacred protein. The proudly worn vial of old Lazarene blood she'd obtained from Akachi had successfully traveled in and out of the Ergosphere a great many times along with her, but that didn't mean it would have an effect on a soul who hadn't imbibed it on Earth if they were trapped in a device such as an E4 during a malfunction. Who knew how hard it would be to get a non-Lazarene out of that place, assuming they arrived at all?

But, maybe it was for the best that such a spirit stay there. After all, the purpose of the old mystic's blood seemed to be escape. That was just how fucked up her Father's world was, Dominia supposed, how corrupt and base—a granule of blood like those in the pills could save a person eternally, even when taken in ignorance.

"Try not to freak out too much, Teddy," urged the General, grabbing him by the arm like a teacher grabbing an unruly pupil. "Gethsemane, Farhad? Ready?"

"We have to be," the pilot observed as their pursuers again howled past. "Activating the BLP, Mahdi."

Amid the sirens of enemy jets and the pleas of Governor Theodore, Farhad filled the cabin with mock sunlight, and the real world dissolved into a figment of imagination.

The amount of time required for Theodore to notice he was not burning to death, and the related amount of time required for him to stop screaming was—well, impressive. While inky black bloomed about the smoking, rattling, beeping E4, the electronics systems failed, and Dominia gave a sigh of relief as all alarms stopped along with the BLP. That same darkness of the Void plunged unnervingly into the cabin of the ship, smiting all vision and leaving the crashed object as nonexistent as the rest of the landscape in the Ergosphere's bleak nighttime presentation. This was why she'd hoped to skip over it: this, and Teddy's ceaseless screaming, now turning into weeping even as Farhad groaned, "Please, Mahdi, will you turn on a light!"

"Just wanted to see if he'd stop screaming, first." With a chuckle, Dominia lowered her head and did the one interesting thing she'd learned over the last year—she spoke the True Word for "light."

If a person asked her in the waking world what that True Word was, she couldn't have told them. Not because she didn't want to but because it was physically impossible. As she had learned before the Lady's union with Her new avatar, True Words in the Void stood beyond language. Rather, they *were* the objects they represented. The magician had once impressed her with his parlor tricks of making fire out of thin air, and when new to this place, she'd regarded his talents with a childlike glee. Now, she understood what he'd done, and understood why what he did was purer than her Father's manipulation of thoughtforms from the dark atmosphere. Valentinian, that saint who was once a dog, was not creating or manifesting anything. He was speaking True Words, which bore so little resemblance to terrestrial speech that, when they were spoken, the mouth did not move. The object but appeared, as light blazed forth across the cabin's interior in a pure golden halo that emanated from the speaker. True Words could not be communicated. They needed be divined, as the Lady had taught Dominia in a series of unrecallable dreams over the previous summer.

"No wonder I understand every word spoken, and all written words," she'd once said to the Lady, after the weight of the ceremony had been given time to settle upon her. The oh-so-generous goddess found regular occasion to greet Dominia in Her chambers for reasons other than bad news, and the General used these meetings for spiritual guidance. Well she understood the magician's pain. Without the Lady, Dominia would have had no one with whom to discuss these matters. Gethsemane had no practical experience, and Farhad, though imbued with an incredibly deep well of religious knowledge, was exclusively devoted to the Islamic faith. Despite her spiteful, PR-related conversion to the Catholic variation over the previous summer, Dominia was interested not in faith but in truth. She knew the Lady would understand her when she said, "The only real words there are the highest ones. Everything else is just ideas."

The entity, kneeling upon a satin pillow across from her, seemed stiller than one of those unfortunate Cairo statues. Nonetheless, Her words rang clear, always seeming to use Dominia's brain stem as Her antenna. *There is no name for the language of the Ergosphere, though many have heard it and tried to put a name to it; but in naming it, it is no longer itself. A named thing is not a wholly true thing. When a thing has a name, it is objectified. It is drawn down into the Earth and into a mere symbol in the mind. That is why, when the truest, highest words are spoken, they will create the object that they evoke, because they are the object. Do you understand? All other words, all human words, are metaphors. The words We speak are the only real ones.*

Her lips parted, Dominia shifted upon the tatami mats of the avatar's room. She thought of the magician, making fire and playing cards and electricity from thin air. "Will you teach me these words?"

You will learn a few in your life. We will teach them to you in dreams. Only in dreams. In waking, We will take them from you. The True Words are not for the pleasure of the living but for those who have burst from the Void into the physical Earth. Were we to speak these words, it would mean the end of reality. Only during such times of flux as on the eve of Our wedding can these words be spoken safely, to any effect. Only during such times can they even be remembered upon Earth.

Dominia was so used to people refusing to give information that she was not even surprised. "Don't you think it will come in handy for me?" she bothered to ask, and the deity's avatar smiled.

They will serve you greater purpose after death than before, child; and after death, it will be the only tongue you speak.

Well, the General had always been the type of kid who wanted to grow up fast. To the Lady's credit, She kept Her promise, and Dominia had a series of weird dreams beneath the peak of the Dog Star and the festivals venerating it. Interestingly, such festivals were common amid the Red Market women and the martyrs back home. Everybody could agree on a few things: to her Father's people, bright Sirius and its nearby companion, Procyon A—the star that hosted the promised land of martyrs, the not-yet-formed planet Acetia—was a symbol of the distant future from which the Hierophant hailed to bring them the protein's good news. To the Red Market, the Dog Star was the symbol of about forty esoteric things that Dominia hadn't fully grasped, mostly because she didn't care. She was more concerned (as had been Akachi before her) with building up her armaments, and rebuilding a body that had suffered a great deal of malnutrition, physical trauma, and battle without rest. Her vision, tunneled by hatred, saw only those moves that would best organize her and her people against her Father.

She was so devoted to her one task that she could not even remember the extent of the dreams that had taught her the Words—but, as the Lady said, that was also by design. Dominia remembered nothing of her dreams but awoke the next morning with the feeling of important information slipping from her grasp. At first proper sunlight, she would hurry into the Ergosphere, and discover to her astonishment that she now knew with a click the True Word for a basic concept like "light" or "pebble." How did she learn them? The aggravating part was she had no idea. Instead, she had the sense she'd always known them, and had forgotten them until the Lady had shifted something in her memory.

By a stretch, the most important word she had learned was the word for "reality," which allowed her to wink home from even the Void no matter where she looked or what the status of Earth's morbid silhouette. She could even take a friend or two home with her— maybe more, they hadn't tried. Such small abilities made the scientists' research in the Ergosphere's nighttime Void somewhat safer, and it had even inspired a few of them to pick up meditation and spiritual devotion to the Lady in hopes that they, also, might be able to divine the True Words and carry on such work without Dominia. More religious sorts might have found such material intent a profane thing, but the General approved of their habits wholeheartedly. The sacred Words were little more than another set of tools to her, and she swiftly trained herself to use them on entering the Ergosphere, where dream and reality were one in the same, and where the raw information of matter's hologram was present in the strange interference pattern legible only with the laser of consciousness.

But was the metaphor (the damned metaphor) a perfect one? Did the laser engaging the playback need to be identical to the laser doing the recording? What did that mean for her consciousness? What was the recording laser? It made the poor General's military head spin; she had spent three centuries religiously avoiding questions of spirituality, and now she'd gotten herself obsessed with holograms, and begun to wonder about the magician and his relationship to not just True Words but *the* Word. The old spiritual symbol of the Logos, for which, Gethsemane had once said, the Dog Star was one of many attached images.

What did any of this mean? The General was getting obsessed with the idea of perfect Words and holograms and blah-dee-blah, as René mocked when she drunkenly confessed this sort of thing to him. But, of course she was obsessed. Maybe some of it would help Cassandra return. Maybe she could divine Cassandra's highest name and speak it, and there she'd be—or somehow a computer could step in where the sacred and the psychedelic could not, to derive her wife's actual consciousness with a sad combination of algorithms and silicone. Maybe, maybe. All she could do anymore was say, "Maybe," even when her little brother's fear turned to wonder at the great blaze of light, and his eyes sought purchase in a place where there was none but the faces around and hints of the cabin implied on the edges of the glow.

Theodore, touching his own face and then releasing the other hand, which had clutched his sister's arm, calmed enough to speak. "What is this? Are we dead?"

"Maybe," she admitted. The first time she had come to this place, after all, she'd stepped into the certain death of the sun. It was a kind of death, she supposed. She glanced down at herself with her single, unpatched eye, at the leather jacket she had not worn in real life since well before the tragedy of Kabul. "I mean, who's to tell the difference between 'dead' and 'alive'? We already died once, after all. Technically."

"But what's happened?" pressed the Governor. "We were about to be shot down just now—right? And then the BLP, and now…why do you look—like you used to? Even your hair, it's so long again! I feel strange." His hand fluttered against his forehead while his seeking eyes darted between Gethsemane and Farhad. The pilot appeared much himself, albeit older, which bolstered Dominia's sense that perhaps things might work out all right. Even Teddy, now that she focused through the Void-muted glow, seemed dressed and groomed beyond his current station.

But—Gethsemane. They had experimented once with taking her into the Ergopshere, and Dominia had halted the experiment soon after it began to whisk her friend right back out. Now, "right back out" meant "back out into the nighttime waters of the Atlantic Ocean," but it sounded almost preferable to standing there and watching her skip like a corrupted video between shards of the earthly woman she was, few sparkling features of the nymph, and—recalling the *tulpa* as much as her wife—expressions and mannerisms resembling those of Cassandra. That was perhaps due to the diamond around Gethsemane's neck, still hanging even in this space where the human's dress had changed and was sometimes a priestess's garb—sometimes nude or protected by wooden armor, as had been the nymph. Elements of Dominia's dead wife were the only visual constants. A lynchpin, or a yoke. Hard to say.

"There's nothing to be alarmed about," the General assured Teddy, and herself, and Gethsemane. Nonetheless, her brother's eyes remained wide with obvious fear. "We've got to get to shore now. Just a little walking to do."

"Walking?" Teddy's eyes boggled, and Dominia nodded.

"The plane's out of commission. They all lose power once they hit the Ergosphere without making it to their landing pad. Electromagnetic devices don't work here. Not by any means we've been able to find, anyway—so we're going to have to cross on foot. But don't worry! I mean, really, don't worry. It's bad for your health here. And for mine."

Of course, such a thing was hard for even Dominia to remember during the next instant, when that spectral face appeared in the window of the cockpit's door.

III

A Sailor Out of Time

What a funny thing, fear! A familiar face when we least expect it is worse to us than a stranger's, as was the face of former *Jun'yō* first mate, Tenchi Ichigawa, whose smiling features appeared half illuminated by the circumference of Domina's glow. At the scream of everybody in the cabin, the sailor screamed, too, and dropped from the window with an unnerving lack of thud upon the Void's un-ground below. Delay induced by the shock sweeping aside, the General dashed to the door, threw it open, and leapt down beside the groaning man before the stairs could lower.

"Tenchi! What are you doing here? *How* are you here?"

They'd discussed this many times over the last year. Tenchi was the reason his cousin knew as much as he did about Lazarus; why wasn't the sailor a confirmed Lazarene? "I don't understand it all enough, yet," he would say. Or: "*Eto*…I'm afraid it will change me, I guess." But here he was, rubbing his head as he sat uneasily up on the implied ground, saying, "Well…I can't explain that."

"Can't, or won't? Have you lied to me, Tenchi?"

"I wouldn't!" Pulled to his feet as the other passengers of the plane leaned out into the glow, the rounder Ichigawa smoothed his sailing uniform and said, "I had to—to take the blood, and to come here, to this spot." After a glance of reluctance back to the watching faces, he fessed up to Dominia: "The magician told me to."

The magician! Valentinian? That former dog of a deadbeat friend? "You saw him?"

Tenchi nodded. "He brought me here. He met me when I came into the Ergosphere and told me I had to help fix your boat."

"This isn't a boat," Farhad told him. "It's an experimental plane."

"Really? I think she looks kind of like a submarine…"

"Forget all that." Hands on his shoulders, Dominia attempted to contain Tenchi's interest because anything less could be downright dangerous. "When did you come into the Ergosphere, Tenchi?"

An anxious expression twisting his mouth, Tenchi tried to glance away at Farhad until Dominia tightened her grip. "I'm not supposed to say yet… He said it will distract you. You'll try to do something— Well. I'm just supposed to fix the ship."

"Plane," Farhad corrected again, stepping down, then helping Gethsemane do the same. The sailor looked at him, aggrieved.

"The magician told *me* she's a ship. Maybe she's both. But anyway, I'm supposed to take care of her."

"How do you expect to take care of a plane you think is a ship?" The pilot stepped aside to let the first mate climb aboard, and all the while, the Governor worried the cuff links of his posh suit jacket the way his lip worried against his teeth.

Teddy asked, "Can the ship get us home once you've fixed it?"

Ichigawa, followed by Dominia, stooped to investigate the instrument panel of the cockpit. "I guess so… To be honest, I'm not sure what the magician expects me to do."

"Had you ever met him before?" the General asked while the sailor settled into Farhad's vacant seat. As Tenchi bent forward to better read the labels of the panel, the martyr rested her hand a few centimeters above it to illuminate the text. "In real life, before the Ergosphere?"

"*Iie*…he met me here, as soon as I came. I followed your—" The little man winced before continuing with a sigh. "I just did what I was supposed to do, to come here. When Earth disappeared, there he was with his red waistcoat."

That was Valentinian, all right. "But what about your cousin? What about the airport, Tenchi? Didn't you catch a flight like we discussed?"

"Well…I really think you should talk to the magician."

Before she could press him further, Farhad called from outside the craft, "There is no damage to the hull, Mahdi. I cannot see well, but I've touched where the damage should be—nothing." The plane's surface reverberated with the knock of his fist. "Hear? Solid."

"That's because it's the soul of the plane," she answered, which made Tenchi look up in some surprise.

"Soul…"

"Didn't the magician explain anything about this place to you?" she asked him, which elicited the shocking reply, "Oh, of course! We've had three whole days to talk."

This wasn't her Tenchi. Not the Tenchi at the dim sum restaurant. This was the Tenchi of the future. Three days in the Ergosphere was closer to three weeks on Earth. Something happened between the restaurant and the sailor's entry into that other space: something that had caused him to become a Lazarene, brave the Void, and meet the martyr saint of death.

Dominia didn't like that one single bit. But she had to pretend she hadn't copped to anything as the cheerful little man clarified, "It was just strange, that's all. I wasn't sure what he expected of me… I can do some basic mechanical things, but to fix a whole ship by myself? In a place like this? But he just kept telling me, 'Don't worry, you'll get it when the time comes! You've got a vivid imagination. That's all you need to speak to the soul of a ship.'"

Hands sliding over the instrument panel, Tenchi said, "I still don't understand what he meant. But if this is the ship's soul…why won't she work?"

"We can't figure it out. This is the fourth craft we've lost to the Ergosphere. Have you seen one of these before?"

He shook his head. "I never got to see the things we engineered… not my department. But it bothers me! Why make a plane, a jet, that looks like a submarine?"

"Well, we did technically crash into the Atlantic Ocean, or come close to it before entering the Void. And, as the Lady says, Her darkness and Her waters are all one in the same." Dominia watched nervous

Teddy ease down the stairs and gingerly lower the toe of his shoe to the dark ground. "Not that it matters here. Anyway, the E4 is built like that for reasons of stealth and speed; it's like its own entry point teleporter, and designed to whip to its end point."

"So it's *meant* to travel into this place."

"Not really…more to pass through it, like a tunnel. The ones that enter this place stay here, because we can't figure out how to get them out. An electromagnetic failure." She frowned, arms folding, and thought of her own electromagnetic field, which was not absent, but so barely visible in the glow from her speech that one couldn't possibly see it unless one looked for it. "Valentinian and Lazarus taught me that souls in this place *are* electromagnetic energies, essentially… Maybe that's why the craft doesn't have the ability to function. Because it has no consciousness, therefore, it has no soul."

"What? No consciousness?" The sailor almost laughed at her, but he caught himself and said, "You Westerners! I always forget…what a stagnant world you inhabit."

Everybody knew more about spirituality than she did—even Tenchi! As he went on to say, "Shinto reveals that everything has consciousness. I guess it's not fair to say Easterners only believe that… after all, that's what alchemy is, right? Crazy old guys talking to the spirits of molten metals. But that's not so crazy. We call them 'kami' in Japan, these spirits, these energies…"

"Thoughtforms," Dominia almost said; but as she opened her mouth, the body of the craft rumbled and groaned, then fell silent once again. The sailor laughed in surprise. "See? She's a living thing like any other spirit in this world…all made by the same deity. Maybe that's why I've been so afraid to come here! I knew I wouldn't be able to see the world the same way. Not ever again."

After reflecting on the notion that the magician would not have set her friend to a task that might endanger her life, the General nonetheless felt obliged to warn the human of the perils of thoughtforms. "Sometimes, imagining things in this place can be dangerous."

"That's only if the thing you're imagining is bad! Or if you don't know what you're imagining. The magician told me that much…but he doesn't have to tell me that the souls of ships are always good." The craft gave another rumble, and to Dominia's surprise, the needle of some dial twitched to life. Tenchi, beaming brighter than the martyr's light, said, "This must be how he wants me to fix the ship! By paying attention to her. Of course, it's so simple… How could she work if nobody knows she's living?"

Interesting question. What was the sound of one hand clapping? If a tree fell in the forest without somebody to hear it, *did* it make a sound? She got those old Zen koans now. Miki would be proud. "I guess that's a good point… Still, I don't understand."

"The ship needs electricity to function on Earth, but here, things function by thought, so I guess…call it a thought-powered ship?"

"Plane," said Farhad, leaning into the doorway. "I do not wish to alarm or interrupt you, Mahdi."

"Carry on."

"There are lights, Mahdi."

"Maybe it's an *airship*," Tenchi muttered, while Dominia patted his shoulder and continued, to Farhad, "What do you mean, lights?"

"Blue torches," the pilot said, to the drop of the General's stomach.

"Those aren't for us." Leaning past Farhad, she glanced out of the E4 and tried to maintain a neutral expression for the path of torches unfurling, as ever, north according to the ethereal guide of her just-hinted compass. She had no desire to follow them, and tried to turn back to Tenchi.

Undaunted, the pilot went on—his tone cautious and respectful, but all the more aggravating for it. "If I may say, Mahdi—" She whirled on him with a dark look that squeezed out of the human man a nervous laugh, even in a place where there was no such thing as death.

"It is just—how do I say—the night in this place is very long, Mahdi, and—"

"And we will make our own fire to rest, away from these. *Real* fire."

"Ah, but it is just that—perhaps these are gifts from Allah, yes? In place for weary travelers…"

After a helpless assessment of Dominia's stony expression, Farhad turned toward Gethsemane, whose glittering features in this place apparently resembled Cassandra's more than ever when she wanted something. (Purposeful? Hard to say.) These sweet eyes reflected from the diamond said with Gethsemane's voice, "We are all very tired, I think, General. Do you know these lights? Know them to be foul? Perhaps they are of the magician."

This, for whatever reason, lit the hot fire of nauseous offense in Dominia's cheeks and gut, and she snapped despite herself. "The magician's lights are real fire. Fire spoken with words like mine. Not lights like…these."

"Whose lights are these, Mahdi," tried Farhad, delicately. The General cursed herself for having hidden this issue from her friends rather than warning them ahead of time.

For one long year, she had been training select men and women in the use of the Ergosphere, and at no point in time had she either revealed or admitted any knowledge of the fairy fire torches that were said to appear in her presence during the nighttime Void-state. All the more reason she preferred the daytime manifestation. Then her Father was only likely to appear when she was alone. In this place, he liked to lure her to him. Her method of avoiding the lure had been a refusal to acknowledge its existence, but that clearly wouldn't work now. Not with all her friends (and Teddy) right here. Gethsemane, who had given up encouraging Dominia to share her worries, watched her now. The martyr tried to indicate with her eye that they were better off not discussing this in front of Theodore, but, of course, all parties only waited for her to speak. Irritated, she cleared her throat and stepped down past Farhad to make a grab for her brother. When Teddy ducked out of her grip, she admitted in a half mutter, "The lights are my— Father's."

"What!" The Governor all but shrieked the word before he was off at a sprint in the direction of the torches, giving Dominia only a second to turn her accusatory look on the humans and tell Tenchi, "Stay here and fix the plane," before she needed bolt after pathetic Theodore.

"Father," he cried, "Father! Oh, *Daddy*"—she could have vomited and actually stumbled a step, giving him slightly more headway and further annoying her—"you've come for me! Even in this place, you came for me, O Heavenly Father—"

"He didn't send those torches for you, you twerp." Dominia's limbs pumped at double time, but the General was amazed to find how fast Theodore was in this place. Perhaps out of terror. "He wants you to follow the torches, but not so he can save you."

In the distance, she could see it. Now more than a door and a disembodied office, her Father's thoughtform study resembled a box. A whole room, as if torn out of a building. The exterior, artfully covered in floral wallpaper, still appeared to float in space. But for that path cleaved through the thick darkness by those wretched torches, it would appear unnervingly unanchored. "Why else would he send them if not to *save* me?" On shrieking this, Theodore slowed sufficiently for the General to snatch the back of his rumpled coat.

"So he can attract *me* here," she told her brother, giving him an irritated mother-cat shake.

"It's all about you, isn't it?" he began—but with his next breath to speak, his nose wrinkled, and his words succumbed to a cough. "What is that *stench*?"

It had trickled into her nose in like time and zipped her back through her journey across the world, and earlier. To the military, to parties as a teenager, to the cloying scent of her human father's clothing. Most of all, it brought her to this place, the Ergosphere. To her Father's study and its most regular unwelcome guest, the prospect of whom made Dominia release Theodore's collar and sprint for that door, herself.

"Tobacco smoke."

As she drew closer, the air grew denser—not just with the scent of cigarettes but the sound of music, wholly unfamiliar and not her Father's classical preference. Perhaps that was why this night, for the first time, she entered the study without knocking and without thought for the fact that she had managed to stay away one year straight. Inside, she found beside the pool table not just her Father but also that bastard, chain-smoking magician, Valentinian.

"Hell," he said in time with the Hierophant, a second before he was pinned to the bookshelves by his jacket's lapels while capping on the belated, "O!"

"Give me a reason I shouldn't shatter your imaginary skull with my fist and send you back in time so far that you're stuck as a dog again."

"Missed you, too, buddy," wheezed Valentinian, almost laughing, while the Hierophant smiled with those inappropriately blithesome fuligin eyes.

"There is my little tiger, at last! A bit late for most of the holidays, but we still have New Year's. I knew if I kept extending invitations, you would eventually come."

"Where have you been?" Dominia continued, oblivious, to the magician. "I gave up Cassandra for you, and now I find you here? With him? And dragging Tenchi into this?"

"Strictly speaking, you *delayed* Cassandra for me." Valentinian continued speaking in a casual tone, either unwilling or unable to disappear with the General's fists clutching the cherry velvet of a jacket she slowly recognized to be new. "We're just taking the long way. The right way."

Dominia jerked her head toward His Holiness. "How am I supposed to trust you, finding you with him?"

Beyond her shoulder, Theodore stood in the doorway and cried with cartoonish relief, "Father!"

"Tut, tut, Theodore." The Hierophant's guileless expression brimmed with self-aware amusement. "I am disappointed in you, lad."

Dominia turned to regard both her Family members, specifically Theodore, and the way his face fell as he asked, "Disappointed in me?"

The Hierophant offered precious more gesture than a solemn shake of his head. "You and all my other children have been warned, time and again, of the horrors wrought by the consumption of the blood of Lazarus. No martyr who has tasted it may be saved."

"But—"

"You have committed the one unforgivable sin, my boy. I'm afraid you are damned for eternity."

Horror filled Theodore's face, and his slightly aged hands clasped one another before tightening like a noose around his embroidered silk collar. "What? What do you mean? Surely you can't be serious."

"I'm afraid I am most serious," said the Hierophant, offering an earnest lift of his brows toward the hairline that, in this place, so resembled Cicero's they might have passed for twins. The cover story of the holy man from Acetia who adopted the appearance of the first human he martyred was the only thing that prevented the General's rampant speculation, because with all the things she'd been exposed to since her flight from the city of San Valentino, she was more open to the idea of her Father's extraterrestrial heritage. As to whether Valentinian's story that he was, in the first iteration of the universe, one of the original discoverers of the sacred protein…Dominia still wasn't sure it passed the sniff test, and somehow that made her Father's story seem dubious, too. Never mind that nobody had explained to her just how it was the fictional saint had gotten himself stuck as a dog, or any animal. It was all so baffling, even after a year in which to absorb it.

Imagine trying to explain all of that to Teddy in any way he'd believe or understand! Now she understood why they veiled so much knowledge from her. She also saw why it was so easy for her Father to manipulate two whole continents of people. His power meant it wasn't some small deal to Theodore when the Holy Father sincerely said, "There is no saving you now. Your soul shall be damned to hell."

The UF Governor took a step forward, his wide eyes watering. "No! No, that can't be."

Dominia said, "He's full of shit," but Theodore didn't seem poised to believe her.

Valentinian told her with an aggravated wave of his hand, "You want proof you can trust me? Let me go, and I can save him."

"Save him from what?" the General asked, but he waved again. She found the change when she followed his hand: the shimmering, wobbling panic that overcame poor Theodore's form. It was as though the ground had quite literally dropped from beneath his feet. He had become a one-man earthquake for as much as he trembled, and as Farhad arrived on the scene along with Gethsemane, it was in time to see the Governor, his mouth a superposition of four dozen different pleas, beginning to disappear.

As the Hierophant continued droning to Dominia (or himself), he leaned upon his pool cue like a cane. "The incredible thing about a damned soul"—his eyes followed Valentinian's dash to Theodore—"is that one must ask oneself whether the person in question could be said to have ever existed once their spiritual substrate is diminished back to its quintessence. When unfired clay is remolded, what happens to the old figure? Does it still exist within the new object, the cup or the bowl?"

"I exist," insisted Theodore at high pitch while the magician grabbed what seemed to be only one of (or part of) a series of shifting fragments that came together to form an impression of a man called Teddy. If Gethsemane was a collage of three women, Governor Theodore was a single man shattered into a cubist portrait.

"Yeah, buddy!" As he would a child waking from a tahgmahr, Valentinian soothed the victim of the Hierophant's mind games. "You exist! Just pull yourself together and keep existing. You don't need his permission to exist."

"Strictly speaking, as I created him in this martyred form—"

Too annoyed with her Father's lectures to suffer another word, Dominia snatched the pool cue from his hand and shattered it over the edge of the table. The Hierophant made a hennish noise of displeasure while the magician continued talking Theodore back to sustainable shape.

"Is that any way to treat your Father after not calling for a year?"

The General's lip curled. "I'd do worse if I could do it in confidence that your whole study wouldn't disappear with you and leave us floating in the night." Now centimeters from his face, she considered the splintered stake of a cue that she'd unconsciously waved under his nose. Had she developed a temper problem? Her Father's pale eyebrows lifted, along with the smirking corner of his lips, as if to ask her what she thought.

Meanwhile, Theodore continued to miserably whine above the tearing vacuum sound of his own soul's struggle to maintain its integrity. "How can I be sure that I exist?"

"I'm talking to you. I—care that you exist." This, from Valentinian, was not convincing. Braced, the magician reached into the holographic form of the Governor as though to hold him in place. "Come on, look, I can touch you. We're in this together."

"That doesn't mean anything," argued Theodore, always poised to shoot down comfort in a time of distress. "You might not exist either, for all I know."

The magician rolled his eyes toward Dominia. "Trust me, pal, things would be a lot easier for me if I didn't. I'd be the first to tell you if I didn't exist. You, though! You're clearly existent. Come on, Teddy, stick with me."

"How do you know my name?"

"Oh, so it's 'your' name? Who's 'you' if you don't exist? Who's Teddy? Cogito, ergo sum, brother!"

"I—don't—" Blinking eyes that came together into but one pair, his body solidifying again, Theodore jerked out of the grip of the magician and said, "Don't condescend to me, please! I'm not a *child*. I know who I am but I—I can't really be *damned*, can I? How can I? I didn't do anything."

"You're not damned," began the magician. As the Hierophant opened his mouth to interrupt, Dominia pushed the cue into his chin until he shut it again. "Nobody's damned, for Christ's sake…you religious types, I swear. You're too gullible, and gullibility is terrible for the soul! Souls need assurance. Confidence! They need substance." Shaking his head, Valentinian removed his pocket watch and handed it to the more-or-less singular Theodore. "Take this."

"What good is a watch going to do when I'm eternally lost?" That said, no matter how miserable he was, Theodore was never too miserable to accept something free. He allowed the magician to clip the watch to his belt loop and said once it was done, "Wait, is this thing broken?"

"It doesn't matter that it's broken. It's something from outside you. It'll keep you grounded, even if you're not thinking about it, because I couldn't have given you that if you didn't exist."

"But what's the point of existing if I'm to be damned?"

Even he had his limits. The magician looked behind Theodore, to the humans who watched in quiet astonishment. "Will somebody please tell me if *I* exist, or if you can hear me? Because he can't seem to. Good Lord…listen, buddy, Theo—the Hierophant's not in charge of deciding whether you're damned."

"He's not?"

"No! Of course not. Who'd let him be in charge? He bullied his way to the top worse than Dominia bullies you." While the General made a noise of displeasure, the magician went on. "You're in charge of your own affairs. Nobody can tell you that you're damned but you. Okay?"

"But he—"

"Is a guy with enough money to run an earthly organization that claims to serve God. But what evidence does he have, outside of money and a bunch of followers, that he's God's servant? Dominia and I and anybody with the blood of Lazarus can disappear, reappear, do all the things he does. You can now, too."

Although he was taken aback, her baby brother was still in the mood to argue. "Well, he has the Lamb, of course." Teddy looked over at Dominia and the Hierophant as though the magician were an idiot and they were in on it. "The miracle-working savior of the martyr race, one of the first two transformed by the blood of the Hierophant! The intercession between Man and God, Earth and heaven!"

"And where do you think the Lamb's miracles come from?" Valentinian gestured around. "Right here. You're standing in the same place where the Lamb does his supposedly holy work. Your Father just wants you to think you'll be damned if you come here because if his secret gets out, everybody will be fighting for a way in."

"What?" Theodore laughed, again looking over at his Family. "No, he—"

The Governor's laughing face fell when he saw Dominia's stone-serious expression and the Hierophant's almost-smiling one, the latter's just barely managing to contain its mirth and thus looking rather strained with or without the pool cue almost up his nose. "Father," tried Theodore, tone delicate as possible, "that's not true, is it?"

"It would be most inconvenient for me to have the whole society of martyrs running in and out of this Void," replied the Hierophant, his expression as innocent as the night he was martyred. "Strictly speaking, from the perspective of my earthly Church, you *are* damned, whether you accept it or not."

"Yeah." The scoffing magician bent his head to light another cigarette. "And from the perspective of objective reality, nobody cares."

"How can you say that? You heard him, didn't you?" Teddy began once more to fall apart until Gethsemane strode up from behind to cuff him in the back of the head. He was more himself after that than he had been once the (now laughing) magician had dealt with him, and seemed more willing to listen as the human waved her arm around.

"How can *you* say that, having seen this place? What is this space, this infinite potential, and what is your so-called Protomartyr beside it? The Hierophant of *what*? My goodness! Do you think anything of Earth matters here? It's the other way around."

Dominia, smiling to hear how Cassandra's emotional mannerisms seemed to infect the normally stoic Gethsemane, relaxed the cue beneath the Hierophant's nose and tucked the wooden shard into his breast pocket with a pat. "Here I was, upset to see you, when it turns out you're able to handle Teddy's deprogramming yourself."

"Is that so," said the Hierophant, behind the glittering of those just-crinkled black eyes. "Silly me."

"So." She whirled toward Valentinian, who loped to collect the abandoned half of the cue and, by his touch and an unheard word, restore it whole—or, more aptly, grow a second half for it, as the original other half still sat in the Hierophant's pocket. "What in the hell are you doing here, with him? Do you mean to tell me that all this time, if I had followed his lights, I would have found you here, too?"

"Not necessarily," said the magician, bending to line up his shot of the blazing three ball. "I do have a life."

"Yeah." The General laughed in a way so sharp that Valentinian scratched and swore to see the lightly bounced cue whirl off, nudge the three, and promptly pocket itself. "Doing what? Because it's not helping me."

"Excuse me," said meek Theodore, "I've had kind of a shock? Can we talk for a minute about—"

"Shut up, Teddy," demanded the General in time with the magician, who then went on to drop his voice and say, "But can *I* talk to *you* a little while?"

"About what? How disappointing you are? Or do you want to try to convince me to make another mistake?"

With a look somewhere between irritation and mild hurt, Valentinian extended the repaired cue to the Hierophant, who traded it for the shard in his pocket. As the magician rendered the cue a panther-headed walking stick—strictly ornamental, she suspected, as he was once a martyr, and wore the face of a late thirtysomething man despite his hyper-advanced age—he fell into stride for the western of the four doors Dominia had only now noticed. Too caught up in fury for Valentinian and concern for Theodore's condition to take in the many new details of the room. This concern became more of a regret as the whiny Governor, over the sound of a knock on the ornate door opposite the one opened by the magician, demanded, "Why won't anyone tell me anything? My Lamb, I've been kidnapped! Drugged and forced onto an *airplane*! An extra-dimensional airplane! Not only that, but a helicopter, one without doors or anything! And threatened! A man was shot in front of me! My soul, condemned unjustly! And now I'm being kept in ignorance!"

The Hierophant, who had hastened to respond to the knock, cracked open the door and made a sound of delight. He threw the portal wide as, in increasing pitch, Theodore carried on, "After all that I've been through, the least—the very *least* you 'people' could do for me is *tell me what is going on!*"

"We can't," answered the guest, who Dominia recognized with a surreal lurch to be herself, exactly as she was, studying her with a kind of calm that indicated she would be prepared for this moment when it next arrived. "We don't understand it all, ourselves."

Pleased as punch, as he himself would put it, the Hierophant looked between his duplicate daughters, then considered the cue in his hand. "Care to close out our dear friend's game, my girl?"

"With pleasure," said that other Dominia, that future Dominia, that impossible-to-explain shadow (or more real) self of herself, who watched the Hierophant turn back to study the best position to place the white ball. Theodore looked the way Dominia felt: confused and nauseous. Though no doubt he couldn't comprehend the awful feedback loop of making unbroken eye contact with oneself. That feeling of being a camera filming a screen of its own output until—

"Are you coming?" Valentinian's words snapped her back to the present and out of the single-eyed gaze of her inscrutable other self. The magician stood at the start of a new path that blazed with healthy red torches, and she hurried to his side.

"She wasn't kidding," muttered Dominia at last, shaking her head. "I don't understand this place."

"You understand it more than you're willing to admit. Hell of a lot of implications to the truth, after all."

The farther they walked from that strange centrifuge of the Hierophant's study, the less dizzy she felt. "What implications are those?"

"I don't know. Religious ones? You tell me."

The General crossed her arms and found she had to consciously slow her step lest she overtake the magician, who was inclined to stroll with leisure rather than hustle as far as possible from her Father. "I'm starting to sympathize with Theodore, scary as that is. I think everybody around here just gets off on denying information, and nobody wants to say what side they're on. I've spent the past year trying to convince myself you didn't use me to get a body."

"Look," said the magician with a belabored sigh, "I can see that you're pissed."

"You left me when I needed your *help*. We were captured!"

"And? You worked it out. Now you run an army."

"For somebody else."

"So? That's what you did before, for the Hierophant. Why's it stuck in your craw now?"

"Because—because I was *done* with this! I was done with the military life, remember? I was the Governess before—"

"Before Cassandra killed herself." The magician studied the General's hard face. "Before you decided her life was worth more than anything in yours."

"And what happened? Everybody made me believe it would be worth it to pick you over her. When will I see her? When will I— when will I be anything but alone?"

Her hand lifted to hide her straining mouth. As the magician said, "Oh, kiddo," she snapped, "Don't patronize me! This fucking place, it makes me so emotional."

"You're always emotional, Dominia. You just can't hide it here."

"Please shut up." Her fingers pinched a triangle over the bridge of her nose. "I could have used your help so many times this year. I've prayed for your help, every night, every morning, like some...stupid girl."

She laughed sharply as he said, "Yeah, I know, and I appreciate it."

"So, why didn't you *help* me!"

"Because you did a fine job helping yourself! You haven't needed my help at all. Look how far you've come in this past year! Do you know how much most people accomplish in the average twelve-month cycle? Practically nothing. If they're lucky, they get a raise at work, maybe they lose some weight, maybe they have a kid, maybe, maybe...but at most, the average person gets one or two big things. You, kiddo, are having a red-letter year. Obtaining an army, instantly doubling its size by working with the Red Market and establishing further ties with the Lady—you run a *city*, for Christ's sake, a whole state from the district of Tel Aviv and east for miles, with satellites in Tunisia, South America, and even a couple in the UF. You keep looking at these things as burdens, but ultimately you have more control than ever. You've got a bright, bright future, and you haven't needed me to ensure that. Yet."

"When I do, will you be there?"

"Haven't I always been since we met?"

The whines of the dog that had led the General to rescue Miki

Soto from traitorous René, the defiant sapphire eyes of Basil while he stopped the train. Her eye teared up but she couldn't relent. "You disappeared during the nastiest battle I've had in a long time, and haven't been around since."

"But I'm here now. Not for too long—things to do—but I want to be here for you, morally."

"You just don't want me to be alone with the Hierophant," she said, sniffing. He laughed as he offered her a handkerchief.

"True."

"Thanks for that. I don't think I have it in me to listen to him drone about…Lamb, I don't know, dreams or history or something."

"He's a walking sleeping pill sometimes, for sure." Chuckling, the magician resumed guiding Dominia west. "Will you trust me, kiddo? I know you're pissed: you go to all that trouble of replacing my dog-body, and both the dog and my body vanish…but I promise it's for a good reason. There's a lot of catching up to do after all that time wasted on four legs."

"Can't you at least tell me why you've spent so much time away?"

"I can tell you that it concerns a lot of people you love, including your little sister." That gave Dominia's attention new vibrancy.

"What about Lavinia? Can you tell me what I want to know?"

"All things in their time. Theodore knows more about her…and you know what Theo doesn't." The magician met Dominia's eye in a way so significant it pushed her heart down to regions neglected, to thoughts abandoned and cut out from the rest of her being. Thankfully, she could not linger there, for in the distance she saw what she first took as a statue of black and silver. Its shape, however, she knew with all the mixed thrill and sorrow of an estranged child for their parent. There, in the distance, stood the Lamb with his silver ram's horns—so still that if she had not known him for his patience, she might have thought him frozen in time. His black cloak did not even stir at his breath.

At her wonder, Valentinian reminded her, "The Lamb is always here. Even when he's on Earth. Always in two places at once. You can't imagine the stress. He can't get very far from his body, but he was able to come far enough tonight to visit you."

Lazarus had discussed this with her once, she recalled. This was what made him so effective when it came to altering probability and sometimes delivering external information in the form of epiphanies. While his body was on Earth, here stood his soul, contemplative as a man staring into a pool of water, his horns reflecting a muted echo of Valentinian's red flames back at the torches that cast them. Surely it was simple for a spirit who saw so much to arrange things—or nudge things—on Earth, much as Valentinian created things from the Ergosphere with the ease of speech.

"The last time we met, it didn't go so well." The General was hesitant to approach her preferred parent when she realized Valentinian would proceed no farther down the path. Gently, the magician smiled.

"Maybe from your perspective. He doesn't care what happened before. There's something he needs to show you. You need to understand that what you're doing really is the right thing, and you need to— Well. Just see."

"And you? When will I see you again?"

"When you need me," said the magician, a twinkle in his eye. The General shook her head.

"You know"—she glanced at Lamb, then back up to the magician—"you people love to talk—

"In useless riddles," she told the open air where once the magician stood. Allegedly stood, at any rate. She could never be completely sure of anything anymore. The General turned back to find with a start that the Lamb now stood a hair's breadth from her face.

"Dominia." He extended his hand. "We haven't much time. Things here move quickly. My body was far from here when my spirit departed to come to you, and it still is, but I will be drawn back when it is forced to move."

There were so many things she wanted to ask. To say. She wanted to reject the hand he offered and argue with him about why he'd felt the need to alter probability so her Father lived on to ruin the world. Why he didn't alter it to stop the blast in Kabul that had killed all those human runners. If the Lamb could inspire feelings, why couldn't he inspire compassion in his followers—in the Hierophant—instead of this intense hatred? The hatred buzzed alive in her ear when at last, saying nothing, she took his hand and saw through the eyes of his body to experience what a head-splitting, soul-wrenching hurricane it was to be the Lamb—especially the Lamb standing at the head of a church, with all the people begging:

Please God

Please, please God

Please! Please please-please! Please God, please o God please God won't you HEAR me GOD why aren't you LISTENING to me God PLEASE LISTEN TO ME no not HIM ME BECAUSE PLEASE GOD I NEED YOU MORE THAN ANYONE IN THE WORLD RIGHT NOW, RIGHT NOW, RIGHT NOW, I BEG YOU, GOD.

The Lamb was not God. But the Hierophant had done a very good job of making martyrs think he might be God, or part of God. Just like the Hierophant, himself. The Lamb. The Son of God. Christ's message was *all* children were children of God, but who would listen to the message in a world like this? Who had listened to Christ, and who would listen now to this sad fellow with the ram's horns—implants that, meant to filter out some of the bombardment of radio-wave thoughts broadcast through the semi-constant low-frequency chatter of infinite minds praying all the time, only served as a funnel for those beggars front and center? In exchange for the loss of fidelity of those wild parishioners on the sidelines of the gathering, the implants amplified those early-to-arrive worshippers whose thoughts were ceaseless prayers for miracles without understanding a miracle's cost—without understanding that the smaller the probability of the thing they asked, the harder it was to enact. Not for the Lamb but for reality, which was always for the Lamb a strange word to describe the trembling of atoms in his fingers. No—this trembling of atoms. There were no fingers. There was the illusion of fingers reaching out to grasp the pulpit, and that illusion made the wood real by way of touch. Merciful touch! It was all the Lamb had to remember where he was.

Swaying behind Cicero, he reflected that it would mean nothing were he to collapse then and there. His brother would carry on using him. Strictly speaking, the Lamb always felt this fluish way because of excessive amounts of both dopamine and serotonin, and altered forms of dopamine and serotonin—created, of course, by the protein, which took an almost-sentient pleasure in warping his psychic abilities beyond the point of any recorded living martyr's. Not considered a problem, then, these spells of weakness, and they never prevented Cicero from hauling him country to country, plastered to his obsessive side as if the Lamb were a child given to wandering off in shopping malls. Mustn't let him wander off. Must parade him around in front of these desperate, empty, sad people who just wanted to meet God, to know their doings were permissible and that their lives were worth something. They just wanted to be terrible people while still deserving love.

Of course they deserved love, even these—but that was not the Lamb's responsibility. It never had been, but, oh! They had certainly striven to make it that way! Somehow they had convinced themselves that it was all God's fault—not anything in particular, mind, but "it," "everything," "anything." To a martyr, the Lamb was God on Earth: the winked and nodded Second Coming of Christ. They could not understand what the real Second Coming was meant to be, could not fathom that it was not a paltry and sorrowful man of flesh and pained spirit who watched the worshipers leap like dogs at Cicero's command: Sit! Stand! Kneel! Sit! Kneel! Kneel! Kneel! He would have told them to *crawl* if there were enough space between the pews, and they would have eaten it up. Cicero would have, too, for that was the kind of man he was. Mad with power and somehow bitter that he had not even more—just as he was still bitter that the General had torn out his eye. So bitter, in fact, that El Sacerdote had made it his mission to make everyone he met see what she had done. He wanted to make everyone uncomfortable with that big, black, neon-pupiled eye that roved at random, filling up Cicero's brain with useless Halcyon information as though it might see Dominia out there, praying, in the audience of his vulgar show.

"In the Churches of Europa," sneering Cicero admonished the crowd, "they are silent when I speak, and allow the Spirit of the Lord to wash over their hearts. Is it so important that your neighbors know how spiritual you are, you who bark and yelp your prayers in response to mine? Shut your mouths."

This was typical for a United Front church and typical for how Cicero dealt with it, for there were always so many new churches each time they swept through the nation that each needed to be taught El Sacerdote expected a certain degree of passivity among his parishioners. People of the Front were often much louder and more boisterous—happy—than their European counterparts, in part because the martyr population was smaller and they were not forced to live with the reality of their situation as much as the Europeans in capital cities who walked down a street and saw through the windows of any local butcher's shop the slaughter and dismemberment of humans. That was how the Hierophant had willed it. He had seen fit to render the human a base animal. To strip all dignity from the race rather than repressing the protein and covering up its existence as Elijah begged of Cicero that fateful night the Hierophant knocked on the brothers' door. He brought with him the false protein they themselves were so close to developing with Lazarus, whose name in those days was no more "Lazarus" than was Elijah's "Elijah" or Cicero's "Cicero." Elijah hadn't believed it a just gift—or just a gift—and was far more frightened to see a man, so towering, appear as his brother's perfect, though slightly aged, duplicate. But Cicero!

Elijah had never seen Cicero so excited as the moment he threw open the apartment door to find himself in the hall. The reformed geneticist turned scornful priest had been so keen to explore his Hierophant-given abilities that he hadn't anticipated the horrors of the martyr appetite—hadn't anticipated that appetite's effect on society, nor that all efforts to cultivate an artificial meat would fail.

Or maybe he had anticipated all that. The Lamb had. He had seen it clear as day and could still see it now, without even turning his head (though that was what it felt like, looking into various probabilities: turning a head that didn't exist). When his beloved brother held him down so the Hierophant could force the change upon him, Elijah awoke from his first death and found he could see all dimensions, everywhere, extending in all directions. Impossible directions. He could see with overwhelming terror that this was the future, this was the future, this was the future—and the future could only lead back to the past until all this could be undone like a knot tangled in the fabric of time. He had seen in that same instant what it was the martyrs truly devoured when they devoured the flesh and blood of man, because it was not a simple matter of the demands of misfolded proteins, or overexcited molecules that craved union with the sun. The protein part of the meat they ate, after all, was easy enough to solve with a bit of stuff from a petri dish! It worked for humans. Why didn't it work for martyrs? What was it that martyrs truly devoured? What was that awful truth in the background of hunts, meals, Noctisdomin Mass?

There was more to man than his flesh.

The Lamb could not explain it, but could show Dominia what he saw when, as usual, humans were put to weekly slaughter at the altar, dragged screaming and pleading in handcuffs and those very same electric collars devised to keep martyrs under control. The General saw through the Lamb's eyes the quivering overlap of an energy, hot and rosy. What was it? Fear? Sorrow? Souls? All of the above: emotion-despoiled electromagnetic energy. Those same fields that bonded the self to thoughtforms and guided the way in the Void—that was what martyrs truly devoured.

As always, the Lamb submitted his own throat to be cut by El Sacerdote, his blood added to the dish as the holiest and most significant portion of the sacrament. That blood was the reason for the Lamb's perpetual travel from church to church and back again, for that blood kept the martyrs who consumed it from requiring human flesh for another week. In this blood, Dominia could see and feel (for she was in the blood, part of the blood, a droplet now trickling out of the Lamb and into the great trough of herself) a substance that rendered martyrs submissive, that altered their brain and addicted them to the Church and burdened their bodies with guilt and shame and sorrow so they could not imagine anything beyond the material world. Heaven, to them, was but a shallow pair of pearly gates sitting on a bunch of stagnant clouds. God was a meaningless word, a faceless old man who kept them manacled like the blood of the false Lamb.

Was it that wretched stuff, not just hatred and shame, that kept thoughts of martyrs bound to flesh—focused on petty things like money and faith, rather than liberation into Truth? That was the nature of the Ergosphere, after all. Dominia had nearly forgotten! The Truth. The Truth, into which she dissolved as all the blood evaporated and there, in the distance, sat the Hierophant's study. Of course, the Truth seemed so impossible to verify she could not trust she existed within it even with perception of herself relative to another object! She shivered as she set out on her own dream-feet toward that distant box that glowed like the two trails of lights leading from it.

What had she and her men spent the last year trying to do but prove all this—yet how could even the greatest researcher prove anything when his instruments did not reliably enter the Void with him? What did technology mean when electric crafts on Earth were powered by imagination in this place? Measuring all this in any meaningful way seemed a process that would take years, if not centuries, from the material perspective. It was stunning the Hunters had cobbled together a formula to figure out how far in the future the exit teleporter needed to be activated for anything to go from point A to point B. Amazing they'd figured out how to make a mobile variant of that technology function even 25 percent of the time. In the time frame with which the Hunters had been working under Dominia, there had been no way to make meaningful progress in this strange new science of dreamtime travel. Asking for some sense of self so soon after seeing through the Lamb's eyes…that was just too much.

The door of the Hierophant's office stood before her, the automation of her feet through the dark leaving her to question whether she had existed until this moment. As if under remote control, her hand extended in a fist that rapped against the office's eastern door. Teddy could be heard shrieking, "A man was shot in front of me! My soul, condemned unjustly! And now I'm being kept in ignorance!"

The Hierophant, who had hastened to respond to the knock, cracked open the door (which she now saw was carved with an elaborate rendering of the birth of Adonis, bursting forth from the arrow impaled in his incestuous myrrh-tree mother) and made a sound of delight. He threw the portal wide as, in increasing pitch, Theodore carried on, "After all that I've been through, the least—the very *least* you 'people' could do for me is *tell me what is going on!*"

"We can't," answered Dominia, studying her own self with that one eye wide as hers had been. "We don't understand it all, ourselves."

Pleased as punch, as he himself would put it, the Hierophant looked between his duplicate daughters, then considered the cue in his hand. "Care to close out our dear friend's game, my girl?"

"With pleasure," said the real Dominia, that present Dominia, that most-real-yet self of herself, who watched the Hierophant turn back to study the best position to place the white ball. Theodore looked the way the past shade of Dominia felt: confused and nauseous. Though no doubt he couldn't comprehend the fascinating feedback loop of making unbroken eye contact with oneself, the feeling of being the output of a camera that filmed its own output. But on what screen?

"Are you coming?" Valentinian's words snapped her back to her own present and out of the single-eyed gaze of that less whole other self who wheeled around, saw the magician at the start of a new path blazing with healthy red torches, and hurried to meet him. As the door (this the tragic hunting Death of Adonis) swung shut, its slam caused the Hierophant to miss his own stubborn fourteen ball. This left the white cue glowing with a shot made just for Dominia to take out Valentinian's missed three.

"Please, somebody"—Teddy sank into one of the seats by the fire— "is there any more of that drug you gave me before the flights?"

"Not here," said Dominia. The crimson ball, a spinning comet, cracked beneath her hand into the gold-striped nine and sent them into respective side and corner pockets. "But we can talk about it back in reality."

To her credit, the General realized she'd abandoned Tenchi in the darkness of the still-deactivated airship sometime before she'd closed out the game of pool. Her human friends assured her that the torches had left the craft in visible condition, therefore protecting the Ichigawa cousin from dissipation. But after her own experiences wandering the nighttime Void in the form of a tiger, she finished that game in three shots (one of which seemed physically impossible even as she watched it) and thrust the cue into the hand of her Father. Even he, to his credit, appeared impressed, and tucked the stick into the crook of his elbow for a golf clap.

"Brava, my girl. Another round? A glass of wine?"

"Wine," Theodore began, even as his sister dropped a hand upon his shoulder.

"We'll pass." She nodded in the direction of Gethsemane and Farhad. "They don't imbibe."

"Such a shame. Spiritual reasons?" As the humans stood, frigid and silent except for the occasional sound of Cassandra's laughter or humming as it jittered from the area of Gethsemane's heart, the Holy Father waggled the cue along with his brow. "Convert to the Holy Martyr Church, my children, and you may imbibe all you please."

"Leave them alone," said the General. "You've done enough damage to Teddy. Speaking of—are you ready to go?"

"But I have questions," the shrill little man said, trying (and failing) to twist out of his sister's grip. "Why would you do that to me?"

"Have to keep Dominia on her toes somehow, don't I?"

"What the— I'm a *person*. Father, I—" With a pained furrow of his brow, Teddy scowled between the two martyrs, then asked the Hierophant the same question Dominia had asked an infinite number of times over the course of not just her journey but her life. "Why did you martyr me at all if you're just going to try to disappear me? If you're not going to rescue me from *them*? Why did you martyr me just to put me through all this?"

"Oh, Theo. Your beloved Father wishes you no harm! No death can come here. I'm only playing a game with a few people who don't concern you, and sadly you're in the middle of it. Don't worry. Since you've made it this far, I'll swoop in and rescue you soon enough."

"Okay," said Dominia, repressing a gag, "we're leaving now."

"No! I want to know!" Now, Theodore was successful in jerking out of her grip, and he stormed up to the Hierophant in a terrific imitation of a more menacing man's rage. "Why are you letting this happen to me? Why bring me this far, then try to kill me?"

How the Hierophant's face changed in a moment like this, when it was time for the truth to come out! She'd seen that ice-cold expression at the same party that had sent her packing to Canada for two sweet decades of no contact with her evil, dysfunctional Family, but there was no memory that could recreate it nor no description that could do justice to that flip of a switch within his offended mind. "Because you're just not that *important*, Theodore," was his razor-blade answer, which left the man visibly shocked, hands spread as if defending a physical assault. "To Lavinia, you are. But not to me. Do you realize, lad, that if I killed you at this very instant, you would awaken back on Earth, floating in the ice-cold waters of the Atlantic Ocean? Do you know how terrible it is for a martyr to drown?"

"What's wrong with you?" Teddy fell back one step, then several when the Holy Father remained immobile. "Are you—are you feeling okay, Father? Don't you know it's me?"

"Don't patronize me, Theodore. Of course I know it's you. Your ability to whine is impossible to imitate. You asked; I but answer. You speak as if all I have ever done was an act of cruelty when you *asked* for this life. *Begged* me for it. I generously rewarded you with the Family bloodline and the platonic company of my most beautiful, purehearted daughter, and you act as if it has all been some burden. I am 'allowing' this to happen to you because you are not as important as the events in which you are involved—and I tried to 'disappear you' just now, as you put it, because Dominia is at this moment responsible for your life. Your death while in her custody would cause her tremendous pain—pain to such extent it might annihilate the remains of her spirit." Now those eyes, obsidian daggers, flicked in the General's direction. She watched with her own blue orb shadowed in hatred. "Never fear, though, Teddy." His attention returned to his shell-shocked youngest child, and his tone of voice lightened just enough to emphasize how black it had been but seconds before. "Soon enough, you'll be returned to safety. And once you're in *my* custody, you will be safe again."

The look on Teddy's face as he glanced toward Dominia indicated he wasn't so sure.

IV

Assume the Port of Mars

An encounter with the Holy Father's true persona had a way of changing his children, as Dominia could have told Theodore. But any warning to such effect would have been lost on a Family member still enthralled by that perfect mask of the jolly old trickster—Lavinia would be crushed by exposure to those treacherous turns of mood, taken with him as she'd always been. Teddy was a close second place for the intensity of his delusions when it came to the Hierophant, and the frightful experience's effect on his mind showed in the hunch of his shoulders and the twist of his silent mouth on the way back to the airship.

For some strange reason, the black sun hadn't risen in the sky. Knowing what she did of time in that place, she suspected some event had yet to unfold. The notion would make no sense to her waking brain, but there it seemed somehow natural that anyone or anything that wanted to interact with her could hold time's march through its day/night cycles. Especially if that thing was the Lady.

Slowing her pace to match Gethsemane's, the martyr investigated her scattered human friend and carefully took her hand. This action seemed, however briefly, to solidify the woman into the state she was on Earth—that beautiful, dreadlocked creature whose heritage was such a combination of countries and cultures that she seemed alien enough without the added aspects of the naiad. "We'll get you home," said Dominia. This was the wrong thing to say; the girl didn't speak, but her throat made a noise like Cassandra's nastiest laughter. "You don't think so? If I can't protect you, surely your Lady will, and She's all this space."

"My Lady will use me as She sees fit," the Bearer answered in a resigned tone. "After your Father's words in the study, I am concerned that you feel responsible for my condition as much as you do for Theodore's."

"Of course I feel responsible. I let you—"

"It is not up to you to 'let' me come or go anywhere," the human said, not unkindly. "I came with you because such a thing was demanded of me—and because I could not have rested with the thought of our last meeting being a sorrowful one where one or both was lost to war."

After a glance over his shoulder for the women, Farhad hurried his pace to increase their privacy while the General said, "I don't see why you have to think about our last meeting at all."

"Our paths are about to diverge, Dominia." The human used the martyr's name so seldom that the latter listened all the harder to her friend's words. "I have thought on the matter some since we came ashore with the Ichigawas last week… You remember the Lady, and how She insisted to you that I come?"

Who could forget? That had been at that meeting in the library basement after Jerusalem's twelfth drone bombing. Sixty-three civilians had been wounded and twenty-two were already among the dead. Teddy's kidnapping, suggested by the Lady a mere two nights before this incident, sounded better to Dominia all the time.

Lazarus, however, had disagreed. In their makeshift war room, the old mystic had sat across from her and defied the Lady's anticipation that he would agree with whatever the General proposed. "We don't need Theo," he said. "There are safer ways to start a war if that's what you want—and if it's really information you're after on a personal level, well…we know everything we need to know about Lavinia. What we don't know can be extrapolated."

"Maybe *you* know about Lavinia." The General stared him down across a veritable ocean of charts, atlases, time tables, flight paths, and one or two example electrodart guns. "Have something you'd like to share with me? With the rest of the group?"

"I don't know." Lazarus returned her stare as coldly as she delivered it. "Do you?"

It wasn't that the General and Lazarus hadn't gotten along over the past year. However, it was undeniable that, as time went on, tensions rose, and Dominia had begun to sense that, day by day, they reached a point for which the many-lived man spent each life waiting.

In service to those tensions, she was careful with her words. Then again, Dominia was always careful when discussing her younger sister. "I know more about Lavinia than the public, but I don't know as much about her as Theodore, and I don't know with any degree of certainty why my Father has kept her locked up. All this time he could have been teaching her how to control her emotions and use her powers responsibly. Akachi was right. It's more than obsession. My Father doesn't do anything without good reason, and he doesn't get attached to anyone on a personal level. That indicates he's keeping her locked up for some purpose, but what?"

"Maybe to lure you back home now," Lazarus posited. The General scoffed and waved the thought away before looking at the Lady, who studied the room with Her unmoving face. The still body, kneeling upon a slightly raised platform against the northern wall, reverberated with the same symphony as Dominia's skeleton.

There are worse things than that the General should face her fear.

"Yeah," Lazarus came back, his expression tight. "Worse things, like what we'll have to do to get her back after she's trapped. We can't risk it. You know better than anybody here all the resources required if we allow her capture."

The same number of resources as will be utilized, anyway. We are already at war.

"And you think kidnapping the Governor of the United Front is going to soothe that war?"

It was a fight nobody wanted to get in the middle of. As the room hovered in uneasy silence, the goddess calmly responded, *Theodore is a weak-willed and sycophantic individual. To rally him to Our cause shall be next to nothing, with rich long-term rewards.*

"Yeah, but he's made out of paper. It's just as easy for him to blow back his Father's way the second we let him. The second—"

This all assumes the plan will go wrong, and the General will be captured. Is that what you anticipate?

The annoyed old man studied Dominia's face (for its own part, arranged in displeasure) and concluded, "I suppose we don't have any better ideas."

With the gates of Elsinore tightly barred and traffic in and out of the city controlled, consider how low the odds of anyone slipping in and out to deliver information, establish a teleporter—or, in a dream, free Lavinia with any measure of success.

"I've already agreed to it, haven't I?"

Looking satisfied for as little emotion as the unmoving face that had once belonged to Miki Soto now expressed, the Lady turned her attention to Dominia. *To soothe the fears of Lazarus, bring Gethsemane with you.*

"She doesn't need to come," Dominia said while the Bearer stood at attention and showed no signs of opinion. "She'd be risking her life for nothing— I've already expressed tonight how wary I am about your suggestion of letting First Mate Ichigawa be responsible for our physical passage to the Front."

Perhaps you would prefer to walk through the Ergosphere?

"That's what I'm saying. Gethsemane *can't.* I've seen her." The General had bristled, nearing the point of dropping the last pretense of respect. "If something goes wrong with the E4 and Gethsemane is there—"

Then it must be Our will that this is so. Would you, mortal, contest Our will? The will of Our Void? We, who gave you sight? Who taught you to speak? Who crafted the world in which you live?

Oh, Dominina hated this. Hated the impotence, hated the genuflecting, hated the service. She was absolutely through with this life of submission to those in power. And it wasn't so much that Dominia wanted power, herself. It was just that she didn't want to watch people in power hurt those she loved anymore. Gethsemane had done much for her in the past year in terms of showing her that she could still bond, at least in a guilty way, with another being. The human *had*, despite Theodore's judgement, relieved the burden of Cassandra in a tangible way. Dominia knew that Cassandra's remains were cared for, adored, polished, and worn in a way that honored them—a silly thing, perhaps, but it was important to her. It made her feel like her wife was alive and…maybe on vacation, somewhere. They had tried that once, about fourteen years in, when Dominia was afraid it wasn't working out. Her wife had gone off somewhere for a year, just to see what it was like to be alone. The Governess had been miserable, sick as a dog. Oh, Cassandra…what a beautiful thing it was, coming home after work one morning and seeing her bags in the foyer. Smelling the edges of her perfume in the air. Dominia still couldn't even remember climbing the stairs.

Somehow, the diamond around Gethsemane's neck made it seem like that moment of reunion was still a possibility. Her human friend even went so far as to accept the burden here, in this place where it added to the shifting of her body (and, no doubt) the shifting of her mind. As that loyal friend called her back to the present with a gently chided, "You have fallen silent, General—take care not to be lost in thought, as you tell me," the martyr stopped her.

"I think it's too much, asking you to carry my wife for me here. I know your strength, but you're dealing with enough with the nymph—I don't know, leaking into you—"

"Revealing herself in me."

"Sure," said the General, trying to chuckle and coming up short. Instead, frowning, she took the Bearer's hands. "Did the Lady tell you something, anything, that we—you—can expect on this journey? Did She send you here to die with me, or for me?"

The human's eyes lowered from Dominia's to study the ground as illuminated by the torches. Ocean waves, frozen in time, felt flat beneath their feet though they visibly rippled across the illuminated portions of the path. "After all that you have seen, do you really still believe in death?"

That old surge of panic, of loss to discover her tears washed Cassandra's blood from her hands—wasted upon the carpet like her brain matter. "If death isn't real," said the one-eyed General, "it does a good job of pretending it is."

"Yes, it does. But you have met him, yes? Death. So have I." As Dominia gathered her meaning, Gethsemane confessed, "In the escape tunnels of the Lady's temple, when we fled with Her—"

Son of a bitch. That was where he'd gone! Of course Akachi would have a handful of of men waiting for the women. Even if he felt the odds weren't in his favor, it would have been worth a shot. Mentioning it to Dominia would have been humiliating for him when his plan fell through, but as Gethsemane described how the half-baked Hunter assault on the escaping women had been foiled by the appearance of the magician, all the martyr could think to ask was, "Why didn't you tell me?"

"Because, I—" Now the woman looked supremely uncomfortable and seemed to struggle for an explanation; it was the most discomforted Dominia had ever seen the stoic human appear. "He turned their guns to birds that pecked and chased them back to the tunnel's exit, and I watched and laughed with everyone, but then—something happened. He did not ask me to keep it to myself, but I...I am a woman of faith, General, and know my spirit is bonded to a fae, a nymph beyond all space and time, but I have no firsthand experience of a thing like this."

Time stopped, she said. The birds in the distance froze midair around the heads of the men they harassed; the women froze midlaughter, midapplause. Even the Lady was still. Only Gethsemane and the magician had remained mobile, and he had turned around and spoken strange things to her. "You are the daughter of the Word," he'd said. "All Bearers are daughters of the Word, and you above all its daughters are cherished, Gethsemane, for it is you most cherished by Dominia. Many times you have died—it is the duty of all Bearers to live many lives and die in miniature as the universe dies in grand, unseeable scale. But no more will you perish, and just as it seems the eve of your death has come, there I will be for you, instead, with one more task for you to commit upon your father's behalf."

When time restarted, it did not simply restart: rather, Gethsemane came to in the Lady's safe house, many miles away, with no memory of what had occurred in between. None of her sisters remembered even the Hunter assault in the tunnels; and the Lady, while not denying the event had happened, had Herself encouraged Gethsemane to keep the event quiet. *Your sisters are not so advanced as you in ways of the spirit—they would be jealous to hear such a thing, not understanding what it means, that you are favored by your father.*

"I have seen the magician in dreams before that time," the woman explained, "but that night was the first and only time I have seen him in person. This past year I grew convinced it was a dream, but…"

"But now you think your time has come."

"It is not time as you mean it. Not death as you know it."

Trying to contain her bitter anger at the forces around her and their penchant for giving friends just to strip them away, Dominia instead tried to focus on practical aspects. "If he says he'll take care of you…I guess that's all I can ask."

"I believe him, General. But I am…reluctant to leave this behind."

"From what I can tell, the other side is just more of the same. But better." With a squeeze of her hands, Dominia released her. The human bowed her head to remove Cassandra's diamond. As the little gem lowered into her palm, it was with the relief of an anxiety the General had not known she'd felt. There was the feeling in her face again. She lifted the gem to her lips to kiss its cold facets, and only on lowering her hand noticed the shocked gaze of Gethsemane trained somewhere behind her. The General turned, and against the distant dark, illuminated without need for her Father's profane torches, stood the Lady.

There is no difference between death and life. Death is an external illusion, as Our Bearer has tried to communicate to you. Walk with me, General.

As the goddess turned away, the martyr hesitated until her human companion cried, "You must go!" and physically pushed her off the path. Dominia, laughing slightly, turned to chide her, but was stunned. Empty space stood before her, the path back to the airship—and her friend upon it—vanished.

Wisdom keeps you from arguing too long with Gethsemane, for you know she has a duty. You know despite your trepidation that you take the right course of action. Irritation bubbled up in the General, who, after putting on Cassandra's diamond, stalked to the Lady's side. *In liberating him from the Front, you will do Theodore—and others—a great kindness, and receive information in exchange. And information is the truly fundamental element of this universe.*

"Where are we going?" As the deity continued apace, each step was accompanied by the eerie rattle of an invisible *suzu* bell, and Dominia felt faint anxiety to see the Lady walk, real event or no. That many-womaned entity smiled but a hair, Her lips unmoving even in the Void.

Have you not yet learned the futility of questions? We are here to show you something.

"But my friends—"

You will meet them again. This is not for their eyes.

A light grew in the distance toward which they marched, far greater than the lights pouring from the women. It seemed at first as though a true sunrise grew over the horizon of the world, but as she remembered they walked through the Ergosphere of a black hole that was little more than the encoded version of the planet Earth, she recognized by sound a black-and-silver block of sea that, animated unlike water for miles around in that frozen camera obscura of a half-world, foamed wildly within its confines.

"Is this some kind of dream?

All things are dream here: especially at night, when all the landscape is submerged in the darkness of Our waters. Even the Earth's waters are no match for them, and Earth's waters are a hungry, violent force. The Lady lifted a hand rendered invisible by the trailing sleeve of Her robe to gesture toward that ungenerous sea. From this distance—if distance could be said to exist in a place where waters roiled in the light of an invisible moon—the wrath with which that ocean thrashed was evident, its waves leaping high and collapsing upon their siblings like overexcited dogs presented with dinner. The closer she drew, the more its color changed—or gained, as its black waters bloomed crimson.

The Lady, unhesitating, made her way to its very edge to watch the waves lap Her feet.

What do you do when you have done all you can, General?

Following the Lady's suit, Dominia gazed into the waters and saw, reflected like a broken mirror by its foaming surface, a face that she first mistook as hers. She was just trying to discern what was wrong with it, this face that sat where she should have seen nothing or her own—until, as his hand burst forth to grab her ankle, she recognized Kahlil.

"You put me here," proclaimed a voice that she did not hear so much as feel. As though it reverberated not through air but through the hand that was joined by another to pull her into the reddened waves. *"I wasn't prepared to die, but you let me die. You knew what he would do. You could have saved me. But you didn't even move."*

Though she drew her gun to extricate herself from the grip, the General was awash with shame. "He would have killed you if I moved."

"You're the expert on killing."

Dominia pulled back the hammer of the gun.

"I guess so."

She had hoped the effect would be something akin to what one saw in old zombie movies—the two-dimensional sort she favored as a little girl, before the reality of being a monster wore away the charm of fiction. In all those stories, there would be moments where something happened like a half-rotted arm was blown to bits by a single, dramatic shot. This was not that. The bullet made contact with the arm that gripped her. At the second of impact, she was back in the Lady's temple, burying sheets of lead in the waves of men who came, body after body, to throw themselves at her like wheat begging to be threshed. All these bodies with families, these spirits with mothers and fathers and no souls, no hope—where had Dominia sent them? Where had they gone when they died?

Her mind flew back to the present conflict. She could not fire again. Could do no more than look helplessly over her shoulder. She hoped to find help from the Lady and instead discovered, in one piece, Tobias.

"Will you kill me again, General?"

As Dominia's mouth gaped in shock, the revenant forced her into the waves.

Time—if time could be said to exist in that place—halted the instant the General broke the strangling surface of the garnet waters. These were not like those waters that had transported her, miraculously, to the Kingdom. A raging tsunami of angry atoms comprised this ocean, a sea whose depth knew no more limit than did the vast collection of beleaguered souls assembling it. As Dominia drowned among them, she sensed their numbers to be very nearly limitless, and marveled: Had she killed so many in her life?

"Yes," was the resounding cry that seemed to come from her own mouth, forced open by the terrible pressure of the waters and filled with their bitterness. *"Yes, you have done this to us."*

A thousand battles, the Bitch of Europa. She had stopped reading about monsters because she had been one—yes, been worse, more pitiful, more contemptible, than one of the Lamb's dogs. Dogs had no sense of morality or consciousness, and dogs loved and cared for not just other dogs but other animals. But Dominia had turned off her ability to love. To care. She had rendered herself as deeply unconscious as possible so there could never be any question of what she did. Never any hard thinking. Any possibility of failure.

But, oh, on the other side of that! How love and caring had rushed into her at the proper time, like the horrors of reality on waking from a happy dream. Cassandra had been the medicant for her ills. A chance to be kind and gentle. An excuse to be a Governess, and stay her killing hand. Yet, she had kept that gun. A badge of who she had been. Of who she would, deep down inside, always be. The General.

"You've already ended the world for thousands of people," accused Akachi's death-paled voice, rattling her brain as her insides screamed for help. *"Why shouldn't you flee to your Father's side and end it for the rest of them?"*

She wished to have the voice to defend herself: to tell them she only did as she'd been ordered and that now—now, too, she was only doing the Lady's will. But there was no way for her to speak, to fight the current that dragged her ever deeper to the abyss.

"Just full of excuses," was Kahlil's response to her struggling thoughts. *"You're a user of people as bad or worse than Iblis, himself. You didn't care enough about Miki to save her. She was just a tool to you."*

Dominia couldn't bear it. She hadn't used anyone—hadn't wanted to, hadn't meant to. But hadn't she done it anyway?

"You have," answered a waver of a voice, softer and more tragic than any she had heard. Horror filled her to recognize Tenchi, of all good people, in that mass of unwashed spirits and corrupted souls. Hadn't he just been by the ship, and before (or after) that, in the Kingdom? It was impossible for him to be here, wasn't it?

"If you proceed along this path, I will never make it to the Kingdom."

But he wasn't more than a mile away, off fixing their airship!

"If you proceed along this path, I will never make it to the Kingdom."

The voice could only echo its one statement over and over, and the General's mind so burned she could only think in patterns—the words "Lady" and "help" over and over until the clamor of accusing, dead voices were hushed by the choir of the goddess.

We have brought you here for a reason. All of this happens for a reason. These spirits that assail you, these waters—what are they?

Her crimes? Her guilt? Her sorrow?

They are the same as anything else. Information.

At last, Dominia's sinking halted, and the waters burst around her. As they cleared to leave her floating in the Ergosphere without even ground, she discovered not only the Lady but, far as the eye could see, characters of various alphabets. It was as if she still possessed that DIOX-I that collected every passing Halcyon account and cluttered her vision with augmented features—but now, the world to be augmented had melted away, and she only saw its data.

"What is this?" The General marveled across this new sea of names, statistics, numbers, and letters arranged in no order or pattern she could discern except most of them were stuck in a single failed process, and many seemed to be nouns that were verbing in one way or another. Akachi swinging (she assumed his arm, up to defend his face from the *tulpa*), Kahlil springing (away from Akachi), Tenchi (tragically) begging for his life. Hundreds, thousands, more she did not recognize, names and functions she did not understand. Most were frozen in permanent stutter.

The conductive nature of salt water permits the transmission of subtle radio frequencies over short distances; it is a carrier for information, and the oceans here in the Void are overfull. As the Lady spoke, the General found her eye could stay on one fact no longer than a second before leaping to the next. *That same dark water of Our ocean is found everywhere in this place. Once a dreamer has been submerged in its substance, the encoded information of reality is everywhere one could look. This brand of perception is where the magician does his grandest work to intercede with the normal functions of reality. This is where you shall do yours.*

"Mine?" asked the General, seeing Tenchi's name again. "But what about him? Tenchi, he's here with us. I just saw him. What is this ocean? How can he be in it and without it?"

Because the Tenchi you see is the Tenchi you have already saved in the future.

The Lady turned to brush a fingertip across some piece of data floating past. A screen could not have been said to appear, though that was how Dominia perceived it, in a way: first one news broadcast, then another, until a great symphony floated across the back of her mind while the Lady activated data point on data point.

"—national tragedy as Governor Theodore del Medico—"

"—kidnapping at the hands of the terrorist organization now controlled by Dominia di—"

"—suspect in custody, thanks to an anonymous tip. Terrorist Tenchi Ichigawa—"

"—detained at the airport—"

"—no word yet on the location of the Governor—"

"—though the stolen jet crashed, no bodies were discovered—"

"—execution to be broadcast live—"

"—suspected to have escaped by boat, leaving Ichigawa behind."

Dominia, on the verge of tears, demanded, "But that's not true! We didn't leave him behind— René was—" Paled, the General looked into the face of the Lady. "René. He betrayed us again?"

René is a martyr now, and not one of your sort. He is not a man with a vision of a higher order, or a better world. He sees only this one, and sees his future in this one as being short-lived if he does not make good use of his new genetics.

"But what about Tenchi?"

If you were to proceed to Jerusalem with Theodore, Ichigawa would not make it to the Kingdom, for he has not yet consumed the blood of Lazarus on Earth from where you stand. He is a religious man, but has been too frightened to gain full initiation into the faith. Perhaps—the Lady's lip twitched—*you would do well to save all souls by tricking them, as you did Theodore. It is the easier way.*

The easier way, to be certain. It was always easier to trick somebody into something, rather than preparing them for what they'd actually have to do. That was why she found herself here.

You cannot prevent Tenchi's capture. By the time of your E4's crash, it has already occurred, and your Father has solidified your presence in this place. But there is time enough for you to reach the location of Tenchi's execution.

With a thought for the vial of old Lazarene blood, around her neck along with Cassandra's diamond even in this place, listless Dominia began to understand her fate. "I'm not saving him. I'm trading myself for him. I'll show up, have enough time to save Tenchi, and then they'll ship me off."

To Kronborg, in Denmark: yes.

The Hierophant possessed many castles, but it was Kronborg Castle in the European city of Old Elsinore he most favored for captives, for raising new family members, and for generally enjoying his "downtime." The climate was favorable to martyrs, and its distance from any (sensible) human-habitable nation was vast. Having grown up around the warm and coastal Mephitolian landscape, with its sweet nights and its dreamlike cities, she had no special love for that dreary place. But, ah, now that she thought on it, how she missed her home! Particularly that real-life Atlantis, Venezia, that drowned city raised from the dead by the Hierophant's passionate love of restoring that which had been beautiful so long ago that people had forgotten it ever existed.

Grimacing, Dominia tore her thoughts from nostalgia and leveled her gaze with the Lady. "You're trying to make me want to go back to Europa."

You want to go back, Dominia. Of course you do: it is your home. Do we not, all of us, long for the past?

"Do you?"

We are the past, and the future. But most of all, We are the present. All things are present in that which We are: therefore, We feel no particular longing for any one thing. But you have the dubious fortune of fully experiencing the present. Of experiencing desire, loss, and all emotions. Therefore, you are more powerful, and more whole, than We are.

Laughing, Dominia asked, "How am I supposed to be more powerful than you?"

Because it is not Our job, or the job of Lazarus, to create the world. It is your job, as much as its destruction also lies in your hands.

"But *really*, why me? Why, why? I don't understand why I'm whipped up in all of this."

Because you are the daughter of the Hierophant. And not any daughter. You are one who commiserates with the Lady and her children. You are a hero who shall bridge both worlds. And the strength and purity of your wish, not only to be someone different, but to rectify what you have wronged…this is something that cannot be matched.

"All I want is Cassandra back. I didn't wrong her. I didn't wrong anyone. I was only ever doing my job."

The silent Lady studied Dominia's face, names and numbers floating between the two of them as though to demonstrate how incorrect she was. At the thick silence of the deity, the General scoffed.

"I suppose you're right…it's my duty."

You have always known it to be your duty. You have denied the weight of responsibility—have run from it. But will you now take it on? There is more at stake than the life of the human named Tenchi Ichigawa. The goddess plucked the name from the air and held it between Her thumb and forefinger. *He is but data.*

As She released the name to fly away, the silent General watched it go, then watched the Lady's unmoving face as She approached in the company of those grave bells. *Now begins the most dangerous phase of your duties. I urge you, no matter what happens, do not forget your loyalty to Us; and do not forget this place. Have you Akachi's necklace?*

The General nodded, and the goddess touched her forehead. *Then make good with your friends when you awake. They will understand.*

"Lady"—Dominia's body dissolved, but she still had a litany of questions before she proceeded forward in this great task. All of them, she knew, would go unanswered if not asked in these seconds—"tell me, please: How is it that Cassandra's diamond comes to this place so reliably—Lazarus's blood, even, or the plane with the blood running through it—when other objects we try to bring within might or might not be with us when we arrive?"

Because the diamond is Cassandra, of course. And the blood of Lazarus— that is like asking why you can carry a key to the other side of its door.

As her forehead burst into a trillion golden molecules, the General started awake to find herself by a fire she had made to crackle comfortably beside the dozing airship. Gethsemane lay in her arms and Farhad snored on the other side of the blaze, with Teddy and Tenchi tucked safe into seats of the E4. Around them, darkness relented to the gray of morning.

Understanding as she did, she wished it hadn't come.

V

Ten Thousand Leagues Across the Sea

Theodore was second to wake that morning. Stirred, perhaps, by the General's soft footfalls as she leaned into the E4 to ensure the well-being of the sleeping men. While she dismissed the fire, her brother crept out to greet her, and whispered in the soft light of dawn, "Get inside!"

"It doesn't burn," she said, hearing Valentinian's soft reprimand of her bullying ways and therefore avoiding tacking on some unnecessary cruel nickname—though a couple did spring to mind. "It's not really a sun that's about to rise. People just call it that because…it's easier. But it looks black."

"Black Sun— Is *this* Father's project?"

With a glance for her sleeping companions, Dominia jerked her head in the direction of the plane's other side. As she rounded the craft with her relative and got some meters away, she asked, "Do you remember what happened last night?"

"Do you not? I went to sleep praying all this would turn out to be some dream…considering the way last night went, I guess it's stupid to ask God for help! What *is* this place? Are we in hell?"

All the old familiar questions. How was she to explain any of this to somebody like Teddy? "Well, it's like—like we're asleep. Do you know how light is a particle and a wave? Consciousness is like that, too. And when a brain is asleep, or dead, the ego enters a low-frequency wave state that can take our consciousnesses here, too—but a high frequency also allows the state, in a more desirable and controllable…"

Oh, the look on his face! She drifted off on seeing her own failure to engage him. Now she understood the dilemma of the holy man and his magical son when confronted by her military mind. Theodore had spent a whole life worshiping money and had sought membership in the Holy Family not out of spiritual devotion but financial gain. There was no celebrity on Earth like a Holy Family member, reviled by some but adored by too many—and literally worshipped by an interesting cross section of both camps. Any car in which the Hierophant rode was bound to be the cause of traffic jams and, from time to time, complete closure of whole towns as people suspended business and camped along his travel routes just to fling themselves against the surface of his car, begging for a handkerchief or a ring or a kiss. Such trifles (the kisses especially) he delivered in abundance, but the devotees he loved best were those humans with mental illness severe enough to buy the martyr lie that the fastest, most guaranteed route to heaven for a human being was to be devoured by the Hierophant. If women screamed to sleep with Dominia, men and women alike emerged in morbid handfuls to beg to be eaten, even in part, by His Holiness.

Failing him, any Holy Family member would do, and the closer they were to the Hierophant, the better. That meant that a martyr on the level of Theodore would never be at risk of starvation. He was a simpering, whining dolt amid his peers, but because he was a famous martyr, he could walk into any club on Earth and attract abundant attention from that most unpleasant subset of Renfielding losers who would settle for a quick fuck and the donation of some blood in exchange for the dubious honor of having been with one of the Family. The General had never been interested in obtaining food from such a source (not to mention the risks of accidentally martyring some stupid fan), but Teddy loved the ease, and although he only had real eyes for Lavinia, he wasn't hard up for company. Earth held for Dominia's stupid younger brother everything he ever could have wanted; and, like most individuals martyred in adulthood, his life revolved around a semisecret terror of death. He'd walked the planet for a hundred years, and nowhere in there had he taken the time for any kind of spiritual or moral insight.

Yet—hadn't Dominia been that way? Lamb! Who was she to judge her brother's ignorance when she had spent over three hundred years doing just the same? Her own wife had taught Noctisdomin school every week for decades before moving on to specialize in music, and never in that time had the General—the Governess—considered such matters, herself. She hadn't wanted to. They frightened her. In that moment, standing before Theodore and called to answer his questions, Dominia wondered for the first time if a lack of spiritual interest was not rooted in fear. The same fear she saw in Theodore's eyes and heard on the edges of his questions. The General knew that fear very well. She, too, was afraid—afraid of what God would think of her many atrocities.

Or was she just afraid of her own opinion? She wasn't sure. She hadn't checked in on herself for years. Too busy taking care of other people. After answering a few basic questions about the substance of the place (and the electromagnetic fields that, with the increase of dawn during their conversation, began to appear in those brilliant alien colors to spur only further queries), she asked her brother, "How are you doing, Theo?"

"Oh, God." He waved both hands in the disgusted fashion of an old woman waiting for Saint Valentinian because she found life too exhausting. "Who knows? Who cares? I feel like I've had my whole concept of existence upended—my whole life! Everybody here is acting like this stuff is no big deal. You know…when I was a kid, I wanted more than *anything* to be adopted by some martyrs."

Here, the General did not smirk, because that was a fairly common dream among a certain brand of human. Nor had she been blind to the way Theodore preened about for his first twenty or so years as a quasi-immortal being. "If only we had traded places."

"If only! Some nights I would pray—really *pray*, Dominia, feverish prayer for hours after I should have been asleep—that my parents would be killed, and all my potential could be seen."

"Prayer doesn't work like that, buddy." With an awkward glance over her shoulder for the jet shielding them from their human companions, Dominia tried to give him an out. "Were they…abusive to you?"

"Oh, no," he said, crushing the last possibility of empathy for his personality. "They would just send me to bed without supper for things like back talk, or what-have-you…but that's a *sin*, you know, denying children food!"

"Is it? That's what Father says. Maybe it's a cruel act to withhold food from a martyr child, knowing what starvation does to us, but is it a sin?"

Teddy wore the answer on his haggard expression. "That's just the thing. I was *sure* it was days—has it been days? I can't tell here, I know we just got here, but for some reason—anyway, I was *sure* of that days ago. And now…he tried to *disappear* me, Dominia. Like I was somebody he didn't even know. First he damned my soul without any recourse; then he tried to make me think I didn't exist!"

"That's the Holy Father for you."

"But he's not supposed to be like that to *me*. I'm a martyr! His child!"

"Welcome to my world. He's culled his children in the past." Before them, extending across the landscape like the kings of Macbeth's vision, Dominia saw the generations of historical Holy Family members who had been martyred and had their martyring completed long before her human birth. She did not ask if her vision was as sensible to feeling as to sight, nor if the vision was only of her mind. There was no difference here, and no real answer. Not even Theodore's lack of response for the image marked it as true hallucination—perhaps it was but a reality only she saw. She tore her eye from those many bleeding and eviscerated Family members whose memorial paintings were forever seared into her brain, and continued her warning to Theodore. They would vanish if she ignored them. "Father's children get too powerful, or get their own ideas, or discover something about him and his society. Then they have to be taken out." There: already gone.

"But not me! Let's face it, Dominia—I'm a gross little sycophant!" While his sister laughed in shock, Teddy offered a small, self-deprecating grin. "I mean, for most of my adult life, I've made it my job description to do whatever he wants me to do. He should know I'm not going to hurt anybody, let alone him! I'm not a threat, not on anybody's side in—whatever *this* is! I don't even want to be involved with all that stuff in the Front. You think I want to be all the way out there, with all those human hicks, dealing with their half-person problems?"

Prickly, Dominia said, "I love the people of the Front. They're good, kind, hardworking people. Hopeful people. Martyrs have been living in their territory for almost two thousand years, and openly ruling it for centuries—but they still believe it's a worthwhile place to live. That being near their friends and family and neighbors is worth the risks."

"Of course you love the Front, Cassandra was there for you! But me? Once I've slept with a woman once or twice, she won't give me the time of night! I have to settle for humans... I guess I shouldn't judge you."

"Maybe your problem is that women aren't into sycophants."

"I *know* that." He sighed pathetically and stared out into the graying Ergosphere, at the peaks of solid ocean water that drew themselves, crystalized, from the darkness. "It's not like I haven't tried to make a name for myself. I'll have you know I graduated—*very* high in my class in my medical program. I had so much *promise*. I knew so much!"

"That's why the Hierophant tried to get rid of you. He knows how much you know, and he doesn't want you telling me." Yet allowed him to come this far—why, she now understood with sickening clarity. Her brother protested on.

"But you *know* everything I do. More!"

"We know different things. And I think there's at least one thing he's sworn you to total secrecy about...I know what it is, but there's something I think you can help me confirm." The edges of an admission ached a jaw she shifted in silence before she continued. "I think it's sort of true, what he was getting at yesterday. I don't think it mattered much to him that we were able to acquire you. In fact...I think he even prefers it. He knows this is the most expedient method of getting his hands on me. Trading you for me."

As he took her meaning, Theodore hacked out a high laugh. "You're going *back* to him? After you went to all the trouble of getting me?"

"I have to. Our man, Tenchi— I have to."

"That sailor? What *about* him? He's sleeping in the plane!"

"Time is very complicated here. I can't get into it now, but"—she thought of brave Gethsemane once more, accepting entry into the Void and taking Valentinian's word that he would come for her—"this is bigger than me. The Lady guided me here, insisted certain people be here with me—She set all this up so that I would have to turn around." With a surge of bitter laughter, the General covered her face in her hands. "Oh, you bitch. It was the only way to make me return to Europa."

"You can't just kidnap me, then leave me with these strangers while *you* get to go home!"

Her hands dropped. "You really want to go home to the guy who tried to annihilate your soul because it would ruin my mental state?" At Teddy's immediate silence, she continued, "Ultimately, I'm going back to save Lavinia, so you should be grateful. At least, so far as *I'm* concerned, that's why I'm going back."

"Save Lavinia! Save Lavinia from what? Herself? Not Father— She's the only person in the world he wouldn't hurt."

No time like the present. Even so, that present seemed long, and her forehead burned with unspoken thoughts. Focused off on the dusty dawn as seen through the warping bands of her field, she wished for but a moment she could be anywhere but the body whose mouth formed the words, "I'm going to ask you a question, Theo. It's something I'd like confirmed before I make this rash move. I just need you to remember that I probably know the answer, so it's okay to tell me. And, anyway—you have nothing to lose after what happened last night."

Visibly dubious at the idea of releasing sensitive information, even cut off from reality and the Family, Theodore asked, "What is it?"

How to say it? How to ask? More importantly, how to ask it in a way that would elicit the truth? She hadn't thought on it much, hoping the words would come in the moment. Thankfully, they did when she opened her mouth. It gathered its sound after but a second of hesitation.

"Does Lavinia understand that she's fertile, or has he somehow hidden it from *her*, too?"

The look on Theodore's face, from the brief, gobsmacked part of his lips to the bloom of his pupils, told Dominia all she ever needed to know from him. For just under sixty-eight years, Lavinia had been in the public eye. Throughout that time, the General feigned ignorance of her condition with the kind of acting that deserved not award but prosecution.

Perhaps because he had nothing left to lose, or because of the way she chose to ask the question, his response was: "No—she has no idea."

She found sweet catharsis embedded in those words. So Dominia was not a fool to do this, this going home. Not a complete fool, anyway. There was a reason for her return. A far more foolish thing would be leaving the world's only fertile martyr at home with the Holy Father until he decided the time was right to start experimenting.

"But how did you know that?" asked Teddy, whose bafflement never faded.

Maybe she did know more than the Governor had ever known. Maybe the problem was Dominia's, for being unable to admit those facts she held. "He keeps her locked away, doesn't he?"

"Well, yes, but she's also *dangerous*. That's plenty of reason to control her movement, it's no reason to think…really, though, how did you know she's fertile?"

With one more look at the edges of her sleeping companions, Dominia waved her brother close. When he bent his head, she cupped her hand and whispered for a time in his ear. Just two short sentences. Two small facts, which Theodore hadn't known, and which so shocked him that he pulled away from Dominia with a new, perhaps visible, appreciation for her evil. Or maybe she was just projecting.

"Please." She glanced at her companions. "Don't tell them. I don't think they'd respect me anymore."

"Dominia…I had no idea you had it in you."

She managed her grimmest smile, which left her eye untouched. "Neither did I, until it was all over."

"No wonder…no wonder." Frowning, Theodore shook his head, and looked at Dominia without a hint of his usual clownishness. She'd never seen him so serious, in fact, and it almost worried her as he stood in contemplative silence for an uncountable time.

"You know," he decided at last, "I don't think I've ever had what it takes to be a martyr."

"Very few people do."

"But you do."

"Yes. I wish I could say I 'did,' and that the person I was then was a totally different person from who I am now, but…I have to bear responsibility for my own sins." With a glance toward the E4, then up to the black sun illuminating the darkness, Dominia realized that sun also illuminated something new *in* that darkness. Beyond and through and within her compass glowed neon threads: thin jet-stream lasers that, thinner than strands of silk, were suspended in the air and seemed, at certain points, gathered in clusters. As she noted these and became amazed, new ones appeared, and others faded. Violet was the color of these new threads, rather than the gentle cerulean of the ones prior. The astonished General looked all around herself, and as Teddy asked, "What is it?" she grew sure he could not see them.

"I don't know." With a delicate touch, she stroked a lavender thread that inspired a fascinating flash of understanding. Namely, that the threads represented digital data. All the information one might retrieve about an electronic device—from its location based on its IP address to its purpose to its user's name—could be divined at the tap of a thread. How *easy* such a thing might make navigating one's way across the Ergosphere! Retrieving information! *This,* or some variation of it, was surely how Lazarus and Valentinian found their ways across this space more precisely than by their warping compasses. Some artifact of her dream-epiphany—if it had been a dream at all. Perhaps if she had dreamed of the True Words while staying in the Void, she might have retained the memories of those dreams, too. She regretted she hadn't.

She was more uncertain of dreams all the time. That moment more than any seemed to indicate dreams may well have been closer to reality than she'd have cared to think, as Tenchi's sudden cry pierced the air. Both martyrs leapt to immediate defense, Dominia out of instinct and her brother out of terror, but both soon recognized the sound as excitement.

"*Yatta! Wakarimasu*, oh—oh, I *get* it, okay—"

Then the air rumbled with the life of the aircraft: no more the stuttering on and off of yesterday's brief efforts, but the prolonged rumble of a plane ready for takeoff. Floored, the General darted to the jet's other side, past her stirring companions, and called to the wide-eyed first mate. "Tenchi! How did you get it working again?"

"I—I don't— I had a *dream*. And I learned the name of the ship, it's—" His words abruptly ended in the manner of someone trying to work a True Word into a sentence, and the lights of the cabin blasted so bright it appeared the BLP might have come back online. As Dominia comprehended in a click, the sailor frowned. "I just said it, but no sound came out."

"Because, you genius, it's not just a name. It *is* the ship." In wonder, Dominia said, "Say it again," and watched Tenchi's face. No hint of movement crossed his mouth, just as no movement might have emerged from Dominia's while she called up light or fire; yet there was another burst of power in the ship, another groan as if from a living thing. The General laughed and slapped the human on the back.

"Look at you, Tenchi! This is incredible. I understand, now. Any ship coming in or out of the Ergosphere has to be—amphibious, you could call it."

"Like me, General," Gethsemane said, sitting up and rubbing her eyes amid all the excitement.

"Yes," agreed Dominia. "Like you…a physical, earthly thing, imbued with the spirit of a Word…or a Word's daughter. Bound to the blood of Lazarus, somehow. But how?"

Farhad, who was not as on edge as the veteran martyr but still a high-strung man of war, had determined the commotion that awoke him was not a threat, and now shifted about, consulting the broad bands of an electromagnetic field that quadrupled in size as the airship—or amphibiship—came online. "If it could give a man like Tobias Akachi a soul, why could the blood not impart a spirit to a plane? Allah would not permit a righteous man who loved his ship to be eternally without her, or a pilot who loved his plane, or a rider who loved his camel. The spirit of your gun is here, Mahdi. Perhaps Tenchi was brought here because it was known he would connect to the plane in an…emotional way."

"Emotional valence," said the thoughtful General, crossing her arms and regarding both the sailor and the craft. "Personality has to be given to the thing…someone has to think well enough of it long enough to produce its real name. You're saying its name, Tenchi, though it doesn't sound like it. You know a True Word, now. Did the Lady come to you in your dream?"

"No," said the sailor, looking and sounding surprised. "You did." At Dominia's start, the sailor continued, "It was so vivid—I thought I was awake! You told me you wanted to talk to me before bed, after everybody settled down. After you started the fire for the night." An event of which she had no memory, but go on. "We walked off a ways with your light, and then you…started showing me these pictures in my head."

Frowning, Tenchi touched his forehead and laughed. "It's funny. It's not that I'm remembering the name so much as…I have to remember the sequence of pictures you showed me leading up to the name, and then I remember it's—"

The plane's radio cranked on, and the disembodied voice of none other than Valentinian carried throughout the amphibiship's cabin. "—for the weather. Looks like another calm day over the Atlantic Ocean, folks, but 'calm' doesn't mean 'short,' so if you have someplace to be and a craft of some kind to travel there in, I'd get along as soon as possible. Never know when conditions will change out there, and especially never know when conditions will change in reality. You'll know you've gone far enough east when your friendly neighborhood magician stops you for the night. And if you're planning to walk"— Dominia's ears perked up, her expression remaining neutral even as the eyes of her companions turned to scrutinize her—"then just be glad your Father shot you folks down well before your intended extraction point, or else you'd be in for an even longer march. Thanks for listening: now back to the music."

Said "music" was just a hissing wave of static. With a frown, Dominia stepped aboard to shut the radio off, then turned to see her friends crowded at the door.

"Are you separating from us, Mahdi?" Farhad stroked his beard before offering, "The men will suppose you a traitor if we return without you. If you are going where I suspect you are."

"I have to help somebody." She glanced at Tenchi. The sailor, flushing, lowered his gaze until she looked back at her other friends. "Several somebodies. Lavinia, my sister in Elsinore—she needs me more than you do. I've been plagued by that this year, and I need to face it."

"I wish you wouldn't go," Teddy whined while she hopped down from the craft.

"I wish I didn't have to. But I do." With brief acknowledgment of the woman who stuttered between, say, half the hair or one of the eyes of the nymph before jolting back to her own features, the General said, "Nobody here needs me much longer, anyhow."

"No," said Gethsemane. "But we want you."

Tender words that took some strength to be spoken from a woman who would put the will of her deity over her own life. It was the will of that deity that had sent Dominia thus—but also the weight of her own guilt. With that in mind, she glanced at Theodore, and asked, "Still want to return to the Family after everything that happened last night?"

"Oh, of course not! Get me as far away from him as possible. But…" He studied the humans before saying to his sister, "After what you said to me back there, you're doing the right thing by going back for her. Somebody needs to."

"Thank you. Travel safe, everybody. I have to—" Her heart sagged in her chest and the General turned to avoid revealing her sorrow. "I should get going. Don't want to drag this out."

Definitely not. She was tired of parting ways with her friends. Once,

Miki and Kahlil had left her by way of that cherry-colored rental car. Now both of them were dead, strictly speaking, though she had seen both—Miki's body, and Kahlil's spirit—last night, in her dream. "Dream." What was a dream in this place?

Maybe just a conversation hidden in a private pocket of the universe within the self. Without looking back at the vanishing point of her friends as the humming amphibiship rose under the hands of Farhad and his spiritual copilot (first mate), Dominia set out east and received help from those threads that had overflowed from a recent pocket of hers. The data collapsed, reformed, recolored based on her intention. Each step, she followed not her imprecise compass but the ethereal veins that guided her directly to Tenchi's execution in America. Three weeks from his capture: this date, implied by the sailor's testament to walking three days, was confirmed by the threads that contained enormous assortments of information conveniently arranged by humans. How incredible it was! How convenient the mortal development of the Internet made navigating this formless space, which was dark even in daylight!

"It is most convenient," agreed the voice of her Father, who startled her only slightly as he appeared to her blinded right.

"Where did you come from?"

"I thought I would accompany you, since it seemed to me you could use a friend in a moment like this."

"A friend, yes. Not you."

"What better friend have you than I, my daughter?"

She tried not to roll her eyes. "Can't you just wait for me to come to you? Do you always have to show up to bother me?"

"Then you would be alone with your own thoughts. Far worse than listening to me drone on." Still smiling, he plucked a metaphysical thread that Dominia could not herself see at that moment, her mind being focused on other matters. "Isn't it funny how all it takes for us to gain a new power in this place is to *notice* something? To apply a bit of attention—of consciousness. So much is revealed when we wake up to what has been around us all this time! At any rate, as you were thinking—yes, my dear, the Internet is convenient for mortals. More convenient, still, for those entities that thrive in multiple dimensions. It's far easier for thoughtforms to enter the human mind when they have the gateway of digital data. All the stuff on your computer is but a physically intelligible form of pure information. To attract a so-called demon once upon a time, one either had to be very sick, or very curious. Now all that attachment requires is the Internet. If I can find any person in the world by studying this stuff long enough, imagine what effects could be had by a thoughtform attracted to some vapid vessel emptied out by a panoply of funny cat pictures and permutations of cartoon frogs."

Ridiculous. "Are you trying to tell me the Internet is a cause of spiritual or demonic possession?"

"It can be. There are a few other ways for one to be possessed. Think about it—that old classic horror-movie method of reading the wrong grimoire isn't a far cry from visiting a nefarious website or adopting the nasty predilections of a terroristic chat room. Anytime one gives up control of one's mind to a concept, that is, strictly speaking, a form of possession: extremist politic groups possess fragile human minds all the time, hence the Hunters and the very UF militias you've put down. However, in a place such as this, one is tempted to symbologize the concept—"

"Please!" The General sighed in exasperation. "Please, I just got up and I had a long night."

"So sorry to hear that, princess. Rest assured, your suffering is soon at its end. With these threads, you can even navigate in the dark, albeit at your own peril. I only mean to say that, even through a digital interface, the mind of the individual is a powerful portal into this place and back. Into the future, and eternity."

"Did you come here just to pontificate?"

"No, my dear. As I said, I came to keep you from being alone with your treacherous thoughts. Would not want you feeling bad about all this, would we?"

"'All this'? What's 'this'?"

"Why, this business of your running away. Of Cassandra. *I* think you did the right thing, darling. Doesn't that matter for anything?"

"Of course you think I did the right thing." Laying her hand across her forehead as though to physically shield her brain from the onslaught of the Hierophant's words, she said, "You corrupted me."

His tone was infinitely calm and inappropriately teasing. "It's always my fault, isn't it, Dominia?"

"It *is*, damn it! It's your fault that I was martyred! That I turned out this way. I didn't ask to be martyred. Fuck—I never asked to be born as a *human*!"

"Didn't you?"

The General's mouth opened to silence, then shut in like fashion, and she realized only then that she had, at some point, stopped walking to focus on arguing with her Father. Nonetheless, the black sun continued its dark journey against its indigo backdrop, as though the contents of their conversation (or perhaps the distant journey of her companions) was enough to move that great dot toward its destination, and the end of Tenchi's life. As she carried on at double pace, she said, "Maybe a past me, my last self, set me up so I could be here, sure. I freely admit that if you ask me right now if I'd do all this again just to be with Cassandra—if that was the only way to be with Cassandra again, I'd do it. But *I*—the 'me' I am right now, with *my* memories and *my* choices and *my* future still open before me—I never asked for any of this. You never had to show up at my parents' house. You never had to martyr me. Theodore has every right to be pissed at you. Why did you do any of that, if you knew what would happen?"

"Because, my dear girl! I love you."

"Oh, shut up."

"Now you're only hurting my feelings. It's true."

"Okay," she said, trying not to roll her eye as he carried on, "Who could *but* love such a scrappy cub falling into their arms, ready to fight them to the death! My good, bold girl with such big opinions. I knew your fate and wanted to save you. I wished to give you the immortality of martyrdom because I think it is still possible for you to make the right choice."

"It's a false immortality! Martyrs die all the time."

"You would know." That ugly little smile! She tried not to bite off her own tongue, particularly as the Lady's voice emanated from her left periphery.

Waste less time tormenting your daughter. You are the murderer of races, of planets, and of a greater number of humans than even the General.

"Yes," he said, with that look of cartoonish innocence, "but all those deaths were necessary, if you ask me. Dominia cannot say the same. Therein lies her problem."

"Are you both real?" she asked sharply, while the two walking behind her carried on with only the Hierophant's unhelpful, "I imagine I'm as real as she is."

You, Dominia, are a distinct entity within the Ergosphere, the Lady more helpfully explained. *Easy to find. A landmark of your own. It is the energy you exhibit. Space bends around you.*

"Me?" she asked, but the Hierophant already carried on. "Since you are so eager to join in on conversations to which you were not invited, O Lady, let me give you context: we were just discussing my concerns that Dominia cannot accept responsibility for her actions and wants, more than anything, to blame the woes of her life upon me."

"I take responsibility for what I've done, but I don't take responsibility for what you've done, or what you've made me do."

"What I've made you do is, strictly speaking, most of what you've done, for most of your life."

No wonder she was such a violent person, as much as she was forced to repress around him! With a twitch of her hand, the General turned her attention toward the Lady. Under the light of so-called day, Her image seemed infinitely more unstable than had Gethsemane's: it consisted of not just Miki Soto but her red-haired predecessor, and hers, and, and, and, until Dominia looked so deeply into the Lady under the black sun that she saw the first, hefty avatar, whose melanin-dark skin was baked further by the sun and whose body seemed immobile (and who, in retrospect, probably began the tradition of the Lady's permanent carriage from place to place in the mortal world). Despite her size, this manifestation glided with feminine ease across the frozen waves of the Ergosphere.

Not shown among all the visions was that black entity that had appeared briefly during Miki's ascension. Dominia realized with an uncanny chill that this was because the being was the substance around them: the black waters of the Lady that contained all forms of data, including the dead, and potentially dead.

"Yes, Dominia," said the Hierophant, again annoying her with his observation of her thoughts. "All the dead dwell here, though I have never discovered the means by which to contact them. Have you?"

"Why don't you just dig through my head and find out?"

"I understand that you saw the dead, yet I do not understand the mechanism. But what potential if one *could*! Why, even bodily resurrection would be possible."

"Please," she begged, but he went on.

"I mean it, my girl, I mean it from love for you! Would it not be glorious to bring your Cassandra back into the world? Even after the crime your cruelty forced her to commit against herself?"

"I didn't force her to do anything. And I wasn't cruel, either."

"I'm not certain your wife would agree."

"Look!" The word was expressed as a hiss while she wheeled on him, having barely fought the impulse to clutch the lapels of his jacket and crack his nose with her skull. "You want to have this fight with me right now? No problem. I loved Cassandra. I did everything I did *because* I loved Cassandra. What she did to herself was a calculated decision to hurt me. If anybody was cruel, it was *her*. Right?" On turning to the Lady, Dominia was deflated by the multi-woman's cold appraisal.

There is no conscious being without fault in the world of the Hierophant. The Lady was polite enough to refrain from offending the General, who deserved to be offended. *The difficulty is not in having faults, or even in their improvement, but in their admission.*

There was the old motherfucker with his Shakespeare: "'The fault, dear Brutus, is not in our stars, but in ourselves.'"

"I can admit my faults," the General insisted, pained, drowning in her own arguments and sorry self-denial. "I can admit everything I did while in my Father's service. I orchestrated genocide. I didn't even do it, myself. I stood like a coward in the shadows, where I helped suggest and design a calculated effort to eliminate undesirables in the human race while trying to attract new, other undesirables for future food. But I only did this because of the values *he* instilled in me."

What else have you done as a result of what you were taught was acceptable?

The General's throat closed as if in allergic reaction to the truth. She turned her blinking eye to the light-bled sky, avoided her Father's gaze, hurried her pace. "I did what I had to do. I did what I had to do for my family, and for my species, and for my own sanity. I did what I had to do for my wife."

"You did it, also, to hurt her," suggested her Father. "Even if only slightly."

That did it. She couldn't stand it anymore. "And I'm sorry," she blurted, eye squeezing shut at a sudden flicker of Cassandra's face across her imagination. Flushed with the pleasure of love, stained with the tears of loss, lifting from the toilet bowl that fateful night after their marriage. That night when it was too late to do anything about the reality of the situation. Too late for Dominia to change her mind. "Yes," the General admitted in the thick silence of the Ergosphere, despite her stinging throat, "I'm sorry. Yes, I did."

She did. She put her wife to bed and left her, ostensibly to go out for some wine. Instead, she chartered her private jet to take her home to Europa, and went directly to Venezia's small but beautiful palazzo. The refuge's lease was awarded to her after her some long-forgotten victory when she was about Theodore's age, and would almost never be visited after the following nine months. After that, it was forever tied to the discovery of Cassandra's pregnancy.

A car waited for her at the airport, having been alerted to her arrival. Would she be staying long? She didn't know. She wasn't even sure what she was doing there. She had nothing to say to the driver. She had nothing to say to anyone. The car took Dominia directly to that old property where she discovered who else but her Father. She didn't mind. It was, ultimately, his domicile.

"What a pleasant surprise." He looked up from where he sat

reading in the parlor of her master apartment, his voice so full of pleasure it could only be described as a crow. "Is Cassandra awake, a martyr at last? Have you and she decided to honeymoon here? I shall be out by midnight, my girl."

Just listen to him talk. She slipped her keys into her suit pocket and sat across from him, in the high-backed chair by the empty Renaissance-era fireplace she studied for a long time—such a long time—before saying anything at all. Then, perhaps because of some particularly empty set of cherub eyes gazing out at her, the General scorned the barren stone mantle and said to the Hierophant, "Cassandra was pregnant."

He did not speak. Did not even move, the book still resting upon his knee with his hand upon its cover. She had a need to fill the silence, much as she wished she could fill that vile hollow that opened in her chest to comprehend this betrayal. "I'm not sure what to do."

"We will do everything we can to support her, of course," had been the Father's answer. Dominia studied him, expression bleak.

"She's very sick."

"She will survive."

"Will the baby?"

"Yes."

"You're positive?"

"Do you wish it were otherwise?"

Her lips pressed thin, the General said at a dark octave, "I wish this wasn't a problem."

"New life is never a 'problem.' My girl"—his tone took a dangerous turn of its own as he rose, the book in his massive hand revealing itself as a copy of *Divina Commedia* as he meandered around the coffee table—"I hope you are not suggesting what I think you are suggesting. Termination is one thing for a mere human—but for a martyr?"

"I don't know what I'm suggesting." Though unruffled by his approach or the danger in his tone, which seemed in that instant an almost welcome threat, she remained still as black marble Juno, gazing with empty eyes up at the book he rested on the mantle. "I just wish this hadn't happened. If I had known—"

"If you had known, you would have waited to martyr her, and martyred the child when it was old enough, yes? A happy family."

"I don't know. I don't want children. I've never wanted children— never wanted to do that to a child. Force it to be in this world."

Shaking his head, the Hierophant said, "Yet, how I wish it were otherwise! I so long to be a grandfather again. You've denied me for too many centuries."

"Would you settle for being a Father again?"

She had meant it as a joke, maybe. At least, that was what she told herself over and over through the years. Joke or not, the second the suggestion left her lips, it was too late. All that mirth in his eyes. He had waited for this moment—had known before Dominia presented him with Cassandra that this was how things ended up. How Dominia hated him for letting it get this far! Her love was a ploy to him. A means to acquire the new child he wanted. And not just a new child. A child born a martyr, rather than martyred in life.

After finding his quiet daughter sufficiently deferent to his soft-spoken threats, the Hierophant strolled to the bar to pour them both drinks. "Do you know, my girl, the true joy of parenting? It is the shaping of not just an individual but of a new generation: the future of a species. The trouble with being a martyr is that parenting is difficult—often traumatic for the child. But what a wonderful world it would be if our race could propagate the same as any other! How much suffering could be saved if the protein did not wreak havoc on the reproductive cells of the body, and we could produce live children."

With two glasses of burgundy wine, he returned to pass her one. "Most pregnant women would never knowingly be martyred. Those in a position to be martyred are not often in a position to be pregnant or are not interested in such things. My own legal restriction on the martyring of pregnant women is one of—well, it does rather pose me a problem, does it not? I am used to reviewing the martyring of chil-dren, or I was before our effort at population expansion these past few decades. We are a highly selective breed. And, frankly, the majority of martyr pregnancies will certainly end in the death of both mother and baby. The amount of nutrition required to maintain both is untenable. Trust me, I have studied this subject. But it *is* possible to maintain the child to birth. And what is possible, to even a narrow degree, our good Lamb can make reality. He could turn the odds in favor of mother and baby; and being given as they would round-the-clock medical care with attention and techniques far in advance of public technologies available at present…imagine the possibilities."

"Why is this so important to you?"

"She must be no more than five or six months into her pregnancy—you met her in July, and we're in September now, so she must have conceived long enough before your meeting for her to have known."

"She told me she's five months."

"Ah…so just before your trouble at Nogales, give or take a few weeks. Very interesting." Acting like he didn't know, as always. She hated him twice as much in memory! But in that moment, what he proposed next was so extraordinary that she simply couldn't feel anything, let alone hatred. "If the infant is a girl, her ovaries will be developed by now, but her eggs may not be complete. Lamb be willing…"

"You think the baby would be born fertile."

"I'm certain of it. The transition sterilizes a martyr because of the death process the body undergoes between their human and martyr existence; normal functions of puberty in a prepubescent are aborted and replicated by the protein, which cannot replicate healthy reproductive cells and cannot, therefore, generate novel life. But when the protein is introduced in the womb, it presents a unique opportunity in the appropriate circumstances, with the right medical care and a mother who can survive to term. In such a theoretical case, the protein is like a third parent. The sperm, the egg, and the protein make equal, early contributions to the fetus, the shock of the death is lessened, and prepubescent functions are uninterrupted. Was Cassandra deceased long?" At the shake of Dominia's head, he continued his thought. "With a child in the womb, there is a longer, enforced incubation period in which the protein can make improvements, and more resources to improve *with*— Cassandra's resources."

Staring out into space, the wine staining her lips more opaque with each sip, the General said, "She lied to me."

"She did not know what else to do," was her Father's gentle assurance.

"Will you help me, really? She can't ever know about this. Can't know that you're responsible for this."

"*You* are responsible for this, my girl. But she will not know. At the opportune time, we will make it all seem very believable that her baby has died. This will not be difficult to mimic. The protein will take advantage of the baby's state of un-life and alter much, causing many physical problems until she is completely developed. But however difficult it is, when the moment of delivery comes, the infant will be out of your hands before poor Cassandra has even had a chance to think about what happened. Why, I'm even feeling inclined to offer you a promotion for bringing all this to me up front. I so value your honesty, Dominia."

"And how will you keep her from figuring out your new kid is hers?"

"Oh, we'll concoct something. Will she have time to think of such things as the new Sponsa Prima of the United Front? As I said, there will be complications in the process, and the child will need be hidden from the public eye for some time. By the time our people become aware of the new Family member, Cassandra will have long convinced herself that her child died. She won't connect the two."

"Do you think she's stupid?"

"Of course not—but do you realize how paranoid she would have to be to believe the truth?"

After finishing her wine, Dominia took a second bottle and returned by the same jet on which she'd left. Maybe on her departure she'd intended to leave Cassandra for good, but now she returned with a better alternative and gentler face, her fury having been purged by the time her wife awoke after a long, dense, coma-like slumber.

"We'll get through this," Dominia swore, smoothing her wife's golden waves. "I promise. We'll get through this together, Cassandra."

By the time the General was freed from the shameful memory that she had ignored and denied for almost a hundred years, it seemed that the Hierophant and Lady had both left her. Both, surely, had business to attend to in reality; and both, surely, knew that she drew near New Elsinore. She had traveled days while plunged in those awful thoughts. Somehow, it didn't alarm her; perhaps because she had no emotional energy left after reviewing that terrible meeting.

Above her, the black sun had vanished from sight. The tangles of red thread were far more numerous, and she wondered if this was not a result of the livestream of the execution. Vultures tuning in to watch poor Tenchi die.

Good. She wanted an audience.

The strings she followed converged at the reflection in the Void of that physical point in space-time that concerned the psyches and phones of so many across the globe. With a chill, Dominia plucked the heart of the threads, and saw uncountable news broadcasts all discussing the same thing: Cicero's demand that the Governor of the United Front be returned, with Tenchi's life at stake. First Mate Tenchi Ichigawa, the terrorist.

More like Tenchi, the good-natured sailor who had never done anything wrong—who had encountered Dominia at the start of her journey and been a friendly, generous, albeit cowardly little fellow. A purehearted and sweet enough man that he could even bond with an inanimate ship, and render it animate. This was a man who did not deserve to die for any so-called cause.

Closing her eyes, Dominia focused on the strings beneath her hands, and spoke that True Word for "reality."

This method was never any less disorienting than her trip through space had been. Particularly not this time, as the black Void submitted to the image of reality that she had half seen replicated in the news broadcasts reflected by the threads. A New Elsinore court building, full to the brim with reporters: with Cicero and the Lamb, and, most of all, Tenchi, who let out a tearful cry of absolute joy as the General tore the vial of Lazarus's blood from her throat, shattered it against the desk where the prisoner awaited his fate, then sprang across to wipe her bloodstained fingers over Tenchi's mouth.

"Drink the blood, Tenchi," she urged amid Cicero's shouts that the guards, already moving in, needed control of Dominia before she hurt one of the screaming reporters. "Drink the blood, and when you end up in the Ergosphere, walk east until you meet the magician!"

"What are you talking about?" he said, instinctively licking his lips at the moment massive hands claimed the General's arms and gun barrels were pushed against her head. She laughed all the same to know that Tenchi was saved, and lifted her gaze to find one intrepid reporter whose cameraman still filmed from where they cowered in the corner. Too devoted to the story of a lifetime to worry how long that lifetime would be, it seemed.

"I am the terrorist Dominia di Mephitoli," she said, grinning in defiance as her face was forced to the table and her wrists, cloistered by the tight snap of electrified cuffs, "and I've come here tonight to surrender."

VI

Jiggety-Jig

On waking in her old Kronborg bedchambers, the first thought to cross Dominia's mind was one of suicide—but the window had been left unlocked, so she supposed her Father hoped for the possibility. Not an option. After sitting up, she absorbed her second conscious element of the room: the bar, fresh-stocked with a panoply of spirits all artfully topped with a cheerful plum ribbon whose attached tag read "Welcome Home."

The third action of the homecome General was the defenestration of most bottles out the unbarred window and into the snowy gardens below, followed by the emptying of another—with a regretful whiff of wasted whiskey—into the roots of some hapless shrub too far beneath to be seen. A brusque knock upon the door attracted her attention as she turned for another. On her call of admission (in Mephitolian, the dominant language of her speech for the rest of that life on Earth), the Lamb stepped inside, a thin smile beneath his close-clipped beard.

"Making yourself at home, I see."

"Good night to you, too, Rabbi. I've come to the conclusion I have sort of a drinking problem." She hefted the nearest vessel of rum. "Want some?"

"This early in the evening? Please, as big a glass as you have." The General permitted herself the luxury of laughter and turned to pour her gentler parent a glass. He, arms folded, asked, "How was the…uh, flight over? Devolving from New Elsinore to Old…"

"Fine. The men Cicero assigned to accompany me only smelled a little nervous, from what I could tell through the muzzle. At least they were polite. How was *yours*?"

"Cushy." Accepting the drink, the Lamb lowered his ram-horned head to sniff the glass's contents. "Suppose you want to know about your friend."

"He's still alive, right?" Not that it mattered, him having had the blood, and her having seen his future spirit. One way or another, he was in the Ergosphere, and that would be true even if he'd been killed on Earth. That said, the thought of Tenchi's bodily death devastated her. Luckily, the Lamb nodded.

"Yeah—Cicero kept his word. You came back. Didn't bring Teddy with you, but execution's still off. Although—I'm sure you know this—it's mostly your Father's doing that stayed his hand. Cicero would love to slaughter everybody who's ever called themselves your friend after that whole marathon thing."

"I was stressed at the time." She jutted her chin in the direction of the door. "So, what's the deal? Am I under house arrest, or…"

"What do you think?"

"Of course not. Free to come and go as I please."

"I'm pretty sure he's having a car delivered for you today. Maybe tomorrow."

The snorting General studied the bedroom in which she'd finally parted ways with those cagey guards following about twenty-four hours' worth of check-in, transportation, and checkout. Had she not administered such hasty captures and deliveries, herself, she would have been disoriented, but to be fair, the bedrooms in Kronborg were disorienting enough on their own. She had always disliked the castle's style of placing its beds so they floated in the center of the floor, rather than standing with the support of a sensible wall. This was a problem with most of their estates, which, aside from a few modifications and the odd added balcony or torture chamber, were fussily maintained in their "proper" condition. Kronborg was the exception in its architecture—whole wings had been added to the castle with the Hierophant's cautious oversight—but the added rooms could have passed for original parts of the building, so carefully they had been furnished. She didn't see why it mattered where the damn bed went, or how the furniture looked. With a palace like Versailles, she could understand, but Kronberg's design had always been more forgiving. Surely the bed could be put in a more comfortable position.

Lord love the Lamb, but she was already thinking about the place like she'd moved in to stay. Time to get Lavinia and get the fuck out.

"I'm glad to see you," the Lamb said, snapping her from thoughts he knew like his own. "But do you think it was the right thing to come back now?"

This room was no doubt as bugged as any other in the castle, with the Lamb two parts concerned Family member and one part sorry pawn. He may well have come to visit her of his own volition, but more likely he'd been sent to butter her up. That was the way things had been ever since she was a kid. Good cop/bad cop didn't even begin to cover dealing with the Lamb and Cicero. No matter how friendly the Lamb may have been to her cause, she could say nothing incriminating of herself, the Lady, or her intention to assist Lavinia. But even if she shared no information, interactions with her Family members could be perilous to her resolve.

In the many histories of infinite universes, the General must have defected a litany of times for a laundry list of reasons, none of which she knew. This meant the Hierophant also knew of the possibilities and may even have known a few of the concrete ways she defected before—which meant she could pretend she was open to the possibility of returning home for good, as long as she didn't come on too strong.

The best solution was, as usual, a concoction of lie and reality. "I couldn't imagine what else to do," she said with a shrug. "I looked at myself and said, 'What am I doing?'" This was true. "I couldn't keep treading water out there. Just waiting for...something. I haven't felt myself at all lately. Then when I heard about Tenchi...it seemed like it was time to come back."

"Tired of waiting for the sky to collapse." The Lamb observed the open window through the murky glass of his drink. "Why sit around when you can collapse it, yourself?"

Best not to answer loaded questions, even from semi-sympathetic mouths. After two millennia of being beaten down by Cicero and the Hierophant, the Lamb was ultimately worth about as much as one of his own dogs. Speaking of: "Add any new animals to the collection since last year?"

"Oh, always a couple…you know how it is."

Yes, she did. The Lamb had a sensitive heart. He couldn't bear to leave abandoned the pets of those humans unlucky enough to attend a martyrs' Mass. Most relocated pets adjusted to their new homes with little problem. Dogs, and especially cats, forgave even homicide given sufficient food and affection. Could the same be said of God?

"Your Father would like to see you, when you get a moment." With one last bob of his throat, the Lamb drained the glass, set it at the edge of the emptied bar, and retraced his steps to the door. "I wouldn't have bothered you if he hadn't asked me to tell you that…not that I don't want to see you, but I'm sure you want some time alone."

The General offered a wan smile. "It's not that I don't want to see you, either."

She caught the barest edge of his upturned mouth as he shut the door. Alone, the General consulted her reflection in the vanity across from that oddly centered bed. No matter how often she studied it in reality, the vision of her body never aligned with what she pictured in her head, or how she appeared when wandering around in the Void—the Ergosphere. (Cogito, ergo…) Yes, she could shower in a downright glorious bathroom of which Hamlet never dreamed, could dress in one of the crisp white shirts and black suit pants stocked in the closet, could smooth back her hair and comb pomade through its dark strands until she looked like the bureaucrat she'd become after the army; but she felt forever her leather jacket, her flowing black hair, the phantom cup of a patch against her shut right eye. This person who she truly was felt like a great secret within her. Some source of power from which she could never be separated. The only consistency between these two selves was Cassandra's diamond. Her little wife who was with her in the Ergosphere and remained with her outside it—even if that wife could not be said to know.

It was that diamond that put her friends on her mind as she strode down the great checkerboard halls (not unlike her Father's dream study), past courtiers, servants, and a few human slaves. All of them marveled and whispered to see Dominia again. Now that she considered it, it had been some months since she'd spent any prolonged time in Kronborg. When she visited it in the wake of Cassandra's death, she'd hardly been of mind to take in her surroundings. Now alert, it was revealed to her that in the time she'd spent living and working in the United Front, the fashion of the castle women had grown stuffier than ever. An elaboration of petticoats and bustiers rendered most female specimen more akin to walking umbrellas in the midst of a windstorm than the sleek beings Dominia so loved. Meanwhile, men's fashion had remained the same over the past hundred years—save the number of breasts given a suit, or whether items such as hats and capes were "in." Seemed like "in" for short capes, "out" for hats. Easy. Was it any wonder the General preferred a more masculine fashion sense, even with long hair? Life was less complicated in a button-up shirt.

Of course, the explosion of suffocating fabrics for women was due in large part to the influence of one particular fashion maven, who was only a maven because no one dared tell her no. This same unqualified influencer dashed around a distant corner with such a furious *tap-tap-tap* of slippers—of both herself and her bevy of attendants—that Dominia fancied a small army of gazelles charged down the hall. It was only Lavinia, who, on seeing her older sister from across the distant moonlit path, let her great black skirts fall swishing around her feet so as to clasp her hands over her heart and cry, "Oh, *Ninny!*"

"Lavinia," said the General, bracing herself much as she would while in the presence of the Lamb's dogs. Lavinia hurtled down the hall and threw herself, weeping, into Dominia's arms with such force that the slim girl might have bowled her over amid the added weight of all those petticoats.

"Ninny! Ninny, I've been so *worried* about you! Oh, I'm so happy you're *home*! Where are you going? We have to talk! Were you scared?"

Hard to answer twenty questions at once. She settled for two. "Father wants to see me. I was never in any real danger." Simpler to lie on that last bit than to point out that Lavinia's beloved "Daddy" was responsible for most—or all—of the danger in which Dominia had been put. Bad personal choices aside.

Granted, were her choices all that bad? Looking at Lavinia's tearful face, the General couldn't help but think there was no possibility for her sister's life to have gone another way. Would the Hierophant have *allowed* Cassandra to keep the child, had Dominia not donated her to him? Would that have been all the more traumatic for her little wife? Hadn't this been the better choice?

"Ninny," said Lavinia, "you're frowning! You've got that little line you get in your forehead. What's the matter?"

"Nothing's the matter, Lavinia. I've just been more worried about you than you've been about me, that's all. And I'm still worried about you."

"Worried about *me*, silly!" As the Princess of Europa tittered, so did the coterie hired to shield her from loneliness—and perhaps, Dominia now realized, shield her from knowledge of her own fertile body. Two of the gutless harpies hid behind their fans while a third, attractive one, made brazen eye contact with the General. "Why would anyone worry about *me*! I'm the most spoiled girl on Earth."

At least she was sort of in touch with reality. Dominia forced a smile. "I guess I was worried about you, worrying for me."

"Oh, that's silly." With a sudden fox-sly look about and a dropping of her voice, Lavinia leaned in to ask, "Do you have to go see Daddy right *now*?"

"I better get it over with, don't you think?"

In an adorable moue of concern that resembled a dilution of Cassandra's soft features, the girl nibbled the edge of her lip, then replaced her lip with the pink tip of her gloved thumb as she gazed through the hall-length windows. Rather than acknowledge what may come of the meeting with her Father, Dominia would have opted to continue contemplating dreamy Elsinore's old world—frosted with snow like this, the town looked to the General like a movie set. She'd been here in summer many times, but she only ever pictured it in winter. Happy and peaceful times, winter. Reality insisted on intruding, much as Lavinia insisted on disrupting her thoughts with the urgent whisper, "Won't he be very angry with you, Ninny?"

She laughed. "That's your second understatement after assuming you're the most spoiled girl on Earth and not the most spoiled girl in this universe—and every other."

"I suppose I'm more spoiled than anyone on Mars. But you're trying to distract me! Don't you think you should come and spend time with me before you see Daddy?"

With a brief spell of nausea, the General eyed her adopted sister. "Do you know something I don't, Lavinia? He's not planning to execute me or anything, is he?"

"Oh, of course not! I hope not— Ninny, Daddy would *never* do that. At least, not since you came home." With her silk-enclosed hands fidgeting anxiously before her, Lavinia glanced once more out the window. "Can't I at least walk you to his office," she insisted.

It came to the General then. This was the worry of a little girl for her older sister's emotions. She was afraid that Dominia was secretly afraid, and trying to be brave. In all fairness…for Lavinia's sake, the General manufactured a smile and squeezed her gloved hand.

"Sure. You can walk with me."

The Princess of Europa's expression flipped in an instant, and she turned to her followers. "Why don't you girls run along and, oh, I don't know…amuse each other somehow!" While Dominia coughed at Lavinia's innocent choice of words and tried to keep her mind from inappropriate territory, the princess waved away her pretty friends as if shooing birds from window boxes. "I haven't time for you now, please! I must be alone with my sister."

"Is it *safe* for you to be alone with her, Your Majesty?" asked that girl who had eyed the General for reasons Dominia's ego mistook as attraction. Lavinia wheeled on this servant with a sharply narrowed gaze.

"Does my Daddy pay you to second-guess my decisions, or does he pay you to be my friend?" (*Slave*, Dominia mentally corrected.) "Run along now! I'll fetch you somehow when you're wanted."

Or put up a big, bratty fuss when they weren't telepathically where she expected them at the exact second she arbitrarily wanted their company again. Though aware of this fact as Dominia was, the girls obediently hurried away in a bustle of whispers—and one furtive glance from that scrutinizing one. Outside the occasional passing courtier going for an evening constitutional around the castle, the women were now alone, and Lavinia became a chatterbox. Oh, she had missed Dominia! She had cried for nights after that awful business in Kabul, but the General didn't need to worry because Lavinia had already forgiven her. Although Cicero—well, Cicero was another matter. He was *very* cross. But that was just like him, wasn't it? Not that he had ever been cross with Lavinia all that much, but, why, she had *seen* how he could be, and she had *certainly* seen how he was after all that business with his eye. Now, just why did Dominia *do* that, at any rate? Didn't she know the Golden Rule? Daddy's testament? "Do unto martyrs as you would have them do unto you"? Remember, Ninny? Ninny? Remember that?

"You know," said Dominia through a strained smile, "for some reason, I've always been bad at that one."

T(he)i(r) talking paused outside the door of the Hierophant's office, outrageously oversize and set at the end of the most strategically imposing hallway in any of his properties. Of significant length, its walls were decorated by tapestries that, one per century, detailed the Hierophant's various conquests and cultural developments. From his early years on Earth dancing between the Russian Federation and the North American Empire of the United States, through the persecution and emergence of the martyr people, past the colonization of Mars, and to the present day. The most recent three contributions prominently featured Dominia's many bloody victories with increasing prominence, until the Battle for the Reclamation of Mexico formed the centerpiece of the latest. It had been commissioned and produced to be ready for the turn of the century, and was revealed on New

Year's Day of 1997 AL, two years earlier than its standard due. When asked at the time, her Father had cheerfully responded he'd "wanted to get a hop on things." Now, the General understood he had wanted it here for this moment. To remind her all she'd done in his name. His psychological cruelty never lacked in detail.

From within the office drifted the eerie sound of music—what else but Mozart's Requiem. With a nervous look for the General, Lavinia pressed again: "You're sure you really *have* to see him now?"

"It's now or later… I'd rather get it over with."

"Will you come see me after, Ninny, and tell me what happened? I'm afraid. Daddy's so frightful when he's cross!"

"Surely he hasn't had many reasons to be cross with you," said Dominia, who now studied her sister's expression in search of some truth she knew not what. Lavinia's eyes dropped from the General's face, and the girl turned back the way they'd come.

"I can't be good *all* the time, Ninny. Goodness! I'm a saint, not God. But, oh, Ninny—" The girl frowned and fussed a moment, then darted back to plant a kiss on Dominia's cheek before she once more hurried down the hall. "I've missed you, I want you to be *here*! Please don't give him a reason to lock you up, or—oh, just don't."

"I'll try not to." The General squeezed out one last laugh, watching her sister go, before turning her attention back to the towering door. With a deep breath that came in time with the voice of *Tuba mirum*'s tenor, Dominia knocked its ivory-inlaid surface.

"*Entrez*," rang his pretentious reply. Steadying herself, she pushed open that great portal with both hands to find the Hierophant writing at his gilded desk with the fire crackling soft (and normal) in its marble place. Cicero, in one of two leather seats across from him, turned both his good eye and the rolling black one against this intruder to his appeal, then froze. His organic pupil dilated while the red one bloomed eerily within his DIOX-I.

"Dominia," acknowledged her curt brother, implied uncle, and least favorite Family member. She shut the door behind her and the Hierophant, in tone far more joyous, also called, "Ah, my Dominia!" and sprang from his seat to embrace her whether she wanted it or not. "My girl, my girl, my poor prodigal daughter"—she thought of the Lady, grimacing in his embrace, and hoped he couldn't read her thoughts here while he stood in the flesh—"mere words are not sufficient to relay my true relief. You're home! My dearest daughter is home, at last. I have spent every second of this year pining for your return."

"Good to see you, too," the General said, glancing but once at Cicero. She, for one, was glad to pretend she hadn't seen the Holy Father since last September's marathon. His immediate uptake of the charade was tacit reinforcement of his prior reassurance that El Sacerdote knew nothing of the Ergosphere, or the true nature of Lazarene blood. As he released her from his hug and she suffered his kiss upon her cheek, she marveled to see he'd even worked up a watery eye. Bravo. "I'm sort of surprised I'm allowed to wander around here, after all that's happened."

"As am I," muttered Cicero, turning his attention to the window behind the Hierophant's deserted wingback chair. "I hope the bruises from your acquisition last night have disappeared, sister."

"More or less," she assured him, glancing at her wrists, then studying that same empty seat. "Hope you're getting used to your cyborgan, 'brother.'"

Said eye whirled in her direction as the Hierophant, tutting, hid his smile on the way to reclaim his chair. Dominia remained in place by the door. "Now, children—this is why I brought you both here for this conversation. I'm sure after all the sordid business of the past year, there's nothing you would both like better than to ignore one another completely!"

Cicero, passive-aggressive as a cat, folded his hands and turned his face toward a bookshelf. "'Ignoring' is not on the list of things I would do to my sister, Father, if I had my way."

"So we're talking about each other like the other one's not in the room?" Cicero deigned to shoot her a dirty look while she continued, "Because if so, 'Dad,' I know a real douchebag with an over-waxed moustache, and—"

The Hierophant snapped his fingers until she stopped. "The same as it ever was, I see. My goodness—how long it takes carbon lifeforms to grow up! I am still engaged in the process, myself." With that twinkle about his eye, the Hierophant straightened the pages before him and set them neatly aside. "With dear Dominia, the odd immature moment is more understandable, at least from my perspective—although you are well over three hundred, my dear. Far too old for these shocking displays of immaturity. We will discuss that in time. But so far as you are concerned, dear Cicero—"

With his brows lifted in a way that mirrored the shocked arch of Cicero's, the Hierophant wagged his finger. "You are the most powerful priest in all my Church, aside, of course, from myself. Old as your brother, the Lamb, at two thousand! Yet, how easily you submit to the very *human* flaw of wrath! Too long you've held this grudge, this loss of your eye. How very many classic passages could either of us quote on this very topic? Each more on the nose than the last! 'Turn the other cheek,' 'an eye for an eye'"—he glanced at Dominia—"although that second is better advice for *you*. Won't you sit?"

Once Cicero scooted his chair as far left as the unsubtle squeaks of its stubby legs allowed, Dominia filled the vacant seat. The Hierophant folded his hands after favoring his children with an approving smile.

"There. It's so nice to have the Family back together again, don't you think?"

"I just saw Lavinia," said the General, licking her dry lips. "I've missed her. It was good to see her again. It's good to be welcomed back by somebody who cared that I was gone."

Worked like a charm every time. Tension could almost always be defused by shifting attention from the conflict at hand to the subject of Lavinia, for she seemed to inspire as intense an adoration in Cicero as she did in the Hierophant and Theodore—perhaps more, and in a way Dominia suspected was far more prurient than El Sacerdote was willing to admit. Mere mention of the girl could bring a bit of light to his beady black eyes. Doubtless moved by the spirit that the Duchess of Florence inspired, he landed a frosty pat upon the back of Dominia's hand. "We all cared that you were gone, my sister."

"You cannot begin to imagine," enthused the heartily approving Hierophant on his son's obvious lie. "How you've *worried* me! Not a night goes by that I do not think of you or what you have been doing. Not to mention the people you've been running around with! Hunters, Dominia? I cannot understand."

"I've been in a very dark place."

"To react to your wife's suicide by taking sensitive information to the enemy—sensitive information about which you knew, at the time, truly nothing!—in pursuit of an obvious dream…my poor daughter, yes. A dark place, indeed." Plucking up the hand that Cicero had touched, the Hierophant pulled her arm across the desk to kiss her unwilling knuckles, to pat them and say, "I am sorry you were so lost, and that I did not see. That I did not think to help you. We failed you, my girl. Poor, troubled Dominia. You have lived a harder life than I ever intended for you."

Though taken aback at the almost genuine tone of his apology, the General reminded herself that no matter how good it felt to hear these things, they were almost verifiably false. Her weakness for his empty repentance was never so much because she believed he loved her, or maintained a single kernel of goodness. Rather, this vulnerability to his gestures emerged because, for centuries, she had paid deliberate overattention to his panache for flattery and placation. How else was she to cope with her circumstances? As a child, she had been a captive, given no choice but to favor his good qualities while blinding herself to his bad ones. But there were plenty of times in those young days when—as she did when he turned to Cicero and said, "Now that I've broken the ice between you, my boy, if you would leave us…I would like a word with Dominia alone"—she was acutely aware of the Holy Father's more frightening capabilities. Blood drained to the bottoms of her feet. When she tried to slip her hand back, the Holy Father maintained his grip with a clamp of his hands effortlessly disguised as an affectionate pat.

"I suppose I must trust Father's judgment," crooned Cicero, who crossed himself and kissed his knuckles in the Hierophant's direction. "If His Holiness sees fit that you should come and go as you please, who am I to second-guess? Good to see you home, Dominia." He threw open the door and, with one arm, yanked the heavy thing shut behind him. "We're just all glad you're in one piece."

Alone with the Hierophant—and not in the dream of the Void, where he either could not hurt her or could only do so negligibly—Dominia willed her pulse to stay slow and calm, because she could tell he took it with that great grip around her left hand. This, she studied before glancing into his bleak eyes as he said of Cicero's comment, "Yes we are. The human world—the Hunter world—is of exceptional danger for a martyr. You know that, Dominia."

"I didn't know what choice I had," she said, unwilling to move even to shrug. "I didn't see a future if I stayed."

"For yourself, or for the planet?"

As her Father released her hand, having no doubt decided that she was sufficiently anxious, she studied the pale teal vein of her wrist. It was true. Cassandra had not been the only motivation in Dominia's abandonment of the Front, the Family. Only the final nail in the coffin. When, after her wife's death the General had grown queasy about an idea that her Father had announced at a secret military conference—that was the lowering of that coffin into the ground. Project Black Sun, which she had not understood at the time, had seemed ridiculous but terrifying, and sent Dominia on a one-woman campaign to flee the martyrs' oppressive religious state.

Now, the plan was only terrifying. She'd no idea back then how it could be possible for martyrs to survive in sunlight, as her Father claimed it would be once the project was fully initiated—but she'd felt deep concern that the attainment of such a goal would mean the destruction of the planet in addition to the human race. The idea of unhampered martyrs seemed unsustainable then, when she knew nothing of other dimensions, the value of virtual data, and her Father's possession of all of it. Did a martyr want to come and kill you? They just had to pop into your living room. No need for threshold technology, what was the use? Just be a good little sheep, don't say anything controversial on the Internet—Lamb, don't even *have* the Internet—be quiet, polite, obedient, ignorant, hardworking. Then maybe—just *maybe*, if you're very lucky—you or the people you love won't be turned into meat. The situation of Dominia's time, magnified to a point of absolute, unspeakable conclusion. Giving the entire race of martyrs the blood of Lazarus with the Hierophant's claws still in their minds would jeopardize reality, the Ergosphere, maybe even the Kingdom.

"You want to get your hands on Lazarus." She settled as far back in her seat as she could, her now-free hand folded over her ribs. "I understand, but I think what I thought when you asked for my help in Kabul."

"Very disappointing, if true. I have concealed the secrets of Lazarus from our people to protect martyrs from themselves until this race possessed sufficient foothold on the planet—and until we had possession of you." While she snorted, he continued. "This is truth. You are key in managing our people and their relationship with that sacred dream-space. Before the crises of your time, our population would not have been prepared to take it with the seriousness and respect required. After this comes to a head, and you are once more at my side, they will comprehend the gravity of the Void within the context of the Holy Martyr Church."

"So you haven't shown them yet because they lack a frame of reference? That's ridiculous. Let them build their own. Why do they have to experience it through the Church?"

He smiled thinly. "Without a frame of reference to apply to my Church, they will not continue to listen to me. I have told you this already—the problem with Regulus, and so many others in generations before yours. My advice is critical if the species is to survive; and if the species remains obedient to our cause, why do martyrs not deserve the blood of Lazarus?"

"It's a cultural problem, mostly. What would they do with themselves, these people—"

"*Our* people, Dominia, *your* people."

"—what would martyrs do," she corrected in irritation, "if given unlimited access to that place? To thoughtforms?" She lifted her eyebrows at the mere implication of that odious Memory Bride that had cleaved to her thoughts and produced a corrupted, ignorant duplicate of Cassandra, then succeeded in transitioning to the physical world, even if only to die at the General's hands. "Do you really want a planet—a universe—full of thoughtform demons and martyrs not limited by the sun, or even physical space-time? How will humans survive? Uninitiated martyrs will run out of food, and initiated ones who can metabolize sunlight—"

"Oh, such martyrs will still be encouraged to follow the same diet they always have. It keeps us bonded to the Church and assists in the attraction and creation of thoughtforms, though such things are possible to accomplish without the aid of anthropophagy. However, it is undeniable that the traditional martyr diet increases the efficiency and simplicity of the creation of thoughtforms."

She bit her tongue, refrained from stating how thoughtforms weren't necessary for a Lazarene who knew a True Word, but she also supposed such a fact was beside the point for him. It wasn't about True Words, or thoughtforms. It was about keeping his species morally and psychologically crippled—keeping them trapped in a cycle of shame, which, in turn, kept them crawling back to the Church. Back to Earth. "You're going to cause the destruction of the human race. All sentient life."

"My dear, small-thinking daughter, that will never be an issue. I have gone out of my way to see to it! Come here, my girl, look with me."

The risen Hierophant pushed in his chair and strode to the window, where he waited patiently for Dominia to catch up to him beside the frosty glass. His breath condensing upon it, he first doubled over his massive frame and angled up his head; once satisfied, he drew Dominia down by the shoulders to point at one of the brightest visible cosmic bodies, its twinkle bright despite the city below. "Do you see that? Mars, my girl. As we speak, thousands—tens of thousands, by now—are working to transform its soil from barren rock to wholesome earth. All to sustain human life! The time of suicide or android missions launched from our lunar base is long over. The negligent ancestor of Carol McLintock"—the General grimaced to hear the name—"has, by now, died and left behind her Martian farm to Carol's optimistic aunts, or perhaps, already, her cousins. They live and thrive and receive monthly shipments that I do not even have to provide anymore! China, that blessed hermit nation, sends them, thinking they are helping humanity.

All those happy colonists, fleeing martyrs for greener pastures…what do you suppose they are doing? They are multiplying—multiplying so that, by the time we martyrs require the services of their planet, they will be ready to generously accept the burdens of their betters—and perhaps even begin another colony elsewhere."

"You're breeding a planet of slaves," marveled Dominia, not astonished by the fact so much as his flat admission. "You're *prepared* to ruin this planet because you've got a backup."

"And many others, though much farther away and in the distant future aside from a few Luna-related plans we're drawing up—but how simple a thing it might be, reaching another planet from the fabric of the Void, rather than through negotiating physical space-time! Imagine." She turned to see that the manic sparkle of his eyes had kindled a fire that burned like the sizzling fireplace nestled between his bookshelves. "A true master race: multidimensional planet-walkers, who, as fertile and sun-loving as any other species, could colonize a planet with little more effort than that required for a healthy hike— even a drive, with toys of the sort you and your friends rode in on. And if you are very good, very dutiful, and prove you've changed your stripes, I see no reason why the former Governess of the United Front might not one night be the Stewardess of Planet Earth, once I have taken off to oversee Mars."

She didn't register that temptation until seconds later, too hung up on a phrase of his that had elicited a snort. "'Planet-walkers'? You mean planet-eaters…it would be one thing if mankind were capable of such a thing; there's a chance they'll go someplace and help the people they find, rather than out-and-out annihilating them. There's goodness in humans, or the possibility of goodness, anyway. But martyrs who believe in your teachings are too far gone. They'll show up and ruin it all. Devour and terrorize the populace."

"Such a thing takes time; and perhaps, in a few planets' worth of experiments, we will come to a more sustainable solution. If only you would pay attention in Church! We provide an important service in God's universe, my girl. We are not mere devourers of flesh and blood—these things are only symbols. We alleviate from the world the pain of mortal sin and take it on ourselves. It is the will of the Lord that we clean the conscious universe everywhere we go."

Frustration tightened her throat, especially as he looped a big arm around her shoulders just before she was able to get out of his reach. "You really think God approves of killing?"

"My daughter, it is God's will! God's gift to us is this universe, and in exchange we keep it pure. We are its custodians, yes, but what ingrates would we be were we to leave such vast swaths of this greatest gift unused?"

"Maybe the rest of it isn't a gift for you."

"True, it is not necessarily a gift for me. But it is a gift for the winner of the game, and I intend to win."

"Whatever bullshit is being played out between you and the magician, you mean."

"Myself, the magician, the Lady, Lazarus, and, of course, you."

"The pawn."

With a gasp of displeasure, the Hierophant cried, "Why, my girl, not at all—not at all!"

She spared him what was intended as a dry glance but found herself reeled in by the earnest arrangement of his expression. "You, my girl"—he jostled her—"are the queen, if you are any chess piece at all. That is not a matter of gender: that is a matter of power. Long before martyrs, the queen was the vizier, you know. He who stands behind the king and overshadows him. But if you insist on feeling like a lowly pawn, never forget that a pawn upon the opposite side of its board *becomes* a queen. Choose a direction, my dear, and move as you please."

"As long as it's back to your side."

"I would be nothing without my finest General. That's why Cicero is so jealous of you, you know! Before you came along, he was my best warrior. After, well, I admit I always appreciate his abilities, but your prowess in battle, and your mind for strategy, is most admirable. How many victories have you delivered our nation?"

"Not enough for you to care about me." Maybe it was stupid to say, but she was on edge, and felt like laying into him as much as she was allowed. "Not enough for you to have stopped me from doing something so cruel to my wife when I was out of my mind with betrayal and grief; not enough for you to have given me an ounce of recognition when I needed it. When I asked for it. Any relationship with you is only ever on your terms."

"I see you're still just as jealous of Cicero as he is of you…ah, my silly children. Would it fix your feelings if I called you my favorite child? Then would you return to my service, and bring me Lazarus?"

Part of her wanted to laugh—bitterly—at his idea that this was a reasonable request. She could just give up the man who had helped her, had given her back her eye and her teeth, had given her his truth-revealing blood! A simple trade. No effort at all.

Feeling helpless and stupid for ever having listened to the Lady— wondering if that Ergosphere apparition of the goddess was not some thoughtform sent by her Father, or something else altogether—the General searched her mind for alternatives, delaying tactics, and mis-directions. In the end, she could only come up with the pathetic insistence that, "Lazarus is my friend."

"Oh, my poor girl! I know he is. I'm sure you left quite a few friends behind! But, if they are still alive when we have completed the operation, I will be more than happy to pardon them."

"Operation?" she asked, weakly. He lifted his brows.

"A preemptive strike of Tunis and Tangiers, and a surge of troops in Jerusalem. In fact, it's been on for a fortnight— I suppose you were in the Ergosphere for a couple of weeks during your stroll across the ocean, weren't you? We're already ten nights to New Year's. Lavinia's Feast Night is but a few cycles away! You came home just in time."

The Lady had not warned her about this. No wonder the landing pad of the plane didn't work: it had as much to do with being too far from a reliable distance as it did with the fact that, by the time they were supposed to appear at the landing pad, the city of Tangiers would have been under assault and all prearranged plans to take its teleporter to Jerusalem would have been cratered. Dominia sickened while he carried on: "After you gave us such a good reason to attack by sweeping away Theodore, why—we would be fools not to take advantage of the opportunity."

So Jerusalem had been falling since before she'd arrived at Kronborg. Hard to keep her mind on the present, suddenly. "And you expect me to give you all the information I can to help you cinch the conquests."

"You have returned to the Family, haven't you?" He arched a brow and tightened his grip of her shoulders. Dominia, for her part, studied the city and tried not to feel the slightest emotion. "It would be a pity to see you defect again after we've gone to such pains to welcome you back with open arms and no questions. Such as, why you have suddenly decided to return"—the phantasmal reflections of his eyes bored into the reflections of hers like black drills—"or why I should believe you won't betray me again."

He shouldn't believe it. She could lie flat in his face without a hint of guilt. Indeed, she felt a certain righteousness: that she might say or do anything in the carrying out of this task, because she was champion of the truth. Her heart was pure, and now forever a captive of humanity, if it had ever truly been otherwise. Thus, so long as she knew in her heart that it was a lie when she said, "If you must know, it was a disappointing experience," she could speak what was needed with impunity.

"My poor girl," said the Hierophant, releasing her with a pat so he could return to his seat. "You will have to tell me all about it sometime. I see from the diamond around your neck that I was right in warning you. The Lady is not what she seems, and Lazarus has no real power."

"What about the magician?" She idled past his bookshelf upon seeing a copy of the *Odyssey*. The characters of its title remained as static as one would anticipate while her Father smiled at her question.

"What the magician can do is amazing, it's true: Valentinian is a fellow of talent. But you, my girl, are infinitely more talented than that."

In this, she was tired of pressing him. There was knowledge there with which he teased her, with which everyone had teased her. The only way she knew to deal with it now was to take her Father's own patented sour grapes approach, which she did by changing the subject. "I appreciate your generosity in…accepting me back."

"My child"—his tone held genuine warmth as he reclaimed his pen and returned to work—"there is nothing you could do to me that could not be forgiven. Even if some gesture is required to prove your sincerity, your Father's unconditional love is always with you. I will see to it that Cicero forgives you as I do. I'm sure, once you have been punished, he will come around."

Ah, yes. There it was! She was wondering. That familiar sweating of her palms, the needle sensation down her neck, the unconscious edging of her body toward the door. It had been centuries. "'Punished,'" she repeated, almost laughing, her faltering smile falling entirely when the Hierophant looked up from his writing with a stern, illegible face.

"Of course. We can't have you running about all over the human world without consequence. People died because of you. Don't you see to it your officers and soldiers are well disciplined for infractions against the rules of your service?"

She had never been so aware of the tick of a clock in her life. Trying to maintain her usual sense of confidence, she arched a brow and dryly asked, "Going to have me whipped? Partially flayed?"

"No, no, of course not. You know as well as I do that corporal punishment is useless. It only serves to titillate those who employ and observe it, while doing nothing to prevent future infractions: far better such activities should be left as the bedroom play they are. As for flaying, well…that is rather dramatic, but somewhat more on target. I have always been in favor of long-lasting reminders—nothing obvious or socially humiliating, of course. Just a small secret between yourself and your Lord. A means by which you can forever remember to be a humble and good servant, rather than a rebellious apostate. Flaying is rather much for that purpose." Returning his attention to whatever he wrote, he suggested, "I think one leg will suffice."

All efforts to keep her pulse calm buckled under the weight of a single second. A scream—her own, or maybe Cassandra's—rose up in her head. "What?"

"Cicero insisted I take both, but I said—"

"No." She felt she stood next to her own body and had to grip the bookshelf nearby. "No, I—You're going to take my *leg*."

"Only one, my dear. A symbolic gesture. I'm sure you can under-stand it. Why, in the end, it will be beneficial to you! I have already ordered a replacement. Some engineers will be by to measure you for it in a few nights. You will find it a vast improvement over your original, and identical in every way."

Her fingers tangling through the chain of Cassandra's diamond, Dominia glanced between the door and the Hierophant and wished she could die on the spot through some merciful intercession of Saint Valentinian's. "But—but I came back of my own will, I—I thought you forgave me. You weren't going to ask any questions."

"Have I?"

"This isn't forgiveness."

"Forgiveness is not free. It requires some effort on the part of those who are forgiven: and there are times when willful penance is not enough. I assure you, princess, I am not taking your leg out of spite. Far from it! It is because I love you, and so intensely wish to forgive you, that I am doing this. How else could I forgive all you've done without some gesture? Some assurance that you will put your best foot forward"—he tried so hard not to smirk that the effort strained his mouth—"and that you will always be with our Family, no matter what happens."

She was too numb to be angry. This was why she had never had trouble on the battlefield, why she had never feared death. Her Father was so much worse than war could ever be.

As cautious as anyone tiptoeing over broken glass, the General wet her lips and pronounced the words, "Surely there's an alternative. If I could say, your forgiveness seems to me"—he lowered his pen and she feared she might vomit—"sort of…conditional. I thought that God's love was…"

"Oh, but I am not God, of course. Though you *do* flatter me…I am but a man of flesh and blood like any other." He rose from his seat and she began mentally searching the room for a weapon, trying to remember whether there had been a letter opener on his desk at the start of the conversation, regretting the lack of a poker in this particular fireplace, wondering about the density of that paperweight, having a difficult time listening to what he said, something something something "—true forgiveness is therefore, ultimately, in the hands of God. The forgiveness of men is a luxury."

"The forgiveness of men comes at a very high cost," she observed, trapped without any defense as he came around the desk and stood before a woman who towered over most men, but who had to crane her neck to see the holy Father's face. "You already took something from me because I left. You took my eye. I only got it back because of my friends."

"Oh, my child"—he gripped her chin with fingers so swift she relived, with post-traumatic horror, the awful feeling of her eyeball being plucked from its socket—"don't you understand? I didn't take your eye because you ran away! That had nothing to do with any of this."

Her eyes, at the visceral memory, at the epiphany, at his presence, filled with a fine gloss of tears. As calmly as she could, through the staggered breath and half smile of terror, she asked, "Then why did you do it?"

"I took your eye because you took mine, first."

Of course.

Of course.

There was no Acetia. He was no alien. The martyr planet from which her Father heralded was Earth in her terrible future: her dark future, where things all went horribly wrong. The General's lips parted. The Hierophant smiled at her understanding and released her chin with a paternal pat upon her shocked cheek.

For a time, she didn't speak. She only marveled at him, at herself, at the whole world and the insanity of reality. A whole globe of people, blinded by logic. The same man could never be two places at once. Time travel wasn't possible. Etcetera.

"How?" She tried asking, just once. He chuckled.

"What fun would it be if I told you that now?" Squinting, she tried to discern a difference between his eyes—any hint of DIOX-brand artificiality—and found none. As she verified both were organic, he continued, "You understand that I must take something from you for what you have done to the Family now, as opposed to what you did to me then, during a marathon, a whole lifetime and persona ago. Yes? At any rate…don't you feel *silly*, now, for flouncing off to Canada! How could I favor any child *but* Cicero? I used to be him. I can understand his anger. Therefore, I require your leg."

There was no way to argue him out of his sense of justice. No begging. No escape. Shocked as she was, the General could not move her legs; for that matter, she no longer saw the room in which she stood. What was she doing? Why had she returned? To face her guilt for—what? Had she really done anything to merit this? Maybe. The Lady must have thought so. The Lady had sent her back here because—why? Because war was inevitable? Because an inside man was necessary for the scheme to work? Because, because, because—but then she remembered she had chosen to come back, not just because of Lavinia but because of Tenchi. The swirling horror of her mind ceased long enough that, finding herself near the door and her Father back at his desk, she managed to ask, "Would you tell me one thing? Where are you keeping Tenchi?"

"Mm? Oh!" The Hierophant glanced up from his work, pen wiggling in recognition. "Yes, yes, your sailor friend—well, it just so happens we stayed his execution and ordered his transport to the nearest consignment camp, but some funny business happened on the bus ride over…I just received an e-mail"—he turned away to awaken the desk-integrated holo-display computer with a wave of his hand and swiped past a few floating windows in that same limp-wristed motion—"something about his disappearance… I've not bothered to respond yet, but I don't expect we'll make his hunt a priority."

"Thank you."

With a tap of his pen against the temple of his forehead in a mocking salute, the Holy Father said, "Close the door on your way out, dear. So glad to see you back."

VII

The Girl with Silver Hands

By her late fifties, Cassandra could no longer stand her urgent pangs of conscience. While she continued to cook for the Governess nearly every morning, and Dominia often returned from work to any number of scrumptious porcine fragrances—her wife a permanent nightdream with that lacy pink apron—Cassandra began to refuse meat. Only at Mass would she consume flesh and blood, she said. That was what the services were there for: why the Lamb gave his blood and why the Churches kept it on hand to be replenished at his next stop. Other than an alleged connection with God and a nontemporal connection to the Last Supper—which was, to put it lightly, reinterpreted in the hands of martyr scholars—the purpose of the Lamb's blood was to give martyrs an option to cannibalism. The rest of the week, well—some martyrs thought it sinful (or at least antisocial) to fast, but Cassandra knew God approved.

Dominia, alarmed, did not approve. For weeks, she pestered her wife about drinking blood, if nothing else. To her present shame, she once went so far as to slip a bit of type A into Cassie's wine one morning. This had only resulted in an astronomical argument and a broken glass, so she didn't try again. She just watched in silence while her wife—a martyr in every sense of the word—fasted, week after week, suppressing superficial pangs of appetite with malnutritional salads, the occasional side of lab-grown beef, or a bowl of vegetable soup.

Each week would begin with optimism and good spirits. Most workers loathed Noctislunae, but it was Cassandra's best night. Each night after, her condition degraded into tremors, insomnia, and, once or twice, a Noctisfrey seizure that necessitated attendance of the Noctisaturnon service as well as the usual Noctisdomin one the following night. This was discouraged. The blood of the Lamb was a commodity, because with so many churches and fifty-two service slots in any given year, he and Cicero could only visit each church so often. So for all her trouble to follow her conscience, Cassandra would sometimes be subject to a sideways comment from the priests and priestesses of their local parish—those same who happened to be her colleagues. The shaming got to be so bad that she had to leave the Bible school business behind. That was when she started to focus on music.

But through all the physical and mental turmoil, Cassandra was in higher spirits than ever. The General's heart broke even now, in Kronborg, to think her wife could only be happy while starving! Dominia wished they had known the truth of Lazarus's blood during her life. Like so many other truths, her Father had hidden that from her. Yes: her Father hid that which could have saved her wife, morally, spiritually, bodily, eternally. Oh! That bastard! How Dominia hated him. How she hated him, and hated that he now wanted to lead the martyr race on a multidimensional march of evil.

Lazarus had explained to her once that she was responsible for ending the present state of the world for martyrs. Things had to change, and change was painful. The right change, Dominia could see, was a complete upheaval of current social values, structure, and even physical presence. There was much to be said for the idea of the martyr race migrating into the Ergosphere once enough research could be done into the subject. But before that issue could even be approached, a complete psychological rewrite of all martyrs was required. The Church, if not in need of destruction, certainly needed a new leader.

And so long as he lived, her Father would never relinquish his position.

Yes—she had thought before how, in the end, her goal was the death of her Father. But now she was confronted with the notion more strongly than ever before. More than that, she was confronted with the notion that it was his death or her death. The issue with her death was not so much any lingering fear of it. She fully trusted that when her body died, her spirit would remain in the Ergosphere. Even if she had to collect herself in the Void, she was prepared for it.

No. Her concern was that if she died, she could do nothing more to stop him. A planet full of martyrs was one thing. A planet full of martyrs who didn't need to fear the sun and who could conquer, world by world, the vast seas of the universe while bringing thoughtforms into earthly existence—now that was a tahgmahr beyond all reckoning. But perhaps it had happened elsewhere. Perhaps it had happened for her Father to find himself with such power and such long memory. When he said he came from Acetia, he meant that he came from an Earth where he was victorious and martyrs had spread their tendrils through reality.

Dominia's head swam as she made her ghostlike way through the halls of Kronborg, thinking through the many General di Mephitolis who'd come before her. What had been different of them? Why had they failed? Though she knew she would persist after, what was the moment of death like? Had she ever sold Lazarus, the Lady, the Kingdom for a leg?

Maybe her standard litany of questions was the wrong thing. Perhaps the best strategy was to imagine the worst possible iteration of herself and strive to be that iteration's exact opposite. It was with great pain that the image came upon her, the trashy cover of a proverbial pulp novel about space piracy or some such business: the one-eyed, one-legged General with the odious Memory Bride draped around her hip as she ruled a hollow world from the depressing city of Old Elsinore. Appalling. Dominia paused against a corner near the primary garden doors to rub the bridge of her nose, and when she looked up, she recognized one of the courtiers gossiping beneath the nearby marble statue of the Lamb. René Ichigawa, who recognized her the same instant and tore off like a rabbit without explanation to his companions. The poor pair looked all the more shocked when the General sprinted past in pursuit.

"René! René, you bastard, there's nowhere to run!"

That wouldn't stop him from trying. After blazing through the vast French doors and down a path more thickly lined with snow than trees this time of year, he recognized the proximity of the General's pursuit and thought he'd get smart by taking a right turn across the pond—the pond that, while frozen this time of year—

"René," she cried, "don't, you idiot!"

Too late. He'd already stumbled though the tree line and now skidded across the ice, trying to take a shortcut in the direction of the hedges until he made his inevitable plunge through a weak spot into the frozen water.

Then, naturally, it was a lot of, "Dominia, help," and, "Please! I haven't been swimming since I was ten!" Sighing, the General took the time to remove her jacket before easing her cautious way across the ice. She reached into the breach, and René, despite his splashing, still had wherewithal enough to try to use her as a ladder rather than accept her help as savior. After at least one kick in his face and a few treacherous warning snaps of the ice beneath her, she managed to extricate René and toss him, wet and shivering, onto the snowbank of the shore. Her own lips slate, Dominia turned him over to the sound of his profuse thanks only to slap him once, sharply, right in the freezing face.

"Listen to me, you little shit. The only reason"—she slapped him again because he marveled too much at the pain of the first slap to pay attention to her words—"the *only* reason why you're still alive right now is because your *cousin* is alive. Okay? Consider yourself lucky—very lucky."

"Dominia—"

"Because if he *weren't* alive, you know what I'd be doing right now?"

"Dominia, please—"

"I'd be yanking out your fucking *leg*, because that's what the Hierophant's going to do to me!"

"I— Jesus Christ, what? No, Dominia, please, I'm telling you! This wasn't my idea—what a stupid plan, I kept telling them!"

"Telling whom?" The General hissed the words with a glance for the lights of the palace. Nosy faces pressed to the glass panels of the doors and a couple of windows down the hall. "Keep your voice down."

"The Lady! Lazarus! Everybody! You think I want to be here? Last time I was around these people, I lost both my eyes!"

Mouth open in shock, she slapped him once more and demanded, "Stop lying."

"I'm not! I swear to you, I'm not!"

"You mean to say that not only did the Lady and Lazarus know I'd end up here, but *everybody* knew I'd end up here? I mean, I've started to feel like the Lady put me here on purpose, but…Lazarus? *You*? Even Tenchi? Oh my God!" No wonder he hadn't wanted to say anything in the Ergosphere. It had as much to do with chronology as it did with his bosses telling him to shut up in advance. Below her series of mortified realizations, René babbled on.

"*I* didn't want to do it. Please! I'm sorry. I didn't want any part in this. You think I wanted to hand Tenchi over to these people? He *volunteered*! You could ask him! You know, if they haven't just killed him anyway. What a stupid idea all this is!"

Dominia pulled away as the English professor's rant continued. "It's this—fucking cult! I can't believe he got involved in that Lazarene stuff. He grew up with Shinto tradition! Freedom fighting, I get, but these religious ceremonies, and then agreeing to drink some old dude's blood…I mean, it's crazy."

"You literally stole my blood."

"Well, *yes*, but that was for *survival*. This is for religion. It's different."

Seeing how he shivered and the peacock tint of his lips, the General retrieved her jacket to drape around his shoulders. "So everybody knows, huh? How many bodies is 'every' body?"

"There was a meeting. Tenchi, Farhad, Gethsemane, the Lady, Lazarus, and I were all there, and a lot—a lot of soldiers, Dominia. Tons."

"Did you count them?"

"Oh, I don't know. One hundred? Two? I'm not a math professor, I'm an English professor."

"Your attention to detail is incredibly helpful." She was about to give up on him when he added, "How am I supposed to keep track? There were people from all over the world, tons I've never seen before. I talked about it with some white guy who lent me a lighter outside the venue."

Lighter, huh. "Tall guy? Thin, dark hair, blue eyes, sort of a shabby red waistcoat?"

"I thought his suit seemed pretty nice, with a jacket, but—how did you *know* that?"

That good-for-nothing mutt. "We've met," she said. Was it worth telling René that the guy who'd lit his cigarette was really the border collie—or had been stored in the border collie, or reflected in the border collie, or bonded with the border collie—that had journeyed with him for thousands of miles? Not when the secular professor wasn't even willing to sit through a Lazarene ceremony. The General busied herself by rolling up the wet sleeves of her white shirt and returned the subject to her irritation. "So everybody knew, huh…"

"Mostly. Bits and pieces, at least. The meeting I went to was an informational one more than anything; everybody else, including me, got some need-to-know stuff in private. My need-to-know was that I had to turn in my own cousin and act like I wanted in with the Hierophant now that I'm a martyr. They won't tell me why I'm here, or what I'm supposed to do now that I'm here. I think I'm supposed to figure it out when the time comes, but I'm freaking out. It's pretty serious, Dominia. And they said the more you know, the more danger you're in."

No wonder they didn't tell René a thing, considering how he'd spewed his guts in a snap. "Everybody around these parts loves withholding." Feeling all the more aware of her right leg, she added, "I'm already in danger, regardless of how little or how much I know."

"Yeah, nobody mentioned anything about you losing a *leg*. I might have cast a no vote after you saved me in Bi'ir as-Sab. I thought I was signing up to *help* you!"

"I'm sure you did sign up to help me, which is why I need to make it look like we're still pissed off at each other."

"Wha—"

The crack as she kicked his jaw was significant, but not as significant as it would have been were she wearing boots instead of oxfords. Even so, René went down like a big sack of satisfying bricks, which she dragged inside by the collar. Not fully unconscious, the new martyr continued babbling through a dislocated jaw that softened his *r*'s to *h*'s and made the word "party" sound rather hilariously like "potty": "Oh, God, will this heal? There's supposed to be a *party*, Dominia! I can't go to a party like this."

"A party?" She paused several meters from doors vacated by the courtiers. "For what?"

"The Hie—you—"

This was getting old. With the thick snap of ligaments and bone, Dominia fixed her undeserving progeny's jaw so he could, after yelping and working it back and forth once or twice, explain, "Your Father's insisting I stay for a New Year's party. I'm worried he's already on to us."

"Of course he's already on to us. That's why I'm not supposed to know anything, and why he's starting to tell me everything. When is the party supposed to be?"

"New Year's Eve."

"Must be my deadline."

"He's going to take your leg at the party?"

"That, or just before. 'Party' is sure to be a euphemism, knowing him. Or it isn't. Sort of a coin flip with these people…I suppose we'll find out." That said, she resumed dragging the yet-dizzied man into the hall. He curled into a wet and bruised ball on the cold tile floor, one hand upon the aching hinge of his jaw.

"How long have you been waiting to do that to me?"

With a stifled grin, she stepped past him, in the direction of Lavinia's apartments. "Don't make me hurt your feelings, too."

Those courtiers, nervous as they were curious, emerged from the nearby lounge to assess the scene, then darted back when the General laid eyes on them. Suddenly, her grin was easy to suppress. All humor dropped from her and she was the General once more, colder than the icy waters from which she'd pulled René.

"Traitors and I don't get along well," was her only explanation. The two glanced at each other before she gave an irritated wave toward René, just the sort Lavinia might have when demanding her "friends" pick up some trash she'd littered in the garden. "Could you take him to his guest room, please?"

Even if she couldn't fully manage her tone, she curtailed her language with courtesy. That counted for something, right?

Jacket lost to René, the General made her damp way to Lavinia's quarters, a set of living spaces and several bathrooms that felt rather like a sorority despite the classical aesthetic and the high, rich wainscoting of the walls. Maybe it was the television in the artful salon that made it seem that way, or the couches, or the proliferation of women's magazines and trashy romance novels left behind when Lavinia tossed her brigade out into the castle. Kronborg bore little resemblance to what it was in Hamlet's day—hell, little resemblance to what it was in Dominia's night! There was a *kitchen* in here, now. Come to think of it, that was why it felt like a sorority. The smell of baked goods emanated from the cramped kitchenette and nobody had bothered to wash the dishes, but neither were there any cookies to be found. Speaking of a bunch of girls who could use some titillating corporal punishment!

Too bad they didn't have a haven of cute women when Dominia was forced to stay in Kronborg. She might have liked the castle's drafty halls a bit better with a few extra skirts swishing around. (She turned her head too sharply at Lavinia's footsteps, and the chain of Cassandra's diamond twisted to choke her; she laughed to think of her jealous wife.)

"Ninny!" Lavinia's voice twinkled with excitement as she emerged from her bedroom at the end of the hall, but her expression soon gave way to a wrinkled nose. "Oh, my, Ninny, you're all—what *happened*?"

"Can I borrow your hair dryer?" asked Dominia, lifting damp arms. "I'm freezing."

After a few minutes—ten, to be exact—spent talking Lavinia out of her "wonderful" idea that Dominia borrow some of *her* clothes, the stubborn princess admitted the hair dryer that had run amid her begging *had* done a fine job, she *supposed*, if the General was fine with looking like a boy.

"This is just how I feel comfortable," said Dominia, shrugging as she might when talking to any unworldly child. "I don't look like a boy; I look like Dominia. But just so you know, a lot of ladies like the way I look. One of your girlfriends seemed to, anyway."

"They're not—*girlfriends*," sputtered Lavinia, so flush that the General laughed. "They're girl *friends*, it's a different thing. I am above such unwholesome activities." Her eyes closed in a stuffy way that nonetheless registered to Dominia as very dear, because she saw so much of Cassandra's sleep in it. The girl turned away before her eyes opened, so she didn't see how sad the General had grown in those two seconds. "Not that it's wrong for somebody else to get up to…*business*, but I'm a saint, Ninny. I can't do a thing like that!"

"And I'm technically a saint, too. Or I was."

"But you're a saint of *war*. Nobody says you can't fall in love with anybody."

"And you can't?"

"Well, of course I could fall in *love*, but it must be *pure* love. Not trivial, fleshly love. No offense."

"None taken." Frankly, she'd been busy feeling astonished by the variety and size of the makeup collection littering the vanity where she sat. Bigger, even, than Miki Soto's before her bridal ceremony. "You're awfully into makeup for somebody who doesn't have a boyfriend."

"*Now* who doesn't know anything? I don't do makeup for boys, I do it for fun. Cicero helps me with it each evening! I can do it myself, of course, but we like to talk. He's such a good brother!"

Good, creepy…a fine line with all martyrs, but especially with the Holy Family, and exceptionally with Cicero. There had always been something indefinably weird about him. Some mixture of incestuous idolatry and profound resentment toward the Hierophant that plagued every room El Sacerdote entered. Now Dominia understood that, and all his fawning over Lavinia, too. And she understood her Father much better. Was that the fate of Cicero? To move on to another reality and make his own? If so, was that because he left to spread his proverbial wings—or was that because he was forced out? The salvation of this world didn't mean the destruction of another, did it?

"Did you have a bad meeting, Ninny? You're frowning again."

"I don't know if I should discuss it with you, kiddo."

"I'm not a *kid*, Nin—Dominia." The General managed to keep a straight face as the girl went on, "I'm absolutely grown up. I know all kinds of things!"

She wasn't in the mood to have an argument with somebody who was so wrong they didn't even have the frame of reference to comprehend their incorrectness. Instead, investigating a bottle of perfume, Dominia said, "I was given a very ugly penance. I just wish there was some alternative."

Her frowning sister leaned forward. "What penance?"

"Lavinia," chided the General, but the girl, literally on the edge of the bed, insisted with her hands upon her chest, "But I'm an *adult*. Really, I am! I've been awake for almost seventy years! When *you* were seventy, you'd already been high in Daddy's army for four decades!"

"That's because that's what I trained for. He bred me for that purpose." And others, she knew now, deeper and more inexplicable. He was a scheming, untrustworthy bastard, the Hierophant, but Lavinia had stars in her eyes for him—loved her Father more intensely than any other child, adult or not. Everything he did was right, so far as the girl was concerned.

But, Lavinia also carried a deep love for Dominia. There had been instant attachment on the little girl's part when she awoke in that young woman's body. So much so that Cassandra had been jealous at times, and Dominia suspected this was because, deep down, her wife always knew the truth. Even before that feast night where the Hierophant's mocking had not slipped past Cassandra's drink-lubricated consciousness. December finished out with an eerie quality and Mrs. di Mephitoli did an impeccable job of hiding her suspicions for a while. But Dominia soon discerned that something was afoot: her wife scrounged through the Governess's old documents one night when the much-demanded politician had been called away on weekend business that ended unexpectedly and allowed her home a few hours earlier than thought.

The General hadn't been that bothered by the awkward return, because the letters she "caught" Cassandra in were correspondences with Lavinia. Despite her sometimes weird bouts of jealousy over how adored by Lavinia Dominia was, the Governess's wife had never taken much interest in the Merciful Miracle of the Holy Father—frankly, the girl was a tremendous amount of trouble when she awoke. At least she awoke with *any* sense of language at all, for understanding if not for speaking: that was a miracle capping even that miracle of miracles, more than twenty years of clinical death spent in a period of growth that ended in crystalized life. Lavinia awoke in a state of physical perfection, that peak at which most martyrs stopped aging. She had never lived at all, let alone lived outside the Holy Family.

And she was immensely lonely. Even living across the ocean in the Front, Dominia saw that. The poor Princess of Europa with her paid-for friends didn't even have those until she was about thirty or forty physical years old, when the Hierophant deemed her socially competent. That meant Lavinia was awake for *twenty years* before she was "allowed" to have a friend, even one subsidized by her Father. Talking to her before that point had been dangerous, especially if the person doing the talking was a young man. Other than the Lamb and the Ciceros, Teddy was the only man Dominia could name who was allowed within arm's length of the Eternal Virgin. It was all a bunch of bullshit as far as the then Governess was concerned, and she showed her protest by drifting away from the Family. This was also an effort to keep Cassandra as far away from Lavinia as possible. But to quell her guilt for this, and for leaving Lavinia alone, she began to write her sister letters. The Hierophant had read them to her, at first, then written back childish correspondences the struggling savant had "dictated"—prompted, edited, and surely augmented by him, of course, but it was a start. Then, as her grasp of language and reason improved, and her rampant emotional problems (along with their resulting memetic contagions) began to wind down, letters had come from her own shaky hand. The confidence in these lines grew over the years to true calligraphy, fine as their Father's—sometimes Dominia still suspected he slipped his own letter into the mix, as talented as he was at everything, forgery included. Even if that was the case, she was glad to know Lavinia got those letters. They were all very boring, and she never talked much about Cassandra in them beyond what her wife's job was like at the time. Nothing of their fights or troubles.

So there wasn't anything wrong with Cassandra reading those letters, per se. The Governess wasn't thinking about Lavinia's strange Feast Night party anymore. She hadn't even connected the events until too late, when she realized in bloody hindsight that her wife had been searching wildly, desperately, for any scrap of information about whether her suspicion about her daughter was true. And—perhaps more importantly—whether Dominia had known.

What Cassandra never could have understood was that Dominia was just too careful. Even with herself, she was too careful. She had worked hard to avoid thinking of any of this since the baby was passed off over ninety years ago. Now, after seventy years of Lavinia's conscious life, Dominia had the opportunity to stop being so careful—and the painful irony lay in the caution that was required when relieving herself of these cares. It would be easiest, the General decided, if she not dive right into the subject of Cassandra's parentage. Better to start with what the Hierophant planned to do to Lavinia's beloved older sister. Perhaps once she understood the gravity of that, the girl would be more conducive to understanding what had happened to her—why Dominia had done as she'd done, and why, in the end, it wouldn't have mattered whether she'd gone to him about the baby, or he'd come to her.

After suffering her nagging thoughts, a reluctant groan, and Lavinia's pleading expression, the General relented. "I can tell you some of what was said at my meeting with him tonight." The girl's eyes, blue as Benedict's, lit like great lamps in the low light of her room. "But you have to promise me you won't tell anyone."

"I won't! Oh, I promise, Ninny, I won't."

"Not a soul. Not your friends, and definitely not Father."

"Never! Please, what did he say? Are you okay?"

Still reluctant, the General sat at her sister's side, voice as low as her head. "I don't want to tell you this because I don't want you to think I'm trying to turn you against Father."

"Nothing could do *that*, Ninny! You don't have to worry." A delicate hand landed upon Dominia's shoulder with that birdlike touch. "I know you know how much I love Daddy! But I also know how scary he can be sometimes."

"He told me he wants to—" Just say it. Say it out loud. Make it real to someone more important than René. "He's going to take my *leg*, Lavinia."

The series of emotions through which Lavinia's face cycled was so unnatural as to be unreadable in the circumstances. The mere sight burned the worst brand of cognitive dissonance across the General's skull. Her little sister's features widened, grew overjoyed, then caved into laughter.

"Why, *Ninny*, but that's wonderful! Don't you see?"

"No." She was numb, more alone than she'd been while lying in the ruins of the McLintocks' china. "I don't see."

"That just means he *loves* you, silly." As the Princess went on, the General paled. Not at the unwinnable battle before her but at something much worse edging into consciousness. "He really has forgiven you! If it were otherwise, why, he'd have you killed and wasted."

The nauseous General regarded the daughter sacrificed on her wife's behalf, and said nothing. Lavinia frowned in the face of that silence, struggling for something to say. Given an epiphany, she sprang to lock her bedroom door, and as she did, Dominia's mind began to scream.

"You know what, Ninny? I know you're scared."

Please, no.

"But since you shared a secret with me, I'll share one with you."

Oh, please, please, no.

"And then you'll understand why this is something you should be happy about!"

Oh, God, Lady, Lamb, please, God, Saint Valentinian, no.

All smiles, Lavinia hiked her many skirts high above her pale leg. After perching upon the edge of her vanity seat, she detached the DIOX limb from the stump of her amputated thigh with the practiced hand of a woman removing a garter.

"See," chirped the girl, all sunshine. Dominia's mouth hung wider than her horror-ringed eyes as the oblivious child continued, "It's nothing bad at all! Daddy loves *me* more than anything in the world. That's why he took my arms, *and* my legs. We're the *luckiest*, to be eaten by him while still alive on Earth! It's an honor, Ninny! Don't you understand?"

The General could think of nothing to say. Nothing.

Nothing.

Didn't she understand?

Didn't she understand!

Her mind, a whirlwind, wouldn't operate. She left her body for a period of indeterminate length and was drawn back by the girl's nervous voice.

"Ninny, why—you're laughing but you look so—"

All of six seconds later, Dominia was stooped over the edge of the toilet bowl in her sister's bathroom, once again plagued by that nausea from the Hierophant's office; nausea which she had not, in the first place, fully escaped. Maybe she would never escape this sickness again. Certainly not as she remembered in a horrible flash of hindsight the very party in which Cassandra came to understand the truth. In her mind's eye hovered once more its glorious centerpiece, of which all the guests, Dominia included, had partaken.

That delicate woman's arm. That—in retrospect—familiar woman's arm.

"That was your arm at your feast night two years ago," she said, lifting her head to slump against the enormous bubble jet bathtub. Lavinia stood, mortified by her sister's illness, at the edge of the bathroom to which she'd hopped. "The one before Cassandra killed herself…that was you we ate for dinner."

"Of course! It was my last limb, so Daddy wanted to share it, and, why—I thought that was just so special and beautiful! Why are you sick, Ninny? Did you eat someone rancid?"

"I…no. I'm sorry, Lavinia." Eyes filling with tears, Dominia lifted her hand to wipe her cheeks and then her mouth and sob, "I'm so— oh, sweet Lamb, I'm so sorry."

"What on earth *for?*" asked Lavinia while her sister bolted up and slipped past her, through the doorway. "Ninny, wait—"

"I can't stay here right now, Lavinia, please. I have to think."

"But, Ninny, don't you see? I'm trying to show you it's a *nice* thing."

There was simply no way for the General to respond. Still nauseous, and now with the taste of bile burning her throat, Dominia stumbled back in the direction of the gardens. The only place for her now was the most clamorous room the entire castle had to offer, and one of its best attended: the kennels.

It was no secret that the Lamb loved his dogs, and the love of dogs—indeed, all animals—had become one of the most popular pastimes of martyr life, right behind alcohol abuse and sadomasochistic sex. Dominia, during peacetimes, spent as many seconds as possible in the presence of the animals, because they did not care what or whom she ate so long as she shared some with them. Nor did they care if she did not eat anything at all. The Hierophant frequently had when she was a little girl named Morgan who, like Cassandra twenty years before her death, could not be persuaded to eat flesh without a great amount of doing. She had been criticized by everybody, and even the Lamb had tried to persuade her to eat normally rather than going by his blood alone. The dogs didn't try to pressure her about anything, though.

This particular group of dogs didn't even care that they hadn't met her before, not once in their entire lives: they simply bounded forth en masse to dance with big dog grins around her feet and spring up, paws bracing against her hips and stomach as they tried to bowl her over in impressive demand for affection. Normally, she would have responded to this behavior with laughter. Given the circumstances, and, seeing that she was completely alone with them, the General di Mephitoli allowed herself to dissolve into nearly hysterical tears.

Being alone with animals had a way of releasing emotion. Even with Cassandra, she restrained herself, forced herself to be the strong one for a woman who needed more support than the Governess. But certainly as a troubled little girl and a supremely surly teen, Dominia had found the company of dogs provided her with unconditional permission to feel. Then, as now, she could let go, crouched in the corner like a real sad sack while a few particularly enthusiastic mutts attempted to love-bomb her out of a sadness whose expression was universal.

"Oh, God." She hugged one at random and covered her eyes with her free hand. "What am I going to do? What have I done? You can't imagine—of course you can't"—she almost laughed—"but, oh, God, I never…I never stopped to ask myself what I was doing. I'm such a horrible person. I—I just wanted Cassandra. I didn't know how to handle her baby. I didn't think…I didn't want this.

"What am I doing? How did I expect this to end? I can't lose my *leg*, but my friends— Lavinia—oh, my heart. I only ever wanted Cassandra."

It was so hard to cry. Humiliating, even alone, as if she betrayed her own self-definition by experiencing an emotion unrelated to a calculated expression of violence. How often she had wept along this journey! This idiotic series of battles like none she'd ever fought. Yet, never had she wept like this. On the floor, every last ignored burden crashed back to her. How she'd changed! How she'd changed and how she'd suffered, and for what? She asked herself what she was getting out of a certain action, not about the nature or consequence of the action. She had wanted Cassandra out of all this mess, but the lengths to which she was willing to go for her wife now seemed foolhardy. She had tossed her life away for a woman who'd killed herself. A woman who could not return to this life, despite all the General had been told. A woman who could only return in the flesh when the universe was born again, and Dominia herself was born again. Would she have no memory of everything she'd suffered to attain? Would she be better off without those memories?

Even if Cassandra could come back, what reason would she have to forgive the General?

With another self-pitying sob, Dominia opened her eyes, about to reach for another dog, and froze in an astonishment that caused her to second-guess her own sanity. The animal before her, which of all its peers listened most astutely to her lamentations (and with none of the concerned supplications of its cohorts), was a most recognizable border collie. Through wet hiccups and soft gasps to stabilize her breath, the General wiped her face to better see.

"Basil?"

Head low, the still, gentle dog leaned forward to sniff her hand and give one affectionate lick. Then, all business, Basil turned on his heels and trotted away, past the lesser animals and around the corner to the next row of kennels. Holding her breath, the General clambered to her feet and straightened out her clothes, then stumbled forward with a cadre of dogs at her heels. As they rounded the corner, Dominia's breath released, and more than half her followers bounded to greet, with barking delight, Valentinian. The Saint of Death stooped to pet the wise-looking border collie before him, a grin already on his stubbled face.

"Aren't dogs the best," the magician said, his sigh one of sheer admiration. "They always know just what to say."

VIII

Dimethyltryptamine

Had anyone ever been so angry at the answer of their prayers? And not "answer" in a monkey's-paw, vengeful-djinni way, but a real, true answer—was it normal to feel, amid the kaleidoscope of relief and surety and sanity and hope, that iron-brand singe of rage? The General could not say. Certainly not in that moment when her anguish transmuted into fury for the magician before her, whose expression, down to the very angle of his eyebrows, remained smug as ever. "Looking a little red there, buddy."

"I am…*surprised*," she managed to calmly articulate, realizing her left hand was bound in a trembling fist. She forced it open to pat the nearest mutt. "Just…surprised to…find you…here."

"And I am *proud* to see *you* are working on your anger management," said the insufferable man, but in such a tone that the General couldn't help but crack the tiniest smirk. With one of his own, he waded through the dogs to offer Dominia his right hand. She shook it while trying to decide how humiliated she needed to be for all he'd overheard, then studied that most patient border collie.

"I thought—"

"What, that Basil would just disappear forever when I replaced him? No, no. I just got a body. He's as much a Void-walking, soul-having good boy as any sapient being I've ever known. Isn't he? Isn't he!" With a few well-placed words and a bend of the magician to ruffle his coat, the noble animal's stoic demeanor melted into playful puppitude that, inspiring like in its playmates, sent the whole crowd rollicking around the rows of kennels like a great canine sand devil. "He belongs in this world, has always had a body here. That can't be taken away by the Ergosphere, although time makes it seem so."

"What happened to your first body?"

"Well, we have an error in reality. Imagine what the first Cicero did when he crossed the boundaries between universes the first time."

"Hence, your deletion?"

"But now I've been given a new body—*thank* you," he added, pressing his hands together in a gracious aside that surprised her. "It means so much to me, I can't tell you. With this, I'm able to alter the closed system. There also happens to be a lot of traffic in the Ergosphere right now, anyway, which can provoke minor reality fluxes. Like with an electric current running through copper wire—electrostatic force pops one valence electron from a copper atom, and that liberated electron finds another atom, in which case the electron's negative charge boots out another electron. These days—ever since the time of my liberation, in fact—people have been a lot more in touch with the Ergosphere. That's our current. People coming, people going; and there's one electron I don't need to worry about. Guess who popped out of existence?" Valentinian drew a circle with his index fingers and Dominia smiled in relief.

"Tenchi!"

"Yeah, buddy, you did good work."

"What about Gethsemane?"

To her annoyance, he smiled and said, "We're talking about Tenchi right now—anyway, he was right to be nervous about taking the blood of Lazarus. Tenchi's the kind of guy who, once he stumbles into the Kingdom, well…good luck getting him back out. He's not dead—I see that look on your face. He's just moved. A living refugee."

"If he intended to leave and come back," Dominia added, "he would have looked a lot older, right?"

"Generally speaking, but not necessarily. Most people have an inner vision of themselves that isn't aligned with their external presentation, and that frequently includes age, whether they picture themselves younger, or older…but creatures without strong inner representation and an excess of emotional desires—an animal, or a primeval or traumatized individual—can be subject to this form of possession. Consider it more like spiritual radio. Of course, try it with somebody who can talk, and they freak out."

"So you intercede through animals—unless the goal is to provoke madness." She needed not think on her Father now. "Is Basil in danger here?"

"He'll feel it if he is, and react accordingly. He's his own man now, for the first time maybe ever. I've always been inside of him, dormant, waiting for you. More…sitting with his data in the Ergosphere and watching it, manipulating it. But it's all the same in the end. Now, after being separated from me and exposed to the Ergosphere on his own, he's a genius dog, in touch with the ebb and flow of information, and knows when he needs to make himself scarce—and when his favorite person needs some comforting."

The General lowered her misting eyes to blink them clear. When at last she could bear the magician's face, she found it strange to see in physical reality. She had waited for his arrival with great impatience over the past year yet been so busy that she had practically forgotten his appearance, if she could be said to have seen it at all in that in that dreamlike Void. For some unnerving reason, she found as much resemblance to her own blue-eyed, black-haired features as those of Lazarus's. "I suppose you won't stay long?" she asked, her tone cool.

"Yes and no. I mean, again, I'm a busy man. But I can't leave you hanging when you're suffering so much, Dominia."

She turned away to study the romping dogs. Valentinian went on, "I want to help you."

"Do I deserve help, after what I've done? What I've caused? God— what I've *done*." She remembered Lavinia's stump with a shudder and covered her eyes as if to banish the memory from their sight, where it would nonetheless endlessly cycle until its horror was reduced to mere fact. Such a process could take weeks, months, maybe years for something so heavy. Certainly a gross amount of tahgmahrs. A shallow gasp wheezed from Dominia's lungs. "Don't I deserve to lose my leg, too? I was responsible for—"

"Not for that," said the magician, his tone more gentle than she'd ever heard. "You did some bad things, Dominia, it's true. So has everybody. But you're not beyond help; and you're not beyond change, or goodness. You're not responsible for what your Father chose to do to Lavinia, or what Cassandra chose to do to herself."

"Cassandra—"

"Was a very troubled woman, no matter what you think you did. Hey." He leaned into her watering field of vision. She forced herself to look at him, forced her expression to remain as stoic as possible. "Listen to me, okay? Everything you've done, everything that's happened— you can make it right."

"And you'll help me?"

"Of course. That's why I'm here. I know you feel lost and lonely and probably more afraid than you ever have in your life, and I'm sorry. Nobody's telling you anything, and when we do tell you something, it's almost always bad news. But I've got some good news for you. Something to show you."

"Everybody's got something to show me tonight."

"But this is a good thing. A really good thing. I'm going to show you why humanity is worth protecting, why staying on the right side of this thing is worth it in the end."

"Why I need to lose my leg."

"Why it's all going to work out okay."

Lips tight, the General glanced to the window and the bright night outside, which lit Kronborg's garden via reflection from the bejeweled blanket of snow. "Trust you, huh...well, I don't know how you expect us to be able to get out of here unnoticed. Can *you* navigate the Void at night? Even you have to stop and rest."

"Well, sure, because it's creepy as shit. But we don't need to go through the Void. That's the wonderful thing about the Kingdom— fairy-land rules." Dominia was awash with mild surprise as the grinning saint elaborated: "When you've eaten food from the Kingdom, you can forever reach the Kingdom directly."

"What? How?"

"Oh, you can reach it any way! It's not dissimilar to the blood of Lazarus. The truth is that a sufficiently practiced person could enter the Kingdom by contemplating a bottle of water." From the breast pocket of that new velvet jacket, the magician withdrew his cigarettes (in a snazzy gold case, no less). "I've noticed you've been returning to Earth using the Word, for instance."

"I can't enter the Ergosphere with it, though. The only reliable method I've found for night travel is artificial light, BLP. I can travel by some music, but not much. I think my Father might go by paintings—his dream study's floor reminds me of Vermeer—but I can't figure out the method and I don't have time."

"Ah, he knows about forty different ways. That's the benefit of fooling around for two thousand years! I'd have to write a guidebook to describe them all...everybody's got their favorite. And you're right, the Word can only be pronounced by an earthly tongue at a time like the Lady's transference, which means it's *no bueno* for getting to the Void from reality. Anything a mind bound to the three-dimensional brain manages to 'remember' is a lesser approximation. That's why I favor this." The smiling fellow offered her a cigarette, which she accepted reluctantly.

"Why do I get the feeling this isn't even a normal cannabis cigarette?"

"Oh, buddy." The magician laughed so that he might have rubbed his hands together, were they not full. "You remember those little cobalt flowers from the Kingdom?" At her visible surprise to find he was able to get them through, he wiggled his eyebrows. "Just because flowers don't have mouths doesn't mean they aren't as much an individual as you, or Cassandra's diamond. Ableist," he teased, which got him a much-deserved elbow in the gut.

"Fella can't make a joke...anyway, those flowers grow around the Kingdom's water sources, but they prefer salt water, and tend to die just as soon as you bring them into the real world. Even dead, they know where they came from—it's stored in the dried cells of their petals. Moreover, they are symbolic here. Another way of thinking of the lost souls of the Void."

There was Gethsemane's ethereal nymph, declaring blandly how many of their pond's visitors were drowned. So the dead were poured into these flowers; they would be traveling to eternity by the contributions of the lost deceased. Better than traditional cannibalism, she supposed. The magician summed up, "When that energy is released with a little bit of fire or a spark of electricity and inhaled by a Lazarene with the substance of the Kingdom in his body, it points out the nearest door to the Kingdom."

"No kidding. And what happens when a non-Lazarene smokes it?"

Inhaling amid the crackling of the cigarette, which he'd tipped his head to light, the magician laughed. "They get good and fucked up!"

While Dominia allowed him to light her cigarette, she glanced at Basil. "What about him?"

"Oh, like I tried to say, animals come and go as they please. I have no idea how it works with them if I'm not pulling them in or out. I've never asked. I assume they're one with the Ergosphere already anyway, and contact with it—such as when a spirit like myself bonds with them—slips them free of time. What am I, an encyclopedia?"

"Sort of."

The taste of the cigarette was a far cry from the standard sourness of nicotine, though some tobacco had been sprinkled in to cut the offensive flavor of the flower. Its smoke, too, burned like nothing she'd inhaled, and she choked as Valentinian said, "You want to try to hold it in as long as possible…won't take much."

On and on she puffed, feeling anxious as a high schooler toking behind the bleachers. She glanced once, twice, in the direction of the door, and all around for cameras, holo or otherwise. Thank the Lamb, there was no one imminently coming for her. No one who would arrive, anyway, before Valentinian's attention was drawn toward one of the kennels. "Oh! There it is."

Yes, like a magic-eye puzzle. She saw nothing at first, but after one long drag, and after he put his hand into it, she saw that not just one but two kennels became from her perception a door into that marble hotel lobby. Reality around her warped, and she leaned forward into an intense gravity that twisted even the colors of the world, yet her vision's position remained upright. As if her senses had separated from her physical body. Within the door, the new front desk clerk of the City's hotel typed at her invisible keyboard with the receiver of a perfectly visible rotary phone jammed between her cheek and shoulder. Dear Miki Soto!

Dominia was so excited to see her friend, and so altered by the cigarette she'd smoked, that she didn't even remember running through the doorway. But, ah, what colors! It all seemed brighter on the other side, with the moment of transition on the threshold the brightest of all—even if she only held it in her memory secondhand. As if the explosion of light and vibrancy had been too much for her immediate observation. Behind her, the doorway had vanished as it came, but the General paid it no mind. The bored clerk looked up, did a double take, and promptly dropped her phone.

"Dominia! Holy shit!"

Completely forgetting her work, Miki vaulted the desk and greeted her friend with puppyish enthusiasm while Dominia responded in like manner. "Miki," she cried, "oh, I can't believe it! You're really here!"

"Hell yeah I am! I—hey, you can't smoke in here!" With a tongue-dampened pair of fingers, Miki pinched the cigarette out before allowing another squeal. "Man, I didn't know you'd be showing up! Not so soon, anyway. You'll never *believe* how great this place is! They gave me a cushy job at the front desk a couple of days a week, and the rest of the time it's just, like…so *chill.*"

It was at this moment that the General realized her friend spoke, as had Tenchi, in perfectly intelligible Japanese. Dominia hadn't remembered more than five sentences of the language since her wartime assault. Interesting how the Ergosphere made all languages resemble one, while the Kingdom rendered all separate but intelligible. Dominia observed that aloud, leaving out the bit about the Ergosphere.

"Oh, yeah," said Miki, clearly "over" that particular feature of living in the Kingdom, "that's a thing here. I can't even tell what language the locals speak. It's this totally different thing like maybe from the future or whatever; I just know I can understand it. But guess *what!*" Looking ready to burst with excitement, Miki waited, and the General realized belatedly that she was actually expected to guess. It wasn't hard.

"You're a biological woman."

"Yes! Dude! Oh my God! You can't imagine— Here, look—" She was starting to lift her skirt, and Dominia laughed, staying her exhibitionistic hands.

"That's fine, it's fine, I'm sure it's even better than your very realistic last one…" She squeezed those hands that she still held. "I'm so happy for you, Miki."

"Thanks, man, me, too! Oh, Dominia, look at you!" The laughing porter slapped her in the bicep. "You look like a seriously bad bitch in this place, *senpai.*"

"Just in this place?" asked the General wryly. The grinning clerk straightened her scarlet cap.

"Yeah! It's the eye patch and the hair. Once you cut your hair on Earth and lost your badass leather uniform, you started looking like a divorce attorney."

"Thanks," commented Dominia, while Miki went on giddily saying, "I can't believe you're here! How did you get here? How long are you staying?"

Now the General glanced over her shoulder and found, to her annoyance, that the door was not the only thing missing. Surprise: the magician was nowhere to be found. Looking back at her friend, Dominia shrugged. "I'm not sure. I guess I'm supposed to see something here? Or do something?"

"Don't you know why you came?"

"Strictly speaking, I was brought here…hey." The martyr followed her friend back to her post and leaned against the counter, trying (and failing) to see the computer at which Miki re-stationed herself. "All the people from Earth who have been stored—or, brought to this place as refugees—they come through this hotel, right?"

"Oh, sure."

"Do you know Tenchi Ichigawa?"

"Why." Miki adopted a theatrical glower. "Are all humans supposed to know each other? Racist. We probably just look like a couple of talking bento boxes to you."

"That's not—"

"I'm kidding, you martyr bitch." Miki tipped her cackling head toward the infinite ceiling, which echoed like a coven of hidden witches. "You should see your face… Hell yeah, I know Tenchi! He's our courier."

Relief! Sweet relief. The General ran her hand over her face with a gratified sigh as the clerk glanced reflexively at her outbox. "As a matter of fact, he just— Tch! That bastard." Miki whipped a letter from the otherwise empty box and brandished it at Dominia. "He missed one! We don't have Internet or e-mail here, he needs to take his job more seriously."

"But you're on an invisible computer," said Dominia. Miki rolled her eyes.

"One computer does not a network make, smart-ass. We're trying to get it up and running… Hey, do you know your way around here?" Turning off her acerbic *tsundere* routine in favor of big *moe* eyes, Miki wibbled her lower lip. "Will you please take this letter to the market plaza and deliver it for me?"

And Dominia, though initially reluctant to wander the City without a guide, understood she needed to do it when she read the name beneath Miki's fingers: "McLintock."

"Sure," said the General, trying not to betray the complex admixture of anxiety and hope growing beneath the breast pocket into which she tucked her cigarette. "Won't you get in trouble with your boss for this?"

"Who—the last Lady? Trisha? No, Tish won't care. Her shift doesn't even start until…well, later. Time is sort of weird here, I can't explain it. Anyway, just run that to Mrs. McLintock for me. And don't lose it!"

"What is it?"

"It's her stipend. The refugees need money to stay in the City, just like the citizens, and so this guy—you wouldn't know him—"

"Valentinian?"

"Okay, I guess you *do* know him—anyway, he funds the refugees' presence in the City through the hotel, and they in turn pay the hotel for their rooms."

"So it's just a big circle, sponsored by the martyr Saint of Death."

"Seems sort of silly, but it works."

"Why can't they just stay in the City for free?"

"What is this, communism? Hell no! If they want to live somewhere for free, I guess there's another City in the desert, way farther West, and it's different? They aren't down with money, so commies can go there. I don't know the deets, I'm a refugee like anybody else. Anyway, I don't think it matters. Definitely not as much as taking Mrs. McLintock's wages to her before the end of the day, so she can pay her way back into her family's room at the end of the night!" With a shooing motion, Miki waved Dominia off. "Gee whiz, the minute you ask somebody to deliver a letter, they want to talk for hours… Some of us have to work, you know."

After a sly wink, Miki resumed her typing, or tried. She realized with a few keystrokes and a sharp gasp that she had left the phone off the hook. After yelping into it, "Hello? Hello?" for a few seconds and receiving only dead air, the girl hung the thing up as if it were guilty of some great injustice.

"Damn…that was the telephone company, too. I'd already held forty minutes!"

"What did you hold them with?" asked the General, who ducked a hurled clipboard on her laughing way to the street.

Above the Kingdom shined a sun more beautiful than Earth's, but just as harmless. Funny: she had been able to move in its rays for a year, yet still she lifted her hand in instinctive shield, wincing back, then, after a few seconds' remembrance, edging out of shade with her good eye still protected from the blaze. Vaguely, she recalled the route she'd taken with Gethsemane and began to head left, its opposite direction. She had no compass here, but if Dominia's bearings were correct and the sun still set in the west, the market lay east.

The City was a sight to behold, with its flowing hills centuries ago covered in masonry so exquisite that the white stone crested like sea-waves. Set decoration to artfully accent the queer-yet-natural variety of costumes that, elsewhere, might seem anachronistic. Here the mishmash was only a natural sign that men's souls had fled to the Kingdom, however it was perceived, in infinite masses and by infinite means since the dawn of existence. The blood of Lazarus must not have been the only means in. Didn't that peplos-draped woman who passed with a sensual smile resemble illustrations of Sappho? Dominia turned her head but could not tarry to see, carried along with the pace of busy walkers all around as they surged, a river, to their destinations: she settled for remembering that meaning-laden final stanza of the poet's "Ode to Aphrodite."

What a miracle to behold a woman of such genius! This place was of a very uncommon sort, to be certain—yet not uncommon at all, for it seemed in that time and space perfectly normal. Each second spent there felt more natural than the last: Not only that, but freer! Godlier! Look at all those good people! Look at all that joy!

What had the Lamb shown her in the Void when she saw through his eyes and watched the martyrs devour the blood and substance of the sacrificial humans? Was it not the sin her Father proclaimed, but that part of the self that, bound by the electromagnetic field of the brain, could for whatever reason not escape when it was devoured by a martyr? That meant martyrs were even worse than they superficially seemed, for each one was a walking prison who contained at least part of the self of each person they'd eaten. Was anyone devoured by a martyr doomed to the fate of those souls her mind had conglomerated into the bloody ocean of her dream? Were martyrs that unsalvageable? The General could not accept that possibility. She could not afford to believe anyone was beyond salvation. If they were, she was surely unworthy of it, herself.

At last, on instinct, the General looked up and found herself at that corner where she'd first seen Tenchi calling her name and running, breathless, through the crowd. Though now she had expected— hoped—to see him, he was nowhere to be seen, and she glanced, with another soft thud of anxiety, at the envelope for Mrs. McLintock.

What would she say? What *could* she say? It was miraculous that such interface with eternity was possible, even for vision—but how could speech cope with the enormity of interaction with the living dead? Especially when that living dead had all the reason in the world for hatred. And who was to say this was even the right McLintock? Carol? Perhaps it was her mother, or her mother's mother, or whatever woman who before her had fled to the Mars colony when it was more than a wild and dangerous frontier. For her part, Dominia could see the appeal of escaping to space long before she boldly entered the gate of the busy market, passed a few stalls in search of the McLintocks' fruit stand, and was struck in place by the incredible sight of none other than young Murph McLintock shouting for their buyers. Forever the eight years at which Dominia had shot him in the head, rather than allow his martyrdom.

Her hands numb with shame, the astonished General was nonetheless more shocked when the boy responded to his own recognition of her not by freezing in terror or running away or screaming for help. Rather, his face brightened, and he called her name.

Every head in that marketplace turned.

It took Dominia a few seconds to register this. By then, silence spread like yet another wave throughout the crowd. A few people shuffled, smilingly, from out of her way. She could not help but think some looked familiar, but became preoccupied by the boy who dashed to hug her, tightly, around the waist.

"I don't understand," she said, her eye wet and batting as people, looking pleased, arranged themselves to murmur softly and watch the unfolding scene. "How did you get here?"

The grinning boy studied her, and said, "Well don't *cry*, please! It's nice!"

"She's crying *because* it's nice, Murphy," said Mrs. McLintock. His very tired mother looked here a little less tired. After wiping her hands on her apron, she emerged from the crowd to accept the envelope from Dominia's amazement-loosed grasp. "Thank you, General."

"You're— I'm so sorry." Her lips strained in a way that made Carol exhale and fan her eyes with the envelope.

"Well, goodness, don't make *me* cry, now. It's— Don't think of it, please."

"But I *do*."

"I know." With momentary reticence touching the eyes above her straining lips, the dead woman patted her hand. "But don't. At least, not as much, or as sadly as you do."

Stunned, the General tried to speak, and failed. It was as she had guessed. What use were words before the dead? Before, worse yet, the forgiveness of the dead? What forgiveness—what at all—did she deserve in life? Her mind was a spinning Ferris wheel, but not so spinning as it was when the boy released her. Then she looked up through the crowd, through its many faces, and, in a crescendo of beautiful glory, focused beyond the shoppers and salespeople and couriers. Rendered that much more beautiful through the stained-glass filter of tears, she recognized the people around had edged wide to reveal, as or more astonished than Dominia, that vision that had driven her each step of her long journey.

Oh, her absent heart! There was its beat again.

IX

Cassandra

Life does not always afford catharsis. All too often, unresolved pain remains an open wound forever, or seems to while we live. But perhaps that is only so those catharses that do arrive—those moments of relief that signal the annihilation of lifelong tension—mean that much more to us as we lie awake, counting each soft breath from the parted lips of a lover we thought we'd never see again.

A lie? A dream? Nothing that felt this way could be either. Dominia and her deceased wife embraced by the overflowing fountain of the plaza, and, weeping, Cassandra succumbed to kiss after kiss. Between each sob and each press of lips rang their words in duet: "I'm sorry, I'm so sorry, forgive me, I'm sorry."

"You have no reason to apologize." Dominia touched that warm cheek. The damp beads of Cassandra's tears burst under fingers that had missed, missed, missed this sensation. "Oh, Cassie, Cassandra—oh, I've missed you. After all I did to you, you don't need to apologize."

"But I do. *I* did that to myself. Nobody did it to me, least of all you. I was just so…angry and shocked and hurt and I—I did the thing that would hurt you the most." Those perfect eyes, big glass marbles of the world, wrapped themselves in a new sheen of tears. "I thought I'd had enough of living, but I was in so much pain! And the depression made me so shortsighted. Death wasn't even real to me until I was already dead."

"Oh, Cassandra…but what are you *doing* here?" Dominia turned her own trembling lips skyward, then back to her wife, whose honey curls were then plastered with laughing kisses. "I thought you were *lost*. That was what they said. The dead wander in the dark night of the Ergosphere forever, get trapped in low-frequency vibrations or… Lamb, whatever, when they have no soul. When they kill themselves."

The hitch of Cassandra's breath made her tighten her grip. "I *was* lost. I was lost eternally. I'm here because you saved me, Dominia, just like you saved everybody else."

Lips parted, the General looked up and saw through her tears the faces of the surrounding crowd. Their faces revealed themselves to her struggling memory now that the first dominoes of recognition were tipped. There was the man who must have been Mr. McLintock, slipping through the shoppers to hold his wife; Sakaki Kurosawa, the cutest of the Japanese nurses killed by Cicero in the hospital massacre, was there with her coworkers; a couple of soldiers she herself had destroyed on the same occasion were there with their wives and Kahlil, whom Dominia almost didn't recognize without glasses. All the people she had ever killed, failed to save, watched die—every single one of them was there. Even that son of a bitch Tobias Akachi, who smiled along with the rest of the watchers. Even Cassandra's first spouse, Benedict, had a misty eye and a gentle smile as Dominia savored her long-awaited reunion. Long-awaited, long-wished, hardly-dared-to-dream! Oh, Cassandra!

"I've hurt all of these people. I hurt you. And Lavinia. She's still being hurt because of what I did. I don't know if I can help her."

"You can. You will." Fire burned beneath the shimmer of Cassandra's eyes, beneath her trembling voice. "I believe in you."

To hold her! Dominia clutched her fair wife to her heart, feeling once again that body as, for over a year, she had only in memory, dreams, sorrow. But this! Oh, this. The General endeavored, somehow, to abate her own tears, and kissed the sweet-smelling head that tucked so perfectly into the crook of her neck. Like home, that feeling. "I don't deserve your belief after what I did."

"Don't say that. We *all* believe in you."

"But I made you so miserable. And I've hurt so many people. I hurt you."

"Dominia…" Cassandra lifted her head, and the irreplaceably soft touch of her fingertips nearly foiled the General's efforts to stave off tears. "I hurt myself. You never hurt me the way I did. You never made me miserable. Is that all you think— that we were miserable?"

"Of course not. We got along. I thought we were happy most of the time."

"We were. You gave me so much. Don't you remember? You made mistakes, and I was in pain, but even so…we were happy. You remember how you used to come home from work, and we'd curl up by the fire and I'd read to you, or we'd turn on the holo-center and the whole room would be our movie, or you'd draw me until I fell asleep? And how you bought me pets, and took me to the zoo, and helped me to start going back to Mass…to start teaching Noctisdomin school. I teach it here, too. Only"—Cassandra's eyes and mouth crinkled with the weight of her smile, and Dominia battled the urge to kiss those delicate webs until they bruised—"I get to teach the truth, here, and it's just Sunday school."

"Less annoying to say in English, not that it matters here…I bet you're even better at it in this place. Those children loved you so much. You were the gentlest, most compassionate person in their whole lives. I know you were in mine."

Her jaw deforming in that sweet way it did when she tried not to cry, Cassandra patted the General's cheek and then, as if not knowing where to lay that hand, her yet-living wife's heart. "If that were true, I would have talked to you more, instead of doing what I did. I just didn't understand. But being here, I learned—the way it was is the only way it could have been."

"But that's not true. I had free will. I made an evil, selfish decision to give away your daughter so I wouldn't have to share you with the memories of the person who loved you before."

"You took care of Cassandra." Benedict approached from the edges of the crowd to shake Dominia's hand. "For a longer time—and in better ways—than I could have. And Lavinia…she's not really mine, now, is she?"

"What do you mean?" Even before her question, the General felt the magician's presence behind her—or smelled his aromatic drugs, more like.

"She's the protein's. And not the true sacred protein…the false, deformed protein held sacred by the HMC. When Lavinia was in poor Cassandra's womb, and Cassandra was martyred rather than receiving the proper genetic treatments—because the Front decided long ago that health care is only a 'right' for martyrs, if rights even exist anymore—the protein went to work on the developing fetus." As the people of the Kingdom resumed their business, Dominia turned, Cassandra still in her arm, to watch the magician. "Your courtship was incredibly fast."

The General averted her eye. "I've criticized myself, but if it weren't for that, I don't think we would have had all those years together."

"Yeah, that's probably true. But I'm not bringing it up to throw stones. Trust me, I know how it goes! You meet an amazing woman— your dream woman—and move right in with her because, hey, you're waking up together all the time, anyway, so you'd might as well! Then some crazy shit happens and it's too late to turn back because your books are mixed on the shelves and you can't sneak all that out while she's sleeping, now can you?" As the women laughed, Valentinian summarized, "Emotions are never a perfect science."

Cassandra leaned that long-lost head against Dominia's shoulder, and the General struggled to focus as the magician went on, "But, like I was saying, Lavinia's DNA was edited even as her body and brain and tiny organs put the finishing touches on something resembling a fetal form. About twenty weeks in…that's why pregnant women and their fetus never survived this before you. Too early and the protein would just edit the fetus out of existence like it was an error. Too late and the changes would be minimal, but brutal enough to cause any infant's death. Between those two extremes, there's a sweet spot that nobody's been lucky enough to hit; and if they did hit it, they didn't have the medical care to maintain the condition. But in that sweet spot? The protein can alter not just a child's genetic and physical structure, but the genetic and physical structure of her descendants. The eggs in her ovaries are the world's only viable eggs containing martyr DNA. She may have technically died in the womb just like everybody else died in life, but she died twice—the first time, the baby died because her mother died. The second time the baby died, she died because that was when the protein began to truly afflict her. It picked a certain point—after it finished stripping out her father's DNA for its own, no doubt—to take her offline until she reached her full development. 'Full development' also includes puberty, and all the finishing cognitive touches of a young adult. Her situation was so prolonged because it was a two-step process of complete transformation. If Lavinia can be said to have a father—or any parents, at this point—it's the malformed protein."

Chilled, the General asked, "Then how can she be saved?" Or, better question: How could the world be saved from her? The magician, looking earnest, stared into her face.

"Lavinia is a deeply troubled girl, but she has a pure heart. Superficially, she is corrupted, because she has no way to comprehend the truth. But if she were to know the truth—if she were on the right side—can you imagine how powerful she would be? Can you fathom what would happen if you were able to convert her to the Lazarene faith, as pious a girl as she is for your evil Father's teachings? Most importantly, the true sacred protein is a hop, a skip, and a jump away from the malformed protein, and she is that malformed protein walking upon Earth. If her body and blood could be set right—healed by a great miracle such as that which gave me a body—consumption of her substance would have the same effect as that of Lazarus."

"How could such a miracle be possible again? No, forget that—the real miracle is getting her on our side. You think she can be turned against him, after what he's convinced her to do? After I betrayed her from the start, before she was even born?"

"Lavinia just wants to be treated like an adult. She wants people to tell her the truth, and she wants to be alive. However badly she's hurt by the reality of the situation, sometimes a little hurt is necessary to wake the fuck up." At the slight scowl of the Noctisdomin school teacher, the magician waved his hand. "Pardon my French. Here: you can't heal from an illness you don't even know you have. Better?"

With a steadying exhalation, Dominia glanced between Cassandra and Benedict. "I think being in this place and having the perspective you do is giving you all an overly optimistic perception of what's possible. But...I'll try."

"You'll succeed," said Cassandra, leaning up to kiss her wife. "I know you will."

"And after I succeed," asked Dominia of that beautiful face, "where will I find you?"

Valentinian, from somewhere in the distance, said, "I'll take care of it," but that wasn't enough. It would never be enough. Nothing was worth this moment, this slight weight of her body, this perfume of her flesh. It was real: so real!

"Couldn't I just stay here? I mean, since in eternity, she's already been saved by the best version of me." She asked it only half joking, and Cassandra smiled at her jest while, irritated, the magician said, "There are universes where you've done that, and it absolutely— *pardonnez-moi*—fucks *me*. That means I have to spend another two thousand Earth years tooling around, waiting for the next 'you' who will hopefully be less of a lazy deadbeat. And a reset isn't a party for you, either."

"I wish you could stay." Cassandra squeezed her hand. "But you *are* the best version of you."

"That's a horrible thing to say!" The General laughed, and her wife smiled.

"You're so much better than you know. Stronger. And someday, you'll be happy, too. But you have to keep fighting. Keep fighting for me. Keep fighting for Lavinia. I know you can save her. You can save us. Somebody has to do it, after all, since we're here."

With a glance for Benedict, Dominia brushed the hair from her wife's face. "I guess you were never really mine. Not my version of you...not the one meant for me, if I'm the Dominia to survive this."

"But how I love you, even so." As Cassandra turned her closed eyes against the General's palm and those soft lips brushed its heel, Dominia strove to maintain her composure. "Even if I'm only the Cassandra you save—only the Cassandra who sets you up for the Cassandra who gets to be yours—everything you did for me…everything we endured and enjoyed together…I'll treasure it forever."

Tearfully, but not painedly, the nodding General bent her head to kiss, one last time, the wife she'd loved and wronged so much that the thought of it had been enough to drive her around the world. To destroy that world. To remake that world. With tears of her own, a hand that patted Dominia's lips, and a mouth that strove to say anything but came up mute before relenting into that familiar smile of resignation, Cassandra took Benedict's hand. After one last look over her shoulder for that particular General, she disappeared into the crowd as if she had never been there at all. But she had. Oh, she *had*.

"Was it everything you'd hoped it would be?" asked the magician while Dominia covered her watering eye.

"I hoped I'd get to keep her when I finally saw her again. That I wouldn't have to watch her go, ever."

"Someday, you won't anymore." His hand landed upon her shoulder, and she turned to look at him as he swore, "I promise you."

"Why are you so intent on helping me, Valentinian? Why have you come here, if you're a wanderer through the universes? The bodiless man isn't obligated to be anywhere. You're liberated. You told me before that you were born into this world as the son of the man now called Lazarus, and his wife, Trisha—that your family, along with Cicero and Elijah, discovered the protein together, but that they stole the credit and power in that first universe. Usually people want to get back at somebody like that because of money, or a sense of obligation of setting things right, but you're the most slothfully amoral saint I've ever met." While he laughed, she emphasized, "I just don't understand why you're helping me. You even have your body, and you're still helping me."

"I'm *especially* helping you because I have my body! Christ, you're so used to constant betrayal that you just don't even understand what loyalty is anymore…poor dude. We'll get you fixed up when this is all over." As he began to navigate through the crowd and back to the hotel, she followed only because she had no choice. "If it would satisfy you to know I have other motives than helping you, then rest assured. You're right when you call me a universal wanderer. I go everywhere, and, unbounded by time as I am in this condition, I see my many future conditions in other universes—see those other universes, and what lies above and below them. When you're like me, you realize how big the big picture is: and the irony is that it's bigger than you could ever possibly realize."

"What was that about 'future conditions' in 'other universes'? You mean, outside of this cycle of the universe where I live?"

"I'm telling you, buddy…this thing is huge. And what I mean about 'future conditions,' well, that's a little complex. To be honest, I stopped worrying about it, though future conditions of myself, as I nudge into the businesses of other universes, might."

"Are you talking about reincarnation?"

"Getting hung up about your own identity is a key mistake most people make, especially when they start talking about the concept of reincarnation. Mostly because they forget that they made a choice to be a part of all this while in eternity. Of course, that's by design. Ultimately, we're all just the Void, imitating people. All thoughtforms, yet all truth. In the service of that truth, I am seriously committed to helping you solve the problem of this world. And, of course, when I do solve the problem of this world, it liberates me from being a part of this particular cycle of existence, thereby freeing me up to be part of a new cycle of existence. A new rung of the ladder."

"So reincarnation isn't being a bunch of sea monkeys before being a smart dog and then finally turning into a man?"

"No, no, that's reincarnation, you're right. I'm talking about transmigration. Different dimensional axis of soul movement, y instead of x."

Lamb, this shit made her head spin. As the saint stopped in an alcove to light his cigarette, the General said, "So long as I'm not responsible for sticking you as a dog."

"Told you, that's your old man. You understand why, now, too."

"No kidding! Having two of the same person in one reality can't be healthy."

He nodded. "Reality itself knows what he's done, and doesn't like it. Every time he shows up, it's around the same time in 1974 CE—the year Cicero was born, years before the creation of the protein. I think I've told you this before—he tries to kill my parents before I'm born, standard timeline interference mistake. Instead, he finds the Lady and her cult, established from the dawn of time in preparation for his coming. This was not anticipated by the first Cicero, because nothing like this existed in the original function of reality. But the next version of him is always more prepared than the last—the output of one iteration forms the input of the next—and his presence inherently disrupts Lazarus's whole ability to form a relationship with my mother. She gets put on a different path, instead of continuing in academia and getting into proper genetic research or dying by the Hierophant's hand. From the first iteration and throughout each thereafter, my mother gets made into the Lady instead of being my mother. Therefore, I'm never born, and my linear-ish stream of consciousness continues working on the system from outside, intervening in small ways such as through dogs and other animals."

With a slightly wrinkled nose to recall the flirtatious behavior of Valentinian toward the (admittedly attractive) redheaded Lady who worked at the hotel's front desk before Miki, Dominia asked, "Why didn't he just turn around and kill Lazarus when he showed up to martyr the brothers?"

"Several reasons. The most important reason, of course, is that, without Lazarus, the martyr race has absolutely zero hope of ever achieving complete universal dominance, and your old man does not dream small. Lazarus and his assistants, the brothers, discover both the sacred and malformed proteins with or without the help of Trisha; but because of the eternal nature of the sacred protein, as soon as he experimentally infects himself, he remembers everything that's ever happened with all of this before and knows to destroy the sacred protein sample before going into hiding. The same night he did this in the first universe, Cicero was creeping around the lab, and stole the only protein which was present: the malformed one. In every iteration thereafter, he never gets that far…the Hierophant gets to him, first. They don't even have to worry about the samples anymore, and Lazarus doesn't worry about destroying them. He just books it into the Ergosphere. Poor old man! In these iterations, he only lives to discover the sacred protein because the Red Market was formally organized for the sole purpose of defending his totally oblivious life. Imagine… stalked by a secret conspiracy of gorgeous women without knowing!"

Dominia sighed. "What a waste."

"Yeah, he was a real dork before he was infected with the protein… now he's still a dork, he's just too angry all the time to seem like one." Chuckling, the magician nodded to a passing individual and stepped from the alcove to resume their stroll. "Anyway, ignorance has its fringe benefits…he also spends his whole human life being stalked by your Father, who, for a solid thirty-ish years, kept tabs on Lazarus—from 1974 until the discovery of the protein—waiting for the RM to slip up. Lucky for us, those women might be more insane than even His Holiness."

"You're not kidding," muttered the General, glancing down, and thinking of the Lady who sent her to her doom. "I don't have to lose my leg in all this, do I?"

"If you did, it would eventually be restored."

"*I don't have to lose my leg,*" she repeated with expectant emphasis, "*do I?*"

"If you do as I say," said the magician, with seriousness enough to raise alarm. "If you follow the plan."

"The plan I don't know about?"

"The plan that you *will* know about, as long as you follow the plan."

Amazing. Not a trace of humorous self-awareness in him. At least, not for this.

In the lobby of the hotel (too soon to leave, it seemed to the General, the powder fragrance of her wife still clinging to her clothes), the magician said, "I've got something for you, but you're going to want to find a place for it as soon as you're back home."

"Does she have to go *now*?" Miki called from behind the desk. Dominia's throat tightened while Valentinian heaved a sigh.

"Yeah, didn't think about that…you ladies should say goodbye."

Dominia, stricken, looked at her friend to see her sorrow shared. "I'm not going to see her?" asked Miki.

"Oh, *you'll* see *her* in no time from your perspective, Miki. This is eternity we're talking about. But from her perspective, she won't see you but in passing, and maybe sometimes in dreams. Not for a long time."

"Man." Miki put aside the phone and rounded the counter. "You're eating up my whole day with this phone thing…oh, Dominia! Dude"—she squeezed the General around the waist with such an iron grip that the martyr grimaced—"I miss you so much! I can't wait until you're here to stay for good. But you have to get your shit right before you can, okay?"

"I'm working on it." She laughed and inhaled once, deeply, calming herself and catching that lavender aura that followed her friend—that very same that followed a great many Red Market women all about the world. "I'll miss you, Miki. But I'm so glad you're happy."

"Thanks, man, me too! I don't know what I'll start doing with myself once I adjust to being here, or where I'll go—where any of us will go—after this place, but I'm looking forward to making my time worthwhile."

"I'll try to do the same with mine on Earth." The General patted Miki one last time before extricating herself from the girl's grip. "Be good, now."

"Maybe," said Miki, waggling her hips as she made her way back to her post. Through years of in-the-moment acting practice, the human did a good job hiding her misty eyes from all concerned. Valentinian, guiding Dominia back to that center sitting area, patted her hand.

"General, General…you're the bravest person I know. Just hold on a little longer: keep pushing forward. When this is all over, however it's turned out—the situation has to be better than the one we're in now, right?"

"I can't afford to stumble into a worse one," she said with a laugh, feeling freer than she had in at least a year and a half. As the magician lifted his lighter and she retrieved her now slightly crooked cigarette to lean into the sizzling blue arc, she asked, "But what about you?"

"What about me?"

"Will I see you again before this is all over?"

"Before this is all over…yeah. Once before this is over—and once, at the exact moment it is *finally* over, because I will have one more thing to ask of you. Which reminds me: I need to borrow something, if you wouldn't mind."

Without stopping to clarify her consent or tell her what he borrowed, the magician reached behind her ear as though to make a coin appear. Instead, he produced a small iridescent coil that, thinner than a hair, curled upon itself into a tiny sphere. This vanished between his fingers as he said, "I've got a project going on in the background here. Science fair stuff compared to my more theoretical business. Still necessary, though!"

"Going to tell me what it is?"

"Later. If I tell you now, your knee-jerk reaction will be 'no.'" While she rolled her eye and puffed away at the joint, the magician took her hand. "But before you go back, I just want to thank you for all you've done. For all you keep doing. I know it's not easy…but we're almost there. Just keep fighting."

"I will," she said. As his gaze fell from hers, she followed his focus, and her breath hitched.

Between the rows of ferns enclosing them, that gold-and-cerulean doorway opened into the Kronborg kennel. The disorienting thing was she did not even become conscious of the intention to walk forward. She simply noticed the doorway, then found herself upon its other side. Yes—back to Earth. Basil at her feet, joint pinched between her fingers, and the magician's hand replaced with none other than a relieving (if shocking) sight for her sore eyes: her lost gun. Still too in the afterglow of dreaming to register the full oddity of the find, she shifted the joint to the corner of her mouth and reflexively checked its chamber.

One bullet.

"There you are, Ninny!" Lavinia's sigh of relief bounced from the corner of the kennels, startling the General out of her reverie (or, possibly, out of the Kingdom, for who was to say that the happenings in the Kingdom were not mere symbols for the happenings of reality). With a surge of adrenaline and hyper-trained reflexes, she stowed the weapon under the back of her shirt before she could savor the reunion. Her sister carried on without notice. "I was worried when you went off like that. Are you all—euch!" The girl's sound was a crossbreed of disgust and indignation. "You can't *smoke* in here, Ninny. Think of the doggies!"

In one swift motion, Dominia pinched the cigarette out and crammed it away, not worried if it broke. The General felt more liberated than she ever had, whatever happened. By the Lamb, she was downright high! (Or by Valentinian's drugs? Hard to say.) The blessed truth whispered to her by the universe that night—that one encouragement she had ever needed—played out in phantom kisses relived by her giddy mind. Cassandra was not lost! Anything else Dominia had learned that night—any threat or horror hanging over her head—was nothing compared to the thought that she had, just moments ago, held Cassandra in her arms. Ah! She could weep had she the time, but she had none, and could not excuse her weeping in front of Lavinia except to misappropriate its source.

"I'm sorry I ran, Livvy. I guess I didn't know…how to react."

With an anxious glance for the door, the Princess edged through the dogs and tangled her fingers sheepishly amid the sumptuous folds of her dress. "Her" fingers—ugh. One wretched remembrance proved more evil than Cassandra's presence proved good, and brought the General's mood down a few notches. Lavinia, innocent to these thoughts, said in anxious hush, "I didn't know how you'd react, but I guess I didn't expect *that*. I've never shown anyone before."

"Livvy…"

"Daddy *told* me people wouldn't understand—even other martyrs. They don't understand anything about me. But I guess I thought you would understand, and that it might help you. You being so scared and all, maybe it would make you feel better to know I'd been through the same thing."

"But *why*, Lavinia?" The General tried to stifle from her voice those notes of natural horror in favor of warm and open concern. "Why did he take your limbs?" She knew his internal reasons, of course. She just wanted to know his excuses, and Lavinia seemed eager to supply them after decades of keeping the issue to herself.

"Well, the first time—you can't tell *anybody* this, Ninny, you hear me? Anyway, the first time I was about…forty, and I was sad that I couldn't marry anyone. I just wanted to be a part of that deep, deep love that a man and a woman share! That you had for your wife. Even Cicero and the Lamb seem happy together, though poor Lambie is always so tired from his work…but his plight just reminds me that being a saint is too important. I can't throw away everything I represent to the Church and to God! Worse, if I had to look outside the Family for a man, and he swooped me away, why, whatever would Daddy do?"

Yuck. Focus, Dominia. Her little sister continued, still in her own, purer world. "He would be so sad without me. But the temptation to have a boyfriend was just so *strong*! I had all these sinful thoughts and couldn't focus—couldn't do *anything* but lay around and sigh. Finally, I asked Cicero for his advice during confession, and he talked to Daddy for me. He's so helpful! They both were, and so understanding…Daddy came to talk to me right that very morning as I went to bed, and said he had a good idea that would solve all of our problems!"

"You gave him your leg because you felt sinful for wanting to be in love? To be an adult?"

"No, Ninny! I gave him my leg—well, you can't tell anybody *this*, either, but I told Cicero what I did in confession because I tried to run away once, too, and after I was foiled by my girl friends…they didn't tell on me, but I felt so guilty. I knew I had to confess to God." At Dominia's visible surprise to hear all this—that the devoted girl ever had one iota of desire to get out of Dodge, as they said in an ancient Western show—Lavinia crossed her arms. "I told you earlier, Ninny, I'm not perfect! And, my goodness…you think it's a fun time sitting around in these castles while you and everybody else in the whole Family gets to run around all over the planet, wherever you want?"

Poor Lavinia. No one in that world could have ever known the sorrow the General felt for this girl, who should have been her daughter as much as Cassandra's. In that rejection, the child had lost not only her psychological self but the greater part of her bodily self. What kind of life would she had lived if Dominia had not sold off the unborn infant to her Father? Would it have been possible, by any stretch of the imagination, for the mothers to make their way to safety anywhere in the world? Could they have ever had any modicum of happiness here? She would only plague herself with the questions she'd neglected for a century if she continued down that track.

"Trust me," the General tried at last, "running all over the world isn't the privilege you'd expect."

"But I want to decide that for myself! I'm sure it's scary sometimes, and that the world is very harsh, especially to traveling martyrs—but, Ninny, don't you love coming and going as you please? Don't you feel so strong and brave? I think you must. You're the strongest person I've ever known." Her voice dropped and she edged in, conspiratorial. "I was very worried about you, Ninny, but I was also very happy for you when you left. I thought—I hoped that you would find peace somewhere, maybe. You've always been so troubled. There are so many books about you, you know? I've read a few, but I don't have a head for military biographies, so they take me a long time to finish…but you've done such hard things. In your letters, you would only ever talk about governing work and the happy things you and Cassandra did, and I always thought…I guess I got the sense after a few decades that you did that on purpose, you know. Being optimistic in front of me. That you were trying to support me, so I wouldn't worry about you."

Aching with the weight of long-suppressed guilt, the General tried to assure herself there was no time like the present. "There's a reason for that." The pure sweetness of her sister's earnest face forced her gaze away; she was no more able to stare into its glow than was a non-Lazarene into the heart of the sun. "Lavinia—"

"—must be in here," interrupted Cicero, as the door pushed open and the cadre of dogs charged to greet him—save for Basil, who, while theoretically no longer possessed by the magician, seemed no less displeased by the prospect of Cicero's presence. Though, admittedly, it was odd for the dogs to be so thrilled by El Sacerdote. They preferred the Lamb, which was why it did not surprise Dominia when both brothers rounded the corner. If anybody was surprised, it was Cicero, who seemed shocked, then displeased, to discover the General along with Lavinia. Any hint of levity scalded straight off his face and left his expression tight beneath his devilish goatee.

"Ah. And our other dear sister is also here. I do hope we are not interrupting you girls."

Although Dominia was about to forge some cover story, Lavinia leapt in so immediately that the General was once more shocked by her younger sister's "naughty" streak: she had a heretofore unknown ability and willingness to lie, which was just more proof she was a natural member of the Holy Family. "Oh, I was just showing Ninny some of the new dogs from this year, and talking about the after-party! I'm so *excited*, Cicero, aren't you?"

"Yes, my dear, it should be very fine time…did you tell Dominia about the play?"

It must have been a special occasion. The Hierophant and Cicero (or Cicero Prime and Diet Cicero, as she strove to think of them) loved having concerts at the drop of a hat—as or more frequent than their parties, though the two were often paired. Theater productions required much more time and effort than the standard gala, meaning that the Ciceros, depending on venue size and location, could only force their actors and crewmembers to pull off about ten to twenty shows a year while working their thespians in repertory. That was to say, ten to twenty separate shows, of which there were sometimes nightly performances, over the course of that year-long season.

A human who had never visited the European theatere might not imagine the size, grandiosity, and variety of shows available in the town of Elsinore, but they frequently did not need to imagine: the Elsinore Theater Festival's shows, like most forms of theater whether human or martyr, were broadcast globally across a variety of monetized streaming services generously open to human countries so they, too, could line the Hierophant's digital wallets with the imaginary bits of encrypted data everyone had agreed somewhere along the line to be a measure of wealth. Every human who considered themselves high-class endured a love/hate relationship with martyr culture due purely to the quality of their theater. As they stood, at present, in Kronborg, and it was the Elsinore Theater Festival, she guessed, "A bit of Willy Shakes, I suppose," to be rebuffed by Cicero, "No, in fact. It is Father's original."

While the General made long-trained eye contact with the Lamb—a sort of brief, exasperated mutual stare used in place of an eye roll when present company made sarcasm unsafe—she maintained a pleasant smile. "That will be great," she said, while the Lamb said, "Pity about the double-booking, though."

"Yes," agreed Cicero, shaking his head. "I should have very much enjoyed an opportunity to see the opening night—but, duty calls."

"I wish you were going to be there, Cicero." Lavinia worried the black lace frills of her overskirt with gloved hands at which the General could hardly bare to look—particularly not when Cicero took one up to kiss.

"You know I shall be with you in spirit, my girl. At future performances. But the Lord does not wait."

The General maintained her smile, thinking happy thoughts of the place she'd been instead of all they discussed now. "You're going to be in the show, Lavinia?"

"Oh, she shall be the star, of course."

"Of course," echoed the Lamb. He stood from where he'd crouched, having mussed sufficiently the ears of the border collie that trotted back around the corner, invisible to the DIOX-I's scrutiny and Cicero's arrogant inability to recognize the animal that had stopped the train. "And the Holy Father had to be sure he had his part, too."

"Naturally, naturally," said Cicero, all happy agreement as he studied Dominia's face like he tried to read her mind. "I'm sorry to say, sister, neither will you be able to attend the premiere performance of Lavinia's play. Though I'm sure we could find a way to access the stream, if you and I wrap up our ceremony soon enough."

"And is this all going to be before the party?" asked the General, to which the priest agreeably said, "Consider it preparation," with that dark, expectant look in his eye. He knew, of course, what she divined. This ceremony was when Dominia would lose her leg, which would probably then be prepared and served for the New Year's party once the Hierophant's show wrapped up.

That was assuming, of course, any of these events were allowed to get as far as that.

"Where is this ceremony?" she asked. Cicero, pleased to tell her, waved a hand in the direction before dropping it upon Dominia's shoulder to guide her along. There she was again, ten years old—human and martyr years combined, mind—and on her way to a beating because she'd snickered in church at some rare verbal gaff of El Sacerdote while the Holy Father was elsewhere on business, where he couldn't make pretentious suppositions about the Freudian roots of corporal punishment. Interesting how the younger Cicero hadn't raised a hand to her in the Hierophant's presence—once she got big enough to hit him back. The first time she broke his collarbone was the last time they'd had a physical altercation until the one on the train. Now those early respites of Cicero's to treat the "bratty" (read: normal) girl as he thought her behavior merited seemed coordinated efforts on the part of the Family to mold Dominia's behavior and establish the Holy Father as a savior force. He was a doting, generous, compassionate protector, His Holiness, until he wasn't anymore.

No wonder the Hierophant was such a jolly old fucker all the time. He got his bad temper out while living the life of that same hateful priest who gripped her now, and said with a sneer-edged smile, "Shall we take a look? Arrangements are being made in the chapel. It shall be a rather more intimate affair than the show, but still quite pleasant. Always a joy to welcome a lost lamb back into the fold."

That hand was so much like her Father's as to be identical. Amazing they'd gotten away with the con for so long! But reality was just so absurd in this case, anything was easier to believe. Why, Cicero and the Hierophant had similar ways of speaking? It was only because Cicero had his nose stuffed so far up the Holy Father's ass—because of two thousand years of cohabitation and co-working. They looked near completely alike, save for the distance of two thousand years or more, which, on a martyr's face, rested like sixty or so without the upkeep of occasional genetic engineering? That was because the Hierophant was an alien, bequeathed with alien technology, and had taken the form of the first man he'd met on Earth.

Incredible, the fairy tales people let themselves believe.

"Do we have to see the chapel now?" asked Lavinia, with a glance for her sister and a clear desperation for someone to tell her something true. "Ninny and I were just catching up."

"I know you wish to chat with Dominia all night—you'll doubtless chew her ear off soon enough—but Father does have a need for you. You've lines to practice, queen mother Bathsheba." At Lavinia's pout askance, Cicero clicked his tongue. "Now, my dear, don't fret. You shall see the chapel before the ceremony, I'm sure."

The Lamb brushed his hands free of dog fur while studying the General. "You can always talk to Dominia after your rehearsal." This meant, "Be careful what you discuss with Lavinia after her rehearsal." She could see it in his face even as he dropped back to let Cicero lead them from the kennels and into the greater building. With a smile for the Princess, Dominia said, "Don't worry. I'll see you soon enough; and if I don't, you can always come to see me."

Anxiously, the girl nodded, then was out of sight.

Kronborg's chapel was certainly intimate by the standards of some of the Hierophant's most ostentatious and thus most favored basilicas. But, to Dominia's eye, it was no less flamboyant, and floored with that same ominous checkerboard tiling she'd begun to assess with particular wariness. Worship had been suspended so workers could prepare for the ceremony of Dominia's alleged contrition. As a few buffed to golden shine Christ and his thieves on prominent display, several human carpenters below slaved over the construction of some wood structure, which, in pieces, went unrecognized by the General.

"I do hate to allow the house of the Lord to be disrupted by such clamor," said Cicero with a distasteful glance for those indentured to the task of construction. "But the dimensions of the crucifix shall be such that constructing it outside our modest chapel is simply not an option. Did you know, my dear, that the Romans may have popularized the act of crucifixion, but they did not invent it? They only learned it from the Phoenicians around the time of the Punic Wars, in the third century BC.

It is thought to have originated with the Assyrians and the Babylonians, but the Persians perfected it…and, of course, your savage Hunter friends still do it to our people all across the globe. Many have had their martyrdom completed in the pattern of the Greatest, much to the Lord's sorrow. Christ died upon the cross, after all, so none of us would have to. And you do not have to die upon it, either: but you do have to take some time to think about what you've done."

The General observed the construction with a new and sicker eye. "I thought that I was just going to be losing a leg."

"That, too, my girl: but all things in their time. It is a *punishment*, after all. Not some simple operation. It is vitally important that you be aware you are about to lose your leg, and even more important that you remain aware the moment you do."

"And how is crucifixion related to the loss of my leg?"

"Upside down," explained the Lamb, looking particularly dead inside as he studied the crucifix, then the face of his daughter. "For a long, long time."

With far greater pleasure, Cicero expounded to the very anatomy-conscious General that, "The upper half of the body lacks in valves to retard the flow of blood, as man was not made to spend his time hanging inverted without a break. After, oh, ten or so hours in such a position, the average person's head will burst from the intensity of the pressure. But we can't have that, can we?"

Tightly, humorlessly, the General bared her teeth.

"We will suspend you by your right leg," explained El Sacerdote, continuing on with perfectly mild expression. "It will soon fall asleep, and quickly thereafter—in the grand scheme of your torture—be dead, for the protein cannot heal your tissues without circulation! Just think of what a clean and easy job the amputation will be when all of this is over. No blood to heal the atrophied fibers of those muscles. But we will take measures to ensure such a thing does not happen to the rest of you, so long as you truly have returned to the Family."

On noticing the depth of her silence, the Lamb said something that she assumed was some dry form of comfort. Dominia couldn't hear his words above the pounding of hammers.

X

The Fourth Empire

Never in her wanderings had the General felt so tired. Though she'd slept when dropped off at Kronborg, the series of brutal revelations—punctuated by that one joyful moment of promise—left her in sore need of unconsciousness to process all she'd learned. Sleep knew, and it eluded her with a sadism resembling that of her so-called Family. Rather than rest while the Hierophant and Lavinia were across town in Elsinore's sprawling Elizabethan theater, she paced her room.

This was beyond the burden of Odysseus's homecoming to suitors plaguing his wife. This time, Odysseus returned to discover the suitors had *always* been there, skittering in the dark corners of his home as cockroaches might inhabit the dwellings of lesser men. The cockroaches here were deceptive, articulate, and alarmingly omniscient. They were also consummate schemers. The air buzzed with the vibrations of their treachery: an only semi-imagined quality palpable to her after her time in the Ergosphere and its nighttime Void.

The Void. She could slip into that Void with such ease. She needed an extra hour or so of rest to think and feel sentient, but she didn't need it to slip into that other place. She didn't even need to smoke the magician's bent cigarette to skip into the Kingdom, if she could tolerate wandering through the dark. A formless Void was almost preferable to staying, especially now that the information around her had resolved for her eye into those digital threads. Failing those, she

could just light a fire and be patient. Then, in daylight, navigate her
way—

Where?

Nowhere.

There was nowhere to go. Not really. In theory, she could wink
back to Jerusalem and join the battle there. Then? She'd be once more
up to her elbows in killing—human and martyr alike. More than
ever, violence did not seem the worthy way. If evil could have been
said to exist, martyrs qualified, but they were only evil because the
Hierophant had carefully groomed them to worship the worst in man.
It was like breeding dogs backward into wolves, which he had also
more or less done, although in the case of canines, he kept the killer
hounds in separate kennels, far away from the gentle family dogs who
only wanted to love and be loved. Nothing of the bloody business of
their cousins.

Remarkable how similar animals always were in the end, though.
When they were afraid, or ashamed. Even animals could be penitent.
After a beloved cat had died and Cassandra had mourned it (Dominia
secretly mourned it, busy being strong for her wife), the General
had talked her into a dog. They had to compromise somewhat, as
Cassandra was partial to small dogs, whereas Dominia felt if one was
inclined to get a small dog, they'd might as well get another cat. In
the end, they'd settled on a miniature shepherd breed originating
from the climate-ravaged prison colony of Australia. The dog in
question was not so small as to annoy the General, nor so large as
to annoy Cassandra. He instead managed to routinely annoy them
both by getting into trash, digging up the garden, and engaging in
other excusable dog faux pas. Each time he was caught, he exhibited
humiliated facial expressions and sulky mannerisms such as leaning
his face sadly against the nearest cabinet: inevitably, the women would
relent into petting and consoling the petulant pooch until his mood
improved.

Even the decidedly not sapient dog had felt shame. The Hierophant
somehow lacked that quality. He may not have been an alien in body,
but in heart and soul and mind, he was one just as much as any little

green man. Perhaps living so long had wrung the decency out of him—but, considering Cicero, it was more likely he'd never possessed a sense of it to begin with. Rather than developing decency, he'd grown a sense of humor. The younger version of the man was more inclined to bouts of rage and intense physical sadism; the older version had gotten all his rage out and just lived for seeing the moment his victim understood what was about to happen. In that light, she was surprised the Hierophant had not been there to see her reaction to news of the impending inverted crucifixion: then again, she supposed he had seen it before.

Yet she struggled to believe for an instant that the Hierophant remembered all he did from the top of his head, however he touted the supposedly lost Roman rhetorical art of memory. It was undeniable that the protein enhanced his faculties in that regard—beyond the point of even the average martyr, it was evident—but there was more to all this than had already been revealed.

It would help if she knew what was going on the night of the so-called party. It would help more if she knew what was happening in Jerusalem. He had given her no television, but if his surge was at all successful in enclosing the Lady's library, supply lines were cut and Dominia's soldiers were trapped. Allegedly. The Hunter tunnel system extended an astonishing length and often incorporated existing tunnels beneath buildings and sewer systems. Even if her Father's militaries closed off the city at the same time as the teleporter in Tunis and the landing pad in Tangiers, many fighters and civilians alike had reasonable odds of evading their death. Many neighborhoods had been evacuated of citizens by her prior efforts, and now by the UF and European armies, but more civilians remained.

And as for Dominia's own inner circle—had the Lady fled, or did She remain? And what of Farhad and Gethsemane? She hadn't gotten back on track to press the magician, she realized now.

It didn't matter, truth be told. Their fate was in Valentinian's hands, and of course their own. For her own part, Dominia's fate began to settle upon her with a distinct sense of nihilism. That unreliable saint had gotten shifty when she'd pressured him about her leg. Seemed like she would have to come to terms with that—and since he hadn't even mentioned the crucifixion to her, well, she was going to have to accept that, too.

All the more reason to do anything other than mope in her room. She was now working on a limited timeline to determine the nature of the New Year's events, outside of removing her leg. Figuring out who would be at each event and what each event was would be key to developing some—any—contingency plan.

Good thing the Holy Father was out practicing his lines. No time like the present to go rifling through his stuff, especially since there was no telling when she'd get strung up on that cross. The trick would be getting to his office without attracting attention.

The castle was thick with spies, whether mollycoddled martyr children or brainwashed human slaves who believed their masters deserved all they took. That was to say nothing of the martyr courtiers themselves, the many painters and poets and sculptors and lords and ladies and distant Holy Family relatives and hired friends and *their* friends and often the lovers of all of the above, each circulating through the many halls to see and be seen gossiping, admiring the great many pieces of plundered art displayed upon the walls, listening to the finest music, or occasionally engaging in a jolly bit of torture—though never without *reason*! Martyrs were not cruel, as the Hierophant assured them. Torture was justified with certain breeds of evil criminals, and, of course, traitors. Given the opportunity, martyrs the world over would tell the General she was lucky the Hierophant planned to leave her with her life.

In a way, they were right. The Lady was also right. So was Dominia's own conscience. Returning home to face this horrific punishment—or, at least, to be faced with the prospect of it—was necessary. There were no better options. After two hundred years of genocide, she had imperiled an entire world by giving her Father access to a fertile martyr. Sold her daughter to the Devil. And for that, he'd made her Governess of the United Front. At the time, she had been too depressed and too corrupt to care. There was no fixing the past from the present. But there was changing the present so the future could be better. There was repentance—not for the world's sake, or Cassandra's sake, or even her own. No: for Lavinia's.

So, for Lavinia's sake, she emerged from her room with that long-missed gun still down her back. The Hierophant and his favorite daughter and whatever "lucky" actors selected for the occasion would be tied up in rehearsal for hours. As to Cicero and the Lamb, she was not so sure. They had parted ways twenty minutes before, after showing her the crucifix and walking her to her door.

She needed to be careful. Kronborg was not the Holy Father's largest demesne, but it was grand nonetheless, and overfull of threats to her security. She needed creep from the hall containing her bedroom and through the church wing without looking like she crept. Then she'd have to pass a series of tearooms—long since converted to more bedrooms and offices, but a great deal more salons, studios, and reading rooms. Those would be better attended, but, like the diners in the train car that first time speaking to Miki, perhaps they would be too caught up in their amusements to pay her attention. Perhaps. Although she would like very much to handle all of this by not handling any of it—that was, by slipping into the Void—the first and foremost thing she needed do was dispose of her weapon.

The sad fact was, the good old gun gifted to her after her campaign in the Pacific (by the Holy Father, of course) now caused her more trouble than benefit. That single bullet meant one of two things: suicide or a lucky shot. And if she kept it on her person, well— perhaps it was her metaphysically one-eyed nature, but the General (not with two earthly eyes *and* her spiritual one all squinting in unison) could see no realistic opportunity for its use against anyone but herself before the undisclosed time of her ordeal. Therefore, if the gun was to be of use against anyone external, it had to be somebody's else's problem.

Though she had not been made privy to "the plan," Dominia had gotten to know the Lady, Lazarus, and Valentinian pretty well. René Ichigawa's useless ass had to have been positioned at Kronborg for a reason. If Tenchi had been willing to stake his life on the bet that Dominia would make the correct decision, it would have been easy for him to get himself caught: but René had been enlisted into the scheme despite his cowardice and skepticism, and had, when one thought it all through, no reason to have been involved in the plan in the first place. That was worth consideration. She did not by any means trust him, but in this situation, she had no choice. It had crossed her mind to give the weapon to Lavinia, but the girl would find the burden unbearable with her heart not fully won—and Dominia was not certain the girl's heart could ever be fully won. Even if they won it enough to win the night (and somehow purify her corrupted blood, as Valentinian had suggested a miracle might), would her leadership be enough to ensure the safety of the future? Was there a way to show her truth enough to prevent backpedaling into a grim extension of this violent path?

That feeling of Cassandra in her arms. *You can do it.*

Yes. She could. Dominia's truth could liberate Lavinia—but it would need to be delivered soon. The more truth delivered at once, the better: and the General was keen to deliver it before the Hierophant had her swinging by her ankle. A thought inspired by the distant sounds of carpenters sealing her fate, nail by nail.

Concern for the location of Cicero's position started to nag at the General when she passed beyond the ominous clatter of the church wing. That concern magnified until she swept through the tiltyard rather than risking the tearooms. Long since converted to an overflowing greenhouse that burst with exotic herbs, South American flowers and vines even in the midst of winter, the altered jousting arena was a good place for somebody who wanted privacy: or somebodies. As she ducked through rows of sumptuous plant life, she spotted the Family's beloathed priest submitting, among a peacock's tail of orchids, to the embrace of his partner. She thanked her stars the Lamb was sympathetic to her interests and passed down a different row, of exotic jungle mimosa trees wrapped with garlands of flowers whose aromas rendered the General unsmelled as the kiss rendered her unseen and Cicero's flurried thoughts (had he emotion enough left to relent to love) rendered her unheard. Praise the Lamb, praise the Lamb: even after her disgrace and reluctant return, the Rabbi remained sympathetic to his daughter.

In fact, as she emerged from the tiltyard and resumed her perfectly casual way to the Hierophant's office, she could not help but consider the Lamb must have been *very* sympathetic to her ends. There was no doubt that he knew the magician had given her the gun. Yet he had said nothing of the matter to Cicero—had he, her weapon would already be gone and she would be confined to her quarters. She had the distinct feeling that, however the bullet was spent, the Lamb approved.

Was this a good sign, or a bad one?

At last she reached the former storerooms converted to a series of guest bedrooms upon the Hierophant's acquisition of the property and his considerable alterations to its size. It was now a matter of locating that particular cell in which Ichigawa stayed—and a cell it would be. While the suites were reasonably furnished and quite elegant in and of themselves, this set of bedrooms and laughably tiny bathrooms were as sizable as the allotment of a favored prisoner: a purpose for which they were frequently engaged. Locating her implied prisoner of choice was not difficult, because even without a martyr's senses, she could have picked his whimpering through any door.

"René." She knocked, courteously warning him as she began to turn the knob. "It's me. I'm coming in, okay?"

"What," he called as she carried through the motion, "not *you!*" The professor sat up from bed and cracked his skull on the bookshelf above with such ferocity that even Dominia saw stars.

"Lamb, René, are you all right?"

"No! Who puts a bookshelf so low over a bed?"

"A sadist," observed Dominia, studying the collection of books with which the Hierophant had decorated René's shelf. Such gems as *The History of Torture*, and a play by the ancient European prisoner-poet Genet. *Deathwatch*. Through these, she thumbed in cursory search of a bug. "Nice of him to provide you with reading material."

"He's very subtle." Rubbing the top of his head with a grimace, the man sat up in bed and searched for trousers to shield his skinny legs. "Do you just come barging in on everyone like that? What if I had been naked?"

"Like I care. Welcome to war, Private." As Dominia recognized her yet-damp jacket had been hung over the head of the casket-size shower, she slipped into the bathroom to reclaim it, then thought better. Instead, she called him inside with faux irritation while looking hither and thither for holo-cameras. Scanners built into the walls, most likely. Plus the showerhead? No: too indiscrete. "What's this hole, René," she said in mock irritation, fingering the yet-damp fabric of the drying jacket. "It didn't have this when I gave it to you."

"What do you mean, hole?" Irritated, the now fully dressed professor marched into the tight space with her, and she yanked the coat down from where it stood drying to brusquely cram it in his hands.

"See?"

"No, I don't."

"Well, never mind. It's not mine, anyway." Still feigning annoyance, she moved as though to put it on and, in a sleight of hand that would have pleased the magician but remained hidden from the perception of even a full-room hologram, slipped the gun from her waistband to the equally black fabric of the jacket while it still hung near the level of her hips. A look of disgust crossed her face. "Ugh, still wet. Keep it." She thrust the jacket and gun back into his hands.

"Of course it's still wet! Did you—" His true annoyance melted into an expression of shock once he shifted his grip on the jacket and felt its contents. "Is—"

Trained by three centuries of battle, her reflexes kept the next three equally loud words from escaping by virtue of a hand that slapped down across his mouth. "Don't argue. Okay?"

Slightly, he nodded, and as she drew back her hand, she asked, "Did the Hierophant tell you what you'll be doing before the party?"

"I don't know…" With an uneasy glance at the damp and dangerous parcel he cradled like a North American football, René stepped back out of the bathroom. "He asked if I'm a religious man."

So the professor's "pre-party" obligation was to attend Dominia's ceremony of repentance. "Aren't you excited! You get to watch me lose my leg. Does that even us out for earlier?"

"What—no! I already told you how freaked out I am about that! And not just for your health, but—I want to be a martyr so I can live forever, not so I can watch amputations. Maybe that's what *some* people are into."

"Like the Hierophant, and Cicero, and a whole lot of other religious nuts who are going to be very torn between a place as an observer of the ceremony or a seat in the Hierophant's play. Speaking of"—the General glanced at the digital clock glowing crimson in the upper-left-hand corner of the room's one smartwall, displayed with a summation of the weather and local traffic conditions—"I have to run. But I need you—"

Faltering, reluctant to speak out loud, she lifted a finger to silence him. From the drawer of the tiny scribe's desk crammed into the corner, she withdrew a pad of paper and a courtesy pen. Anxiously contorting her arm and back to shield the pad from anything suspect in the room (cupholders, lampshades, certainly the aforementioned smartwall along with any stupid ones), the General scribbled a note while René leaned over her shoulder to watch.

This thing has one bullet. If you are for sure going to the ceremony, try to sit where you'll get a clear shot.

"Of whom?" he asked. She flashed him a grim little smile as she wrote: *If you can't get Cicero, then I guess me.*

"You want me to—" Lips sealing in agitation, René snatched the pen from her to scribble in elegant-yet-illegible scholar's cursive: *You want me to shoot Cicero?*

I like that you're more concerned about him.

With an annoyed look for Dominia's lame attempts at humor, René jotted: *I'm concerned about me.* Several underlines, and a very emphatic wave of his hand on slamming down the pen.

Starting to feel annoyed, herself, Dominia tore the top three pages from the pad, folded them, and tore them apart while she flat out asked, "Do you think he's going to let you live in his world if he gets his way in any of this?"

Mouth open but soundless, brows knit in deep irritation, the professor relented with a sharp sigh of disgust. "*C'est naze,*" he muttered. Awash with relief, Dominia clapped him on the shoulder, then strolled into the bathroom to flush the scraps of note.

"Thank you," she told him on her emergence.

"Yeah, yeah…get out of here. Now I have to figure out…" He waved his free hand and shook his head with a stifled Japanese curse. "What a liability…Dominia…"

The smiling General slipped through the door and left him to his muttering. Too bad, in retrospect, she hadn't been able to bring the jacket: it would have been a fine alibi, the laundries being relatively close to her Father's office. But there was no time to look for a better solution. The thing to do was to look like she had every right to be walking where she was—and that was true. She was allowed anywhere in the castle. Only her intentions were suspect, and who knew? She might very well change her mind at the last second. Unlikely, but such a line of internal nonsense helped her look less sinister.

Only once—one time—was she noted with any scrutiny by any-one she saw. Near a depiction of *The Breaking of Saint Severian*, wherein Valentinian gleefully bashed the limbs of a man upon the wheel, the General rounded a corner and ran almost face-first into Lavinia's sharp-est little friend. Their martyr reflexes prevented collision. Nonetheless, the scrutinizing girl, wig askew, recoiled as if they actually had impacted and regained her composure with a narrow-eyed, "Oh." As in: "*Oh, it's you.*"

"Sorry," said the General, continuing apace toward the chancery, gritting her teeth to feel the girl's gaze boring into her back. She forced herself to amble all the way to *The Interrogation of Saint Titania*, seven paintings down, before looking back. There, she found the cour-tier gone and took a breath that echoed beneath the soft music filling the chancery wing.

Paranoia wasn't bad in Kronborg, but even there it had its excesses. Within grasping distance of her Father's office, this was the ideal time to slip into the night-blackened Void and steal her way behind his lock. She just had to convince herself it was the right thing to do. What good was that place, after all, if not to allow her passage through solid walls? She needed caution—a single step in that place meant a variable number in reality—but she now possessed means of navi-gation. Information. Regardless of whether the Hierophant had left a computer running in his absence (unlikely), that room was full of information. His sleeping computer, yes, but more analog information: books. Was it not possible that information kept in books could be seen in the Void with perhaps greater ease than information encoded as ones and zeroes?

Confident she was alone, the General let her body slip through the atmospheric religious music of the chanceries and into the formless, unlit nighttime of that other space. Working with the Ergosphere, whether day or night, was not so much about learning how to create anything as it was about carving the rules of its workings from its own strange substance—and the more that was revealed to one, the more could one reveal to oneself by way of reason. Much as thoughtforms could be fished from the darkness by the magnetism of thought, so, too, could Dominia's consciousness sculpt from the Void's black innards a new perception of the data around her.

As she contemplated this in the darkness, the information adjusted to her thoughts. No longer did it appear as threads demonstrating the connectivity of electronic devices. Rather, information pulsed all around, massed together in great golden clots of foam. Bookshelves. Though each office held an abundance, the General needed only find the brightest assortment of lights. No room in that castle contained more books—and a greater wealth of information—than her Father's study. In the center of these bright clusters, she spoke the True Word of "reality," and dropped back into her body.

Yes: like disorienting magic, there she was. Standing on her Father's desk instead of the floor, perhaps, but all the same, she'd appeared within a locked room without so much as touching the knob, and laughed at herself in astonishment.

Then, she was back to business. Careful to keep her shoes from touching another centimeter of furniture, the General dismounted the desk and looked for clues of her Father's foul intent. The (literal) desktop computer—a hologram PC built into the Hierophant's otherwise untouched antique desk, a device that amounted to a projector lens set responsible for projecting both images and keyboard—had no doubt been locked, and if it wasn't locked, then it was a bigger trap than his whole office. If there was a single room in the castle not being constantly recorded, it was this, but she wouldn't have been amazed if he'd made an exception for her imminent presence and gotten scanners installed the week before.

In other words, Dominia knew she would get caught. It was a matter of gathering as much information as possible before in the hopes that, somehow, in a dream or the actual Void (maybe even after her death if that was what it came to) she could transmit the knowledge to her friends. Even help herself. If there was any evidence of past efforts or future plans, it was worth the risk.

Perhaps unsurprisingly, she needed only look far as that desk on which she'd manifested. Papers sat, still arranged as they'd been during the earlier meeting. Those papers front and center were none other than *The Curse of Bathsheba*, the final treatment of the Hierophant's play. He'd been working on it while she spoke with him, and the scene in question was troubling: drawn not from the human Bible's story of queen mother Bathsheba, but the martyr variation. In the Old Testament, Bathsheba was mostly an unfortunate married woman who was lusted after by King David when he saw her bathing. Whether or not she was raped as so many mythological women was unclear, but she and David were nonetheless punished unilaterally by the death of their first child. May have had something to do with David angling her husband to the front lines where the man died, thus allowing the king to marry Bathsheba—but that was a matter of debate. Whatever the reason, after the first kid, many others followed: including the future king, Solomon. A magician, Dominia noted wryly. In the human version of the story, this child claimed the throne by peaceful means, through his mother's influence on the still-living David.

All that was in the Old Testament, though. The Post Testament revisited the queen's story, and many other stories, with purportedly true versions handed down from the priests of Acetia. Hogwash: from the Hierophant's degenerate imagination. Beneath his pen, everybody in the Bible had their bad qualities ramped beyond reason, and there was quite a lot more amputation, cannibalism, slavery, and black magic than in even the Old and New Testaments. One had to admit this was almost impressive. When it came to the story of Bathsheba, the focus was on her rise to power as queen mother, assisted by the prophet Nathan. David died more or less at the start of the story, and a few—one might say, "liberties" had been taken with the essential natures of the characters in the story. Not to mention the means by which Bathsheba and her son attained power! Mostly, as one might have expected, this was through the mass slaughter of their enemies.

The play evidently meandered for some time before it got to that point, because it looked like it was Act III or IV before King David was confirmed dead. In the scene Dominia's Father had been touching up, Bathsheba was responding to news of her husband's intended heir—Adonijah, the son of another of David's wives—with an anger most humans might have considered extreme. In her rage, martyrs said she wished the children of mankind to die before being talked down to simpler solutions by Nathan; but before his intercession, her wish was not for death by simple means like flood or plague.

ACT IV

SCENE III

(Queen Bathsheba's chambers. She paces in agitation while the prophet Nathan watches. Smoke rises outside: Adonijah sacrifices cattle in a public demonstration of his claim to King David's empty throne.)

BATHSHEBA
The constancy of od'rous meat poisons
A scent meant to call us to the table,
Emulating instead death's fecund stench
And rend'ring that which was once called "sweet," foul.

NATHAN
The sacrifices of Adonijah.
Fatted calves and oxen for the Lord,
To celebrate—and thus cement—his rule.
Haggith's son always thought himself the king.

BATHSHEBA

Let no one think this impudence will stand.
To dream! My son, his royal seat displaced,
Standing at odds with uncertain future—
How can the Lord allow me such a slight?

NATHAN

His retribution comes in subtler ways:
Namely, within the actions of His men,
Acting without knowing themselves actors.

BATHSHEBA

And doth the Lord not possess women, too?

NATHAN

Aye.

BATHSHEBA

Then find his retribution in me.
Find justly rage within this breast, Prophet,
For I burst with it, as Death's bloodied air
Marks a battle lurking on dawn's rose cusp.

NATHAN

You would do violence in your good son's name?

BATHSHEBA

Why should I not do violence? After all,
'Tis what my husband imparted on me
When, by his violent passions, he conceived
To lure me from my poor Uriah's home
And first, to trick the man—then see him die.

NATHAN

Of these acts, Queen, our Lord did not approve,

Nor now does He approve of this ascent.
Monarchy is given divine consent,
Which Adonijah hath not in this case.

BATHSHEBA
Yet he burns oxen at my son's altar!
Those wretched sacrifices rot the air
So Valentinian's perfumes plague my mind.
All I can think now is of sweet Death
For those who are the source of my cruel grief.
After all, the Lord hath punished me, too,
Taking my first child by David's loins
And killing him, unnamed, soon after birth.
Even now, God grants me no recompense!

NATHAN
Being the king's best wife, no recompense?

BATHSHEBA
Not when my real power is a fraud
And I'm belittled by that very might
That, in hollow victory, comes with crowns—
And costs the lives of my husband and babe,
Firstborn through no fault it could name
To death that keeps me awake counting stars.
The Lord hath let so much slip from my grasp—
I will not lay down and let this go, too!
I will not long suffer this rancid stench!
Ah, how my breast burns with fury, Nathan!
That's the flame that boils my blood to venom
And fills me with a wish I'd dare not speak
Were David not in Death's red velvet hand
While remnants of my power ebb away.
Canst thou not see it in my very eyes,
This foulest wish of which I am not proud?

Look! Look into my eyes. Look deep in them.
Lookst thou in my eyes and see my pure wish:
That every human know firsthand my pain
And by their own hands murder their children—
As David, by his treachery and lust
Marked our first child for death by the Lord
In a cruel retribution for his sins.
Let no firstborn escape their parent's clutch
Until the heart, once started by love's hands
Is culled to silence by the very same.
May second, third, and fourth, and so on thrive.
My Solomon, wisest of my litter
Was fifth from my womb, yet he is the best:
While first born of me soon thereaft' withered.
There were no such problems with all the rest!
Much as Adonijah is Hagitth's boy,
A harlot David met while off in war:
And how much trouble he causes me now!
You see? Those firstborns robbed us first of joy,
And to an altered life they formed our lure.
Therefore, cave in their skulls! Make sure they're dead!
Slay all God's firstborn children in their beds.

NATHAN
Surely you don't mean that, Your Majesty.

"Do you like it?"

Her Father's voice, unexpected at such an intense moment of the reading, startled her into dropping the page. His movement across the study was so quick that he not only caught the paper before it fell but also caught her hand before she sprang away. Holding it there and staring into her frozen face, his own bearing the smug expression of a cobra, the Hierophant spared the briefest of glances to the text. "The atmospheric alteration rockets are ready for the climactic storm sequence, the orchestra has practiced until their hands malfunctioned, and every seat in the house is sold out. Yet, with the premiere right around the corner and rehearsals nearly wrapped, I can't keep from making the odd change here or there. The language must be perfect! This word, that dash—Shakespeare would understand."

"I wouldn't call this Shakespeare." She assessed the hand whose bones he could snap by tightening his fingers a quarter pound of pressure more. "Webster or Ford, maybe. Very dark."

"Perhaps, but who could blame poor Bathsheba? She did suffer a lifetime at David's hands, and by Act IV we find her on the cusp of seeing her lineage denied its glory. After all she endured, it is only right the throne go to her favored son. Her reaction may be rather extreme, I admit, but the Bible can't be corrected, can it?"

"No more than can its author's brain."

With a banal grin, he said, "At any rate, Nathan goes on to talk her down into a subtler scheme. She is only mortal! All mortals say things that they mean with only fleeting emphasis. I don't think Bathsheba's reaction is all that irrational. We all know what it is to suffer a broken heart, don't we, Dominia."

"I didn't know you had such an organ." As she studied his hand and her own within it, her twisting mind formed a blender of terror. "Lavinia is playing Queen Bathsheba."

"And all those people—hundreds of thousands of human families from all across the globe—will be paying to watch."

The General mentally catalogued the room in search of an actual, physical exit, and was as relieved as she was disappointed she had already gotten rid of her gun. This play, this scene. He had left it out to mock her. Left it out because he knew she would come looking. Because he wanted her to know that, buried within the text of his play, was an order designed to come out of the mouth of a girl capable of controlling the minds of watchers who made eye contact with even her recording. Some weaker willed wouldn't even need visuals. The words would suffice. Lavinia was being taught to give an order of genocide.

And the Hierophant wanted Dominia to think there was nothing she could do about it.

Her lips were dry as they parted to form hushed words. "Don't you understand this is a war crime?"

"Of the highest order! In fact, if I get the prose to a fine enough quality, I am not sure the condition will be curable. You know how it takes fine art to overcome Lavinia's mental viruses; but when the virus itself is embedded in fine art, well…"

"Why?"

He released her hand to study the page in the lamplight. "I have been waiting for an opportunity like this for quite some time. It was important that tensions already be high before I made my move, that war already be underway. No sense in ruining a perfectly good world! Better, in my opinion, to let you stir everyone up first. Give them a reason to get curious again about the martyr world and give them a night when, burning with curiosity to know the fate of the surrendered General, they tune into the paid livestreams and end up with their own family's blood on their hands."

"You think it will be good for the martyr population if their food source dies out?"

"Now, my dear, try to be less dramatic. It is only the *first*born that parents are being urged to euthanize. The second, third, and so forth, these will all be safe, and many deaths will be inconsequential ones—of older generations who turn on their adult children and suffer. Although I do wonder what shall happen in the case of stepchildren…"

"You're an animal," said the General, not even thinking of Tobias as she spoke.

The Hierophant smiled. "Aren't we all, in the end? Animals capable of crafting consciousness, and consciousnesses capable of crafting reality—nonetheless, housed in animals. But think of what this will *do*, Dominia, aside from imparting a sense of seriousness in the humans and sparking interest where political isolation has been the rule for centuries—China and India, in particular. All the other Asiatic countries have overflowed into ours, and the South American ones. Think how this will ease the burden of mankind upon the Earth!"

"Not all martyrs are as strong willed as Holy Family members. What if they kill *their* children?"

His hands spread in a mild shrug. "Then they hadn't will enough to be martyrs in the first place, and will be arrested or turn themselves into their local police in the aftermath. I fail to see the dilemma."

She didn't know how to argue with someone so completely insane. She could only remain quiet and calm as he lifted his brows. "You think me some super villain, but rest assured, I did not come lightly to this decision. The most important point imparted by this method of extermination is clear: the evil resting within martyrs is that same evil resting within humans."

"Of course it is," said Dominia. "Because martyrs are just humans."

"Yes, well, you know I prefer to discourage that line of thought. We are so much better than that! This has always been a matter of dissent between us. It was from the start of all this—from the moment you began to pout about my Project Black Sun. Do you not understand what it is of which you are a part? This is the Fourth Roman Empire, my girl! I dare not speak such a thing aloud, dare not announce it to the world—the last man who did was a racist, petty methamphetamine addict. Although I have more claim to the Empire's lineage than he, to speak such a thing before the geopolitical stage would be as conducive to diplomacy as Lavinia striding into a party while announcing she's the prettiest girl would be to her making friends. We all know what this is. The humans know this is beyond them—this destiny of the Empire to revive eternally—and that is why the Caliphate hunts our kind. Not out of a humanist ideology but an envy for our power. Even these wretches, my child, these murderers and terrorists with whom you've run for a year—even they believe martyrs and humans are different creatures." At the obvious tension of her whole face to be captive of another lecture, he lowered the page.

"But there is no reason why the differences between martyrs and humans need remain a controversial topic for you, or the few like you who insist on belaboring the point. You have changed, of course, after seeing the world. And I know the tender part of you that has always struggled with its empathy for humans may well never be the same after these changes. But the humans have emotionally manipulated you and beaten you, badgered you off the righteous path I and Cicero and the Lamb placed you upon all those years ago. How we wish for you to be willingly guided back! Because, you see"—his attention was caught by something outside the window—"I cannot help you if you insist on remaining with the losing side."

Pushed to her edge, the General lost her respectful tone along with any hesitance. "You can never win. As long as the magician exists, you'll never win, ever. Hell, Valentinian doesn't even need to be real. As long as a new world somehow appears, that's all it takes. And people keep telling me I'm the one who makes this new world happen, so—"

"If you refuse to remove your thoughtbody's eye patch in life, the world is recreated by default when you die." That was a disturbing bit of information hitherto unshared with the General. Enough to deflate her sense of power. "If I martyr you and you are wise, a world is created. If I martyr you and complete your martyring, a world is created. You understand now why I cannot afford to leave you unmartyred, no matter the trouble you cause me. With you, I always have an exit strategy when things become troublesome."

Fine, fine. All well and fine. "But you're still failing in some way. Still failing to sustain the lives of martyrs. The life of the planet. Your own life." His black eyes glimmered without moving from the window while she fished through his psyche, looking for that key. "You haven't won an iteration yet, or you—some version of you—would have stopped this game when you had. Some Cicero always moves forward. In a perfect world, wouldn't your whole Family—duplicate of you included—stay together? But you don't. Something is wrong. You're still trying to find your perfect solution, the way the magician looks for the best version of me."

"Just like you look for the best possible reality. Just like all the rest of the players, of course, search for theirs. But I am in a unique position, for there is no reason Cicero or I need go to another world yet. Things have not become so bad as to require abandonment. You could remain perfectly alive, all of us happy in this world, living life the way it was before. You, my General. My daughter."

She did not speak, studying with narrowed eyes the blurred text of his play. Now, he deigned to glance at her. "Do you suppose you are the only woman in the world who has lost a wife?"

"Shut up, please."

"If I were you, I would not address me like that at this moment in time." Her blood turned to refrigerant gas as he continued in perfectly casual tone, "I mean it for your sake, Dominia. Do you think this is a healthy mode of dealing with grief? Running away from it? I will be the first and most wholehearted in telling you that trying to find joy in a new world ends in more crushing disappointment than the initial loss."

"It wasn't the grief I was running from. I was running from you."

With that perfect, blasé smile, the Hierophant waved her over. The reluctant General stood beside him to see what had caught his attention through the window. Her stomach lurched: its frame enclosed the slithering lights of a *tanque* caravan. She could sense what had happened even before the Hierophant told her.

"Though you likely think I returned just to catch you in the act of snooping through my office, try to be less self-centered. I admit I received a message that one of Lavinia's friends thought you up to no good, but I had already been forced to leave rehearsal early after getting a phone call of actual importance. Jerusalem has fallen, Theodore has been rescued, and some of your most important friends have been captured alive. We didn't need your help when I asked you before, about turning in Lazarus. I just wanted to see if you would volunteer. As usual, you stooped to my expectations. How tragic! You could have saved your leg at the cost of nothing not already lost."

While she pressed her forehead against the cold glass to watch the procession through his taunting reflection, he said, "You know, I have always found the name 'Israel' to be a fascinating one. Jacob's name, after that angel ruined his hip in their wrestling match. The name of the promised land—this iteration of the political state was founded with primarily Jewish intentions, you know, before it began accepting religious refugees amid the Holy Martyr Church's success. Yet its etymology is controversial. Though some Hebrew scholars argue it means 'God strives,' 'Israel' really means 'He who struggles against God.' A more appropriate name for a man who tricked his brother out of his birthright and grappled an angel!

"It is in the nature of the chosen to struggle with their destiny of service to the divine. Perhaps that is why the religion of Islam—'submission'—had so many historical arguments with their Hebrew brothers before I came along. Perhaps that is why you were drawn to that rebellious house. My chosen daughter, my dissatisfied Israel. If you would but learn to submit! Then, you would find peace."

The block letters of that old Tucson mosque upon her liberation from Nogales: "HAPPINESS IS SUBMISSION TO GOD." Her Father patted her shoulder, then turned to answer the knock of prearranged guards upon the door. "Seeing how restless you are," he told her on the way, "I'll make sure your crucifix is prepared by sunup. Nine nights may seem like a lot, but we can't have you getting into even more trouble, now, can we?"

XI

The Plight of the General

Within her first hours hanging from that cross, Dominia's thoughts turned so often to her human childhood that she began to think this was that famed pre-death flash of life before the eyes. Perhaps it was not the rapid-clip flashback she had always pictured. Perhaps, rather than the snapping back of the mind to the beginning of the next iteration, it was only the stultifying cycle of treacherous memories churned by the sorrowing ego near the grave.

Once, many years ago (oh, so many years!) when the General had been a human girl named "Morgan," she was a morbid thing. To a child still so close to the fresh side of the Void that the realities of existence seemed more dreamlike and unreal than the concept of nothingness, death and its uncountable manifestations held profound intrigue. There were so many, seemingly *benign* ways in which one could die, or find oneself mutilated, or endure some other sudden shock of tragedy in this brave new world.

She had also, like many children around the age of five, been fascinated by those few forms of consciousness alteration available to small minds, namely: spinning in rapid circles until the house twisted upside down and she crashed in the middle of the living room to the sound of her mother's criticism; or standing too quickly and stretching with too much vigor so as to produce that dizzying starburst behind her eyes; or hanging upside down over the arm of the couch until all the blood collected in her head and the room began to vibrate.

"Don't do that too long, now," her father (the real, lost one, not the capital-F fucker who stole the title) said to her one afternoon, not long after she had mentally applauded herself for beating her own "record" time.

"Why," she had asked, before leaping to, "will I *die?*"

"You'd want to sit up before you were likely to die," was the response from behind the slim glass tablet on which he perused the news with a slowly scrolling finger. "But, yes—if you stay like that too long, it's possible to die."

Young Morgan's mind had turned in eager fascination to the question of how a person might look after dying in such a way. Would they bloat up like a big grape? That was what she had pictured at the time. A child's cartoon. Not this.

Dominia had already pinpointed the places in her forehead where blood might eventually shoot out in little jets: mostly around her temple and cheekbones, but certainly from her eyes, which felt after only four hours as if they would burst. Electrified manacles binding back her arms notwithstanding, the inversion had not been a totally unpleasant experience for the first twenty minutes. It wasn't so bad, she told herself. She had one leg free—her left—and by means of this she was able to brace herself against the fifteen-foot-tall crucifix and do something like a sit-up. Held for a time, this relieved a bit of the pressure of her eyes, and gave her an opportunity to think of something to do. Of course—it also exhausted her, so she needed do so sparingly.

To be honest, if not for the electrified manacles, she'd be slipping into the Void. A small current would have been beneficial in this regard, but threshold technology could produce one with a voltage and respective current high enough to stop a human heart. The physical pain therefore prevented the escape of a Lazarene into the Void, as attention was fundamental in their flight. But there wasn't much to be done about this collar of hers, any more than there was much to be done about escape, or about—well, anything.

Because the reality was that the infamous General Dominia di Mephitoli was going to die.

There was no going back. She understood that with new clarity when strung up by her leg, which she already could no longer feel but for the occasional needle-buzz when it jostled with her efforts to sit up. One leg free or not, this movement was no easy feat: she had been given a stiff leather bodice to protect her modesty, and a one-legged pair of like trousers. This allowed her—along with any visitors—to monitor the intensifying purple tone of flesh visible through the straps of the harness that clamped her thigh, supported her knee, and extended up the length of her shin, where it was attached by the ankle piece to its swinging tether. Its black coloration served as the frame of a vile window to the status of the doomed limb.

Yet, it was not just her limb that was doomed. Her heart was as fixed as the molecules of the diamond she had been allowed to keep, draped around her wrist rather than her neck so that it would not fall but be forever there, with her, while she endured. (And promote a healthy current in case of electrocution!) There was nothing the Hierophant could offer to tempt her to his side: nothing he could say to enlist her in putting down the Market or squelching the Hunters before tying Earth up for him in a big silk bow. Not after seeing Cassandra, and not after seeing what he had done to Lavinia. He knew that, which was why she was here.

There were other reasons, too. Given nine days to work on the softhearted princess, the General may well have accomplished her goals of liberating the most brainwashed girl in the world. The Holy Father knew that as well as he knew Dominia had no intention of helping him take Jerusalem, or Lazarus, or any damn thing ever again.

The situation, which had been entropic from the start, could only hasten its degradation from this point. Somewhere in the castle—in the rest of those cell-like guest rooms, further cementing René's position as honorary prisoner—her friends awaited their fates. So did Theodore, that useless asshole, although she supposed she couldn't be mad about it. Letting himself get captured again—he wanted to go home. It was her fault for thinking he could change. Disappointing he couldn't, of course, but it wasn't like he'd made any promises, or anything.

Who had been delivered to the Hierophant? Which friends sat in the castle? She had gotten to know so many people in the human world while on active duty for the first time in almost a hundred years: Which of these had died, and which yet lived?

It was not very long, to her surprise, before she was given partial answer. After she had begun to understand her sit-ups did more harm than good by not only exhausting her, but bruising her ribs against the cage of the stiff bodice, she succumbed to her hanging condition. At least she could savor the odd wiggle of her free leg. How long did they seriously intend for her (or her eyes) to last in this state? Lamb, she wasn't going to lose her sight, was she? Not again! As though he knew her thoughts, the Hierophant picked that moment to enter, midconversation, with none other than René Ichigawa, whose restored eyes widened as they rested on the chapel's ceremonial centerpiece.

"Dominia," he automatically said, while the Hierophant assured him, "Oh, yes: which is why I brought you here."

Ever given to inappropriate cheer, her Father waggled his hand at Dominia in a finger-wave on his way to collect the tall ladder against the matroneum. "You see, René, poor Dominia has gotten herself into a bit of trouble—nothing good ever comes of snooping around, you know—and, being her friend, I thought you might like to help her out."

"Help her how?" The professor warily assessed the General, who was not interested in wasting words before the Hierophant.

"Crucifixion and suspension are useful tortures, you see—not because of the convenience offered when bleeding a corpse or preparing to amputate. The true cruelty of crucifixion comes from its asphyxiation. Not breathing very comfortably by now, are you, Dominia?"

When she did not respond, he paused to lay a broad smile on her. Then, he directed his attention back to his guest. "In upright crucifixion, prisoners exhaust themselves by having to push their chest up in order to catch their breath. Hard enough as it is! The eventual cause of death is almost always asphyxiation. In this case, however, additional pressure is being put on our good General's lungs as a result of gravity's involvement in her predicament. She knows Peter's pain now, in part. But we need her to last nine days, or she'll miss the New Year's celebration! And martyrdom, miracle that it is, can only battle gravity so long. So, I've come up with an idea. Every twelve or so hours, I shall send someone in—or come by, myself—to help her breathe. Yes, that's right, Dominia. Your friends, who love you so dearly, will be given an opportunity to prove their love for up to an hour at a time by getting on the ladder and holding you upright. As far as they can, anyway. You'll get a chance to breathe easily and get a bit of blood flowing back into that right leg, since we can't have it rotting off before Cicero claims his prize—and your friends will get to see you one last time before their deaths. Isn't that generous of me?"

Her dry lips, swollen with blood, at last suffered themselves to part. "Hoping we'll crack? Talk about something vital in front of you?"

Shrugging, he said, "Your operation has no vitality left. What does it matter if you do or don't discuss your hopeless dreams? The result will be the same. Enjoy your hour, Ichigawa-sensei." With a self-satisfied little bow and an eyebrow wiggle for Dominia, the Hierophant whisked off through the nave and out the chapel doors.

Alone with the General (more or less), Ichigawa asked, "How did you stand that guy for three hundred years?"

"You know how it is with family." Dominia left it at that, using her free leg to swing herself aside and give René a chance to place the ladder against her cross. "You don't seem like much of a heights man to me."

"I'm not afraid of heights. I'm just not sure about ladders." Easing his way up a few rungs, René got level with her head and then, after some consideration, looped an arm around her shoulders and said, "Sorry if this is awkward to you."

"Don't worry," she assured him while he folded her up toward her leg, much as she had been doing with her sit-ups. Each careful rung higher, he pushed her uncomfortably up the length of the crucifix before him while she continued, "I'm completely past the point of caring about a concept like dignity. I just appreciate your help."

"Any—time." Huffing, René scaled the ladder to its height until, in the most painful relief she'd ever experienced, Dominia's body folded up past her legs. Blood—cherished blood!—crashed into her right leg with such a vivid, physical drop that the General cried out.

René asked, "Are you all right?"

Through a pair of stinging tears, she laughed.

After a few minutes' shifting and one occasion of almost dropping her, René determined that, by gripping the crossbar of the crucifix with that arm that cradled Dominia, he could support both himself and her with relative surety. "An hour, huh," he said, and she snorted.

"Poor you. Try twelve. Try nine *days*."

"Look, I'm sorry. But I'm trying to help you."

Agitated, the General studied the leg that, shade by shade, faded to a grayer variant of its usual tone. A step up from the raisin color into which it had settled. "Sorry to be short. I just feel…helpless."

"I can imagine."

"Did you hear about anybody from our side being brought in?"

"Oh, yeah." Dominia turned her head enough to see René's bafflement. "But I don't—well, I don't know."

"Don't know what?"

"They're reporting weird things about the Battle for Jerusalem. I caught something on the news yesternight—actually, right after you left my room—about some kind of unidentified object plummeting over the Lady's library and taking out a bunch of Hierophant soldiers…" While Dominia struggled to avoid any external expression of relief, love, joy at the mere thought of the E4 returning from the Ergosphere, René sweetened it by adding, "And then something about people coming out—like a saint the martyrs are superstitious about? I don't know. No offense, but war makes people crazy, and I think they were seeing things. But whatever it was that came out of the…crashed plane, I guess they've started to call it, it caused the martyr forces to retreat and regroup."

Bless Valentinian! She was close to praising him out loud by sheer accident when the professor ruined it all again. "I guess by the time the martyr forces returned, their confidence was back because they'd turned the omen into something in their favor. They even closed in on the Lady."

"No!"

"No, no, it's— She got away or something, I think. The news is playing it off like it was misreporting, but they were damn certain when I saw the broadcast that Her capture would be any minute. She must have shaken free from their clutches."

Thank the Lamb—for the Lady's sake, and for the world's. If there was any truth at all to the Lady's footfalls upon the Earth being the indicator of imminent apocalypse—whether causal or correlative—she could only imagine what a disaster it would be when her Father's troops tried to force the goddess's avatar to walk.

Trying to turn her thoughts to more pleasant issues, she asked, "Did you happen to see or hear who *was* brought in?"

"I think I did, but I'm not sure whether I saw everybody. It didn't seem like many prisoners were brought here: I only saw Farhad and Lazarus."

"And Tenchi? Gethsemane?"

"Nowhere I saw."

That filled Dominia with relief as much as trepidation. Hopefully that meant they were alive and in the Ergosphere—Saint Valentinian, walk with them. She was sick enough as it was that the True Protomartyr had been brought in. "You're sure it was Lazarus."

"Definitely. He was placed in the room four doors down from mine. I don't know what happened at the battle to land him here, but I know he didn't look happy."

"He never looks happy." Under normal circumstances, she might have smiled while she said such a thing. Now she had no energy. Drained physically and emotionally, Dominia could only try to keep her mind from her condition by asking René the first thing she thought. "Have you ever been happy, do you think?"

"Always asking the hard questions, Mephitoli-sama…" The professor glanced away, to the gilded pulpit that seemed to float above the room. "What is happiness? I don't think I know what it is…I don't think it's real. I don't think it's possible to be happy. It's not—" His arm, straining, required that he shift her, like Atlas, upon his other shoulder. "It's not a condition you attain. It's like…a field."

Smirking, Dominia asked, "The happiness field," and he reacted with a defensive tone, not understanding she only smirked because his supposition was so apropos after all she had lately experienced.

"Yeah, a field. Like an electromagnetic field, or something… You know how when you run electricity through a coil, you get a magnetic effect—but in this case, the electricity we're talking about can be anything that engenders happiness, and that magnetic effect attracts more positive things. So, when you ask me if I've ever been happy, the answer is no. I guess I haven't been happy, because I don't think it's possible for anything or anyone to actually meet the human ideal of happiness. Nobody can 'be' happy. We can't even 'be' ourselves, for God's sake."

"Why weren't you a philosophy professor, instead of an English professor?"

"Because I don't have the patience to waste my time with anything that can't be proved…if I'm going to be spouting improvable nonsense, I'd rather write fiction. Philosophy, it's all a bunch of talking in circles."

"But sometimes we experience things that can't be proved. Things unique to our own existence, or beyond the capacity for description."

"There's always an intelligible explanation for any mysterious phenomenon."

Thinking of the gun that she had passed to him, she asked, "Is there?"

How she wished in a way beyond wishing that she could know he'd kept the weapon safe! That she could know for certain that he was on her side. But one could never be too careful. She would have to suffer in agonized curiosity and turn her attention elsewhere: for the remainder of their hour, the two discussed literature.

Too soon—much too soon—that hour was up, and the Hierophant made his reappearance to wave Ichigawa down the ladder. His Holiness jeered to Dominia as her body sagged back into the hanging position. "I hope you enjoyed your break, my dear. I shall see you again in another twelve-ish hours, yes?"

Twelvish hours. She could do that. She had passed many hours in total silence, in the military and as a prisoner of war. This was the same. She was a prisoner of life—her Father's life. Would death not come as liberator? That was how Saint Valentinian was depicted. Why he was the patron saint of slaves and prisoners, as well as death and artists. Was she not freer than she had ever been, hanging by her once-more purpling leg, knowing that no matter what happened, the end drew near? Indeed, the longer she remained in her inverted position, the more correct such a notion of freedom felt. It seemed to her as if her Father's world had always been upside down. Perhaps her death by this means, trickling back through time to the beginning of her life, was why.

If her death produced a new world by default, did the creation of a new world mean her death? She was fine with that. How tired she had grown of this life! Of this place! Look at this garish chapel, begging to be seen. The source of such strife, such incomparable heartache! It was one of the most beautiful rooms this life had to offer her, and it was built of human bones and plundered gold. There was a higher, truer world than this. She had known its substance. She had held Cassandra.

She had held Cassandra.

Nothing could undo that notion. Nothing could convince her it was only a dream, or a fantasy, as the Hierophant tried to when he ascended the ladder at the end of those twelvish hours and offered her blood-throbbing brain a momentary respite. As he held his daughter upright as easily as most men held a baseball, his attention turned to the Kingdom. She endeavored to avoid so much as the slightest reaction when he indicated knowledge of its existence by asking, "Has the magician bothered to teach you how to come and go from the Kingdom this time? You know—if you taught me, I'd set you free this instant."

Faced with her resolute silence, he filled the air with preposterous theorizing. Oh. That was René's problem with philosophy. She got it, now.

"I personally suspect the Kingdom is a hallucination instilled in subjects by the magician, which is why I cannot seem to find a way into it."

"I believe you will be there," she opened her mouth to generously say. The Hierophant appeared almost surprised by that.

"Oh? Because you will show me how to get there?"

"No. Maybe. I don't know." But, by the Lamb, she had seen Tobias Akachi there. A human to rival her Father for the evils he had committed—yet he, too, had been in the Kingdom. Wry humor quirked her lips even in a time like this, and she turned her aching head to lift her eyebrows at him. "You keep trying to get any piece of information you can out of me to get me back to your side—Lazarus, the Kingdom, anything—but I should be the one trying to appeal to you."

"To my better nature?"

"You have no better nature."

"Ah!" He chuckled and patted her back. "You took the words from my mouth. To what would you appeal, then?"

"Your soul." The statement elicited a patronizing coo as though it had charmed him, but she had thought much on this over the past twenty-four hours. "Your soul can always be saved."

The Hierophant's jolly humor faltered not one iota. If anything, he seemed moved to sheer delight. "You would preach to me while hanging from the cross I put you on!"

"I would save you."

"Wouldn't you rather save yourself?"

"That's not possible. I've thought this through, Father—and, remarkably, I'm not so sure you have. What good are your thought-forms when you have no body? They wish to work through the soul to manifest on Earth. What good is a soul with a dead body? Your study, your books—hell, even your torches and your fires will abandon you. And you know that. That's why, when whatever apocalypse I bring destroyed the culture your forebear built in the last iteration, you fled to this new world. Cicero." His black eyes sparkled in merriment to be addressed by his secret name, as close to a real name as anyone could hope to know of him in this life. "But you could change all that. Make the choice to change yourself, before Saint Valentinian decides it's time to force the change."

He was unflappable. The head games her Father routinely turned on others broke against his frontal lobe like waves shattering against rocks. "I must say—I have always found it interesting that the magician is capable of using you to suit his needs when he feels. Yet here you are, allowed to hang from a cross. Allowed to lose your leg! A fine way to repay you for all your hard work. Not unlike Bathsheba, no? Perhaps I'd ought to have given the role to you."

He wanted to get her into an argument. Wanted to get her passionate about his immortal soul, or the Kingdom's reality, or the magician's righteousness. As if it were the magician's fault that she swayed back and forth like a tetherball, starving, trembling, thinking with increasing fondness of the moment when all this would graciously end.

Seeing his cursory efforts to seduce her into his service were for naught, the Hierophant lowered her at the end of the hour with a few solemn *tuts*. "How much trouble you would save yourself, if only you would be reasonable. You are afraid to betray a dream, as if it were more real than reality. As if it were worth more than your Family!"

"Cassandra is my family," said Dominia, defiant to the end. "More my family than anyone. And I will never betray her again. I've let her down enough."

"I suppose you have."

If she weren't upside down, she might have spat to watch him walk away. Instead, she tried to breathe and focus on that memory of her wife's gentlest smiles. Oh! Cassandra. She had to believe they would meet again at the end of this. That it would be in the flesh, in reality. Not, as her Father had said, in some dream.

Because he did have a small point in that. Whatever the Kingdom was, wherever it was, it was a conception of eternity, but it was not linear reality. Its time and the feeling of its time functioned like a dream, and Dominia could not help but feel that if she lived there, she would never accomplish anything again. Nor would she be able to leave after a certain point. The world would need to end for that, and in that case, she wouldn't remember anything. So, she might theoretically have Cassandra, but she would be forced to lose her once more even if Dominia would again have the pleasure of reliving (in ignorance) that beautiful moment of their meeting.

The General couldn't stand the thought. This had to be the last time. If it meant this was the last time, then she could withstand this.

She could withstand anything. She would have Cassandra, and there was no alternative.

After twelve more hours, Dominia was startled from a dreamless sleep into which she had not meant to wander, nor known she could wander in her current position. Farhad was brought to her, and struggled more to support her weight upon the ladder than would any martyr.

"You are deceptively heavy," the pilot exclaimed, his laughter nervous as the ladder rocked back, then forward against the crucifix, while he used both hands to support the General. "You do not look as if you should weigh much more than my sister."

"It's muscle mass, and the fact that I'm dead weight right now. But thank you for doing this, Farhad."

"*Afwan*," came the grunted response. "I am sorry to see you in such a situation as this. Iblis is a coward who would eliminate you by easy means, rather than honorable ones."

"There are no honorable deaths. Just stupid ones, and expected ones."

"Which is this?"

"No reason it can't be both, right?"

The slightest smile lit Farhad's voice. "Even in a time like this, you are a very funny person, Mahdi."

"I like to make people laugh. When I do, I almost feel something that's not…awful."

"Have faith, please." To hear him say it with such insistence gave her pause, and the General glanced over, her blurred vision etching out Farhad's bearded features like a camera's slow-to-focus lens. "You will survive this, Mahdi—this trial on the cross like the prophet Isa, who is alive in heaven and waiting for you to heighten the war against Iblis and ad-Dajjal. He will come, then, and unify the world."

"He doesn't need to wait on my account," said Dominia, much too tired to argue and never having been interested in doing it when it came to religious matters. She had never had particular belief or disbelief in Christ, and now that she understood the workings of the Ergosphere, the fact that Jesus of Nazareth had been possessed—sorry, "descended upon"—by a pan-dimensional archetype now seemed as self-evident as the color of the sky. This simple detail of the nature of reality could trash even the most devoted martyr's belief in the HMC for just the reason that the Hierophant had carefully limited their understanding of the Bible to a violent brand of semi-literalism. The martyr position on the matter of Jesus as the Son of God was that he was, most certainly, that; and, especially since the Roman Catholic Church had fled Italy (for, sadly, Israel), the Holy Martyr Church had claimed it *was* the Catholic Church. It was merely an extension of that most revered and historic institution. The real, human Catholic disagreed with this notion, because the Post Testament added a whole new set of blatantly sacrilegious beliefs. Namely, that the Second Coming of Christ had occurred in the earthly form of the Lamb, who was the martyred son of the Hierophant—himself, merely God's highest servant ever in pursuit of the clearest light of divinity.

When she mingled among religious humans, particularly Farhad, she learned that the popular human conception was quite the opposite. Oh, sure, she'd heard people call her Father "the Devil," because he called himself that for a giggle and cherished the title. But what had surprised her was the depth of the demonology that had been applied to the Holy Family, and the almost universal understanding of these theological positions across Christian, Muslim, and Hebrew faiths. (The Catholic Church, treating the Bible—especially Revelations—on a symbolic level, was one of the few ironic holdouts who denied the Hierophant was anything of supernatural power, infernal or divine.) In the eyes of most human faithful, the Lamb was not the Second Coming, but the anti-Christ, and the slave of a foul demon who called himself the God of this world. This had been Kahlil's belief, but it was all pretty far-out stuff to her, especially when she started asking Abrahamians about their particular stances on Jesus Christ. With perspectives differing so vastly on the subject, it didn't seem possible to the General any one religion should be more correct than another. Nor was she thrilled at the notion of waiting around for the Second Coming of a Messiah, alive in heaven or not.

Though she had to admit, the Islamic notion that Jesus never died on the cross was pretty comforting in the given circumstances.

"Have you considered, Mahdi, that the tether might be undone?"

"A deficit of free hands aside, they'd be all over me before I made it to the doors."

With a reluctant glance over his shoulder, Farhad studied the restraint around her ankle as she had herself studied it closely over the past cycle. Its substance was flexible, with a bounce not dissimilar to bungie cord. Given her position and the fact that one leg was free, it would be easy for her or anyone dropping her to dislocate her leg before it was even amputated. Any effort to free her required guaranteed success. Further, the tether was secured at the top of the cross, strung through the metal loop of a weighted cap that had been slipped over top the two-barred crucifix to render it the horned variant preferred by the HMC. The whole thing resembled a bisected version of the old astrological symbol for Mercury. Maybe she could pull her way up and chew through the tether, but she was increasingly weak from the effects of starvation, and she suspected the tensile substance was as durable as it was conductive. This last thought was posited to Farhad, who looked shocked when she mentioned her hunger.

"I did not know. All this time, I thought you shook from fear. I should have known better than to think you afraid." Looking around his person with irritation, he said, "They have taken all my weapons, of course, my knives and guns, but I might withstand the pain of your teeth if they are sharp enough—"

"No, Farhad." She tried to smile for him and just couldn't physically manage it. "But thank you. It's just better. Trust me, being in this position for this long…"

"I see."

"Only about a week more," the General observed. "I can do it."

"You can, Mahdi, and will. I believe in you." Cassandra's voice echoing with Farhad's managed to elicit the corners of Dominia's smile while the pilot went on, "Please: believe, also, in us."

"I do…after you were able to get back from the Ergosphere, especially. I hope I get to hear that story some night." Hesitant to discuss it with all the monitoring resources the castle had to offer no doubt focused on them, Dominia nonetheless felt obliged to ask, "Did Gethsemane return to Earth with you?"

Pending a soft exhalation, Farhad shook his head. "The magician you've told us about—the man from the study of Iblis—he flagged us down once we had flown for a day, as he promised on the radio. This man…perhaps you do not know this story. He reminds me of the servant of Allah, Khidr, who met and challenged Moses. I do not know why he does the things he does, Valentinian. But I believe he does them in the service of Allah."

"What did he do to Gethsemane?"

"He took her out of the plane with him, and when Tenchi and I emerged, the magician was alone."

"How was she looking when he took her away?"

The man's expression grew hesitant; he glanced up at Dominia's leg, perhaps deciding whether it was worth burdening her with the truth in her current circumstances. "When I was a small boy in the state of Syria, my uncle was an imam; he could answer any question about the Quran and tell many of its stories from the top of his head. The one I remember best is the one everyone remembers best. The story of the Seven Sleepers. These men, Mahdi, these Christian shepherds, they enter a cave near Ephesus to hide from Roman persecution, and by the grace of Allah, they are allowed to sleep for three hundred years. Their dog lays across the cave's entrance"—she recalled Kahlil's aggravation over dogs, and wondered what he would think of that story—"and even he survives for that phenomenal length of time. When they leave the cave, they return to the city and find it changed—now Christian—and their story is proven true because the coins with which they try to buy food have not been in circulation for three hundred years. After they realize what has happened to them, they die on the spot, praising Allah."

"I love a happy ending."

Farhad chuckled. "That was always my problem! As a boy, I thought, 'Why didn't they just stay in the cave! They had to face death anyway. If they had stayed in that cave forever, they never would have died.'"

Dominia saw where he went with this even as he cleared his throat to say, "I think—perhaps the best thing for your lieutenant is that she remain in that sacred cave. I did not recognize her by the time the magician led her from the E4."

That was surely so, but it did not make Gethsemane's earthly loss any less difficult. In a way, it would have been easier if the human had lost her life in a battle. Instead, Dominia had lost Gethsemane to the magician's machinations. What was intended for the nymph's vessel? The General might never know. She had accepted that already, but it stung her to think such a thing when she considered she might have protested.

All this horrible groping in the dark. She was used to depending on herself; to getting herself and her men out of anything. Lying down—upside down, to be precise—and allowing all these losses to accrue was challenging in and of itself. She couldn't be sure, but she suspected she'd had at least one seizure while hanging, sometime after Farhad was forced to return to his cell. She had been unconscious and had only realized it when she'd faded back in with an awful headache and the taste of blood in her mouth. Food deprivation seizures didn't usually start so early into the martyr's starvation process, but she had a suspicion the stress position worsened it. She'd have to take drastic measures to keep track of her consciousness. The General had begun to fill the time with singing. This humiliated her, so she kept it soft. At least in Nogales she had been able to walk around her cell, or rest. She could talk to Benedict through her cell door during his shift. There was a similarity here, her jailers and friends taking shifts with one another as they were. Her Father came alone at the fourth respite of her ordeal.

"I was quite impressed by your decision to spend all this time fasting, Dominia. Are you hoping to purify your soul in this process, as you made your last-ditch effort to save mine? Religions worldwide have a proud history of sacrificing food in exchange for higher wisdom."

"I want no part in leeching human spirits to feed my own. Willingly given, or no."

"You are going to spend the rest of your life refusing to eat when you cannot spend time in the sun? Some things never change."

She did not voice her suspicion that the rest of her life was worth, by that point, all of six days. That would encourage him to drop the number to five. Instead, she sternly said, "I've seen what it is we really eat."

"Sin and fear and doubt."

"*We* fill these people up with fear and doubt. Martyrs do."

"Had we nothing to frighten, we could not exist—and fear is not an objectively ugly thing. Fear's only object is to end its own existence, for when we fear, we are repelled from the object that instills the feeling in us. Fear is a beast that lives only to die, and when it possesses a human being to a point said human conflates themselves with their fear, the result is the kind of fatalism that keeps martyrs well fed."

The Hierophant considered the sallow face resting in the crook of his arm, his own features arranged in an expression that was, for once, convincingly genuine. "You look at your life and see only my greatest cruelties. Creating you, and this exhausting sprint on which you've forced yourself. These two alleged crimes of mine bookend your existence as if to drain that existence of all meaning—but your life, the life I gave you, has contained much more than this. And it is a life that can go on from this point, if you let it."

"And then what? More of this someday, in some other form?" She laughed bitterly—a noise that in this case was more like a low, wheezed "ah-ha"—and was then overcome by a wave of convulsions. Clicking his tongue, the Hierophant cradled her to his shoulder and patted her back. Doting as any parent presented with an ill child.

"It does not have to be like this. Nothing ever had to be like this, my girl. You chose this."

Her eyes shut. "Please, go fuck yourself. That must be why you spend your time with another Cicero, anyway."

"I know it upsets you to hear, but you must face the truth."

She did not respond. When he was certain she would speak no more that night without his provocation, the Hierophant patiently said, "Now more than ever, I see you are jealous of your brother. But remember: knowing all this trouble would come about, I martyred you just the same. Because I can use you, yes—but wouldn't it have been a simpler task to martyr and slaughter you right off? I have allowed you to outlive many of your forebears. Only Cicero and the Lamb are older. All the pitiful whelps who preceded you, whose martyring I completed years before your human infancy—they were too base and unworthy in the end to meet my needs. Going on evidence from past iterations, it seems no matter what assortment I select, the results are more or less the same. I, like Goldilocks, am caught between children: this one, too vain; that one, too indolent; the next, too unpredictable. The list of flaws goes on. But you, Dominia—what a good girl you were, *always* were, for centuries! Your problem has only ever been, in my opinion, Cassandra. Oh, you liked to fuss with me as a small child, loved to argue and debate and scowl and stomp your foot when nothing you could do managed to infuriate me. That was why I frightened you so much, I think. Why I still frighten you now. Because I am calm. Because I know what is going to happen."

"How do you know? How do you remember? Did the last Hierophant tell you?"

"Aside from the protein, and methods of Roman orators lost on a world that prizes smartphones and personal assistants, I find the best means of securing memory is by writing things down while they are fresh. When I reach a new world, the first thing I do is begin a new notebook listing my crucial points—points on which the Lamb's predictions are, for one reason or another, obscure."

"But why go to a new world at all? If this keeps happening again and again, why this consistency of a Cicero moving across the boundaries each time?"

Merrily, that hateful bastard laughed. "Why, because I have outgrown the old world. You know how tight a leash I keep on you and your sister. Imagine how carefully I confine myself!"

XII

La Pittura Infamante

Oh, for a glimpse into her Father's mind! Perhaps he *had* shared with Dominia some hint of that specter that pursued him world to world. If so, she struggled to divine it. To say that Cicero had left the last iteration only because he wanted his own sandbox in which to toddle, well—that was not all there was to it, surely, but good luck getting anything more. It wasn't worth fighting through his layers of obfuscation. Her energy was better spent elsewhere.

Things were only bound to get worse from here on out, and that was a horrible thought, because she was already having seizures. Her right foot, bound within the iron manacle in which the leg brace terminated, was now permanently discolored to the shade of cement. The limb had begun to follow suit. And, oh, how tired she was! When she included the time before the dim sum restaurant and her restless half doze upon returning to Kronborg, she had gone something like four, almost five, days without real sleep. Well—she was able to recount one period of sleep she'd grabbed, because when she awoke from it, she found her vision had spontaneously inverted itself. The dizzying effect of perceiving the world as right-side up while the body hung suspended was so overwhelming that she cried out upon perceiving it. Aside from that instance of waking, there was no way to know when she was asleep, or what night it was. She had lost track of even her own consciousness.

And she had lost track of all time, but she did have to admit the hours, of late, felt shorter than her 333 years already made them. Sixty-minute blocks of time dilated into seconds. Perhaps she slept and was just not aware of it, but it certainly did not feel as such because, ah, how her muscles ached, how her teeth itched, how her body trembled and her stomach seemed it might rupture from its own acids as they ate into its tissues. A few times in that third day (she tracked any semblance of space-time by chanting in a dreadful mantra the pattern of her visitors, an act that occupied an unpleasant amount of her mind and was also, at times, alarmingly hard to recall), she tried to tamper with the binds about her wrists and received a nasty, high-voltage shock. After she had recovered from that, and her body moved reasonably again, she set about suffering herself (literally, suffering herself) to tangle her bind around her sleeping ankle. By wrapping the tether, again and again, around her leg—an act that caused the dead limb terrible pain and caused Dominia to gnaw on her already bitten tongue—she could draw herself up that loathsome frame custom-built for her torture. At the top of the cross, she found the flexible tether was one solid piece that had been looped through the great metal circle and had been attached somehow inside her ankle's metal gauntlet; in fact, as she looked, it seemed the tether had been attached at the time of welding. She'd hoped there was something to tear or unhook, or perhaps that in their haste the carpenters had not securely attached the horned cap to the top of the crucifix. Alas, their craftsmanship was sublime, for it had meant their lives. There was no easy way out of this. She was in the careful process of lowering herself back when the doors opened and the General, gritting her teeth, slipped. The nasty fall of the final four feet did not dislocate her leg, but did wrench it and leave her more physically out of sorts than she'd even been before.

"Didn't mean to surprise you," said Lazarus, looking over his shoulder at the shutting doors, then the ladder he almost unconsciously retrieved. "I'd save my strength if I were you…there's not a lot of good to be done. Not from your position, and certainly not now."

In spite of her pain, the endorphins released by her brain at the sight of her friend were on the level of any street drug. "It's good to see you. And good to see you in one piece."

"For now, anyway." With a wan smile, the tired old man edged the ladder beneath Dominia at a slightly sharper angle than used by the others and, cautiously, backed his way up it, informed by experience that the best way to support Dominia's body was back to back. She saw what he was going for and urged her weakened muscles to sit up, her burden relieved when she felt the old martyr's brace. For the first time in days, her body could relax as he continued up in a backward, crab-like fashion. The act left her in the fetal position but at least more upright than before, and like this, she could endure the hot agony of blood rushing through abused ventricles. "You look tired already," he said.

"I feel tired already. I've been here for nights, after I was busted trying to get a glimpse of the Hierophant's script."

"He'll do that…writers are so sensitive about showing their work around. You know the truth about Cicero and the Hierophant by now, right?"

"Top contender in the category of 'things I wish you would have told me any time over the last year.'"

"What good would it have done if I had?" He shrugged against her back, his shoulders pushing hers and provoking a sting. "Knowledge is only so much power. Sometimes it's a catastrophic burden. You can't fix the past that's happened, so you can only change the future; and you have to trust you'll know what you need to know in order to make that change at the right time. Just like everybody else in the world—except your old man, anyway. The Hierophant's always lived through this before, so he's always one step ahead."

That would mean, in the proverbial Mandelbrot equation of reality, that the Hierophant was the variable under iteration.

But if Dominia was not a variable, what was she?

Her mind could not trail after the thought. Eyes closing and brow furrowing in sorrow to lose its thread, the General asked, "Then what are we supposed to do?"

"Rely on you. Like I said a couple of seconds ago, sweetheart." He talked to her now as he never had—a gentle grandparent—and it made her body tremble with inexpressible tears because she knew and he knew she was dying. "You'll know what to do when the time comes."

"When I'm dead."

He said nothing. She regained her composure and exhaled, inhaled, tried to enjoy breathing while she could. Tried to learn what she could while she could still learn. "I saw Farhad. Did anyone else come with you?"

"Other than Ted? No. They thought they had the Lady, until the men who had Her realized their terrible mistake. She's elsewhere now."

"Why did they bring Farhad?"

"He was one of the four beings that emerged from the E4 when it crashed into the Lady's library in the middle of a very intense standoff." This aspect matched the report René had mentioned, with the story that had started off as a UFO, then turned into a downed plane. "You can guess who the four were, I'm sure"—Farhad, Theodore, Tenchi, and Saint Valentinian—"and also guess why only two were obtainable."

"Because Farhad would have leapt into the fight, Teddy was meant to be caught, Tenchi has other interdimensional fish to fry, and Saint Valentinian's never around when you need him."

Lazarus laughed, lowering his head so as not to bump hers. "You know well as I do that's not true, but it does feel that way sometimes."

Yes, it did. But, he was right. She had needed him more while weeping in that kennel than she had in the entire year spent praying for him. More than she needed him now. Frankly, she didn't want to see him now. Because the next time she saw him, she suspected he would be acting in that most grim capacity for which the saint was responsible.

Funny to think of him now in that role. Funny to think she had ever regarded him as fictional. But had he ever been a man? She sensed he was more than man or fiction and probed the sage on this point. "Do you have any memory at all of the magician being your child? Even a dream?"

"No. Either the magician has stolen those memories on purpose, or he's lying, or the sacred protein failed to retain its own memories of the initial world because it wasn't expecting it would have to. Do you have any inkling, any static memory, of what happened in the last iterations? It's not written in your brain, but for me, it's backed up in my blood, and my blood rewrites my goddamned memories every time after that first time. Christ, oh, Dominia! Do you know—something like ninety percent of martyrs return to life without anything special about them at all. Of those who do, maybe half of those powers are more impressive than basic parlor tricks. I think Cicero does have a gift—memory—but it pales beside his brother's abilities."

"And they really were brothers in life?"

"Yes! That's my *point*. Their starting genetic codes were just—*that close*"—she could imagine him holding his fingers a hair apart—"yet the Lamb inherited all he did and Cicero got the ability to remember everybody's birthday. If my own genetic code was just microscopically different, I always think maybe—"

"There'd be no saving the world, or a single life. Because there would be no way for us to enter the Ergosphere."

Lazarus sighed. "Yeah. Yeah, I know. I guess I just look forward to someday being able to relax, and enjoy a life, or something. Or enjoy being dead! You know, I've never been to the Kingdom?" At the General's shocked noise, the man said, "I'd become a citizen, for sure… but I guess I just never have time. I'm needed here. But someday, Dominia—I'm going to get a sweet slice of eternity. Maybe Trisha and I…well." He chuckled. "I don't know what she'd think of me now, with the beard and all, but I'd hope that in eternity I'd have a bit of youthful charm returned to me. It's the blood, you know. Memory ages you."

"That's why the Hierophant looks so much older than Cicero, but why is he so much larger?"

"You'll laugh."

"Try me."

"Okay. Every iteration is a little smaller than the last." She did laugh. "It's true. Ask the magician. He'll explain it."

She might have teased him more, but then she thought about fractals, and how, to find the Mandelbrot set hidden within the edge of the Mandelbrot set when viewing the function as a colored image, one had to zoom into the fractal for an unnerving eternity before finding the miniature duplicate. It only pushed to mind that trail of thought she hadn't the wherewithal to follow before. "If the magician stole your memories of that first time, Lazarus—"

"I don't know that he did."

"But if he did, why would he do such a thing? And if it's not true, why lie about being your son?"

"Maybe because the weight of the actual truth is too much for us to bear. I don't know that he's lying, necessarily. Valentinian does look a lot like me…anyway, I'm pretty sure he's not evil, per se, but I am pretty sure by now that it's his fault all of this happens on repeat."

"Yeah?"

"Oh, yeah. I don't think the universe was always caught in a loop like this. I don't think martyrs were always a problem, and I don't think they will be if we can set the universe in order again."

"And you think it's Valentinian's fault?"

"Usually, when a thing like this starts, it's because somewhere along the line, somebody screwed up, and screwed up bad. You may be responsible for remaking the universe, but where did you get the power for remaking the universe? *How* do you remake the universe? I'm sure you've asked yourself that enough already, so I won't. But I just mean…I think it's a bunch of bullshit that the responsibility is on you. If anybody's responsible, it's the magician."

"I've missed you, Lazarus."

"Well, I'm here now, kiddo," said the old man. "For a little while."

Little, indeed. Too soon he was gone and there she was again. Alone with her thoughts, her trembling, the ceaseless calendar of her memories, and the awful anticipation of her fate. Three days hanging, longer without food. Far longer, still, since she had felt safe or comfortable for anything more than a handful of seconds at a time. Dominia could not feel her face, which was good, because if it was anything like the rest of her, it would be in agony. Her flesh was tight against degrading muscles devoured by her hungry body. By the proteins that could barely maintain a functional, noncancerous shape. She tried to focus on one thing Lazarus had told her during his visit: what had come when she'd asked him if he expected her to die. If the instant of death would be worse— more painful—than this.

"You know where you're going after death. Most don't. You can endure this, Dominia. If I can endure living over and over, you can endure suffering this way just once."

"Just once I can remember."

"Isn't that as good as experiencing it just once?"

She supposed. Still—what a depressing thought! To be yet another in a long line of failed Dominias. How far she had traveled! Across the very globe, in pursuit of a dream that she had known to be ill-fated from the moment René appeared in her office. Yet, she could not help but dream it, pursue it, for nothing else bound her to the world after so many years of sordid living. Nothing but Cassandra, who weighted her to reality. Who she fancied she could, with increasing clarity, feel. As if she were with Dominia, there, in the chapel.

If only. If only she were really there. All this would have been unnecessary. If only this were the more dreamlike of the worlds the General inhabited! Alas, this was not the case. Her world had become suffering, marked by throbbing skull and cheeks not felt for quite some time. It was endless, nagging pain, and a parade of friends and relatives sent to mock her with their brief relief, their sudden absence.

To her surprise, the fourth day saw Theodore sent into the chapel, looking fretful. Even he proved relief to see, though until she knew for certain he hadn't contributed to her friends' capture, she couldn't help but feel a bit standoffish. Hence, rather than joyful greeting, she asked, "What are you doing here?"

"Father sent me in— I have to climb up there to do this? There's no other way?"

"Are you really asking me that?"

Sighing, Theodore took his turn on the ladder, and at Dominia's question of why the Hierophant had seen fit to torture her with Teddy, of all people, the Governor exclaimed, "Because he doesn't *trust* me! Because it's a load of— He thinks I want to help your little human friends! Frankly, he owes me an apology after the way things went down in that— *wretched* place, that Void— and Jerusalem! Hah. I'll tell you about it sometime. The explosions! I was almost shot. Frankly, I think I was in more danger from Father's own men than I ever was from you and your cronies! But you know how it is, hoping for an apology from him… Anyway, he did get me out alive, so I guess I have to be grateful. Thank goodness he saved me from your band of criminals! I was worried. Not for me, of course. For Lavinia."

This clumsy lie, told at a rapid clip and nervous pitch and packed with unnecessary, meandering details all in response to her simple question about why the Hierophant had sent Teddy in to prop her up, reassured her that her friends—and Theodore—had come intentionally. That the Lamb was not confirming these notions to the Hierophant was a very curious point that emerged again on day five, when the ram-headed man in question was the next to mount the ladder and give her support.

"You've been awfully quiet since I returned," tired Dominia observed, head rolling back against the shoulder of the Lamb's black cloak. In her sleep-deprived state, even this fabric felt too rough. He considered her statement—and its true sentiment—a few seconds before responding.

"I guess I just hate getting in the middle of all of these things. I'm sorry to see you up here, but things will work out the way they'll work out. There's nothing anybody can do. Certainly nothing I can do."

"But that's wrong. You manipulate probability."

"Sometimes, in little ways. I can't make a big change for anybody. Not out of nothing. And the changes I initiate are only…entropic. I can't turn water into wine, or straw into gold. I can't heal a person, but I can increase the odds of them becoming well."

"Still—you see so much. And hear so much. Surely you can do more than you've ever let on."

"I've done enough. I helped your Father gain power."

"But why? You've never been like him. You were always kind to me. A better parent than he was, no matter what he'd like to think."

His eyes trailing from the General, the Lamb said, "I've been by Cicero's side since I was born the first time. The human time, if you can say Cicero was ever really human. He was always a little like a robot, I guess. But the protein changed him as much as it changed me. Power changed him. And—well." His lips turned up in a dark smile at some taboo reality. Some act that changed the Hierophant into the free-spirited tyrant he was, which could not be spoken without consequence. The man once known as Elijah settled on saying, "I can't explain it any more than I can explain to you why I've let him do the things he's done. We're brothers. We've always been brothers, but since we were martyred, we've been closer than brothers. We can't help it, you understand. We're each the only person the other can trust and—he helped me. When I was first martyred, hearing all the voices and seeing things from the Ergosphere that weren't present in reality, he took care of me. Evil as he is. And so I help him—because I love him. I know you can understand that. I love him because I have to believe that, somewhere, something inside him is redeemable."

Her attempt to save the Hierophant's soul fluttered back to her with genuine sorrow. "I guess I know what you mean." Glancing over at the Lamb's dark curls as she tilted her forehead against the cool metal of his right horn, she asked him, "If there are two of Cicero, why aren't there two of you? If only one person can slip into a new universe, how could he stand to leave without you?"

With a macabre smile, the Lamb repeated what he had said at the start of her questioning. "I guess I just hate getting in the middle of all these things."

She understood why.

Her next tormentor, after the nightly visit from her Father, was none other than Cicero—but she was so tired, so beyond function, that the best she could manage was to focus on the rhythm of her breathing while the brother who was but the seed of their Father gloated, "How right it is to find you thus, Dominia, after all the trouble you've given us. And all the difficulty you've given me, personally, over the years!"

Baffling. "I never did a damn thing to you."

"Aside from spurning my authority, and that of the Church, at every turn? Why you've so stubbornly resisted attending my sermons and accepting Father's grace, I shall never understand— You are a *martyr*, woman, better than anything on Earth and deserving of glory. Yet you would scrape about in the mud with the humans! As if their lives could ever amount to anything."

"Humanity did just fine before us. Better."

"They destroyed the very planet. Before Father raised it from the waters of the Mediterranean, Venezia was drowned by rising seas thanks to the negligence of men. Rising seas that saw the deaths of many fish, replaced by his own well-funded programs. Why, the very waters of the sound around Kronborg would have ruined this fine castle had His Holiness not seen to its restoration and protection."

The place had survived a fire before him; she would rather Kronborg had seen a flood than fallen into her Father's hands, but this was like wishing the sky were yellow, or that Cicero would shut up. "Humans abuse the world," her brother continued. "So we have taken it from them, as your rightly took Lavinia from Cassandra's irresponsible hands."

"Is now the time for this?"

"When else are we to bring it up? You and I both know you are destined to lose more than your leg. A time like this is worth some self-reflection from the both of us." After consideration, El Sacerdote said, "You know, Dominia, I never hated you."

"Oh, please."

"I suppose if I was a bit strict with you, it was because I was trying to save you from this. Prevent it."

"Father told you this was coming?"

"Of course. He told me everything." At his sister's snort, the Holy Martyr Church's most notorious priest adjusted his grip on her to demonstrate a shrug. "What else would you expect of him?"

"Nothing less. It's just sort of funny I don't even have temporal privacy. You remember that summer we stayed in France, and he took down all the doors in my apartment in Versailles?"

"You were doing an awful lot of drugs that summer, my sister."

"I was nineteen! An adult. And I still found ways."

"Yes, well, you have always had trouble with connecting conse- quence to action. That's why you insist on blaming Father for what happened to Cassandra! Why, he wasn't even the one who talked to her on Walpurgisnacht."

How amazing. Even in a situation like this, even battered by a chain of horrific revelations, her faltering heart still managed to drop. Yes, that strange and uncomfortable feast night—normally one of the best of the year—wherein Cassandra exited the annual "Raven" recitation to have a crippling panic attack in the nearest bathroom. They had caught a silent jet home, had a bizarre fight, made up (so Dominia had thought), fallen asleep on the couch—

She could not finish her thought. Could barely open her lips to ask, "What happened on Walpurgisnacht?"

"I'm shocked you hadn't heard. She confronted me, Cassandra. A fine time to do it, too, in the middle of my favorite holy night!" As Dominia's practically disembodied spirit was nonetheless struck by bolts of pain, the priest explained, "Amazing she'd been able to compose herself the whole night until that point, planning to say all she was."

"Let you have it, did she?"

"As I've never experienced!"

"Good."

While the priest chuckled, he said, "As my ego recovered from her dressing-down of my every quality, she bashed me with the fact that she knew Lavinia was her baby, and that we had conspired to take the infant from her, and that we had wanted her to think she was crazy…"

Oh, no.

"And, why, she was off on such a screed, I had to bring her down somehow."

Poor Cassandra.

"So I just told her, 'You should be having this conversation with your wife,' and left her on the balcony where she'd dragged me. And then…"

And then, the recitation. And then, the silent jet home. And then, that bizarre fight the second they hit the front door. Dominia asking over and over, "Why won't you tell me what's wrong? Why won't you talk to me? Cassandra, honey, please."

"It doesn't matter," had been her wife's only response, over and over, for thirty dysfunctional minutes before her broken tone changed. Her watering eyes locked on those of the Governess like a pair of lasers, she asked, "Would you ever lie to me?"

Would

You

Ever

Lie

To

Me?

The words rang through the chapel even now, bringing Dominia that same surge of alarm such a question always brought a liar. "Never," she had lied. "I would never lie to you. Never, about anything. Why would you ask me something like that?"

Cassandra clammed right up again. Saying only little things like, "I guess I made a mistake," or, "There was a misunderstanding," when pressed as to what had caused her change of mood or the sudden silence through which Dominia could not break.

Only now, the General realized she could have. She could have broken through that silence and maybe even saved the life of her wife. All she had needed to do was tell the truth when it mattered.

And she hadn't.

"Please leave," Dominia said, so softly that Cicero didn't hear it over the sound of his drone. She raised her voice, repeating, "Please leave," and adding, "I need you to go, right now, go, please," adding the same words in all the languages she knew: English, Mephitolian, Spanish, that smattering of half-remembered Japanese and her year's worth of shitty Arabic. "Get out, get out, get the fuck away from me, Cicero!"

In time with her words, she had begun to thrash so violently—at best, a half-deliberate set of movements—that before Cicero could react, she'd succeeded in knocking the ladder, along with its occupant, sideways across the chapel. While the priest, his foot tangled in the rung upon which he'd been perched, crashed to the floor with a terrible cry, the dryly sobbing General felt the joint of her hip slip with the full-length fall and suspected her leg had finally dislocated.

Oh, Cassandra. If only Dominia had been a better person! While the priest, bruised and cursing, limped out of the chapel with only the briefest of sneers for his sister, the General thumped her head against the crucifix, but soon lost strength for even self-abuse. Such a thing would do nothing but harm, anyway.

Lazarus was right. Nothing could be done to fix the past. But the future could always be made better. Dominia was determined to make it so, and her heart sped with that determination when the door opened but a few unscheduled hours after Cicero's departure. The hinges' squeak punctuated the pain of a familiar voice.

"Oh, Ninny."

She couldn't believe it. The Hierophant had brought Lavinia? While the General blinked stars from her sleep-deprived eyes and tried to lift her head, the girl hurried up the chapel—accompanied by, of all God's good creatures, Basil, who already crept near the base of the cross. Her back aching as she spared energy to see him, Dominia uttered the words, "You shouldn't be here."

"I know, Ninny, but I couldn't *stand* it. I had to see you. You know this doggie, don't you? Isn't he the one from the train? He's been with us for weeks, but I only recognized him when he was next to you. I won't tell, I promise."

Dominia believed her, but the holo-cameras tucked in the chapel ceiling wouldn't stay so mum. "I'm sure our Father would be unhappy for you to see me like this. Especially without his permission."

"Daddy can pound salt," said the sassy girl, eliciting a real smile from the General. "Look at you up there! Oh, that's not *right*. I didn't have to do this when I tried to run away."

"Well, you also weren't successful in running away. You didn't help the enemy. You're too valuable."

Frowning, Lavinia glanced around and, spying the ladder, sheepishly said, "If *I* were the one who took you down, Daddy wouldn't be able to do anything about it."

"He would find something to do about it, all right. Just, please, Lavinia, go back. I can't stand to see him do anything more terrible to you."

Frowning down at the dog she stooped to pet, the Princess, up well past her dawn bedtime, studied her own pale hands. The hands she used, anyway. The same subject must have rested heavy on the girl's mind, for she soon said, "You know, Theodore is safe! I'm so happy. I was worried, but I…after you and I talked the other night…" She faltered, and frowned. "He doesn't know. At least, I don't think he knows. I haven't told him, and you know—these darn things are so realistic…I can feel with them just the way I could feel things before, so it's all the same. This fellow doesn't know the difference, does he?"

Basil did not wag his tail, because he knew the difference very well, but continued allowing the girl to fawn over him with her mechanical hands while he assessed, as reverently as an animal could, the woman suspended above. Dominia held the dog's eye contact in perfect understanding of his respect for her plight while Lavinia went on. "People will know the difference, though, when I tell them. They'll suddenly see it the way I do…little differences. Sometimes I move too fast, or I'm too strong, even for our people. And if you reacted the way you did, as close as you are to me and as long as you've known me, why…I suppose I can't expect somebody like Theodore to react differently, can I?"

"You love Theodore back, don't you?"

It had been the silly source of a lot of teasing over the years, but the way Lavinia glowed with the innocence of true love just to have the question asked told the General all. "He's so gallant, Ninny. Of course I love him. You know—he probably doesn't care, or think it's a big deal—but he was the first person I ever remember seeing, even before Daddy. Can you believe that?"

"Oh," said Dominia, "I think he cares."

"Really?" Hope sparked bright in Lavinia's eyes before she smothered it with a wave of those delicate hands. "Not that it matters. Our love must remain the pure, courtly kind. What I symbolize to everyone—it's all too important. I can't let it be thrown away because of some silly crush, can I?"

The General had the feeling those words were not Lavinia's but Cicero's, drilled deep into her head. Yes, Theodore was absolutely silly: one of the silliest people Dominia had ever met by any definition of the word. But, Lavinia was right. He could also be sort of kind, even if he was a selfish idiot who let himself be a tool of the state. The flaw in his compassion was that his moments of kindness were not rooted in hidden goodness but naïveté. In fact, that was his problem. Theodore was too naïve to be evil.

In that respect, he and Lavinia were the perfect pair. Dominia's cheeks hurt with her effort at smiling, so she stopped. "I think you should live your life, and make yourself happy."

"I don't think I'd know how to live my life if I could." Still in fair humor, Lavinia laughed the words while she stood to brush her hands free of dog fur. "I don't know anything about the world—anything at all. Do you know how excited I was to ride the Light Rail? Oh, Ninny, it was so fun! That must be what you feel like all the time. Well…not right now, but you know what I mean."

Dominia did not respond—could not, until she was pushed by Lavinia's regret that: "Everybody treats me like I'm made of spun sugar because I didn't wake until I was grown up—but I know things. I'm not stupid, Ninny."

"No, Lavinia. You're not. That's not why our Father keeps you confined."

"Oh, I know why he does *that*. It's because he wants me to be safe, but—"

"No, Lavinia, please. Please listen to me." The girl quieted while Dominia, struggling for breath from her position, arched her ruined shoulders to fill her lungs. "I don't know what you're going to think of me after this, but I don't think I'm going to be around much longer. I'd might as well tell you now, and make it fast, since he'll be here any minute. Probably watching us right now…I'm sorry, Livvy. I haven't told you the truth. No one has ever told you the truth. Not about yourself, and not about your life. You're fertile. Our Father doesn't want you to be out on your own because you'd discover that, or—far worse, in his opinion—you might find a nice, human man and make a child without his knowledge."

Though the stained-glass windows of the room had been shuttered against the light of day, Lavinia's eyes seemed to glow as they widened with her sputtering mouth. "How…but—that's not right, Ninny, he wouldn't do that. Daddy wouldn't— I'm not a *dog*, Ninny. He wouldn't *breed* me. Not even if I could get pregnant. But that's silly. That's silly, Dominia, and you know that it's silly. Martyrs can't get pregnant."

"He keeps you at home because you bleed every month, right? Other martyrs would know."

Humiliation, along with horror, lined the girl's face. "Why would he tell you about my—my illness—"

"It's not an illness! It's menstruation, Lavinia."

"What is—" The girl frowned, her perfect brow furrowing with bafflement. "I know an awful lot of words, Ninny, but I don't know that one. 'Month'?"

Sweet Lamb, but the Holy Father had managed to shield her from *that*. Dominia shouldn't have been so shocked—the girl never lived a human life, never had a female parent, never read anything that wasn't in her approved Biblioteca reading list and never spoke to anybody who wasn't paid by the Hierophant to keep their mouths shut. Yet, for the girl to have been kept in the dark for almost seventy years about a basic fact of her own body—it was so abhorrent it was almost impressive.

"That bleeding means you can have a baby." At the girl's visible skepticism, Dominia pressed, "You *can*, Lavinia. You can, because you weren't ever a human. You were born a martyr. You're Cassandra's daughter."

The ninety-year-old tumor of the General's lie dropped from her mouth, and in that instant revealed to her how burdensome its weight had become. She had never realized it—never once felt its creeping mass build until now, free of its pressure, she was confronted with the faded image of Lavinia's eyes growing big, bigger, her brow furrowing and her mouth uttering, "But I don't understand," in a voice so soft the General barely heard it. Not over the thud of blood bearing down on her ears.

Gently, as if trying to talk an eggshell out of breaking, Dominia tried to explain. First, about Benedict. Then, about Dominia's loneliness. Finally, about Cassandra. She thought about trying to make some excuse, like that the General thought they couldn't give the baby a good life—but that would have been another lie. Cassandra was a natural mother.

Dominia was always the problem, Dominia and her fear and her lying, and so Dominia said, "My heart was broken, and I wanted to break hers, but I couldn't bear to give her up, or reject her child to her face. Not when she was so lonely and afraid. So desperate for my help. Those vulnerabilities that brought her to me in the first place, those were the reasons I loved her. They were why I wanted to protect her. Yet, I punished her for them. I told our Father about you, and I thought, until recently, that I had made the right decision. But last year, everything fell apart. That was why Cassandra killed herself, you see. She knew. She realized what had been sitting in front of her face for almost a century, and she was destroyed by it. The weight of my lie…what I did…I killed Cassandra, Lavinia. I killed your mother. I took your arms and your legs."

Tears falling upon the tile floor and the fur of the watching collie, the General shut her eyes. "I am so sorry."

For a time—too long, by Dominia's reckoning—there was no answer. She was too frightened to behold the girl's expression. But when that soft voice did reach her to reveal itself full of astonishment, she forced herself to behold its stunned speaker. "Then you would have been my mother, too, wouldn't you?"

"Yes," admitted the General, whose despair paid no heed to the light of Lavinia's face, or the way she stepped forward with hope in her smile. "But I failed you."

"Oh—*Ninny*. I wish—I wish I could hold you, Ninny, I—" Lips trembling, the girl glanced down at the dog, then gasped as conversation rose from the hall outside the chapel doors. "I think you're right, Ninny. I shouldn't be here."

"No," Dominia agreed. "But I'm glad you came."

"Oh—oh." The fretful girl took another step toward the General, tugging her cloak around her. "I can't leave you *now*. I can't let this happen."

"You have no choice. You'll be busy acting in a play that will kill half a planet's worth of human children."

"I—it's only a little cull," Lavinia defended, almost admitting she was a willing participant in the proposed murder of the firstborn. "Daddy says…Daddy…"

The furrow in the girl's brow said it all, and Dominia managed to raise both her own.

"The Holy Father says a lot of things, doesn't he?"

Looking stricken by the notion of their Father's fallibility, Lavinia glanced around the room and, at last, turned to follow Basil's loping route to the door. "I don't understand why he never told me any of this before," the girl murmured. "Doesn't he love me? I thought—"

"The Hierophant does love you, I'm sure, in his way. He most loves what gives him power: and you are the most powerful person he has ever known."

That was certainly the first time Lavinia had heard a thing like that. If any notion of self-empowerment had ever come upon her, nobody on Earth had paid it any heed. The girl cast another reluctant glance for her hanging sister before hurrying away, and it was with an awful lurch as the Princess and the dog slipped through the door that the General caught a glimpse of her Father's massive frame. But the truth had been disseminated, and he could do nothing.

"I think we will make that your last visitor," declared her Father, leaning into the chapel. "You do have a way of violating those few privileges you are given, my girl."

"Don't you hurt her," shouted the General. Her Father only chuckled at her outrage.

"Why should I have to, when you have done such a fine job? I'll see you at your next break, my dear."

The slam of the shutting door echoed through the chapel but could not compare to the sweet opening of Dominia's soul. Crucified or not: she had waited too long for this moment. The truth had fermented within her, and now drunkened her to private tears that she, dehydrated, could not afford to weep.

XIII

Suspension of Disbelief

Eight days. Eight nights. A human being, as Cicero had pointed out, seldom made it one day in such a state. Even with respites such as hers, a human being by now would have expired. At the very least, their leg's necrotic condition would have spread farther up their thigh. No, no. Dominia's dark flesh ended just above her knee (or below, spatially speaking—she'd lost track of up and down long ago). How much longer could she have lasted beyond even her torturous nine days? Without blood, the protein inhabiting her muscles and skin could not long maintain its resistance of tissue death. Every drop of blood was localized in her head, and had been there for a while. That leg looked long, long gone.

It was safe to say the General felt unwell.

She had gone this long without eating or having the blood of the Lamb before, she thought, maybe. She couldn't remember. Numbers had become meaningless. How long had she been stuck in the dungeon with René? Maybe not this long. Or maybe longer. Her life was an uncanny blur. Each passing second contributed to the disintegration of her neurons as they self-consumed, dissolved, or were reedited into cancer cells. This alteration of her physical brain reduced her inner life to little more than an uncontrollable chain of abstract images that blossomed without meaning or warning, sometimes grating on her nerves in a physical way and occurring again-again-again-again-again.

Those cogent thoughts retained were the same thoughts over and over. Her mind was trapped by itself and cycling into a horrible whirlpool that would not, could not, end so long as she was trapped in this body: this hanging body: this suspended body for which everything was oblivion yet eternal: this prison of form where each minute, each second, peeled off far into the distance of infinity. Each time her fading consciousness found, within the substance of her atrophying muscles, joules enough to control her thoughts, she willed the second of her death that much closer, begging for its shadow as a pastor begged the miracles of the Lamb.

Perhaps God despised her for the crimes she had committed against mankind, her wife, herself. But she had no lingering fear of hell. Hell was not the Void. Not being nothing for all eternity. *This* was hell. This material compilation of the abstract data of the black hole at the end of being, this place of her Father's, was a waking tahgmahr. But that may have been a self-possessed notion. Material chauvinism, perhaps. She had to remind herself that she had seen the suffering of the souls hovering in the Very Low Frequency variation of the Void around Jerusalem—all those many unfortunates who had conflated that which was heavenly with that which was substantial and could not, even in death, shake themselves of their delusions. They would rather have felt themselves betrayed by a negligent God than dare connect with the entity on a personal level.

Understandable. Dominia, personally, was terrified of God. The experience of God. The idea of plunging into that highest, unspeakable godhead with her naked soul made the top of her head tingle even now—maybe more than ever—in a kind of spiritual inkling accessible even in these physical chains. To contemplate what the Jewish Abrahamians called "Keter" while in the Void—surely that was to invite a kind of annihilation, for better or for worse. What soul, especially those bound to the VLFs, could bear to realize this mating of the godspark to its source?

This was why the religions of the world employed clerics. Much as martyrs, whether knowingly or not, craved to know that dark aspect of God through the evil works of the Hierophant, so did humans seek

God through the intermediaries of priests, imams, and rabbis. The Red Market women who served the Lady likewise could not have been said to seek God directly, for they pursued only the feminine aspect of the divine, and only through the vehicle of the Lady's avatar. Dominia felt safe with the Lady for that reason. One could argue She was God…ish. Maybe that was the origin of "goddess." Had she energy, the General might have laughed at that thought, then been spat upon by a hoard of angry feminist historians and etymologists. But what did she care of history, of gender, of politics, of language? She stood on the edge of death and her only thoughts were of God.

There was only one person she knew who had, so far as she could discern, sought with true tenacity that which one might call God. Not her Father's perverse idea of it. Not society's, either. The term was often condescendingly accompanied by stereotypical images (man with beard, clouds, harps, angels, snore), yet remained so deep in true meaning that its casual use curdled the blood of those most militant atheists. But somebody she knew had wandered the universe—proven fundamental in rerunning the universe again and again—and in the process had, she suspected, come to intimately know the divine essence propelling the movement of everything. That same seeker was the only entity she had known to intercede in the world. Wretched as she felt, with her hands having been forcefully folded by her bindings for eight days, the General did what most hopeless people do, and prayed.

"Saint Valentinian"—she exhaled and inhaled and laughed in a hollow, hacking sound that caused real agony at the base of her ribs because her lungs were compressed to shapes like little prunes—"I need help."

The church was so perfectly silent that she heard the distant footsteps of a guard charged to watch the hall since Lavinia's audacious visit. Somehow bolstered by the quiet, Dominia lifted her head and batted the watering eyes that bulged with the pressure of her skull. When she spoke, her swollen lips felt they might crack, or, to her absurdly working mind, fall off. "I know you're busy, like you keep saying every time I see you…and I don't even know what you can do. What the limits of your intercession are. But I—I wish I were dead."

She allowed her head to drop back against the wood of the cross and gritted her teeth. Her eyes shut to a phosphene mandala of pain. "I wish I never have to live again. If it has to be like this…if this is what life is—why was I ever born? Why am I worth nothing more to you, or my Father, or anyone else, than any other tool? I'm as much a person to you sons of bitches as the hammers that made this cross. Is this *nothing* to you? Is this suffering nothing to you? I understand what I've done—all that I've done. I know I'm a horrible person who deserves to suffer, but please, please, let it end!"

You would accept eternal failure to save the pains of one last day?

Astonished to hear any voice not her own—let alone this choir reverberating from within her degraded auditory cortex and broken Broca's area—the General allowed her blurring eyes to open. Nearly blind as she was with the pressure of the blood in her skull, the Lady was as clear as ever. Perhaps clearer. More real and substantial than reality—though there was a wrongness to Her that the General only recognized as She began to make Her way down the aisle. Halfway, Dominia twigged to the problem. The Lady walked, though this was, ostensibly, reality. With each step, the goddess gained an inch of height, until, before the General, She towered the twelve feet necessary to stand above the head of the hanging woman.

"I heard if you walked it meant the end of the world."

It does. You seem surprised that your prayers were answered.

Before the goddess, the General needn't struggle to organize her thoughts. Her mind was sharper than ever, as if she'd eaten and slept and bathed and engaged in about a decade of cognitive behavioral therapy. Happiest of all, she could speak without pain. "Surprised to have them answered by you, maybe."

The magician and We are closely allied. You and the magician are closely allied. You are closely allied with Us. We have come to help you, as you asked. If you truly wish to put an end to all of this, We can take you now: but this will all occur again, and this iteration will be rendered obsolete.

And another iteration would take its place. She felt all the sicker at the thought. "I can't go through all this again, knowing it or not."

Then We will give you a far more valuable gift.

With Miki Soto's head, the Lady bent to place a kiss upon Dominia's aching lips. In what could only be described as a miracle, she felt not her death, but the death of all pain, as if agony was a skin that shed on the Lady's contact. The General's actual physical condition had not improved. Her leg was still dead—so dead that it *required* amputation at this point—and her body was still bound, but she had no sense of it. This was not a matter of numbness, or endorphins. It was as though the General observed herself from outside her own body; and as she copped to that sensation, she sat upon the nearest pew. Watching her own swinging body, meeting the gaze of her own helpless, blood-filled eyes.

"Are you sure I'm not already dead?" asked Dominia of the Lady. The entity sat, in normal scale, directly to her left. Did they speak in words, or Words? What was the difference?

You are no more dead than any martyr whose martyring is not yet complete. Look: here comes your Father.

As the Lady said. The doors opened and, per usual, in strolled the Hierophant for his anticipated mocking session. He said something unintelligible. Only as she focused in on him did his words clear themselves. Presently, he dragged over the ladder with the assurance that, "I suppose you'll want to know Lavinia is in good order. Be relieved, she is."

"Is this my soul I'm in?" Dominia's nose was a sharp closed parenthesis that abruptly ended the world: the hallmark of her missing eye.

It is always your soul that you are "in." Reality is the hologram cast by the projector of the black hole, said the Lady, eyes never leaving the crucifix. *The travel of the soul through this space is less akin to the movement of ghosts through physical space, and more akin to the result of a physical entity navigating a holographic field. This experience of bilocation is more likely to happen when one is asleep than at any other time, due to the wave flight of consciousness from the low-activity, low-frequency electromagnetic field state of the brain before rapid eye movement begins. But such a phenomenon is also likely to happen in meditation, as well as instances of great physical trauma or duress. There are many who follow Us who use the term "astral projection" to refer to such a phenomenon, but that term more appropriately describes reality, yes? It is all a series of projections produced by the mind.*

The General could not think to respond, fascinated as she was by the experience of being outside her body in so distinct and lucid a way. While the Lady spoke, Dominia rose and walked straight up to her climbing Father. Remarkably, she was poised just below him, yet he noticed nothing. She asked of the Lady, *"Can I go anywhere this way?"*

Yes. But beware, General. To enter even the daytime Ergosphere without one's body is a treacherous proposition. Without physical root, as without consciousness, the soul is as good as drunk or drugged, or worse. A flailing ego, run rampant without its guards.

"So a black-out drunk is a total suppression of consciousness in favor of rampant egoism," observed the General, turning away from the crucifix. *"Explains a lot of my own drunk behavior. Did he mean what he said? Is Lavinia really okay?"*

You may see for yourself, as it pleases you.

The nodding General intended to step toward the doors and instead found herself propelled forward. It was as if she floated in the womb of outer space. Astonished, she rose to the high ceiling and then, truly ghostlike, wafted through the wall of the chapel—to the office, where Cicero's right-hand man busily arranged El Sacerdote's vestments for the ceremony. Farther down the hall, in the gallery, humans decorated for the party to follow on New Year's Eve that Noctisthor. If Dominia had her way, that party would never happen. The year 4044 CE/1999 AL would ring in with the death of the Hierophant, or the death of Dominia, or the deaths of both: but there would be no cause for celebration on a day bound to mark the beginning of a culture's destruction. The question was, would the destruction be of martyrs, or of mankind?

It was not an easy decision to make. While flying through the castle in pursuit of Lavinia's chambers, the phantom General saw so many martyrs along the way. Plenty she knew, in passing if not as friends. For the most part, these were just regular people. Stuffy rich people, but still people. The average martyr had no hand in the hunt and slaughter of humans, had no part in the genocide orchestrated by the Hierophant. That genocide Dominia had supported and helped him envision. Globally speaking, the average martyr was much like those in the town of Elsinore, and less like Dominia: and though she wished to write off the desires of adult humans to be martyred, she recognized now that these were but people with passion such for life that they were willing to trade every scrap of their humanity for a chance to enjoy it just a little longer. They were artists and friends and lovers and siblings, children and parents.

But the humans were all of that, too. And long as the Hierophant was in charge of European and UF society, there could be no chance for humans to live in peace. Not without their rights and lives infringed upon by the mere existence of their predatory counterparts. There was hope, the General believed, that martyrs could change, and the world would improve—but this cancerous growth in the brain of the global organism needed to be removed as soon as possible, or the whole creature was liable to die.

At last, in lonely Lavinia's chambers, the General found the girl, while better treated, in no small amount of trouble for her decision to visit Dominia. Who knew what the truth had provoked the princess into doing or saying? At the peaks of her tantrums, Lavinia was capable of frightening behavior. But now, like most girls who'd worn themselves out with a tantrum, she cried in her bedroom. Alarmingly, Basil was not with her; nor was the girl in the mood to rail to herself in convenient Shakespearean monologue about the injustices that had befallen her, so as to give the General some easy insight into what had happened before—or what would happen next. The watching shade could only take solace in this vision of the girl alive and well, unhurt in anything but spirit. That ghostly hand of the General lay upon Lavinia's golden curls, and, as though feeling it, the princess's tears ebbed to a few indignant hiccups.

"*I know you feel betrayed,*" said Dominia—sure, if nothing else, Livvy's soul heard. "*But it's because you see you have a chance to do the truly right thing after such a long time of being told you were already doing the right thing. And you will do the truly right thing. I know.*"

She had to.

As the General was about to leave, she noted through the wall a most curious thing—aside from the notion that she could…well, not see *through* walls, for she also saw the walls. But her senses were beyond their usual limits, and strange effects were undeniable. Plain as if her consciousness mimicked the omniscient, camera-style sight of a dream, she watched merry Teddy stroll through the emptied suite to knock upon the door. The girl, anxious and not knowing her Father visited Dominia's uninhabited form, called, "Who is it?"

"Someone who wants to brighten up your night," sang Theodore. While Dominia restrained a spectral eye roll, this announcement elicited a gasp of joy in her sister, who sprang from bed to throw open the door and dive into del Medico's arms.

"Oh, *Theo*! I'm so glad you're home. Just knowing you're back in this castle makes me feel secure. If it wasn't for knowing you were safe, I—oh, what a state I'd be in!"

"I wasn't ever in *that* much danger…" Nice to hear him admit it now! "Once we were out of the plane, anyway. What's the matter, though? I can't remember the last time I heard your rooms so empty."

With an anxious nibble of her lip, the girl studied the reading nook where the General's spirit happened to hover. "I sent my friends away for the evening. I just can't bear it… You saw Dominia, didn't you?"

Theodore nodded, his face full of uncharacteristic tension. "A few days ago, but I saw her."

"I wasn't supposed to, but I did… I thought Daddy would be mad, but we got to talking, instead. Theo—Theo, did you know Cassandra was my mother?"

Shock, pure and clear as the ringing of any bell, reverberated through Theodore's features before it faded to anxiety based on the weight of his conversation with the General. "No. Dominia told me only after—the kidnapping."

"So you didn't know…" Relief visible in her blue eyes, Lavinia caught Theodore's hands in hers and frowned in contemplation. "I don't think anybody knew except Daddy and Lambie and Ninny. It was Ninny, she…she was sore at Cassandra for lying to her. But now she—" Her lips trembled, a look that shot the General through the heart. "You don't think Daddy means to kill her, does he?"

"I won't let him! He's been out of *hand* lately, that man."

"You can't say that about Daddy." Even now, Lavinia's voice hushed with concern. Theodore, glancing around, guided her to sit upon the edge of the bed. There, he held her delicate artificial hands in his doting, oblivious ones. It was only beside Lavinia in this way that the General recognized the slight dishevelment of his otherwise vainly kept hair and clothes; and she certainly had never seen him defy, or imply he intended to defy, the Hierophant's will. Yet, this he did when he leaned in.

"He's *just a martyr*, Lavinia. Just like you and me. Not some alien sent by God! I can't even begin to tell you all the things that have happened to me, all the things I've learned. But…" He lifted his hands out of hers to move them at a rapid clip, and the General recognized the sign language in an instant; it was that same she and Lazarus had used on their first meeting. Elsinore alone was home to quite a few deaf human slaves punished for gossip, theft, or eavesdropping. Some martyrs even had all their slaves mutilated from the start. Dominia never thought that was right: privacy was the price you paid when your commodity could speak and hear. But the price was compounded, because Lavinia had learned the silent language of these unlucky slaves, and Theodore, if he had not learned it in school, would have no doubt learned it just to speak to her in private. Assuming she didn't pressure him into it, desperate for a friend who wasn't a paid servant liable to run off to her real boss at the first whiff of thought crime.

I've seen some things you wouldn't believe, bunny. Dominia tried not to gag at the private choice of sign to avoid the cumbersome spelling of "Lavinia." She focused on his words. *And I've experienced crazy things, but the long and short of it is that Father tried to* kill *me!*

Once the shock wore from her face, the girl signed, *If that's true, why are you still alive?* A fair enough question, especially of Theodore, who audibly stammered in annoyance before going on in silence.

It's—complicated. It seemed like it was a half-hearted attempt. He also "playfully" excommunicated me, but I haven't heard him mention it since we got back here. I think he's just hoping I'll think I was crazy.

But when was this, Lavinia continued to press. *Before you got kidnapped?*

After, he let slip, and he and Dominia winced in time. *Like I signed, it's complicated.*

That's not possible, though. After you were kidnapped, Daddy was already here at home. Matter of fact, he hasn't been away in months! How could he have threatened you?

I don't think it's safe to explain, Theodore signed, much to Lavinia's exasperation. In that moment, the General sympathized with her more fully than ever. Dominia had, herself, been confounded left and right by constant refusals to enlighten her. Even Miki Soto seemed to have known more than she. Now, she could not help but think her enforced ignorance was a kind of karmic retribution orchestrated for her behavior toward Lavinia. And, of course, Cassandra.

Pained, the General looked away—and her keen senses, unhampered by material walls, detected the figure of Cicero looming down the distant hall.

What to do? She could not interrupt them, not as Lavinia signed, *If it's unsafe, if he's planning something against you, you should flee!*

For once in his life finding some bravery, the (former) Governor of the United Front expressed, *But I came back for you. I couldn't leave you alone here, because I—I love you, Lavinia.*

Awe passed over the girl's face in a tender crimson wave, and the General felt terrible guilt. As if it wasn't bad enough being voyeuristic party to a private moment the princess had so long awaited! Dominia had to find a way to break it up before—Lamb forbid—Cicero did. Now they embraced, and it was as sweet as it was ill-timed. Violent panic rose over the specter. She tried to sweep a vase of white tulips from a nearby table like some horror movie ghost only to find her powers to interact with the material world were limited. Perhaps nonexistent. What could she do? How could she alert them?

Another knock answered her prayers and startled even her, for she had not seen this body move through space toward Lavinia's chamber. Both would-be lovers tensed in cunicular anxiety before the princess stood to straighten her dress. Amid the rustle of fabric, Theodore tiptoed in the direction of her bathroom. "Come in," she called when he was well out of sight, and the door opened to reveal—praise him!—none other than the Lamb. The ram-horned man assessed his daughter with the sort of bland expression he'd worn while remonstrating a far younger Dominia for things about which he had no personal concern, but which he knew were hot buttons for the Ciceros.

"Hello, Livvy." His eyes trailed not in the direction of the bathroom but in the very deliberate direction of Dominia's spiritual body. As his head turned back toward that bathroom to say, "Hello, Theodore," the General saw, as if in double exposure, a second jaw and mouth upon the Lamb that ran in sluggish time with the first. A spectral jaw that said, *"Hello, Dominia,"* before catching up to merge again with its partner.

While Theodore leaned into sight from the bathroom, the Lamb told Lavinia, "Just thought I'd come chat with you before Cicero fetches you for dress rehearsal…your Father will meet you there."

The General drew the Lamb's split attention toward her spirit once more. *"Was it the horns that kept me from seeing you through the wall?"*

"No end to their utility," said his second mouth.

Meanwhile, Theodore shared an anxious glance with Lavinia. "Is Cicero already here?"

The Lamb said, "In about ninety seconds."

Face rapt with horror, Lavinia looked at the Governor and, then, at her closet. "Get in there," she said, not just leading him into the walk-in space—more like a hallway used to store clothes—but cramming him, with those too-powerful arms, into a mess of chiffon and silk and lace hanging from the left set of shelves. "Stay quiet, Theo. Oh! I'm sorry. Leave when they're gone. I'll see you at the performance, at least, won't I?"

"Of course! I wouldn't miss it."

The girl's face glowed. Had Dominia ever known young love like that? She feared hers was a jaded brand before she'd even been kissed. Acute gratitude infused her body to know Lavinia was not so scarred. *"Will you keep her safe?"* The disembodied General asked this of the Lamb, whose physical eyes again traced over her spectral form before focusing on Lavinia's bookshelves.

"Nobody is safe until you've killed your Father."

"Why are you helping me," she pressed. His gaze glazed off into infinity.

"I hate to see you upset, Lavinia," said the Lamb aloud. "Your Father can be obsessive to the point of destruction…and so can Cicero. I know because he's been that way with me my whole life. We're special, you and I—in different ways. And if he can't use what's special, then he doesn't want to know it exists."

"I thought you loved Daddy," said the sheepish girl. The Lamb smiled.

"Of course I do. But that's the hard part of loving an evil person."

"What's that?"

"Figuring out what to do when you realize that all along, you've been good."

Cicero knocked upon the door and, much as Dominia had with René, did not tarry for answer from within. Rather, he opened it immediately, chiming, "Time for the theater, my pet! Are you ready for the final dress rehearsal? I simply cannot wait."

With the tensest smile the General had ever seen her wear, Lavinia offered her hand. "At last, my servant has arrived with my royal litter. Let us hence!" With a wave of her free hand, the girl seemed as though to laugh, but the sound rang hollow. Cicero, too self-absorbed to note his little doll had feelings, simply smiled at the Lamb and played along with her.

Was Lavinia won? It was difficult to know, but Theodore's position seemed certain. Dominia watched with relief as he crept into the vacated room, mopped his brow, and exited once he was sure the trio had left. Her friends had indeed come here of their free will, and Theodore had been a convenient means and reason by which to do that. She thought of the *tanques* that had brought them in and could not help but wonder how deep the operation went. Had they thrown the Battle for Jerusalem? No wonder they didn't tell her what they planned, if that was the case. She never would have agreed to it, ever. Call it stupid pride.

Still—what a relief to know the General still had an army behind her. A small one, and described as "ragtag" by only the kindest, gentlest critics…but, an army. She had to consider—had to hope—they had something planned for this occasion.

In the castle tearooms, the General traveled cell to cell and confirmed the presence of her friends. She confirmed, too, that Basil had been given his own cell. This meant it was possible her Father did not realize the dog and the magician were bodily separated. (She tried not to distract herself with visions of the Hierophant mistakenly lecturing a border collie as though it were his nemesis, but she did need to laugh at *something*.) Lazarus and Farhad were still well and alive, and truly, Gethsemane was nowhere to be found.

Perhaps Dominia was better off investigating elsewhere—like the stage meant for the ill-fated play, with its storm-bringing rockets and its vast orchestra pit. The Elizabethan open theater, off on the southern side of Elsinore, rested upon the artificial isthmus of a glorious, darkly wooded boardwalk thrusting out amid the cold Baltic Sea. The stage itself was separated from the audience by a trough of water allowed to lap through for a bit of scenic interest; but aside from that, once one entered the confines of the reception area, the open-air theater's only relationship with the ocean was the view through its lobby windows. How she longed to see it from above! But it was as she contemplated flying off to admire it that she finally felt something, anything: her Father's brisk pats against her earthly cheek as he said, "Dominia? Dominia, my girl, have you even been listening to me at all? Are you there, Dominia?"

"Not really." Her response was automatic. In the nauseating blink of an eye, she found herself held "upright." Blood flowed into her legs and, praise the Lady, she remained unable to feel anything of substance. "I guess my thoughts have been elsewhere."

"I would encourage mindfulness, given your circumstances. These are the final hours you will have this leg. You ought to cherish them."

"Not like I can do anything with it, can I? It's already dead."

"I suppose, if that's the way you insist on looking at things. But a more optimistic mind-set would go a long way. What is death but the opportunity for rebirth? You know that as well as all martyrs. When this is done, and you are unburdened by your guilt, you will have a new, pure life stretching ahead. Won't it be a relief!"

Nothing he gave her would ever be relief. She would accept no gifts from him if they both somehow survived. All he gave was evil—poisonous. He had existed at least four thousand years and in that time managed to, with varying degrees of control, undo two iterations of Earth. There had to be some way to stop him or his duplicate from destroying another.

Muddled though her thoughts were, it seemed to the General that the best way to stop him was to stop Cicero's transmigration. But how? From her position, how?

Her friends. She would have to rely on them. Had to hope against hope that somehow, improbably, something would go so right that it didn't matter how wrong everything else was. But how difficult it was to be so helpless! Helplessness was a plague on the senses, the psyche. Its cloak whipped her back to that awful instant of Cassandra's death; it made her feel as she had when, a little girl, she awoke to find her family on the verge of ending. There was nothing worse than helplessness. If it was true that the best ending to all of this would leave her alive with her wife, then, by the Lady, the General would never let either one of them feel helpless again. She would do anything in her power—everything!—to stop that from happening. For three centuries, she had been beholden to her Father's every whim. She had been his slave. Literally, his Bitch.

She would never let that happen again. No matter what it took.

More uncountable hours passed, lurching ever closer to that fatal one. The ceremony of her alleged penitence might have been smaller than the *hieros gamos* of Miki's ascendance, but it still managed to be, in every way, infinitely more pretentious. That was the way the Hierophant's ceremonies were. Some people found martyr religious ceremonies to be of exceeding beauty, as much as any Catholic Mass from which they derived nine tenths of their symbolism and habits. Dominia, however, never found them anything but stuffy. If God was anywhere, it was as far away from this bunch of pricks as possible.

Although, in all fairness, the General was so desperate for a change of state that her heart was consumed by joy when Cicero and his priests, accompanied by the silent Lamb, entered the chapel in such flurry of movement that the doors seemed to have burst. The gaggle of godly men spoke loudly about their preparations, as if she were just another decoration.

"Let's have a dry run, if you all will indulge me." El Sacerdote strode past Dominia without sparing her so much as a glance. He deposited his sacramentary upon the altar and called, "Positions, lads, our imaginary *Introitus* is ending."

Struggling as she was to see through her own eyes, the General had to squint and do some creative reconstruction of the scene to recognize the objects held by the priests. They were not merely censers and books: one was a small dagger made of, or plated with, gold, and one was a bastard sword whose hilt had been encrusted with jewels.

"Now, after our *Introitus*, I intend for us to open with the *Confiteor*; then, Deacon Greholda, if you would read from the Gospel of the Lamb…"

But she, thinking of these weapons—in particular that largest weapon, which consumed her attention now as it would later her leg—she could not focus on Cicero's words. Not until the priest holding the sword got out of her way and allowed her to make eye contact with the Lamb; not until she was able to make out, amid all the underwater audio effects of her near-bursting eardrums, the word "Lazarus."

At that, the Lamb stepped up to accept the dagger from the priest. There was Cicero in her vision again, miming the space on the floor before the Lamb as if Lazarus knelt for the slaughter. Cicero, still senselessly, ceaselessly talking, strode to take the sword from his compatriot, then turned to demonstrate (in slow motion, with no physical contact) how he would hack off the General's leg, right there, above (below) her knee. There were distant words to the effect that it would take several blows, so, in the case of excessive thrashing, her bindings would need to remain until the ceremony was over—but it would be in poor taste if the penitent was also electrocuted as consequence of her natural struggles, not to mention of no small consequence to the sword's bearer. Therefore, the electrical component of her bindings would be deactivated before the ceremony.

"I hope you will not let us down, dear sister," said Cicero, at last condescending to address her.

She did not condescend to respond. She just made hard eye contact with the Lamb, and chose to pray to him by means of his favorite form of prayer: not thinking at all. Instead, she took it on faith that he was as supportive of her as he had pretended to be all these years.

The Lamb did not look away, nor did he make any move to comfort her, nor give any indication she should expect comfort. All the same, she took strange comfort in his gaze, and allowed this comfort to carry her through to the start of the ceremony. The priests returned in their vestments to open the doors and welcome those few lucky, noble parishioners given the honor of seeing firsthand Dominia's act of penance. Anywhere from one to five at a time, martyrs made their slow ways in, openly gawking at the nine-day-rank and tortured General. After they averted their eyes from the inevitable glance at her face, they'd cross themselves and genuflect before their entrance into a pew from which they strove to stare at the victim without further eye contact.

Let them look. She didn't want them to be completely disappointed. Not after all the good money they paid and time they'd wasted and asses they'd kissed to get them to this moment, invited here. At least they would have the pleasure of seeing her strung up, if they weren't going to witness an amputation.

Hopefully. Hopefully. God, willing. Magician, kind. It was already an encouraging development to hear that her bindings would be grounded. She nursed that sign the way she nursed images of Cassandra. When it was time for the long, drawn-out ceremony to begin, and perfumes of frankincense announced the procession of priests and prisoners— Lazarus, Farhad, and, amusingly, Basil—she was emboldened to see them. Shackles and doom be damned. Her friends were there with her, before these insufferable bastards. Alongside them, she was invulnerable.

And then, to bolster that hope—here came René, looking as shifty as he ever had. Late—disrespectfully and embarrassingly late—wearing Dominia's jacket, scurrying in after the procession. The doors closed as he snatched a seat in the back with a genuflection so half-assed that the laughter of the General interrupted the *Introitus* and led to a lot of uncomfortable coughing and shuffling among the parishioners. This was visibly echoed by the aggravated thrash of Cicero's black eye on his otherwise stoic march to the altar. The cyborgan whipped to Dominia, then to the back of its owner's head in search of the disruption's source, before El Sacerdote got it under control.

She wasn't sure what her alleged brother had expected from her. True penitence? Perhaps the prior Dominia had shown such, and the Hierophant had assured Cicero that this would be the case—but this Dominia was through with every bit of the sorry institution that was the Holy Martyr Church. How annoying that the final hour of her life should involve her in a religious ceremony!

Annoyed as she was at the tail of the pompous introduction, the General felt her teeth might snap in her skull at the force of her grimace. In the hands of one of the priests was not the aspergillum usually used to contain holy water but the globus flask used by Lazarus to collect and transport the waters of the Ergosphere. This, they wasted in sprinkling upon perfectly healthy martyrs, taking it up and down the aisles as was generally done during Easter Mass with so-called holy water. You could get that shit out of wells so long as you had a priest around. To get the Lady's water, you had to go to a specific well—or a geyser, she supposed it was now—and bring the stuff back to Earth. Pouring it on these tools! It made her chest hurt even with the deity's blessed pain removal.

Cicero, meanwhile, opened with that rambling confessional prayer he had threatened to use for the occasion, delivered while standing before Dominia so as to stare at her while he rattled off the long list of sins called by name in the longer and more Hierophant-favored variant of the Latin prayer. The worst, most tedious one, in which parishioners agreed with the priest that thrice, through their faults, they had "*peccavi per superbiam in multa mea mala iniqua et pessima cogitatione, locutione, pollutione, sugestione, delectatione, consensu, verbo et opere, in periurio, in adulterio, in sacrilegio, omicidio, furtu, falso testimonio, peccavi visu, auditu, gustu, odoratu et tactu, et moribus, vitiis meis malis.*"

Blahdiam blahdione blahdoio blahdavis. Modern Mephitolian was identical to Latin in many respects save for a lot of German roots and loanwords, yet in this context the stuff was somehow still dry enough to put her to sleep.

"Sin rots the relationship between the soul and the Lord," Cicero surmised, the prayer having been completed once the priest carrying the stolen waters halted outside the General's periphery. "One need look no further than my eye—the eye of your own humble servant of God—to see its effects upon the world. Its effects upon the self, and the selves of one's fellow man! Dominia's sin was what took my eye from me, children: but the Lord, in seeing her penance and my suffering, saw fit to provide us with the circumstances for a miracle."

Now she understood why the Holy Father's DIOX-I, from his time as Cicero, was undetectable. It was because he had no DIOX-I. Both his eyes were perfectly real. She understood so well—and was, for her part, so fatigued by horrible tortures and emotional revelations—that she was not the least bit shocked or surprised (as were those many screaming parishioners) when the black DIOX-I of the priest faded into a deactivated state and was, by his own hand, yanked out of its cavern with a scream of victorious agony. After hurling away the bloodied cyborgan, the half-blind priest wrenched the waters from the hands of his lesser assistant. Before the worshipers, Cicero tilted back his head to waste the remainder of the Lady's water on the restoration of his own eye, rather than the healing of the lame or the curing of disease.

What a surprise. Even less surprising was how, after demonstrating his new, healthy eye to the roaring martyrs who abandoned horror and shouted their praise for the Lord, he resumed his pedantic sermon on the subject of sin as if he had not just committed the most egregious one Dominia could name.

She had sinned against no one this past year, save those people she had been forced to kill in righting her Father's wrongs. Her sinning—her conscious, intentional sinning, at least—had ended with Cassandra's death. Though Cicero and her Father loved to pretend they were arbiters of sin, Dominia had learned only she could tell herself what was a sin and what was not. A sin was a crime one committed, ultimately, against oneself. It was not one's neighbor one truly hurt.

Not the families of the murdered or the victims of rape. Not even God was hurt by one's sin. Rather—each sin, no matter how ignoble the soul, piled against the spirit of the sinner until it boiled out of the body and took the form of physical recompense. Because that was what it took for the truly depraved sinners to cease their sin. It took arrest, or execution, or, in Dominia's case, the loss of the one thing that ever gave them any scrap of joy.

René's face appeared intermittently as he leaned from time to time around the oversize hat of the woman before him. Dominia thought of his summation that happiness was a field—and then, she was forced to wonder whether Cassandra had ever really given her any joy. Was joy but a chemical reaction? A state temporary as any other? Was the entropic world too cruel a place to sustain the feeling long-term?

She didn't believe it. Couldn't believe it. Happiness was possible. Cassandra was possible. The end to all of this was possible. Across Elsinore, Lavinia recited lines that drew them ever-closer to the boring play's surreptitiously deadly climax—yet such a thought arose with relief in the General. The end to all this lingered so close as to be surreal. Once more, she fell out of the body that she had not felt since the Lady's visit one day prior. Once more, she observed herself from outside. She stood just within the shut chapel doors while, across the room, the chanting priests arranged their prisoners. Here was Cicero, accepting the sword. There was Lazarus, forced to kneel before the Lamb as El Sacerdote called to his worshipers, "This moment is the moment for which all our ceremonies have been mere preparation. The blood of the Lamb, mere metaphor for the forgiveness of the Lord, is the means by which we wash away the sins of this world—but with the Holy Father's guidance, the blood of Lazarus is the way we higher men will open ourselves to the next." Here was the Lamb, being handed the knife. That was Cicero, brandishing the sword. The bite of its metal edge should have chilled Dominia's physical thigh.

"Sin is a dead limb that weighs us down," summarized the maggot to her Father's botfly.

Unwilling to wait a second longer, cagey René Ichigawa stumbled up from his aisle seat with Dominia's gun in his hand. How funny.

Poet, professor, political dissident: ultimately, history would mark René as an assassin. Too soon for anyone to notice and too far from anyone who could stop him, he tripped to the exact spot where stood the General's phantom and clumsily fired her old weapon at the second Cicero said, "Luckily for you, my sister: belief is a sword."

In their analysis of what happened that night in Kronborg's chapel, those brooding historians would be forced to come to one conclusion: the murder of the Lamb and the freeing of the General Dominia di Mephitoli (therefore all the events of the night that led to her permanent disappearance, the death of the Hierophant, and the final destruction of the Holy Family's vile institution), was initiated by one highly improbable bullet trajectory, and one very coincidental power outage. The rest was a mess of conspiracy, paranoia, and implications that were downright magical.

Certain basic facts were agreed upon. The Lamb, who had noted sway over probabilistic outcomes, saw the shot being fired—and, more importantly, had seen it was fired at Cicero. He, along with two other priests, moved to cover his brother; only he was fast enough to get between El Sacerdote and the would-be assassin. Not that he needed to, or should have. René's bullet—the single bullet remaining in the gun returned to the General by means the textbooks could not comprehend—ricocheted off one of the metal horns of the Lamb, snapped the tether hanging the General from her crucifix, then ricocheted once more—this time, off the metal cap of the crucifix, which altered the trajectory enough to allow the projectile to bury itself in the Lamb's brain.

It was also a fact—mere coincidence, most impressed—that Kronborg Castle's power died along with the Lamb. Elsewhere in those frigid walls, security PCs lost their connection to the prisoner's cuffs, and the remote-controlled devices, already grounded, sagged open around the wrists of the prisoner, Dominia di Mepitholi.

The speed with which all those events occurred could not be communicated by any historian, no matter their effort. Women screamed; the General fell; Cicero uttered for the first time in two thousand years a noise that Dominia's spirit interpreted as a cry of horror the instant before impact with the cold tile floor returned her to her flesh.

"My brother," El Sacerdote screamed as worshipers poured through the doors. "My brother, oh, Elijah! No, no, oh—that lying bastard!"

Her leg was beyond saving; though, perhaps thanks to the Lady's water across the floor, or her first chance to be upright in over a week, the General felt better than she had in days—even if her heart ached to see the death of a Family member who had treated her with a decency not found in any iteration of Cicero.

There was no time to mourn. The rattle of chains muted the sounds of chaos as Lazarus bent over her, hastily seeking to keep her awake and slip her hands from the parted cuffs.

"You'll be okay," swore the mystic, not able to move his hands within a particularly wide range, but able to touch her face well enough. "You've got it from here, kiddo."

There was no time to ask. Not even time to cry out. Her friend's face changed; his body slumped. Cicero withdrew the sword he'd plunged into Lazarus's back and fluid streamed after it. Not blood. Not that good, sacred blood that saved so many souls, human and martyr alike. No: in a strange miracle she could not then explain, her friend's fatal wound wept water.

Without giving in to amazement or redemption or the urge to make some gloating speech, Cicero nudged the mystic aside. The priest plunged the blade between Dominia's ribs.

Steel pierced her heart.

XIV

Anamnesis

For several seconds, the General could not place the nature of the silence where she stood. It was not the silence of the Ergosphere, nor of any other thing she recognized. Why, she could not even well remember where she had just been. She only knew that, like a sleepwalker on waking, she found herself upright, on two good legs, with darkness all around—except a disembodied row of ghostly faces that floated before her.

She could not recognize the silence until a white moth flitted past her eye. With its help, she pieced together where her spirit stood: visible in this moment of her death in what was, truly, a miracle. Upon the Elizabethan stage, the manifestation of Dominia turned to see Lavinia. Too astonished to pretend she gave a fig for the show she was in, the princess stumbled forward a step.

"Ninny," she whispered, while the Hierophant pressed, "Say your line."

As quickly as she had appeared in the spotlight, the General disappeared into the more familiar silence of the Void and left in her place the seventh avatar of the Lady, who raked Her steely gaze across the crowd. This information did not come to Dominia by any brand of firsthand sensory experience, for she was not there to see the Lady's body flicker into her empty place. Rather, she felt the abstract knowledge as if by some organ she could not place. She could hardly place herself! Again, again, again, she was consumed by the piecing of the sword through her flesh and against the muscle of her heart. Again, again, again. As if that was all she'd ever been: pain, burning pain. And failure. The darkness around her replayed it with detail so cruel that the nothing that was once Dominia was forced to remember that moment again, the way memory cycled through the tail end of a terrifying tahgmahr even when one was clearly awake, safe, in bed. Lazarus's face, then Cicero's. Then, the point of the blade. As bad a dream as any.

Dominia had suffered many tahgmahrs as a girl, waking often to the sound of her own screams. While she remained a child, on the instances the Lamb was home for these terrors he would arrive to comfort her almost before she was awake—but as a teenager, or during his many transcontinental trips with Cicero, she had been forced to learn how to rationalize, on waking in a cold sweat, why the images that caused her to shake were false, and now absent. Then, as now, she felt deeply alone; but then, as now, that feeling resolved itself into her own sense of space and bodily security. Dreams of being kidnapped from her parents and murdered by the Hierophant resolved into the truer, parallel reality; dreams of her own failure and murder by Cicero resolved into much the same. To have died, she needed to have been alive. And to observe her own death after the fact, she had to have some basis from which to do it. Therefore, she could not be dead in an eternal sense. Therefore, even after death, her soul was swiftly derived from the darkness of the Void and the trembling of her trauma.

There was now a certain comfort in the Ergosphere's dark night. The absence that it marked was not the absence of Dominia. Thanks to experience during her life using the blood of Lazarus, any postmortem confusion about her Self had been brief as she'd been promised. She perceived her thoughtbody as she always had—and, though she stood in the dark with no so-called black sun of Earth's stolen light hanging above to illuminate her path, she did not feel at any more risk of disappearance than she might have in reality. Yet there were still risks. Still traps. And the simplest trap of all was walking anywhere.

If she did not move, time would not pass. This, she knew as well as she knew that, on Earth, she was dying. Should she return to it, that body, she could not imagine what would happen. Her high-frequency consciousness floating around in wave form now would collapse into particle form on entering the vicinity of her brain's fading electromagnetic field, and then, what? How would she perceive it? Was it possible to perceive at all if one's eventual fate was simply to fade into the dirt like the rest of matter? Better, was a return to such a dying body even physically possible? Was the brain's electromagnetic field what kept her consciousness in place?

Was her awareness—particularly her continued awareness now, in this place, in this moment—not, in and of itself, evidence of her permanent security?

"There is no such thing as death," answered Saint Valentinian, behind her. Yet if she looked, she knew she would not see him. On he spoke. "Not from an eternal perspective. There is only the illusion of death. If you are aware enough to see that death is an illusion, you can never really die; and if you were never aware enough to see that death was an illusion, you were never really alive. Those unconscious individuals who have not crafted souls, whether by blood of Lazarus or any other means, cannot experience death in a way that matters."

"That doesn't make it right." Dominia closed her eye as if to shut out the notion. "Every death matters. I've caused more deaths firsthand than anyone I've known or read about. That matters."

"Death is more a dream than this dream-space."

"Then something—someone—needs to wake those people from the tahgmahrs of their deaths."

"Will you?"

Dominia opened her good eye, and the dark night of the Ergosphere lit with crisscrossing beams of information. To her death-opened mind, they represented every possible arrangement of physical information— in every color, too. Even colors the General had never seen before. As she touched a cerulean thread, the information represented once more changed. Now, to a vast collection of lights. She found she could, in a delirious way that she could not retain and yet did in a way beyond knowing, reach into these lights and absorb their content: books, albums, films, private journals, tattoos, blueprints, legal documents. The entire creative capacity of Earth represented in a swarm of potentiality. So many lights filled the darkness that they appeared less a collection of individual orbs and more a vast mist of will-o-wisps stretching through the Void.

"There is an infinite variety of ways to view the information of eternity," the magician told her. The lights refolded themselves (for that was the only verb Dominia could use to describe a process so beyond description) and became a series of objects resembling crystals, all of them in some way interlocked with their neighbors. These revealed tangible data about every physical object, imparted to the General's consciousness in a brush. For example, she laid her hand on Kronborg, and knew then not just the history of the building represented, but the history of all the pieces of wood and stone that built the building, and the history of their trees and quarries, and the genetic lineage of the seeds and sediment they once were, stretching far, far back into the dawn of time. All the builders who were involved in its making, all the coins that financed it and whence they came—

"This is incredible." Dominia marveled, pulling her hand away, feeling herself falling too deeply into a well of information she sensed was of limitless length. Traveling far enough into any one single jewel could reveal the entire array. "Valentinian…is this God?"

"I don't know how to answer that, other than to say, 'If you can describe it with words—even True Words—it's probably not God.' People are always looking for God outside themselves. But 'God' is a word invented by Man, to distinguish a phenomenon Man needed distinguishing. Everybody has a different vision of what it means. Is consciousness God?"

The crystals around her collapsed into dust, and she saw fewer lights scattered about, but still a great many: each of infinite brightness, arranged in the dark like blinding stars. As she turned her head to find the one that she thought to glow the brightest, the General marveled to find it emanated from within her.

"I don't think the question is one of God's substance," said Valentinian. "Even from this height, God is an unknowable force of nature by definition. At least, by my definition. What's your definition of God, Dominia?"

Hearing her own name in that place sent a palpable ripple through whatever substance could be said to form her body; the external reminder firmed her spirit as once it had when she was lost. She closed her eye and said, "I don't know. Somebody like you, I guess."

"Woah. Thanks, buddy, but I have to worry about your standards."

Chuckling, Dominia said, "I mean, you're versed in all of this. You maybe even are responsible for this, on some level. It's hard to tell with you."

When she opened her eye and found him standing there, she expected it, and was not the least bothered. "*Are* you responsible for this, Valentinian?"

"Sort of. Does it matter?"

"I guess not." Exhaling in a breath that was only theoretically necessary, the General asked, "Is this it, then?" She met Valentinian's eyes. "Is it over? Am I dead?"

"With that attitude."

"What can I do?"

"Anything other than 'nothing' is a good start. One advantage you've given yourself is taking zero steps. You remain suspended at the instant when death is imminent—when Cicero's sword pierced your heart. Consciousness always leaves the body when the brain knows death is a foregone conclusion, and it perceives its flight in different ways depending on the persona's level of awareness for these matters. For some people who aren't going to experience their own death, or can't, it engages in a sleight of hand to tuck them off to bed in a way they won't mind so as to use the light of their consciousness again next time around. But for most, the veil tears in one way or another, and we experience the truth."

"What about those people who don't have a conscious light?" She thought, as she asked, of Cassandra. "Those who don't even have souls to be bound to the Very Low Frequencies? Do they just disappear?" She imagined a confused soul taking a step beyond the moment of their death and leaving themselves irrevocably stranded in the mists of the Void, but then realized these soulless individuals had not even vessels with which to step.

The magician, unconcerned, emphasized, "You can perceive this information *any way* you want."

Frowning, Dominia contemplated death. Throughout the course of her life, the General had carefully venerated the dead. The dead she made, and the dead she knew. She lost soldiers to the battlefield, friends to depression, and, as her human family aged, all artifacts of her humanity to Chronos. She had not been a praying woman until her final year, but she had been a respectful woman, and had kept in her mind a long list of names that the DIOX-I had offered to digitize for her while in her possession. This, perhaps, was what she expected to see when the information of the black hole resolved itself into a form representing the dead: some list, or the wide variety of floating names awash in the ocean of her dream about the Lady.

But that had been a nebulous pool of information that included potential deaths. It was more abstract than that which she sought now. The organization of the black hole's information into the dead of *her* world, from *her* iteration of *her* reality, was a different and more specific request that yielded a different, far more startling result. Nothing but the Void, and the magician, standing before her as he had.

"Where did the information go?" she asked, even as she began to understand.

"Did you ever ask yourself what dark energy is? That force that hastens the expansion of the universe; that energy with a proposed scalar field called 'quintessence'—it changes over time and is attractive or repulsive, depending on the ratio of its potential energy to its kinetic energy."

Reaching into the darkness of that place's night, the General marveled as he said, "The information stored in the black hole is only an abstraction of what we would consider physical objects. Unsouled people, for purposes of the Ergosphere's categorization, are the same. The information and energy of these unilluminated beings cannot be physically destroyed any more than it can be *abstractly* destroyed. It only seems to be destroyed. In reality, it has been stored."

"In the cloud," observed the General wryly, which made the magician laugh. "Dark energy is really…"

"There are a lot of beings with psychic substance in the universe, and a lot of things that seem to die or get destroyed—including inorganic and non-sentient beings or objects. One of the reasons quintessence changes over time."

"'This quintessence of dust'?"

"Science, Shakespeare, and metaphysics have been involved in a torrid love triangle since long before Willie picked up *The Triumphal Chariot of Antimony* in 1604 CE and started going even heavier on the alchemy references."

"But how can anybody distinguish one member of the dead from the other in a format like this?"

With the giggle of a goofy teenager, the magician shrugged. "I know, right? It's not only like finding a needle in a haystack: it's like finding a needle in a haystack that's been covered in tar, and the needles and the haystack are also tar, and you might become tar if you spend too much time monkeying in it."

"Okay—so what do I *do*?"

"Try praying," said the man, winking again into nonexistence to leave the General, as usual, annoyed and alone. Of course, it was when the magician was at his most annoying that he was usually imparting a very important truth. This somehow made it all the more annoying.

But, it did make sense. When she was lost in the Void, her form exchanged for that of a tiger, the prayers of Miki led her back to herself. They reached her and she heard them—and, just now, when Valentinian used her name, the General felt a great many degrees more substantial. Was it not the desire of the dead, surely, to be remembered? Honored? Called out and spoken to? No wonder so many cultures practiced careful ancestor veneration. Even if, in the course of the physical universe, the expanding collection of unsouled personas separated from Earth were unable to hear the prayers of the living, in the black hole they would know.

What strange complications were inspired by eternity; in what strange circles it forced the mind to turn! But it made perfect sense to her now. Still in place, the General knelt, and bowed her head until it touched whatever could be said to form the ground. She had asked Farhad to teach her the proper posture for the prostration that Muslims called *sujud* one night when she could not sleep. After observing it in the quarter of the encampment's men who practiced the faith, she found the position to be the only way for her to approach the godhead.

Now, in the hour of her death, she was glad she learned it. Here she was, less than nothing, asking for the world. Upon sorting her disordered head for prayers, she selected her long since memorized one for the dead on behalf of Saint Valentinian. There were several other she knew, actually, including one adapted from an old Catholic prayer for souls in purgatory, but they were too short.

Though the words to that Catholic one finally made sense to her! Purgatory made sense to her, now that she found herself here. And how *many* souls there were in purgatory—how many souls there *must* have been in purgatory! She remembered Dante's travel through it guided by Virgil. Did the writer imagine the scale of the place? A place that, by definition, had to encompass the righteous pagans of tens of thousands of years' worth of good people who, through lack of opportunity or lack of interest, did not cultivate their soul while on Earth? And what of hell, the VLF bands of the Void? There had been *so many souls*, such a great many. Who would pray for them all? Which of them, the lost, had hope to find themselves in this world where consciousness forever waxed and waned, where humanity eternally suppressed itself in the form of martyrdom or something—anything—else?

This notion struck Dominia so severely that she found she could not complete her third simple prayer, which had been generically said for all the souls of the dead. But now…well, now. After considering the vastness of the operation before her, and her position frozen on the cusp of death, the General said to herself: It's a good thing I tried to memorize all those names.

She also said to herself: If I don't have names, I have faces, and occasions.

And she also said to herself: I think I'm going to feel like I've been here forever.

But she also said to herself: All things can be accomplished by doing one portion at a time.

So, one portion at a time, one prayer at a time, one name at a time, the General Dominia di Mephitoli, former Governess of the United Front and the notorious Bitch of Europa, began to beg the forgiveness and freedom of the dead.

There were so many names. If she had given the DIOX-I permission to catalog them for her, its software would have crashed. The General had fought a thousand battles (okay, more like eight hundred, seven hundred and ninety-five…she'd rounded up) and usually killed no fewer than fifty men, herself. That was a staggering number of dead, and a staggering number of names; and she wasn't sure that, forced to recount the list on Earth, she would have been able to remember them all. Indeed, as she herself had just considered, many names had been irretrievable on Earth due to time or severe destruction of dog tags and facial features—or, in some very awful cases, the mass destructions of cities and/or encamped individuals. But, in the Void, as she repeated the same short prayer with each iteration single-mindedly devoted to one person (often more than once per person, for she could never pray enough), the names blossomed without the least effort on memory's part.

It was the other way around. Effort was required not to produce but to endure the memories arising with each name. Though on Earth thoughts of killing haunted her with increasing concern until her conversion to decency, here, memories of each death came upon her like an accusation made by the dead—or made by her against herself on their mute behalf. The more innocent the person, the more painful the memory. Working back from the officers killed on their escape from New Elsinore and the martyrs she'd allowed to die in the dim sum restaurant, she wasn't off to a great start. By the time she got back to Tobias Akachi, she heard his chiding.

"Now you feel bad about killing me, eh? You did not seem to feel bad about it at the time. Nor did you feel bad about it at all during the last year of your life. Not until now, this very moment. You expect me to forgive you?"

Feeling obligated to respond as though he were really there before she continued on to her next prayer, she licked her lips and allotted, "Well, no."

"Then what do you expect, General?"

What did she expect. What did she expect? "I expect you'd want to be some place better than this." In the immediacy of that place, she re-experienced the surprise of seeing Akachi's big smile in the crowded market square. "Someplace that's not just miserable death, floating around in the vacuum of space with only your memories of the end."

"What do you actually want from me, General," asked the spirit, or Dominia's memory of Akachi, or something that borrowed his voice. "If it is not forgiveness that you want, why bother to feel guilt over all these deaths?"

That was a good question, in a way, although it oversimplified the emotion of guilt into an option. In the General's opinion, it was the furthest thing from. Guilt was like pain; it was not a bad thing in and of itself, but it was a sign of something wrong. Both guilt and pain seemed to thrill the masochist and antagonize the sadist. She did not dwell in guilt because she wanted to, or because she expected forgiveness. After all, what would she do with it if she had it? What would the forgiveness of her victims matter if she had yet to forgive herself?

"I guess I need help," she decided. "I'm appealing to you, Tobias, because I need help, and I know that you do, too. Neither of us liked the other in life, but it doesn't have to be that way here. Nothing matters anymore."

The spirit gave no answer. She went on, emboldened by his silence. "I don't want you to forgive me—but if you would help me pray, maybe that could help us both. You're a Christian man, right? You can help me call out the dead. People I don't know. Since you're here, you have your own guilt, too. Might make you feel better, right?"

"And you think my dead will want to hear from me any more than your dead want to hear from you?" Tobias's voice was now so clear and direct that he must have stood before her. She did not lift her head to look.

"Of course they won't want to hear from you. You did something to them that you need to pray about."

After a few seconds' silence, the dead dentist scoffed, and his footsteps echoed around the General until he found a place to kneel behind her. "If there is one thing I do not like, it is a martyr who is closer to God than I am."

The softly smiling General restrained her desire to tease him for the wording of his comment and resumed her prayers by throwing out one for the dead *tulpa*. (Not too many, though.) Name by name, falling out of the rough chronology and instead allowing them to emerge as they would in her mind, the General prayed for the souls of the dead. The lost dead, the historical dead, the influential dead. All those many martyr saints depicted in paintings, real and false. All those who had died by her Father's hand before she was ever born. But, most of all, she prayed for her dead. In the distance, their lights bloomed awake in acknowledgment. How was it she could even know so many names? They were incredible to her, these prayers pouring out at a rapid clip. The most recent ones felt just as raw as the oldest ones: those first kills on battlefields long since rendered simple farms and normal cities, as safe and happy as any others.

"It shouldn't surprise you," suggested the Lamb as she realized she'd forgotten to pray for him, although she had been responsible for his death in incidental fashion. His horns were gone—she had never seen him without that false silver halo. "It's always given me headaches, the way you worry things over in your head, again and again, even when you tell yourself you don't care about them. Of course those old wounds seem fresh, Dominia."

"Sorry," she said, not without a trace of humor. "And I'm sorry about— I'm sorry you had to die."

"I'm not," he assured her. "'Long-suffering' doesn't begin to cover my experience, being Cicero's brother. And the Hierophant's... If it mattered to me, and I wanted to live, the bullet would have missed. Actually, I had to nudge it toward me a little. Your friend is a terrible shot."

He was trying to be funny, but the good Rabbi's downright desire to die broke her heart. Who could have blamed him? Paraded around from town to town to have his throat slit every Noctisdomin…she'd want to die, too. "I'm sorry that living is such misery for you."

"'Was'—in this state, anyway. But it's all right. The next state will be better. Probably. It can't be worse. Do you want me to help you pray?"

"Could you, please? I've got a lot of ground to cover."

"Then it's a good thing," said the Lamb, kneeling beside Akachi, "that we have so much time."

He wasn't kidding. Dominia was grateful they had all eternity to shuffle through the masses of the dead. The list unfurled in all intangible directions while her mind leapt across time from one battle to another. Once, she looked over her shoulder and found more people—many more—than had announced their presence to her. Some, unrecognized, had perhaps been summoned by the ruminations of the Lamb or Akachi. These spirits also prayed for those they had known or wronged; and of those spirits, a few came forth to add to the effort. Their number grew before her eye, and the General, chilled, returned to her fervent prayers with renewed vigor. When she could not remember or did not know a name, she pictured a face, and evoked a battle, and remembered the impact of her weapon or the sound of her gun's discharge.

The way she figured, at least one hundred thousand people had been put the slaughter, directly or indirectly, by the General's hand. This did not touch the many destroyed en masse in the Black Night. Yet, this was not a fraction—not a seed!—beside that multitude of souls forming the quintessence from the beginning of linear time. Still, she needed continue; still, she prayed, though her heart despaired that the task before her was impossible. As this despair reached its peak, a hand touched her head. She looked up, and found Kahlil.

"Jeez, will you relax." He said that, perhaps, as much to himself as to her, for in this space, no spirit was yet purified of their anxious death memories. Emboldened by the sorrow in her face, the young spirit knelt beside her. "Try to look at it like this. If you save everyone in the future, then they're already saved in the past—so they're praying for you, too, forever and ever. What is that? 'Teleological' thinking?"

"Every moment," she murmured. "Every prayer, shaped to a purpose."

Yes: that notion was, somehow, very encouraging. Prayer did little perceptible good other than serving as a kind of spiritual cell phone, but it did have a way of bolstering the speaker in a time like this. In an eternal time like this, where the information making up reality went unmoved, yet the veritable army of souls behind the General grew to limitless expanse. It was a good thing that time did not exist in that place, however, and that issues of thirst and hunger did not matter: based on the time it took an individual in reality to recite the prayer on behalf of Saint Valentinian, it would have taken the General 3,472 earthly day/night cycles to complete her penance.

If she did not eat.

And did not sleep.

And did not excrete, or move, or think a thing that was not a plea that the souls of the dead be granted the eternal rest of paradise and comfort of Valentinian rather than this state of nothing. This state of suspension. Perhaps it was those great many unheard prayers of eternity that had helped the General so quickly find her soul after death, rather than her year of training in the Ergosphere. She could not be sure.

Just over nine years of prayer and penance, densely packed into a single instant. A single instant of death. The only movement the General made—which, while hypnotic, also kept her aware of her thoughtbody and maintained its integrity apart from the Void—was the movement of her waist, up and down, as she bent to the floor for each new prayer, then up again to cross herself. Then, again, back down. On Earth, even the martyr General would have collapsed from exhaustion, but there was no exhausting her now. Not here. Her legs, quite literally, became one with the base of the Void, but she did not cease for an instant her meditations save for those brief splits in which she grew aware of the overwhelming noise of the crowd, the murmur having long since grown to a persistent buzz, clamor, roar. She prayed; they prayed; in the Kingdom, their eternal selves surely also prayed.

And, as Dominia neared the beginning of her career—those long-lost nights of Lieutenant di Mephitoli, Private di Mephitoli, and all her many variations—a change overtook the Void that was, in and of itself, miraculous. Without any spatial movement on the part of the General or the passage of a single second in reality, the black circle of Earth at the edge of the Ergosphere rose as though they sat at dawn.

Or perhaps—perhaps it was not so much that, as it was that the quintessence around them evaporated. A vast army of souls chanted their prayers behind her, drops of water condensed from that bleak mist of indistinctness and fear.

Around her neck, the diamond of her wife beat back and forth: a pendulum whose sways marked another soul, another soul, another soul. Reminding Dominia each time, *I'm here, too.*

I'm always here with you.

All this continued until, so suddenly it surprised her, the General looked up, and saw all the darkness had cleared from the sky. She understood why the Void's darkness was said to be unclean even beyond its radioactive signatures, for it was filthy with the psychological toxins of all these unpurified souls. But as the place grew cleaner, so, too, did its cleanliness hasten, the prayers multiplying exponentially until a whole world of people, past, present, and future, had been derived by the connections and good wishes of those lost spirits whom the General pursued—of those *nous* who saw the labors of Dominia and were moved by her anguish for the person she had been. Those individuals had distinguished themselves from the quintessence, and the quintessence was no more, and the beauty of clear space revealed to Dominia a glorious truth. Even the darkness of the black sun had disappeared, as if the black hole returned the light it had stolen from the planet's face. There was the glory of Earth, the radiantly mossy soul of itself resting upon the edge of the Ergosphere.

"The black sun of your Father's is a fiction." She tore her eye from that great swirl of blue and green only when her periphery noted Valentinian's form. "Just like death. Here we are, suspended at the end of the planet's history: eternally frozen in this moment of destruction, when that which was once Sol of Earth ravages, in an eyeblink, its already dead infant. Then this black hole will be devoured, and that one; in other galaxy clusters, other black holes will devour other black holes. Yet I say again, the black sun is a fiction. There is no such thing as death."

"The Earth looks so new, and alive." The General's eye filled with tears to see the glory of the planetary atom hanging above her head. "Like it was just born."

Kneeling at the side unoccupied by Kahlil, the magician crossed himself and prostrated as had Dominia. "Because the moment of destruction is also the moment of creation, and it is also an eternity. Can you imagine what eternity is? What it really is? What maintains it?"

"God," she supposed.

"But what is God?"

Even now, annoyance for him crossed her face. "I asked you that."

"If you'd stop asking other people that and think about the question for a while, you might astonish yourself with the real answer."

The General dared not interrupt his prayers to press him further, and intended to resume her own: yet she realized with an uncanny feeling of relief she had but one more prayer to utter. When she tried to remove the necklace from her neck, it was with an urgent chill of panic that she found it gone. Had it fallen off, somewhere into the Void? Her head lifted to see where it dropped, and then—there.

Ah, there.

There!

"How can I deserve your prayers?" Cassandra, wan from her time in the Void, stood before her—not yet brightened by the peace of the Kingdom. "How can I deserve to live at all? To have lived, and thrown my life away…oh, I didn't understand until I saw your face. Until it was already too late. I didn't understand until that second that, as long as I was alive, I could recover from anything. That I could adapt. I didn't realize until the second it was too late that I could have hated you, and you still would have loved me, and stayed with me, and taken care of me, until I didn't hate you anymore. Or even if I hated you forever."

"That's the way it always is," said the magician sadly, "in that last second. All our errors become so clear."

"It's why I can't—I can't possibly deserve better than this." Cassandra wept, the back of her hand against her lips.

For the first time in the equivalent of nine years, the General rose. Behind her the prayers had hushed, but she'd stopped hearing them, anyway. Step by step, Dominia closed the distance between herself and the spirit of her wife.

On Earth, Basil licked her face.

"You did what you did because you wanted to hurt yourself—and me—worse than I hurt you. I'm so sorry, Cassandra."

While the body of the General di Mephitoli eased open its half-blind eyes to study the dog above it, the muted sounds of Cicero's weeping filled its ears.

"In those seconds you first appeared to me, I thought you were perfect. Your body, your face, the way you smiled, the way you held yourself—the way you looked at me. Everything about you in that second was so perfect. It's how I always think of you."

Beneath the hand of Lazarus's sprawled body lay the dagger intended for him.

"But nobody's perfect, Cassandra. I should have known that, and accepted it, instead of reacting to your imperfection like it was a crime."

The earthly body of the General relied on what was left of its muscle memory to claim the dagger. With this ceremonial weapon, it slumped toward Cicero's back.

The true body of Dominia touched Cassandra's face, so cool and soft that it was like touching the meniscus of a glass of milk. "I hurt you, then spent a lifetime trying to make up for it with the force of my love. But instead I made you the prisoner of my lies. And I have to—" Dominia fought a hiccup of tears to no avail, and her facade crumbled to trembling lips in an expression that, as ever, was mirrored in her empathetic wife. Especially as the General forced herself to say, "I have to let you go."

Dominia turned to see Benedict stood in the spot where she had prayed. She took one step to the side.

As Cicero sobbed over the body of the Lamb, the General plunged the dagger into his ribs.

"Benedict." Weeping Cassandra covered her face. "I can't be seen by you this way."

"What way?" He hurried to his lover's side and took up those hands Dominia longed to take, herself.

"At my worst. My cruelest, my stupidest."

"Honey," said Dominia, at the same time and in the same cadence as Benedict. This elicited a wry smile out of both before the man allowed the martyr to go on, "I don't think there's anybody here who hasn't been cruel or stupid at some point."

"We're all just people," said Benedict. Cassandra's lips trembled in that rapid, familiar way that ached Dominia's jaw with the urge to kiss her calm.

"But I don't deserve people," protested the woman. Dominia wiped tears from her cheek, at last drawing back her attention.

"You feel that way because I made you feel that way. And I'm so sorry, Cassandra. You deserve people. You deserve happiness. You deserve a family. All the things that I couldn't give you here."

"Maybe," Cassandra continued lamenting. "But I took from myself any chance I had to live a happy life."

"Happiness is still possible," insisted Benedict.

"Eternity is a long time," said Dominia.

Although, for a glimmer, hope lay in those doe eyes, Cassandra squeezed them shut. "How can I be happy, thinking of my daughter? What a fool I was. She was right in front of me all those years and I never saw it. Of course not. I didn't want to see it. The things he's *done* to her, Benny, oh! To our daughter." The woman emitted a sob that broke the General's heart.

"Dominia will make it right," said Benedict, but Cassandra wailed, "How? How can anything that's happened to Lavinia ever be put right?"

"Tonight is a night for earthly miracles." The magician rose to his feet. "Tonight is a night where anything is possible."

"If that were true—if all this about eternity were true—then where is my daughter now?" Lifting her head, briskly wiping her eyes to reveal their defiance, Cassandra demanded, "She should be here, if this is eternity."

"This is more a holding cell," Valentinian said. "For you immovable individuals with too little soul and too much grief keeping you from transcending someplace higher. Your daughter isn't here because she doesn't need to be."

At last! A spark caught the dampened tinder of her spirits. Cassandra stepped past Benedict, toward the magician. "Where is she?"

"You'll see her. But Dominia won't see any hint of you for quite a while—and this you, the you that remembers everything she does for the world, she won't see for a long, long time. So…you know."

Her hand a fist at her breast, Cassandra turned to see the stoic General, who tried with every fiber of her being to remain stoic. "You've done so much for me," Cassandra said, coming to hold Dominia's hands.

"I would do so much more for you, if I could. If I could change the past."

"You don't have to. Even though I hurt you so badly—even though I killed myself—you still looked for me. You traversed a whole planet just to find me again, and died, and came here. You spent an eternity in this place, just to remind me that I used to exist. That I used to be a person. That you used to love me."

"I still do love you," Dominia swore. "I will love you forever. I'll never love another beside you."

"But I wish you would." Color returning to her being degree by degree, Cassandra blinked her wet eyes and touched her wife's face. "I wish you would let yourself forget me. Then you might be able to be happy."

"There's no such thing as happiness without you," said the General, who bent to kiss those perfect satin lips, which pressed back; parted into a breath of air like Dominia's name; dissolved into atoms of light that embraced her, then filled her. In the space of a second, her senses were overwhelmed with the infinity of her wife's existence, of her kisses—of, not that sad death, but a long life joyful in the face of many sorrows. The warmth that filled the General was indescribable, as was the force that punched her chest as she was penetrated by this…what, if not soul? Spirit, she supposed. She could not fathom what it was in truth, in its highest form, this essence of Cassandra: nor could she imagine why it flew into her as if to settle there.

But, as the personas—those consciousness-less or consciousness-tainted egos—of Benedict, Akachi, Kahlil, and all those others began to dissolve into light and do the same, the General understood. This was how a soulless spirit might be bolstered for eternity, might be given a soul. She had more than enough consciousness to go around. Her lungs winced while her mind was barraged by more entities than she had known to exist. With each spirit came each one's reality. Before the feeling of one existence could pass, another burst through her like a gunshot, and another, and another: a great chain of people all plunging into her, and all of them, spirit after spirit, reminding her that there was one dead spirit outside of herself for whom she'd yet to pray. Barely enduring those glowing bolts, Dominia eased to her knees and spoke one last prayer for Lazarus.

"Do you think I need it?" asked the old man's spirit.

She laughed, moaned in pain, closed her eye against the cold tears of divine ecstasy. Before her, the True Protomartyr knelt. "Praying," he said with a chuckle. "Salvation. I just want to rest! The way I see it, I'm already saved. Same way you are."

"The protein?"

"'By you,' I was going to say—but the protein, too. Maybe you're right, though. Without the sacred protein, after all, you wouldn't be able to save anybody."

As that soul dissolved and entered her, she found that he was right. The true sacred protein was a greater hero than she was. An eternal connection to this place, to the divine. Was there any point in praying for a set of friendly cells? She thought of the E4, which had a name, a True Word—and dear Tenchi, who believed all things in the world possessed some form of spirit. So, as those effervescent spirits plunged into her, the General rationalized that she owed it to the protein to pray for it. Perhaps she might ask it for its help.

Perhaps it, too, had a true name that might reveal some avenue of assistance.

Her forehead against the cool un-ground as she submitted to the ceaseless flow of intrusions, she plunged into the depths of herself and prayed for that very same protein that had led her this far—prayed it might continue to lead her, and that it might spread itself beyond the reaches of its malformed cousin. That it might teach her to do the works of the Lord. That it might act to her as a friend and companion. That it might see her Father's regime collapsed into the dust from which it had been built.

And then, as the True Word for that which was known to men as the sacred protein bubbled to the surface of her opened mind, Dominia's memories of the past rose with it.

More than any, it brought the memories of the first function. The same as this iteration, or nearly. Without the organization of the Red Market, without the Hierophant, without the foreknowledge of her hateful Father. The Family: it had been Cicero and Elijah, Dominia and Cassandra, Lavinia and Theodore. And what a terrible, violent mess all of it had been! What an endless sea of sorrows worse even than this world. Then, as now, Dominia had died after seeing to the death of the Lamb. Then, as now, she had found herself praying endlessly for all those she wronged. But the prayers in that place had been different, the Catholic prayers, for then Valentinian did not exist in even the fictional sense. Again and again, she pled for the eternal rest of the damned and lost and lonely beings of purgatory; then, as now, she had prayed for the sacred protein, and determined once it revealed its True Word that it, too, had a soul.

Valentinian, the martyr saint of death and the incarnated form of the sacred protein, genuflected down before his mother at the instant she sat up. He asked, "Do you get it now?"

"You are the sacred protein. Its spirit."

"You didn't create me. But I was born of you, Dominia. Your Word." The surge of white energy blazed into her with such force that she was rendered speechless, and could not even comprehend the irony of discussing the Word at such a time. "You derived me from the sacred protein's bond to your soul. Gave me life here. And now you've given me flesh. Because you've given me flesh, I can help you trap your Father.

"Do you know how much information you can store in a hard drive while respecting the structural integrity of the universe? You don't have to answer that." He smiled doggishly into her eye, unseeing above her pain-opened mouth. "The answer is ten to the sixty-ninth power bits per square meter. The standard Earthling brain—martyr or human, for those keeping track at home—has one hundred trillion neurons, which is an incredible amount of storage space. The brain is the only storage device that must run a twenty-four-seven program simulating an entire world. Almost, anyway. Without sleep, we'd be in trouble! Have to dump that RAM somehow. Do you know how much your brain is doing for you during your waking hours? You look at an apple, and you don't see the real apple. Your eye is interpreting it, coloring it, flipping it right-side up, then you go, 'Oh, that's an apple.' Every day, you walk down the street, and you see a thousand apples: a thousand things, a million things, that your brain is perpetually constructing and interpreting, then selectively presenting faster than I can snap my fingers. Not just that, but all it remembers! All those once-glanced faces that come to you in dreams, or those fragments of chatter invented just for them. Every mind contains infinity, but the infinite contains every mind; and that which contains every mind *becomes* infinite, you understand."

She fancied her limbs dissolved, overwhelmed by the force of the souls plunging into her with their flowers, their straw hats, their fishing boats, their starry nights and beautiful mornings and all the things they once had and wished to have again. She felt it all; and what was "it"? The world, she supposed, swiftly passing the point of supposition. The General had been forced to her knees and needed to be held upright by the magician, whose arm she gripped with such a viselike hand she was surprised he did not wince.

"Every person you know, everything you've ever experienced—it's all part of the black hole, Dominia. It's all a part of you. If I am the soul of the first True Word, you are the soul of that vast, encompassing spirit: the Lady. You create new iterations of the universe, new models, to trap your Father there. Instead of moving into the afterlife or transmigrating to a higher state of being, the old wretch is so broken up about the death of his brother—and, now, so addicted to power—he'd rather flee to our simulations of the original universe and delude himself they're real, tangible iterations. Ever since your first death, I've helped you do this. Helped you physicalize it all for him, to give you another chance to end his life and set right what you've done.

"You asked me once what you were in the metaphor about movie theaters. I let you think you were the projectionist, but you're not. I am. You're the screen, kiddo. And we're about to run this film one final time."

The vibrations of her rib cage made her feel as if her very internal structure sought to drill through her flesh. "It hurts," she said. He embraced her, her friend, her son, her personal manifestation of the Holy Spirit within the sacred protein as projected through her genetic code. Still the spirits flowed. "Why me?"

"Because that first time you died you didn't do what everybody else does and start praying for yourself. You started praying for everybody else. You, that first time, realized the formula of consciousness plus ego equals a soul. You, that first time, invited them into you and became infinite in the process. You realize you could have moved on to the Kingdom by now and seen Cassandra? She's already there. It's eternity. But that idea never even crossed your mind. It was worth more to you to trap your Father and liberate all those spirits than it was for you to be happy. In the infinite probabilities of infinite people, it's infinitely easy to take the lazy way out. You refuse to allow that—maybe because I keep coming back and pushing you," he added, chuckling. "But that's one of the reasons you derived me. It doesn't have to hurt."

At last, the river of souls ceased. The impact of the final spirit was so thunderous that the disoriented General returned to her senses to find the magician disappeared. His voice from all around her—from within her—said, "Take off your eye patch."

After all she had endured for the sake of keeping it on, and all she had been warned of its removal, the moment arrived to a very reluctant Dominia; but neither could she stand the pressure, for her intuition cried that if she did not find some relief, even her powerful thoughtbody would be lost among the screaming masses within her. The weeping masses within her. All those souls of the world who wished, in the purest way of wishing, only that they could live again. It didn't matter whether they did it a little better, a little worse, or just the same as last time. And if she could make their dreams come true—if she could give them a chance at redemption—it was worth her own suffering through the same.

The General of the old world removed her eye patch and the Lady's eye opened. The hyper-density of the spirits within Her collapsed Her form, that old self bursting beneath the pressure of the knowledge contained: bursting, yet, reforming with the dark substance of the Ergosphere that very material world. An eye opened in Her that was not an eye at all—it saw beyond all information, all structure, all time. Above the howl of the geyser that streamed from Her un-eye's socket, the magician said, "I prefer to derive reality through a mathematical model, because it's so streamlined. But what I find works best for you is true sight."

The darkness of the Void that had returned on its emergence from Her skull now swirled back upon Her to crush Her body in a wave: as that darkness inhabited the very substance of Her flesh, She saw it for what it was. Ink, or phosphors untouched by electrons. But, more often, ink. She looked beyond this ink, into the shapes they formed around her, with her, beneath her, and read their words in a way that was not the absorption of new information but the remembering of old. Or, better than remembering, the revealing of what she had always known. Broken through, she read the Words upon the pages of her life and found she spoke them aloud, True Words forming reality from her invisible mouth in the Void while the vanished magician said, "Once you have words, you're going to need numbers. That's easy, because they're implied right in front of us. Anytime there's one, there's an infinity. Though frankly, you don't even need one—.999 repeating will do, since it equals 1, but we're lucky we don't need to concern ourselves with that. Since I already know I'm a given, we have to distinguish enough other numbers to fill a number system. And since we—or I, anyway—have ten fingers…"

In the vastness of space, the magician reappeared. "One," he counted. Then: "Two." A beam of light pierced the darkness, then another, then another. Nine he counted them, before the Lady repeated their names. From these lights emerged the souls of the Bearers, the first beings of the Kingdom, which, in turn, revealed the existence of the Kingdom. As the Lady's opened eye transmuted into the waters of that crystal pool, the magician drew through it those souls desperate for refuge from the bleak landscape of Ergosphere. Within that same desolate plane, that pool was envisioned not as a perfect mirror of water but as another world. That world spoken, eternally, by the voice of the Lady.

Now, She understood how long—and how infinitely short—Her journey was to be.

XV

Anno Domini 1974

Trisha Robbins was twenty years old when a then unknown cabal of prostitutes began seducing her from academia to fulfill her destiny. Of all seven avatars before the Lady herself manifested upon the Earth in that distant, fatal future, one could easily argue Trisha was the most significant—and most visible. Yet she was not affiliated with a spirituality, as had been Her previous embodiments. Nor was she of a distinct race or cultural affiliation, which was a trait particular to the people of her place and time. She was a modern woman living in the United States of America, a nation of immigrants founded upon the backs of genocidal religious separatists. Therefore, religion was in her DNA, but far be it from the geneticist-in-training to acknowledge such a thing! Not before she began to understand her role in the world.

Ironically, though she studied biochemistry and would, in another place and time, have been responsible alongside her husband for discovering what martyrs called "the sacred protein" ("Our only child," she would have joked at the sundry cocktail parties upon its discovery, before her worthless lab assistants stole a malformed variation and took it in secret by terrible mistake), Trisha had never been as interested in her genetic background as in her mental lineage. She venerated no more ancestors than she did deities. The spirits she praised were Newton, Darwin, and the wise words of then living sage, Dr. Carl Sagan. His book, *The Cosmic Connection*, had spoken to her from a bookstore's new-release section just the year before. This man wrote in a way that made her believe science fiction was possible. Imagine, terraforming a planet! Imagine, a race of people who never died, but might voyage out into the far reaches of outer space like an infinite collection of dandelion seeds! It was not an American that Trisha foremost considered herself; it was an Earthling first, a human second, and a scientist third.

Budding scientist, at least. In her Pomona College dorm room, she dreamed every night of a future that seemed as if it would never come—not with so many years of study between it and her. Her roommate majored in French in a way that mostly involved drinking at parties, missing her classes, and occasionally remembering to show up for exams, but Trisha worked so hard through her first year of study that it took a month into year two to realize a fellow was making eyes at her. That crossroads of time, October 1974: her roommate, while unwrapping a vinyl album sent to her by her mother, said, "So are you going to *do* anything about that guy?"

"What guy?" had been the redhead's oblivious response. Her boggling roommate lowered the cardboard sleeve, allowing a glance of the cover—the band Styx had released an album lazily titled *Styx II*, and Trisha had been blissfully unaware of its existence until her roommate started humming some song she'd heard playing in her home radio station in Chicago. Tish had a feeling she'd like it even less played twenty times a day from the poor students' turntable in the corner of their room. She had zoned out into thoughts of the device's cost when her roommate told her the name of the man she'd noticed admiring the pensive, analytical Robbins girl.

Oh—him. Yes, she did know him. A very fine-looking fellow, with dark hair and piercing blue eyes, who (nervously, she would realize on future pondering) inserted himself into her campus library study group. She hadn't realized it was because of her. Her roommate's annoyance on hearing this gave Trisha the sinking feeling that something would "be done" about it. Sure enough, a day later, the quiet young man asked her out to ice cream. Like it was the 1950s! So wholesome. And, well, he was too good-looking to pass by. Trisha was very good-looking, herself, but it was a confidence issue with her. She had never expected to have the pick of the litter, so she usually didn't; her focus was so plastered to her books that there was no time for something as frivolous as boys.

Almost.

They tend to say opposites attract, but this same cliché-prone "they" also tells us that birds of a feather flock together. With him, Trisha felt what she could only explain as, well—a cosmic connection. Sure, sure, they both had very similar dreams for their futures. Both came from similar socioeconomic backgrounds, both had similar political ideals in that period of sweet, post-Nixon relief. But nothing felt quite the way it did when she found his paperback copy of Sagan's 1973 book in the bedroom of his off-campus apartment. Then, she *knew* it was love. She'd never believed in love, or fate, but here were both, and neither would be denied. Of course, it made perfect sense she should meet another budding biochemist in college courses that led down that career route, but the similarity of their dreams—to heal the sick, to perpetuate the human race through the stars, to believe beyond all doubt that death was defeatable—before the presence of that book felt, for lack of a better description, like a sign.

They talked for hours. Only talked, the way people did in movies. Then, like a gentleman, he offered to walk her back to her dorm in the still-warm darkness of the Claremont night.

Claremont. What could be said of the place where she spent so little time? It was *safe*. She had never felt threatened there—not once—so it was a great shock when, from the darkness of a storefront along their meandering route, two figures stepped into the sidewalk on their passing. Trisha's body tensed, although she told herself she was a fool; but, before she dispelled her fear by turning to ask the shadows if they wanted to pass, her would-be lover made the mistake for her. He had enough time to utter a cry before the blackjack fell upon his head and his body crumpled from Trisha's arm. A scream began to peel past her lips as she turned to see the assailants for herself, but she was so shocked when she found them to be a pair of stylish women in military coats that the noise tapered off like the expiration of a leaking balloon.

"He'll be fine," said the woman with the afro. Her Latina sister whisked a few strands of hair from her tanned face, then stooped to drag Tish's boyfriend into the building from which they'd come. While Trisha, senses somewhat regained after the start, began again to cry out, the black woman sucked a tooth and closed the distance between herself and the redhead.

"Please quit it with that racket or we'll have to do the same to you, Miss Robbins. Then you won't feel there was any choice in the matter."

Confusion after confusion! It felt as though confusion were the wave, panic the medium, and Trisha the shore upon which it all broke. "How do you know my name?"

"We were told to watch you, and to be ready for the moment to move. The time is now; we are changing history tonight."

"'We'? Changing—what *is* this? What are you doing with J—"

"If you go back to your dorm room in the next fifteen minutes, you will die. You and your boyfriend, both. This is his only opportunity to do it. When he misses, it's over for him. To rise to power, he has to get started yesterday—metaphorically, I mean—and that means he can't afford to botch it up by killing you late in the game. He shows up in 1974 and tries to kill you sometime in the course of that year. Tonight's the night this time. It's now or never."

What did these words even *mean*? "He," who? What sort of stranger just walked up to somebody on the street, incapacitated a man, and started *saying* things like this? While a limousine whipped around the corner, the dark woman turned to greet the reemerging comrade, who dusted her hands to indicate she'd relieved herself of their burden. Trisha managed to grasp hold of her thoughts enough to ask, "Who? Who wants to do this to me?"

"A man not yet called the Hierophant," answered the black woman. As the limo slid to a halt and fluttered open the women's military coats to reveal the shimmer of bright fabric beneath, she popped open its back door. "Will you come with us?"

Trisha, with an anxious glance over her shoulder for the building where her suitor had been dragged, wrapped her arms around herself. "What about him?"

"He's being taken care of. In a few hours, we'll drop him off down the street from his apartment. Make it all look like a mugging."

"What am I supposed to say to him?"

"Please." The dark woman pulled the door wider while her compatriot stooped to get in. "Just a ride around the town. Half an hour. Let us show you something."

"What?"

"The truth."

Her skin crawled. She'd rather have been anywhere other than there. To do anything other than get in! But she sensed there was no alternative. With a reluctant step toward the car, she asked, "Will you at least tell me your name?"

For the first time that night, the black woman smiled. "I'm Gethsemane."

Tish had seen vehicles like this in movies, but even so, it was hard to believe the little minibar rattling behind the three other women already in the car. Hard to believe the shag carpet, the smell of pot, the disco ball, the specialty cocaine mirrors lying out on a couple of knees, anything—anything about it. Especially not the women themselves, who seemed an arrangement of not so much models from a runway in Milan as tropical birds from a mysterious jungle moon light-years away. Absolutely stunning and…not particularly shy in their choice of wardrobe, to put it politely. While Trisha cleared her throat against improper thoughts, Gethsemane and her friend removed their coats to reveal equally elaborate (and slightly less suggestive) dresses beneath. The black-and-white sequins of Gethsemane's illuminated the cabin as though it were a light of its own.

"What *is* this?" asked Trisha of the three new women. They looked between themselves, then studied her.

"It's a conspiracy," suggested the one with hair so pale blonde it was nearly white.

"Like a cult," said the third, whose curly black hair, arranged in an immaculate bun, received the occasional pat from a fussing, jewel-covered hand.

"No," said the woman in the middle, a Native with her long hair in simple, elegant plaits, "it's just some criminal organization of—"

"Hookers."

"Whores."

The one in the middle looked annoyed at her sisters. "—Prostitutes."

"Independent working girls," clarified Gethsemane patiently. "On our way to a convention, of sorts. You are not invited."

"I wouldn't want to be," insisted blushing Trisha, hands upon her chest, while a few of the other women smiled. Gethsemane, their apparent spokeswoman, went on.

"Not tonight. But another night, perhaps. Our sisters are all correct; the women in the service of the Lady are all of those things. A cabal, a cult, and a conspiracy. But the truth is the *real* conspiracy, sister, you dig? It embodies everything around us. It is the oxygen we breathe and the food we eat, and is in itself embodied by those things. The Lady is nothing more than the sentient embodiment of the truth, and She has appeared throughout time in an infinite number of ways."

"'The Lady'?"

"She is that which the Hierophant wishes to suppress and kill. She has been hidden since the dawn of time, asleep within all of us: man, woman, and child. But only some can contact Her, and fewer still dare host Her. She lives upon the Earth in the form of an earthly woman and guides us from the shadows. Not all women who worship the Lady are ladies of the evening as we are; and not all women who worship the Lady worship Her in Her highest form; and not all women who worship the Lady in any of Her many forms believe that the avatar is the Lady; but I have seen that She is the Lady, and know it, and urge you to believe it. We, all of us, are Her keepers; Her Bearers."

It was all so very laughable. She might have, nearly, were it not for the circumstances at hand. "You gave my date a concussion and told me somebody plans to kill me so you could try to recruit me for your cult?"

"No," said Gethsemane. "We did those things to save you, so you will be our next Lady."

When silent, the vehicle was a whole new car. While Trisha's brain churned into fifth gear, she asked, "Excuse me?"

"We believe there are certain requirements to be the next avatar of a Lady at a given period," said the Latina woman. "You fit the requirements of the era, but you are an unusual case because you were not chosen by the Lady or Her followers. You were chosen by the Hierophant. Because he wants to kill you, we wish to save you. And what will happen tonight—"

"What *will* happen tonight?"

At Trisha's pressure, the five women exchanged a web of glances.

"Tonight," said Gethsemane, "when you return to your dorm room, you will have proof that what we say is true."

Her stomach sank into a foul pit of quicksand. "My roommate," Trisha said. Gethsemane placed a hand upon hers.

"I urge you not to think of her now. The Lady—"

"This is ridiculous," snapped the student, emotions exploding with every furious word that peeled through her lips. "I believe in science. I was never even a *Christian* growing up! I've never believed in anything I can't see, and now you're trying to tell me to believe in this? This is *crazy*. You're all crazy, let me out of this—this crazy car!"

It was the only adjective with which she could articulate her thoughts. It *was* crazy. It was one thing to have cultists try to recruit you. This was the seventies, the heyday of cults and inexplicable murder. The practice of hitchhiking had disappeared that year, along with a bunch of girls up in the state of Washington. America's cultural landscape was such a fucked-up death trap most places that it was better to avoid all eye contact and hope the scrub you passed at night wasn't the next Charles Manson. But this was *Claremont*. And these women weren't recruiting her to join their cult; they were recruiting her to be its leader. To make it stranger, these weren't cult members of the weird, gross kind you read about in the news—neither did they fit the pervaded cultural image of prostitutes. The Latina woman all but confirmed that when she said, "I used to feel the way you do. I'm a trained anthropologist, and when I was young, I believed in only what I could see in physical human history. But then, I saw the pattern in many cultural artifacts and mythologies across the world, and saw who I was inside. Then the Lady showed me the way to Her, and to the truth."

"What is the truth," pressed Trisha. The women smiled as the limo pulled to a stop.

"Like I said." While the door opened from the outside, Gethsemane pressed against Trisha so all those women could pile out into the populated night. The open door allowed their chatter to mix with the clamorous sound of tens or hundreds of other women making their excited way into the grand hotel and its surely packed ballroom. "Tonight, you're not invited. You're not ready, sister."

"Then what in God's name makes you think I should be your next Lady?"

"You don't believe in God, yet you protest in His name; you see what power society has given men? Even language is a tool of sub-jugation in this world." The door shut and left them, now just Trisha and Gethsemane. The car once more began to move. "Language was once made to elevate mankind, men and women both. It is said by our faith that a woman was pivotal in forming the first spoken words more intricate than simple sounds, and that the Lady first came to this woman, in whom She longest dwelt, and through whom She first revealed assurances of the spirit and eternity.

"But language since then has been perverted. Rather than revealing the truth, it veils. We speak the truth in every word we say and every gesture we make. We see it everywhere, in such a proliferation of sym-bols that we could never begin to collect, experience, or understand them all in a single human lifetime. But you will, because you are the Lady. You thirst for knowledge, for the solutions to life and death. You will have them."

Trisha was still concerned about feeling like a hostage, though the car was gentler (at least quieter) when absent the other women. "I'm not trying to be rude, but I just feel like, if your organization has been watching me, then you should know—"

"That you're going to be a hard sell? Oh, yes." Gethsemane smiled. "We know. But we also know that you will come around."

"And how do you know that?"

"Because, it is written."

"Okay." Trisha laughed, glancing out the window. Sweet relief! They'd turned around the block to reorient themselves toward campus. "And that's supposed to convince—"

Glass shattered across the cabin of the flipping limo, which, with an explosive metal cry, rolled, then skidded out of its lane amid the honking of cars and the sound of someone else's scream. At the crash of the stretch vehicle into the corner of the nearby building, all noise was obliterated. That would be what Trisha gathered later, from the news. At the moment it happened to her, the crash was but a crescendo of animal terror: Wondering, hoping, begging, please, not tonight. Not here. Not like this.

She'd hit her head on something. What, it wasn't clear; nor was it clear for how many seconds she'd lost consciousness. It must not have been long—Gethsemane had just begun to push herself up from where she'd collapsed within the upended vehicle when a foreign hand, huge by the standards of any person of the day, slithered in to pluck the Bearer by the neck as though she were a kitten. Out of the limo, that splendid woman was pulled screaming, and there that beautiful embodiment of Gethsemane met her end amid the torrid snaps of bones. Trisha was too tired and too blank with shock to react. She lifted her head an inch and let it fall again.

A face peered into the vehicle: a man's face, so pale and androgynous from that angle that it seemed to bleed into the face of a woman. A Lady, who stood before Tish in a strange, dark place that had no sound yet was sound, itself. The eye could not take the Lady in, stunning as She was. Sometimes it seemed to Trisha that She had four arms, sometimes three eyes, sometimes a halo or a crown shaped like the moon, or a warrior's helmet, or a wingéd sun that blazed in glory a few inches above Her head. Those uncountable eyes glowed like the light from Her mouth, which spoke words Trisha knew at once to be beyond anything terrestrial.

You will bring the truth into the world to lay the path for me, She announced to Trisha. *And when this has been accomplished, I will leave my present body to take on yours—and you will live forever.*

"I must be dreaming," insisted the stubborn student, who in this place did not wear glasses, and did not realize it until she reached up to adjust them. Laughing sharply, she looked down at herself and found herself buxom in a way she had always been but now for the first time experienced. She had never felt confidence before, but here, her lovely nature was a simple fact and exuded from her being as glory from the Lady's. *"I don't believe in ghosts, or a god or the devil, or witches, or magic. I don't believe in you."*

My existence does not hinge on your belief, human, or your lack thereof. You will believe soon. Awaken now. Return to your room. You will be protected.

"Why is all this happening?"

The world where all this did not happen proved this one's genesis. Therefore, all this must occur infinitely to create a world where it does not happen, where it cannot be caused. We all must sacrifice ourselves to protect all other universes from our reality.

"I don't understand."

You are a woman of science, and yet you do not understand the oscillations of the universe, or the implications of relativity, or the secrets hidden within the human's genetic code. I do not fault you; no woman or man of science will fully understand the latter for a very long time. But the secret of a repetitive universe—the secret of my existence—has been encoded in the products of the human mind since that first day's dawn. Every story ever written contains My same substance. You will see, but not with your eyes.

"How?"

The Lady did not speak. She only turned and, with a wave of her arm, revealed to Trisha that which six other avatars had seen before her, and in as many guises; but she saw it not as a palm tree, or a beehive, or a column, or a ladder, or a twisting serpent, or a spiral staircase. She saw the double helix chemical rungs of a towering strand of DNA, which coiled into the infinity of space and tugged at Trisha's very bones.

"What is this?"

This, said the gently smiling Lady, *is that thin wall through which God speaks to mankind.*

A series of gunshots interrupted the Communion with the Lady so suddenly that, though the conversation may have continued in eternity,

Trisha snapped back to her body. The androgynous face from the window was nowhere to be seen. As women called out and someone uttered a distant cry, footsteps clattered down the street, and a siren yet many blocks away began its mournful howl. The twisted door was forced open after a few seconds of grinding and struggle. Trisha covered her face with her forearm as a few more glass shards twinkled down like falling stars. "He's gone," said the woman, whose face resolved into that of the anthropologist. Trisha struggled to maintain even this level of focus. "Come on; we need to get you out of here before the cops show up."

"But Gethsemane," she began. The woman looked pained and reached into the vehicle.

"Please, not now. We need to go."

The accident must have happened on the other side of the block from the hotel. Surely, he knew about the meeting. Knew where to come after he found Trisha's roommate alone in the dorm room. That was what Trisha would eventually decide, anyway, when she realized there was credence to all these strange tales. For now, as she was helped out of the crumpled limo, the twisted neck of morbidly still Gethsemane was sufficient evidence that life could never be the same. Not after tonight. While Tish held back tears, another smaller car squealed up to the scene. The Native woman didn't wait for the doors to shut after her passengers before she peeled off. Shaken in every sense of the word, Trisha tried to hold on to the pure feeling the vision had left within her breast. Tried not to lose it amid all the horrors of reality. "That crash—"

"That was the Hierophant. He is not of this world—this iteration of the world. Were it not for him, the Lady would not exist, and the man with whom you spent tonight would be the husband with whom you discovered a reality-altering pair of substances. But you would also be responsible for many terrible things."

"How do you know all of this?"

"The Lady has made it very clear. We are on the cusp of a silent war. In truth, we have fought this war for many years already, and laid much groundwork for it. The truth is all around you, Trisha. You will start to see it when you look closely."

"What about Gethsemane? My roommate?"

"Life is temporary in this flawed place," said the Native woman. "In truth, it is eternal."

"So you're saying you don't care that people are dying tonight?"

"People die every night, everywhere. We are sorrier to lose Gethsemane now than you could ever know; but someday, we will see her again, and later still, she will be born again, here again, in this iteration of the world. This is the way with Bearers."

Trisha was in such a daze she hardly realized it when they pulled in front of her dorm. From her clutch purse, the anthropologist withdrew a business card. "There is a library here. A very small one. There you will find many books on these subjects. Please study. When you are ready, and you understand what you must undertake, we will be here for you."

"Where will I find you?"

"You will know when you are ready," said the woman again.

Trisha glanced anxiously in the direction of the dorm.

"You will be safe," said the plaited woman. "We will watch over you in the coming months to ensure your safety while you embark on your true studies, and while you come to us. As it has been said—if he does not get you tonight, then you will never die."

The cloud of horror that had settled across the dorm building was evident from the moment she stepped foot within. Her body, already burned out from adrenaline, yet endured another pulse of the stuff. She doubled the pace of her steps to reach the third floor when she found people murmuring in hallways, doorways, common rooms, and every corner of the building like a cluster of terrified cockroaches. Worst, all regarded her in a way that stopped their conversation and hastened her steps. She knew what she would find, but she would never believe it until she arrived at the peak of proof she would receive about the reality of the night. She jogged through the hall of that destination floor while crying her roommate's name. The crowd of attendants, police, campus security, and nurses all tried to keep her out. They failed.

The matchbox-size studio was thick with the scent of death, which seemed impossible to her, as the death had only just occurred. Perhaps it was the smell of organ meat? She couldn't think when every thought in that awful scene was had to the beat of a skipping record: that very same her roommate's mother had sent just a few days before. "Lady—" cried the record, an uncanny chant while Trisha wept over the bloodied body of her dead surrogate. "Lady— Lady— Lady— Lady—"

Her roommate's mother gave her that record while tearfully sweeping off with the final box of her daughter's things. Seeing Trisha's wary eyes lingering on the album, the older woman said, "She would have wanted you to have it," thinking in the good-natured way of a grieving parent that her little girl might live on in her friend. She did not know the significance of the album, whose particular skipping song was overlooked as evidence by the police in favor of the fact that it *was* skipping, mere effect of the obvious struggle.

Only Trisha understood it was a message to her—only Trisha *could* understand. And even though she understood, she felt mad in thinking it. Yet such a coincidence was beyond mere happenstance. Her roommate's killer had selected the point in the song down to the very second.

She was almost glad he had. The objective taunt bolstered her resolve that the events of that night had happened. Otherwise she would have been adrift in a sea of questions. Not that knowing was better! Such tangible confirmation of the Lady's presence haunted the student. Trisha was expected to ease back into classes with the help of a great deal of counseling and the sorry reassurance that her dorm was watched (and she was sure that it was, by agents a great deal more competent than campus cops).

But night after night, she lay awake analyzing the contents of that vision. That woman (Was it right to call such an entity a mere woman? Of course. Trisha was a scientist, not a cultist.) and that great spiral of DNA, and the place—and the *feeling* of that place! She could not understand it, nor could she understand why she so longed to experience it again. Why she had felt so whole in those seconds of interaction with something in which she did not fully believe.

It was a few weeks before she went to the metaphysical library. Mostly, she was embarrassed to be seen someplace so goofy. At the time, she remained naively firm in her skepticism and could not see it had become her personal brand of fundamentalist thought. A true scientist understood critical thinking did not involve the automatic rejection of a challenging belief; and Trisha was, at that time, only a scientist-in-training. Some training, anyway. She had become so preoccupied by the nightly memories of her vision that she'd started missing classes. It was around that time, just before winter break, that she decided to take the plunge and visit the weird strip mall "library."

The first day she was there, the librarian behind that counter—though a stranger to her—seemed to recognize her. Instead of paranoia, Trisha felt a relief that came from so deep within her she could not be sure it was from her own nervous system. The books populating shelves in that rented storefront were not of the sort Trisha usually read, and she turned up her nose at titles by figures such as Aleister Crowley to such an extent that she began to edge her way back to the library's entrance. How was she to leave without offending the librarian, who tried not to stare at her only visitor? But it was then Trisha noticed it again: *The Cosmic Connection*, sitting on a display labeled "Staff Picks." Beneath this book sat four others: *Synchronicity*, by psychiatrist Carl Jung, another book published just the year before; Robert Anton Wilson's (again, brand-new) book on goddess worship, *The Book of the Breast*; the cumbersomely titled but intriguing work of a Dr. John C Lilly, *Programming and Metaprogramming in the Human Biocomputer*; and—much to her displeasure, for she had already resolved to check out all the books on that display before she laid eyes on it—Aleister's *Book 4*. His guidebook on magic with a *k*. Screw it. As she collected the books, she told herself that she did not enjoy every book her university professors crammed into their curriculums, either.

When she dropped the tomes on the front counter and asked, "How much to join the library? It's private, right," the librarian perked.

"For one week only, it happens to be free. You picked a lucky day to come in!"

The penniless student strongly suspected luck had nothing to do with it, and the contents of those four books would confirm it—not just their printed contents, but their actual, physical contents. The great irony of it all was she would, in some months, come to hold Crowley in high regard; the entity that he called the Scarlet Woman would then seem the Lady to her in all but name. But at the end of 1974, with those first four books fresh in her dorm, what should slide out of the Lilly volume? Not a proper bookmark, or the usual haphazard replacements for one such as the standard receipt or old grocery list or expired movie ticket. Nothing usual by any means when the baggie containing six cartoon-printed tabs of LSD dropped into her lap. Extremely considerate on the part of the last reader (or that librarian), since Mr. Lilly's techniques utilized the chemical. Such a thing could have been dangerous, but Trisha was (almost) a scientist. Though she had not so much as smoked a cigarette, she felt, in the wake of her vision, that she already had experience in the neighborhood of psychedelics.

Alone, she took two tabs of the acid; two weeks later, she ceased her classes in favor of more important studies. Four years later, while intermittently working a few menial part-time office jobs, Tish volunteered a handful of hours at a battered women's shelter—a new inspiration that had come to her the morning after a later acid trp. All the workers, she sensed, knew the Lady. They put on a very good act of pretending they didn't know her when she first started coming by; but there was a deliberateness about all the things they said and did that Trisha's senses declared to be somehow false. The shelter, like her new apartment, was in Claremont, but whether out of his embarrassment, her shift of interests, or the manipulations of the Lady, she never bumped into her would-be suitor after the event he surely remembered as a mugging. Just as well; he would have monopolized her valuable time, which she increasingly sensed to be short.

Then, one day, she saw him on the news. The Hierophant. Not being interviewed, featured, or anything like that. A blink-and-miss-it glimpse of his familiar face looming in the background of joyous Catholics celebrating the election of Pope John Paul II. Just there, smiling, filling some space in the news broadcast's B-roll. Maybe wondering if Trisha saw him.

The next day, she began to write a book that would be published in secret by a company suggested by that librarian, who had become

Trisha's best friend since the tragedy of 1974. Every month, Tish came in to return her books, and lo! There would be a new display, with new, auspicious texts to elicit in her frontal lobe a kind of urgent itch. Any guilt for abandoning her academic path was tempered by the notion that she had replaced it with another—one more in need of an objective, scientific mind than any discipline she had seen.

At the same time, she began to understand why so many occult books descended into rambling, or why its practitioners seemed crazed fools. It was impossible to describe the experience in a linear way. It was impossible to recognize what the anthropologist had called "the pattern," this great chain of symbolic similarities spread across culture, medium, and intention (or lack thereof). Cultures that had never known one another bore profound similarities. Historical figures superficially unrelated became linked in subtle ways that often related to magical practices or drug use. She at last understood what Christianity was secretly speaking about, and recognized it was identical to the thing everybody else spoke about. Her reflexive anti-religious stance began to relax. Trisha at last saw spirituality for what it was: a model. A model for reality, like a mathematical model, or any other.

Finally, five years to the evening of the incident, she returned to the hotel on the off chance that the worshipers of the Lady communed again that night. Behind the counter, why— who should be there but that little librarian. Five years of chatting, and Trisha had never realized she had a night job. As she had the first time they met, the girl perked, and Tish could only think to ask, "I'm inquiring about the convention."

"Yes, Miss Robbins. An invitation for this Saturday's event has been left for you." Smiling, the librarian-slash-concierge placed a red envelope upon the counter between them. "I was told to say they look forward to seeing you."

"'They'?"

"The convention members, of course."

"And what is the name of the convention?"

"Our hotel's administrative staff is not permitted to divulge such information," said the chipper young woman. "They look forward to seeing you there."

Was the hotel in on it, too? They must have been. Who *wasn't* in on it? The day came and she glitzed herself up as much as possible while still maintaining modesty, more anxious every second. Suppose it did just turn out to be a bunch of prostitutes? Some weird trap? Human trafficking? Yet as she parked her car down the street and trotted up to the growing influx in her awkward heels, a few women turned to greet her. In that instant they recognized her, and she, also, recognized them: the Bearers, they had called themselves. The Native woman, who this year sported the most elaborate of all her sisters' updos, extended her hand.

"Well," said that woman, whose name was unknown, but who could not be called a stranger. "Are you coming?"

XVI

Enthousiasmos

If somebody told young Miki Soto that, as an adult, she (or her body) would lead a battle that would end the world as man and martyr knew it—well, suffice to say she'd have been pretty dubious. She had never believed she would be in a battle, period! Tell her to march, and she'd have laughed in your face between bites of a burger that never seemed to affect her delicate weight. Secretly, she worked hard to keep off the excess pounds. Her mother had always told her if she made exercise part of her routine, she would never have to think of it; and that had been a necessary advisement, since she'd been a pretty chubby kid! But, then, she'd also been a very depressed kid, and food had been her most comforting and nonjudgmental friend. A sandwich neither recognized nor cared what gender she was, so a sandwich didn't obliviously remind her, sentence after sentence, reference after reference, conversation after conversation, for the first seven years of life, that the whole world—even her own mother—thought she was a boy.

Oh, she never *blamed* them. It was a natural, though flawed, assumption to think that something with a penis wanted to have that penis, or felt like that penis belonged to it. But Miki had hated, hated, hated the thing from the instant she was conscious of the difference. Potty training, a time of trauma for all children, had been a horrible revelation for her; and as her interest in dolls or her mother's elaborate wardrobe was spurned as "weird" and "effeminate," she could not but feel a constant sting of pain, which turned into bitterness against God, which was easy to transmute into self-loathing. Maybe this was because she felt her mother would have loved her from the start if only she'd been born into the right body. Then Miki wouldn't have had to deal with seven years of displaced misandry and deep resentment for which Yoriko would spend the rest of her daughter's life repenting once the truth was fully communicated.

To Yoriko's credit, Miki had given up trying to communicate her gender around the age of five, so for the two years in which the child most grappled the issue, there was nothing Yoriko *could* have done. But the ultra-popular geisha—who spent vast amounts of time busy in e-zine hologram shoots and meetings to approve overpriced galactomyces-based beauty serums for her growing brand—might have had a chance to correct the problem had she picked up on the five years of clues exhibited by an increasingly emotional child. She had reacted to Miki's mischief involving her clothing with fury for a boy who had no respect for his mother's things, rather than with the relative impatience she would have shown a girl who only wanted to imagine she would someday be as beautiful as her very splendid mother.

But no matter how cruel and blind that mother was, Miki did not blame her; Miki blamed the divine, and herself. Only the cruelest of deities would put her into this body, this wrong body, so that the whole world would mock her without even knowing it. She decided perhaps she had done something wrong in a past life to merit such an existence—a tragic thing for a child to think, but natural given her culture's teachings about reincarnation. She wept every night for how hard an otherwise easy existence became when one was told every day they were someone they weren't. Amid her weeping, she sought an explanation. There had to be some reason, damn it. She couldn't accept that the universe was so unjust as to do this to her for no reason—to take from her the thing she felt would make her existence the smooth ride she deserved.

It would take Miki many years to understand that the life of a woman was hard. As a child in the wrong body, biological females seemed to have it so easy. The issues were all so simple then. If they wanted to look pretty, no one would stop them; if they played with dolls, that was fine; if they lived in the culture Miki did and fantasized about being a beautiful, famous geisha like Yoriko, people thought it fairly normal (though not necessarily ideal). Of course, there was something deeper to Miki's envy of biological females; something that she could not articulate at such a young age. They were allowed to be themselves. That was all she saw of women, and it slayed her with jealousy. She did not understand then that the life of a woman was still, even in 4012 CE, rife with danger. Issues like rape and sexism were not time-specific problems, or even human problems; they were *mortal* problems. They were problems with exist-ence, and would always be there so long as conscious beings had free will enough to make the wrong choices.

When Miki was seven, Yoriko was raped by a client. The geisha decided to retire from her career to focus on her skin-care line, whose profits she now partially dedicated to a foundation responsible for investigations that Kyoto police did not prioritize. That was to say, sex crimes against sex workers. Yoriko did not approve of the "lifestyle" of women who sold their bodies, she explained to Miki once, long after she had learned her daughter's identity. The geisha thought the higher ideal was to make oneself into an untouchable piece of art, like a painting behind glass. The rape, therefore, had not just been a repugnant invasion of the temple of her body. In Yoriko's mind, the rape was some strange slight to her vanity—and Miki could tell you that vanity was Yoriko's foremost trait. The assault "reduced" her to the level of "mere" sex worker, which was perhaps why the old bat began to deal more compassionately with them. It was certainly why her anger problems exploded.

Miki did not understand all that at the time, of course. She only understood her mother was home much more often, sleeping much more often, and angrier than ever when she was awake. A bad grade or a missed chore (keeping in mind Miki was barely seven years old) could now elicit a slap once reserved for back-talking or outlandish displays of disobedience. Those few activities they enjoyed together disappeared. Very benign things, like visiting Kyoto's elaborate rooftop gardens, or taking the train to Osaka's amusement park, or going up to Hokkaido for some fresh crab (oh! Natural flesh from the sea was better than anything fake modeled off land mammals)—no more. Miki was more alone than ever in their big, empty, Western-style house, and struggling with more self-loathing, too. Day on day, she told herself none of this would be happening if she had only been born in the right body. Then, her mother would be warm—friendly to her the way she was to women, not cold and businesslike the way she was with every non-client man Miki had ever observed. Clients got the warm treatment from Yoriko until her retirement—but even while she worked, she would come home at night, swipe off her makeup, and complain to her child, "Men! They're all such bullying, tedious wastes of space. Thank goodness for artificial insemination! Don't you ever grow up to be like that, Minoru-kun. Listen to a woman now and then, instead of yammering all the time. Ugh! I thought if I had to listen to him for another minute I was going to vomit all over the tatami. Finally I fed him so much sake he fell asleep, the idiot. His wife will have to come drag him home…her problem now!"

These things would have been cruel to say to a child who was really a boy; but to say it to a child who was secretly a girl was the height of spitefulness. Every night, Miki learned with increasing clarity that her mother could never, ever love her for as long as the child was called "Minoru." At least, this was what Miki convinced herself—and it was not far from the truth, but it was still a mistake on the child's part to allow these negative feelings, seven months after Yoriko's retirement, to drive a suicide attempt.

Of course: Was it a total mistake? Without that night of despair, elicited by a slight so small in the grand scheme of life that Miki couldn't even recall it as an adult, she might never have had her vision of the Lady. She might never have gone on to become Her avatar. One second, the girl was hanging from the handle of her closet door, and the next minute she fell through her floor, slipping between Plancks into another space. Into a Lady's arms.

Oh, Miki, said that glowing kami upon whom the child trembled to look, and upon whose face was written a compassion surmounting that of any living being. *I didn't know.*

Miki? How strange. If she was startled to hear herself addressed by a name she had never heard, she was all the more startled to find she *knew* the name was her real one. It was in her surprise that Miki looked down at her body and hiccupped into tears. She was not a child at all, and certainly not trapped in the body of a chubby boy. She was a beautiful woman, dressed in a kimono more elaborate than even those in which designers begged to dress her mother. As her watering eyes disrupted the vision of the herons upon the gossamer fabric, she cried, *"I'm a woman!"*

Of course you are. This is your real body. The kami released Miki, for it knew she wished to hold herself. *The body you will have in the future.*

"The future…my future." Lifting a sleeve to hide her tears, the girl said, *"But I don't have a future. I can't live like this, hidden away. I can't live with her. I'd rather die!"*

You are a butterfly, Miki, as is every caterpillar. Time has yet to unveil it, and you have many more years before you will make your cocoon. But caterpillars can be very beautiful; they can be themselves.

"I can't," she lamented. *"My mother hates me."*

She doesn't understand, and is an unfair woman. Would she but loved you no matter who you were! But she does not see that she abuses that which she most treasures. It is the caterpillar's mother, sweet Nature, who grants her beautiful colors before she even has wings. Show your mother that you will someday be a butterfly, and she will color you. At the girl's fearful silence, the entity urged, *She will understand if you tell her in the moment she finds you.*

"Who are you?"

You don't know me yet. Someday…but that is not me. It is a version of me. I am more than that, now; and I never will be that again.

"Then, what are you now?*"*

The kami did not speak. It merely wiped a tear from Miki's cheek, then cast that tear into the black abyss around them. There, the droplet expanded into a form that Miki would never find concrete words to describe. A tesseract, perhaps, or the E_8 lattice—both were the close concepts upon which she would someday come, but even these did not describe the visual experience of the object. This lotus of intense beauty that possessed an infinity of shimmering, shifting petals, each containing an infinity of its own. To look upon it, Miki felt the weight of all of time, and could feel for an instant her own future understanding of this, this experience, which at that time was simply alarming and hypnotic. Someday she would understand that this object was the same that Trisha perceived in the form of the DNA double helix; but she would still not fully, personally, manage to articulate what it was, even when living in the Kingdom with Kahlil.

Nonetheless, looking upon it in that place, she could sense her life was but a pinpoint in the timeline of existence. Smaller than a pinpoint—smaller still. She sensed that the length of time between herself and her true body was not so great as it felt to a mind that had lived not quite eight years. Indeed, Miki was practically nothing at all. But it was inarguable that she was something, for there, in a facet within a facet within a facet, behold!

The worried face of her mother, shaking her awake.

There were many other things she saw, too, in little half-had glimpses: another life as a maid, the motion of hands and a clatter like keys; but all these she forgot as the face of her mother gained in clarity. The many lotus petals of that multidimensional fractal folded the rest of the universes away and left her with the one called, to her, "reality."

"Minoru! Minoru!" She had never seen her mother cry. In that moment when she became conscious of Yoriko's warm arms and the splashes of her tears, the girl felt *this* was the true miracle vision. Forget the tesseract! She was so dazed she nearly forgot the Lady's words, until hers bubbled up of their own accord.

"Will you call me 'Miki'?"

Her mother, half laughing for a brief second of relief through her tears, managed, "What?"

"It's just—if I have to be a boy here, can't I have a name that's more like a girl's?"

"Oh!" The motions of Yoriko's hand, which had been mechanically rubbing away the impression of the belt in her child's tiny neck, froze in a comprehension that was also quite possibly the grown woman's very first experience of shame. "Oh," she said again, new tears springing up in those beautiful eyes, "*oh*, I didn't know!"

While her weeping mother clutched her (weeping, surely, out of joy as much as embarrassment to have missed every one of a thousand signs), Miki also heard the lamentation of the kami. It had come in the same tone, with the same depth of sorrow. The words had even sounded Japanese, in a way, but she knew they weren't. They hadn't even been the English her mother insisted they speak around the house. She sensed they weren't a human language. At some point, she tuned back in on her mother, who had been repeating variations of, "Forgive me! I've been an idiot—a total idiot! When you were littler and would argue that you were a girl, I thought—I thought you were just too young to understand. I didn't realize you were really…forgive me, oh, forgive me!"

Miki had just been saved from suicide *and* had come out as transgender—and here she was, patting her mother! Comforting *Yoriko* through *her* tears! The life of a narcissist's child: small wonder she should someday get on quite famously with the infamous eldest (living) daughter of the Hierophant. But, narcissist or no, Yoriko was the best possible parent for Miki, especially from that point on—though her maternal value may have peaked in those moments after her apologizing, when, collecting herself with a birdlike laugh, the former geisha sat up and daubed away her tears with the edge of a designer handkerchief.

"'Miki' is a very pretty name. Have you wanted me to call you that for long?"

Miki shook her head. "I've always wanted you to see who I really am…" She frowned, and could not think of a cautious way to say it. "The name…a kami told me that name, before I woke back up with you."

"Kami *desu*," repeated the woman in wonder. "You visited Yomi but didn't eat the food there. You're a smart girl." Being called a girl by Yoriko in such a casual way was so flabbergasting—so validating!—that a sheen of tears brightened Miki's bloodshot eyes and made it hard to focus on her mother's questions. "What was the kami you saw?"

"A beautiful woman. She—" The thought of having had and lost that marvelous body drove Miki out of her post-death daze and into a profusion of childish weeping. "She showed me my body. The body I'll have someday. I'll be so beautiful, like you."

"What woman," pressed her mother. "Izanami?"

"Maybe," agreed the girl, before her intuition gave an unpleasant twist, and she decisively shook her head. "No. Or maybe, this goddess and Izanami are sometimes the same, but she wasn't Izanami now. She couldn't have been, because I wasn't afraid. Even if I met Izanami at her most pure and beautiful, I think I'd be very afraid. This Lady, she was so perfect—bright—"

"Amaterasu," breathed Yoriko, and this elicited a more agreeable chill.

"Yes," the little girl hummed, removing from the unstable shelf of childish memory her culture's fables, which she remembered better at that time than her mother's Halcyon contact number. "Definitely, Amaterasu—but, in her cave. Before all the gods throw a big dance party to bring her out." The girl could not help her grin. Of all the stories she had by then been told of the ancient Shinto gods, that one most filled her with joy. Yoriko smiled, too, and mopped away her daughter's tears with that same fancy handkerchief.

"And how do you know that?"

"She was in a dark place, trapped—and sad. Susanoo should apologize for breaking her loom, and hurting her friend."

"Yes, he should—but he never will." Rocking back upon the heels of her stylish slippers, Yoriko said, "She'll need help coming out, won't she?"

"I want to help her," said the girl, holding back bold tears. "I want to be like Uzume, and dance so well that I make everyone happy. To call her out again."

"Then," agreed her mother, "we'll need to make you a pretty bronze mirror."

Few children experienced such an overnight change for the better. The very next day, Yoriko took Miki out of a school where she didn't get along with anyone and began to work on her transfer to an all-girl's school, where she could transition superficially without much fuss. It was far easier, and more sensible, than trying to get children to accept their current classmate's change. Even in that day and age, the subject of what to do about transgender children caused fierce debate in the Empire of the Risen Sun. Like opinions about women, homosexuality and other issues of human rights, these things waxed and waned with the centuries. It took a martyr's perspective to understand how little any of that mattered in the long run, which was often why such identities were considered inappropriate; but those same small-minded people usually eschewed genetic engineering and croaked, turning the tide back and forth every fifty or so years.

Socially speaking, things looked up for the Japanese transgender and homosexual communities around that time, but the subject was still iffy, so Miki had to be cautious yet adamant about the true nature of her identity. She was tired of being misgendered by well-meaning peers, teachers, and strangers, and she wasn't about to let those same individuals turn around and tell her she'd grow out of her own soul. Even Yoriko, after all, had mistaken Miki's initial protestations as some kind of phase or misunderstanding on the part of a toddler not equipped to comprehend gender. But when, in those weeks off of school, Miki's haircut appointment was canceled, and her wardrobe was completely changed over, and even her bed was replaced without warning to one with frills and curtains like a Western princess (maybe even *the* Western Princess—you know the one she meant), it was like a whole planet fell from Miki's shoulders.

Oh, her mother was still incredibly—sometimes shockingly—passive-aggressive ("No wonder she was such a *homely* boy," Yoriko once chortled in Japanese to a friend during tea time, right in front of Miki. "Her really being a girl and all! Isn't she pretty now?"), but that was just the way Yoriko was. It was all bearable when Miki could play the little-girl games from which she'd been ejected, or consigned to male roles. Now in "House" she could be the mother, and be a downright bitch just like Yoriko. Ah, childhood! Many pretend husbands, daughters, and dogs were slapped across the face with fans, slippers, and rolled-up paperbacks. In retrospect, it did explain her adult specializations in sadomasochism.

Somehow, in spite of how quickly Miki took after Yoriko when allowed to be herself, the girl made scores of friends in her new school. Friends! She'd never had any before. Slowly but surely, she started to have places to go that were not her own (still slightly oppressive) home. Meanwhile, Yoriko assuaged the girl's body image frustrations with mountains of gifts and more validations than the selfish old (okay, middle-aged) witch had ever given anybody. But it wasn't the stuff, the support, or the friends that kept Miki going as she blossomed, through the help of hormones, very mild genetic therapies, and—at the long-awaited age of eighteen—surgery, into a beautiful young woman.

The Lady was always there with her, after her suicide attempt. She couldn't explain how she knew it. She never *saw* Her, after all. Never even in dreams, though these did become more vivid after the experience. There was one time, though, that rocked her world and made her question her whole interaction with the entity.

It happened a couple of years after her vision. For some reason, the news always reported tabloid gossip about the martyrs and what they called their Holy Family. Ostensibly this was done to give people a glimpse into the existence of the enemy, but there were plenty of Japanese women who kept their eyes on Lavinia's current wardrobe. Yoriko was one.

Miki hadn't ever given a shit about the enemy, to be honest, for better or for worse. Japan was a safe place these days. Martyrs weren't welcome after the Pacific Conflict, and Miki lived in a happy snow globe of assumption that she would never, ever meet one of those predatory fiends. Hell! Even if she left the island nation, the odds of encountering a martyr were fairly low. Something around getting attacked by a shark or being struck by lightning. Okay…not that low, but *still*. No way was she going to have to worry about something like that! Consequently, she would laugh and roll her eyes when her mother, like all Japanese mothers, would use the boogie(wo)man that was Dominia di Mephitoli in early, ill-fated attempts to get her child to behave. She was still out there, the Governess of the United Front, always waiting to appear on the island with her Father and snatch up disobedient children when the supply of immigrants ran thin.

W-H-A-T-E-V-E-R. Especially once Miki was allowed to be a girl, there was no getting her to behave. Not even the infamous General/ Governess/etc. could threaten her. Nobody!

Except—with a bored glimpse up at her mother's program playing in their holo-corner one afternoon, Miki dropped her portable video game in shock. There, with Roman nose pale beneath her stern lapis eyes, floated a clear vision of the Lady.

How? It was more static and mortal than that vision, yet—Miki knew. The shape of the face, of the non-glowing eyes...it was all the same. "Who is that?" the girl asked her mother, who admonished her in surprise.

"Miki! Don't you pay any attention to the news, or social studies? That is the Governess of the United Front, that devil, Dominia di Mephitoli. I can't even stand to look at her damn face! Ugh." While the hologram's muted lips moved, Miki stared into the floating face with wonder before her mother plucked up the remote to fast-forward with a sigh.

"Just get to the Florentine...blah, blah, blah..."

Miki hid in her bedroom for a while after that. Now there was an experience to keep her up at night! The Lady was a martyr? Not just a martyr but one of the worst, most evil martyrs in all history?

She couldn't understand it. In that other place the Lady's image had been beyond comprehension or explanation. Yet when Miki thought of it now, there stood Dominia. That kami, awash with light, had the same face. She confirmed it with research that impressed her mother and earned her a couple of valuable history books that she wouldn't crack open until the Red Market expanded her interest in self-education. Even if she'd been into reading such heavy shit at the time of receiving those tomes, it would have been too much. It was already too much to sweep through her hand-me-down e-reader after doing an image search for "Governess of the United Front" and seeing image after image of the goddess from her suicide attempt.

There was no telling anybody about this. Ever. She had to keep this to herself. This was insane. She might have been seriously unhinged. And at such a young age! What was wrong with Miki? Had she just seen the

Governess in the background of news broadcasts, and been presented that image by her brain? Why? Why would her brain choose this evil martyr to represent Amaterasu? Why would Amaterasu take this form before her? The idea was a source of great spiritual consternation.

Yet, she knew she was not wrong. The Lady was real, and had chosen her. Had saved her. Why, she didn't know. She didn't know that any more than she knew why or how the martyr was tied to the Lady. Why she could not unconvince herself—why she eventually came to accept— that the two entities, no matter how evil one seemed, were one in the same. Maybe there was something to her mother's suggestion of Izanami, after all.

But it could not be Izanami. Could not be something evil, this kami, this Lady. No matter whose face She used, She was good. And She did not directly communicate with Her human charge, but She did seem to send some messages, somehow. Sometimes, going about her daily routine, Miki would get a flash of inspiration to do something drastic—eat fewer sweets, start working out, start wholeheartedly venerating Amaterasu—and Miki felt compelled to follow the action through. Good thing she wasn't being told to, like, stab somebody, or something, right? Though, admittedly, one of those impulses did lead to a pretty vicious falling out between herself and her mother. See, what had happened was, Miki was about fourteen when she started expressing real interest in following in the footsteps of her mother's work. After her experiences, Yoriko was reluctant but knew her daughter was smart and driven enough to make it in the ancient business of Japan's most fetishized class of women. Therefore, after school, Miki's schedule was crammed with music lessons, dancing lessons, elocution, etiquette, calligraphy, flower arranging, foreign language lessons, posture—for the Lady's sake, she had to relearn how to *walk*! It was about two years before Miki realized being a geisha absolutely, unequivocally sucked, no matter how romances written by Westerners tried to make it seem. Why did her mother do it? Miki asked her once, and, outside of the fact that her mother began training her around the age of seven, Yoriko had insisted that the career of the geisha was a living art that was to be kept alive.

Miki wasn't so sure about all that anymore. It was the opposite of her personality to be quiet, demure, and obedient—to sit and pluck her shamisen like a boring doll. Was this what she wanted to do all her life? Snore, snore, snore! No, thanks. About the time Miki was supposed to be promoted from *maiko* to actual geisha, which might have been a little more interesting, one of her fellow *maiko* mysteriously quit. That was all the incentive the admittedly lazy girl required to leave, herself, and put her skills of being an amusing beauty queen to work in hostess clubs. Yoriko wasn't happy, but what could she do? Her daughter, who had adopted the last name Soto while apprenticing as a geisha, was free to do what she wanted with her career, and working in hostess clubs wasn't so different from that most ancient of doll-like women's arts. So, her mother put up with her change in career until the day Miki was at the market picking up a shoulder of lab pork. That day, her abruptly missing former coworker bumped into her—or, more appropriately, came running for her while screaming, "Soto-chan, Soto-chan," across the crowded stalls. Always got a couple of hilarious stares from the Japanese, that name. Miki grinned at the strangers who returned to their business, then at her approaching friend. While nursing the stitch in her side, the tanned young woman stopped to kiss and hug Miki, and tell her (in the semiprivacy of fluent English) what she'd been up to: prostitution.

"You're Red Market," whispered Miki, trying not to be visibly disgusted but letting her shock remain. "Isn't that dangerous?"

"No, it's great! The women all take care of each other… Actually, I know a couple of girls who know your mother—from the foundation, isn't that funny?"

"You didn't tell them about me, I hope!"

"Of course not, of course—but, *Miki*—" The girl's voice dropped even lower, and the hostess was forced to lean in. "You have to come meet some of them. This industry, I'm telling you, it's much better than being a geisha. More fun. When you're a geisha, every man thinks he owns you. It's like he's renting you out for party decoration or something! But when I'm working for the Red Market, I'm so free. The Market and I are the ones in control."

"Sounds like some kind of weird, sexual pyramid scheme. But I guess a weird, sexual pyramid scheme is just a cult, huh?"

Though the girl's made-up and childish sticker-accented face flashed with annoyed, her expression regained its sly quality perhaps too soon. "Actually…you might call it a cult. A lot of the women involved, they do their work for religious reasons, to reach out to men and connect them with the divine."

"What do they worship?"

"I don't know. They're really obscure about it! They won't tell me its name, they just call it 'the Lady.'" The title, which was the same she had privately applied to that kami, shot a chill straight up Miki's spine while the girl went on. "I think it's Amaterasu, or something… I don't know, I don't care. I'm in it for that *money*, girl!"

"Good money?" asked Miki, as if she needed convincing now that the compelling nag of intuition built an electric tingle in the front of her brain.

"*Girl*," emphasized her friend, waggling her bleached eyebrows in a way that Miki's natural-colored ones echoed. "You don't even know."

She sure didn't! Hot damn. Yoriko threw Miki out as soon as she discovered her daughter had reacted to two nights spent shadowing a pair of experienced Red Market recruiters by quitting her stupid hostess gig, which was a-okay. It was time for Miki to spread her little wings and fly. And did she ever. She moved in with her *ganguro* friend and started turning tricks, which was weird at first but quickly became a total blast—especially when she discovered that most masochists didn't even expect or want the gratification of getting laid. Then she talked to her manager (aka, the woman who took a "small finder's fee" on behalf of the Market until Miki was a formal member, which wouldn't be until she was vetted for an interest in the Lady and trained as a priestess) about becoming an exclusive dominatrix.

Then, much to Miki's delight, she spent ten solid years embarrassing her mother at every turn. The young woman took particular joy in slipping work anecdotes into speeches given for the women's foundation, which she was often expected to do "[…]so some good [could] come out of [Miki's] [expletive] stupid career choices," as Yoriko put it one very drunken New Year's.

But, even if she didn't approve of Miki's lifestyle, Yoriko did seem proud of her daughter. She was proud of Miki because she knew Miki would do whatever Miki wanted to do, and there was nobody on Earth who could stop her.

What Yoriko didn't know was that Miki's actions were a compromise. Oh, yes, Miki did whatever she wanted to do; but she did whatever she wanted to do with respect to the wishes of the Lady. She worked hard—very hard—and, after receiving basic training as a lowly assistant priestess, became recognized as one of most valued (and valuable) members of the Red Market Kyoto branch when she was—well, an age older than twenty-six. Do we have to use numbers? Such *constraining* things…genetic engineering and martyrs in general meant that age only got relevant when it was advanced, anyway.

As her demand increased, another Market privilege revealed itself: travel. Meanwhile, her bank account grew as men literally paid her to take vacations outside of her claustrophobic island. Yoriko, of course, didn't approve, and was nervous her daughter would get swooped up and devoured by a martyr as soon as she set foot on foreign soil. But Miki knew she had nothing to worry about—the Lady was a martyr! How could a martyr be allowed to hurt her? Her fate was sealed. She knew she would be okay. Too bad Yoriko hadn't traveled some, herself! It might have done her good. But, no. The old crow believed she'd heard enough about the world from her clientele. She didn't even want to visit Europa! And she idolized that place, damn *seiyō kabure* that she was. No skin-care product could cure that Western rash of hers, but travel might have.

To the isolated nation of oppressive China; to the techno paradise of India; to the perfect restaurants of Unified Korea and; and, of course, to the glorious historical sites of the Middle States—Miki went everywhere, did everything, and met everyone she could. She always sent her mother a postcard, and would always later see that postcard hanging up in the kitchen. Things were fun and it was good to have her mother's tacit support, but then Yoriko began to express concern about her daughter's well-being again, and Miki sensed this was out of Yoriko's own fear of age. After a bit of soul-searching, Miki made the decision to reduce those trips, and intended to settle back down in Japan. Not to quit working, mind—just to stay in one place.

But, then, she got an invitation to a seminar. That was a pretty big deal. As a Red Market priestess (or priest, for there were plenty) moved through the tiers by donating time for various organizational efforts, more information would gradually be revealed about the nature of the religion. Like any good cult, of course. Miki, much like her former roommate, didn't really get into the religious aspect. She had her own personal connection to the Lady and was happy to help unburden the men who came to see her for spiritual reasons, but she couldn't help but look at structured religion with a skeptical eye. Who was anybody to tell her about the Lady, and who was she to tell anybody, in turn?

Still…the Asian Retreat, as that seminar was called, was in Hokkaido. How could anybody say no to that crab? (Or that glint of intuition that pushed her for it, but more importantly—the crab!) So, promising to bring her mother something tasty, Miki packed a bag for a week and took the Red Market's offered economy LRT pass to the meeting.

And, oh, boy, was it as predicted. The touchy-feely-let's-get-to-know-each-other New Age shit started the second her toe breached the threshold of the private grounds, and it didn't stop until she was ready to burn the place down. Playing games like "What color is your name" and "Attracting your spirit animal" were, to Miki, pointless corporate icebreakers rather than spiritual exercises. She was miserable. They even had classrooms, with syllabi for the various "classes" she was forced to attend. The best was the yoga thing, and even that was pretty tedious when they tried to work spirituality into it.

But the worst by far was the one on the fifth day, where all the people in her group sat around in a circle, closed their eyes, and were told to visualize the Lady.

Miki *almost* laughed. Almost. Somewhere, the Lady laughed for her.

When it came time for the women to go around the circle and share their own inner visions of the Lady, she couldn't handle it anymore. Slumped in her seat, hand cradling her forehead, Miki listened to woman after woman drone on about imaginary versions of the Lady that made her want to puke. Inevitably, She was described as having no clothes, or blonde hair, or no hair, or She was Asian, or She had cat ears (that was one Miki actually did laugh at, which earned her a few unpleasant glances), or had pixie wings, or She was made out of flowers, or, or, or…urgh! Finally, it was as another ditz described the entity as a Barbie doll with a cotton-candy-pink aura or something equally ridiculous that the opinionated woman could no longer contain herself, and into her shielding hand, muttered, "*Martyr desu.*"

The instructor may not have heard her, but the woman beside her did—and, oh, boy, did the look on her face change. Miki couldn't have been assed to learn a name at that retreat if they paid her to do it, which was why it was extra infuriating when this person who she didn't even know tapped her brusquely on the shoulder. "Excuse me," the stranger said, eliciting a groan from Miki along with the attention of the instructor. "What was that?"

What was that? "That" was it! Her whole—something-something-year career was about to be blown up because she was surrounded by idiots. A lifelong secret about her vision of the Lady, spilled now because of her own lack of self-control. Maybe her mother was right about her mouth.

"Nothing," Miki lied. The girl's tone grew all the hotter.

"You did! I heard you—you said the Lady is a martyr!"

Gasps! Theatrical, melodramatic gasps! Miki tried not to roll her eyes and wondered if they were going to start hissing her out of the room. Above the clamor, the instructor snapped to full attention and took a step that rattled her many beaded necklaces.

"Is it true?" demanded the instructor of Miki, staring her dead in the eyes like Yoriko finding drugs in a sock drawer. With a blasé glance for the women around, Miki crossed her arms and shrugged.

"Yeah, it's true. I did say that."

"How *dare* you," began to puff the tattletale. Thankfully, the instructor stopped her with a well-manicured hand.

"I think you should go to the Welcome Center, please." As another, softer set of gasps from the girls who liked Miki filled half the room, the instructor slid her digital glasses from her nose, regarded the younger woman, then nodded. "Yes. I think that's for the best. The Welcome Center's check-in quadrant, please."

She slipped the glasses back on and blinked their screens into operation—no doubt to give admin a heads-up that Miki was being ejected for having an opinion. The younger woman sighed, shrugged, and slid out of her chair. "I wasn't any good in school, either. Later!"

Outside the bungalow classroom, one of seventeen scattered across the grassy "campus," Miki's bold steps slowed to a pensive pace. This was why she chose that name—"Soto"! Even once she was herself, pretty, and popular, she was still an outsider. Her thoughts: they were what made her an outsider. Her thoughts, and her damn connection to the Lady. What was She? That vision…a kami, or an *oni*? Had the spirit guided her through all this, led her to this point, just to see her ejected from her career and sent with no professional training into the humdrum world of—*ugh*—the Japanese salaryman? No fucking thanks! Somebody just shoot her.

The Orwellian Welcome Center was divided into four quadrants, each with its own color flooring. She needed proceed no farther than the one in which she was deposited on her entry. The cheerful evergreen carpet made her feel like a kid waiting for the principal, and her foot's wiggling was so incessant that it had clearly begun to bother the secretary by the time the ominous office door opened. Maybe it shouldn't have been a surprise that the looming figure behind the frosted glass was revealed to be one of the most jaw-droppingly beautiful women Miki had ever seen: her head heavy with light-colored and elaborately beaded dreads, the mixed-race Amazon spared no time scanning the waiting area before locking eyes with the hapless Japanese priestess.

"Please come inside, Soto-san," implored the woman in fluent Japanese. "Shut the door after you."

Yes, that was it. So sad! She never thought this day would come. Miki had been fired from a restaurant job her mother made her work after catching her with "the dope" (dastardly cannabis! What a drug fiend, Miki) and had hoped she'd never have to repeat the experience, because the truth was it sucked. There were a billion ways to play it off and laugh about it, but at the time of her firing, she felt as small as she did while across the teak desk of a woman who introduced herself as Gethsemane. Or the desk at which she sat, anyway. The name of the person who belonged there was written in kanji on a plaque, and was nothing close to "Gethsemane."

"I'd like to talk a little about what you said today," began the fragrant manager, whose specific position remained unidentified for now.

"Please." Miki sighed so deeply her body sagged forward in her seat. "If I'm going to be fired, or disciplined, or whatever—"

"That's not what this is about, Soto-san." At the smaller woman's visible surprise, Gethsemane lowered her voice. Her professional tone now carried a reassuring, almost sisterly edge. "I'd just like to ask you about your thoughts. How you came to this conclusion."

Panic started to rise upon Miki. They'd think she was crazy. If nothing else, this was not a subject to be discussed lightly. Of those few times (before her journey with the General) where Miki experienced true fear, none were as palpable as that moment of being pressured into giving up the secret of the kami who had saved her. Was this what the Lady wanted? It wasn't a mistake she could make. She leaned back in her seat. "I don't know if I should really…talk about this."

"I understand." From the black cup beside the holo-screen computer, Gethsemane removed a pair of pens. Then, tearing apart a sheet of paper, she said, "Do you believe the Lady to be a specific martyr, or just 'a martyr'?"

"I—" At the woman's glance, Miki felt compelled to admit, "Specific."

"I'd like you to write the name of the individual on this sheet of paper." Sliding the scrap across the desk to Miki along with a pen, Gethsemane said, "I will also write the name of the martyr with whom I identify the Lady. Then, we can trade. Okay?"

The smaller woman's heart fluttered. "You think—"

But Gethsemane already wrote. With a trembling hand, Miki scribbled in English the words "Dominia di Mephitoli," then folded the scrap and exchanged it for Gethsemane's. As she opened it to read the katakana characters for "The Bitch of Europa," Miki's eyes filled with tears.

"What…" She looked up at Gethsemane, who glanced at Miki's paper before putting it through the shredder in the corner of the office. "Is this—is this real?"

"You write in English, Miss Soto," said Gethsemane in the language.

"Yes, my mother—but—"

"That's good. I prefer it." From the hands of the baffled Japanese woman, the foreigner lifted the scrap of confirmation and destroyed it, too, before returning to her seat. "I would like you to tell me how you came to know this information, if you wouldn't mind."

"Forget *me!*" Thrilled, now—validated in a way she hadn't been since her mother first realized her gender identity—Miki leaned forward and begged, "How do *you* know? Do *other* people know? Does your secretary out there know?"

"No. Twenty-five women within the Red Market organization understand the true nature of the Lady, and all of them are scattered across the seminars this month; none but my eight sisters and I know who exactly She is. Therefore, I would greatly appreciate it if you would tell me how you came upon this information."

Gladly. Miki spilled her guts right there in the office, confident that this was meant to be. Her heart sang with the release of a long-held beatific vision, and Gethsemane just listened. Listened patiently to every word of Miki's rambling tale, from her life's start in the wrong body and the suicide attempt that had revealed the truth, to the recognition of the Lady's face in the holo-corner, to the bursts of intuition that she sometimes received and that had ultimately led her right to that very office. As her long story wrapped up, she pressed the woman, "So, do you think it's real? What do you think all this means?"

"I think it means," said Gethsemane, "that you're the next avatar of the Lady."

What? She seemed to have lost her English comprehension for a few seconds there. But then Gethsemane said it again, and flipped open a hitherto unnoticed file with a petulant sniff. "Oh—wow, you're not in management? Then you don't understand."

Briefly, Gethsemane explained the true belief of the Red Market, which was hidden from all but the highest priestesses: that the Lady was not some metaphor or some dream consigned to a distant sphere but an entity responsible for maintaining the physical integrity of Earth—and that Her presence upon the planet, though required, was also unstable. For this reason, the Lady needed a body to inhabit.

For this reason, Miki was stilled.

"You want to take my body?"

"The Lady will, yes."

That was a startling notion. "Like, possession?"

"Like the divine descending upon you, emerging from within you. Your entire mind and body will be given up to the Lady. You can refuse, but—"

"No, I'm not—" Miki frowned in search of the words. Had she ever considered the point to her life? She'd just been living minute to minute for most of it, helping herself, and sometimes other people. She loved other people. For a long time now, she'd felt her only real point for existing was communicating with other people and obeying the whims of the Lady. If the whim of the Lady was that she should relinquish her body to this goddess, well…especially after getting a confirmation like this, she couldn't reject the request outright.

"Does it matter that I haven't always…you know." She nodded down at herself. Gethsemane shook her head.

"No. The second historical avatar of the Lady, during a time when goddess worship was at its height, was a cisgender man—albeit a pretty one. Physical sex does not matter. Her avatar always represents the compensatory principle in a given period of society. As the dominant aspect of society is, and has been for the past two thousand years, religion, our current avatar was a woman of science."

"And what will I represent, then?"

"If I had to guess, Miss Soto, I would suppose you represent transition in a world that struggles to maintain its dissipating status quo. And biological transition will be the reward for your valiant sacrifice. While your mortal body continues on in the world beyond even the point of a martyr's resilience, your soul will be rewarded with its true form. Given the miracles that tend to occur during the transference of the Lady between Her avatars, I would expect your body to be altered on a biological level in reflection of your self-image."

"So, my surgery, and all my…"

"Your body would become naturally feminine, yes."

If a sense of spiritual duty hadn't been enough of a stick, the carrot of two X chromosomes made her ask, "What do I have to do?"

Smiling for perhaps the first time since they'd met, Gethsemane slid another file, this one red, across the desk to Miki. She flipped its cover open to reveal several pages of information about a young Afghan man whose first name was Kahlil. "This young man, a regular customer of many Red Market women working Kabul, is in over his head with the Hunters. Of all members of that organization whose pride survives by our silences—and there are many—we believe that Kahlil is the perfect intersection of our needs. He is a man with important knowledge about the Hunters—perhaps too much, given his proclivities, and his tender heart."

Miki's whole expression sparkled with unbridled delight. "You want me to run, like, a honeypot operation on him? Like a *spy* movie? Oh, shit! Dude! This is crazy!"

"Please take this seriously, Miss Soto. This conversation has revealed you as the single most valuable member of the Red Market, which makes you the second most important woman worldwide. Third, I suppose; but the Lady's highest manifestation, within her avatar, goes without saying."

"Why is the Lady in two places at once? As the avatar, and as Dominia di Mephitoli?"

"Many mythologies throughout history chronicle the plight of the demiurge created by Sophia, or the horned man trapped by the great goddess…Demeter, bearing Typhon. The Governess of the United Front does not, cannot, understand that she has done the same with the Hierophant."

Dazzling Amaterasu's sunlight, bursting from her cave. "But the goddess—she's been trapped, too."

"Yes. She sacrificed Herself to Her own trap that we could all be saved from the same, even the Hierophant."

Prior excitement began to fizzle. Miki wrinkled her nose. "That sounds like Christian Abrahamianism. But, like, with a feminist gloss."

Gethsemane chuckled wryly as she rose, taking Miki's personnel file and leaving Kahlil's blackmail one. "That's the greatest secret of all, Miss Soto. Something *only* I and my sisters know…we are all describing the same thing. Abrahamians, martyrs, Red Market, none of the above. We are describing the Word, Logos, who also arrives on Earth to lead the Lady to victory. You know—" She had looked about to leave, but paused a foot from the door, beside Miki in that cramped space.

"When I was younger, I believed Western thought and Abrahamian faiths were incompatible with belief in the Lady. But a spirit descended upon me when I was seventeen; a spirit I was not. This spirit brought me knowledge of which I had none, and this same spirit brought me to my sisters. I am no longer the self that I was. I was shown the truth—that there is a man who stands with the Lady, as the Lady, as mentor to the Lady, and as the son and servant of the Lady. The spirit ordered me to sleep and in my dreams showed me many things, including a great book: the words "the Queen of Peace" were written there. A title for Mary, but the voice of the spirit with me said, "This is also a title of Christ when He is upon the Earth."" Gethsemane studied Miki's face carefully.

"Do you understand what that dream told me? I did the instant I awoke. Christ *was* Mary. Christ was God and fully human, so the Christians of my village taught. Therefore, his human DNA, his body, had to come from somewhere. From a physical, scientific perspective, unless the Holy Spirit brought with it the DNA of an earthly man, Jesus of Nazareth must have been a masculinized clone of his mother. A perfect genetic duplicate in every way, physically presenting with a dick and a beard." Miki grinned at the woman's playful obscenity in proximity to spiritual discussion as slightly smiling Gethsemane asked, "Dig me? The sacred androgyny of Christ is real. The Logos is real. And our Lady, Dominia di Mephitoli, will use his help, and yours, to save the world. But first, she has to change."

Change, for sure! While Miki spent months sowing seeds with Kahlil, apologizing to her mother from afar for her false homecoming, she watched the news and waited as she'd been instructed to by further contacts with Gethsemane. She was a real secret agent! And, like most real secret agents, she succumbed to her damned emotions in that little honeypot scheme of theirs.

Oh, Kahlil. It was never his fault that Miki shut him out! She just had trouble with feelings. After he got comfortable enough with her to start falling asleep near her, she'd watch him sometimes, and think, yes, there was something very cute about him. He had a lot of bad habits and had spent an unfortunate amount of time trying to get in good with the Hunters, but she could see that he, like a lot of men, was just perpetually disappointed every woman he encountered wasn't also his mother. (Personally, Miki was relieved every woman she'd slept with wasn't her mother, but that was the difference between men and women!) So, she mothered the bullshit Internet- and Hunter-instilled misogynistic expectations right out of his sorry ass, showing him that her skills extended beyond artful spankings and good—well. The point is that Miki spent a lot of time with Kahlil, cooking for him, seeing movies with him, listening to him nonjudgmentally, spoiling him with gifts like he was just any old friend or family member. And as she saw his gradual drift of interest from the Hunters and onto her, she discovered her own feelings had developed somewhere along the line.

What was she supposed to do with those? Especially once she considered the business nature of their relationship—and the aspects about which he was unaware. But she got him to open up to her about all he knew, and soon enough she abused that knowledge by passing it along to higher-ups. Then May Day of CE 4042 came around, and, well…there was that change she'd been waiting for. While the red-eyed Governess struggled to hold it together during her wife's globally televised funeral, Miki pulled the rug out from under Kahlil.

The fight! Was it worth recounting? He had accused her of using him, of abusing him, of crushing his very heart. All this was like a series of stabs in Miki's, but this was why she'd kept as far away from those kindling emotions as she possibly could. In as calm and businesslike a fashion as she could manage, she'd laid out the conditions of his future: he would help her and the Governess reach Lazarus. They'd fought and fought until he asked her why she was doing this. She told him about the Lady, withholding her gender identity, because he hadn't figured her history out and it was none of his business if she didn't tell him. Then he'd turned on misplaced sympathy. A Hunter, telling her *she'd* been brainwashed!

This religious aspect allowed him to forgive her, somewhat—especially when she admitted she did love him. But he was still being blackmailed into betraying his affiliated regime, and that wasn't pleasing to any man. If he'd been in a proper relationship, it would have been time to rethink that relationship's whole foundation; but poor Kahlil had thought himself only worthy of the love that he bought, and, well…

Miki was more loyal to the divine than to romance.

Of course, sometimes she wondered if she was on the right path. The boy continued to love her in a disappointed way, and Miki couldn't help but ask if it was worth hurting him to do all this. She questioned right up until that fatal September, when the Governess abandoned her post, and an order came through from Gethsemane: to return to Japan, to say goodbye to her mother, and to prepare to bring the Governess to Cairo in preparation for the Lady's renewal ceremony.

The finality of it all…somehow, Miki almost couldn't manage to see her mother that last time. Yoriko suddenly looked so old! All the skin care in the world, all the mild therapies to which she'd opened up after her daughter's plight—none of it could save her from the fact that she was still someday going to die.

Miki, too, would someday get old and die.

Did she want that? She asked herself while her mother, after dinner, presented her with that same shamisen which had been her partner throughout her famous career. Did she want to get old and die—or did she want to live forever with her consciousness split across two planes of reality and her body hosting the spirit of an immortal goddess?

The choice was obvious; but, in the cab back to her hotel room, Miki couldn't help but cry. They felt the same as the tears she'd spend with Dominia, in her room before that ceremony. Those forty days in Cairo had blurred by, and Miki, still reeling from the physical existence of her imaginary friend and the sacrifice that she was about to undergo, could hardly understand Kahlil's bitterness toward her. She loved him, damn it! Wasn't it enough for her to love him *and* be sorry that she couldn't spend her life with him? Wasn't it enough for him to be there? But he didn't even want to be at the ceremony.

That was why it was so surprising when, as the ringing of her spiritual transference cleared away and she had said goodbye to Dominia, Miki became aware of a body—her *body*! That body she had seen before the Lady! *Oh*, what a body!

But she was aware of this body because of the body across from it. Kahlil's body. Joy filled her to see him, and sorrow, and Kahlil, tears in his unobscured eyes, said, *"I made such a terrible mistake. I'm sorry."*

Everything he had done: she saw it now. In fact, she saw *everything*. Somehow, it was as if she'd always known everything—everything in the world. As if she'd put it there, herself. But that was the Lady in her, she knew. The Lady, and the higher spirit behind Her. Miki's own pains for her crimes filled her breast and she took her lover's hand.

"And I used you. Kahlil…I played with your heart like it was my shamisen. You know—I don't regret anything in my life, my career or any of that. But I wish somehow…it would have been nice to be your wife. I couldn't have had your kids, though. I'm sorry I lied to you about that, by the way."

"It's okay… I knew."

Miki's eyes widened, and even there, in the Void, she smacked him across the face for her embarrassment. *"You cad! Why didn't you say something? I thought you didn't know!"*

"Of course I knew. I can't explain it. I just spent a lot of time with you, so of course I figured it out. But…I didn't care. Why would Allah care if you really felt like a woman, and presented as a woman, and thought like a woman? I was thrown for a loop about it for a while, but you know, I just loved you too much, and you were always a woman to me, so…"

"Oh, Kahlil." As always, when at risk of emotions, she had to turn them into humor. She hid her face behind her heron dotted sleeve. *"Well, it's paid off for you, now! Would you look at my figure?"*

"You were always perfect." His smiling faded into hesitation, and he glanced down at her hands as they slipped into his. *"Would you be with me now? After the way I betrayed you, got all those women killed?"*

Your own death was punishment enough, I believe.

The starburst of the ascended Lady struck the two lovers through with the glory of Her light. These same crystal beams dissolved Kahlil through Miki's hands; she knew without a hint of fear that she would see him soon enough. Instead, she threw her arms around the Lady's neck and embraced the deity with unabashed joy.

"See why I had to kiss you when we first met." Miki laughed. Even the radiant kami smiled at that. *"I'm still a little sorry, though, to leave it all behind."*

I want to show you something. Something I saw when the True Word was first unveiled to my exposed mind.

With Miki's arms around Her, the deity rose high through the Void. They penetrated that sphere of darkness and a brilliant and beautiful light—more brilliant than even that of the Lady!—was left naked all around them. Their pace only increased, the speed so vast that it tore away the flesh of the goddess and revealed, one by one, those beautiful pillars who maintained Her physical presence: first that vast woman found in many an ancient statue, success and happiness where there was famine; then a beautiful man who would someday inspire stories of Adonis; then a glorious beekeeper who became known variably as Astarte, Isis, Ishtar, Inanna, and a bevvy of other titles; then, across the sea, a slender young native woman who traveled through a region later known as the Ohio Valley and, amid varying tribes of people sometimes lumped together as the "Adena," sowed a language of cultural symbolism full of weeping eyes, and animals becoming men, and the sinful horrors of cannibalism; then, in Europa, as Christianity crested to its height, a schizophrenic barbarian girl babbled herself full of the Lady, and would someday give way to the science-minded Trisha Robbins.

Then, of course, Trisha peeled Robbins away and revealed the body of Miki Soto: and Miki realized she had never been Miki to begin with. That body chipped off as the unnamed watcher observed on, and lo, Dominia di Mephitoli ascended through those many spheres of reality, those many highest heavens, until Dominia, reaching up, found she was but the eighth vessel of that electric entity known in human tongues as "the Lady." Beyond that highest sphere against whose membrane she paused to press, the fingers of a ninth, unseen, untouched, too-close Lady wove a lightning that cracked the General down, down, down into the body of Miki Soto, in whose form she dwelt until the fateful night of Dominia's death.

XVII

The Battle for Jerusalem

It was not possible to express all Dominia now understood. She had, since the nascent turnings of the planets, waited. Suspended in that edge-of-sleep superposition of existence/nonexistence until consciousness began to take root in what could be called "humans." As the substance of the physical hologram representing that iteration of reality, she lay present in all things. "All things" included human DNA. The Lady was to the human genome what Saint Valentinian was to the sacred protein, perhaps. Where the tail ended and the head began on that strangely orbiting ouroboros, the physical mind could have hardly gleaned. Speech was inadequate to transfer the experiential information; even writing had its shortfalls. Take, for instance, that taboo place with a thousand names. That realm between the living reality and the storage of the Kingdom.

After all, it was not proper to call this space the Ergosphere. Even that image, devoid of face, possessed too much substance. The true form of that taboo place could not be perceived, could not be thought—for, in thinking It into the shape of any one thing, It craftily made that thought the smoke screen by which It got away. Dominia had existed in a perpetual state of It, even when she dwelled within her avatars and was able, minimally, to interact with that world she supported. Through their hands she guided the flow of human events so that, by the time the Hierophant arrived in 1974 CE—the year of his old self's birth—he was perpetually entering the iteration midgame.

He thought it was his wish that brought him to this new iteration of the world. Had he say in the matter, of course, he would have arrived at the dawn of time just as Dominia had. And, in ways, he had. His shadow had, at any rate. Dreams of him emerged in the collective dream of humanity long before he fizzled into existence in this particular plane. Even the Lamb, whose earthly body was not born until soon after that fatal year of 1974, had the ability to afflict probability for such a vast expanse of space-time that his probability field, the Lady now understood, encompassed a great period of time both before his birth and after his death. Many improbable events had occurred in human history, and it was impossible to say which ones had been nudged this way or that by his brother's future requirements even before that evil brother was physically upon the planet.

Because the Hierophant was not present until she allowed him to be, and until the hologram of reality could accept the existence of his genetic code error. From the moment of his arrival, he had total freedom. Access once more to all the sweet potential of the unconquered world. A mouse had no say in where its neck would someday be snapped, nor say in the bait or placement of the trap. He was a miserable wretch who had lost the only thing he loved in the world—his brother—and who deluded himself with the notion that there was a way to get him, it, life, back.

Now, more than ever, the Lady understood Cicero's plight. But she had no sympathy for his means, his choices, his cruelty. His *cruelty.* Only after receiving the full input of all those souls within her did the hyper-dense spirit of the former General understand the depth of his horrors. Two thousand years of people, brainwashed from a state of childhood innocence into a race of sexually violent reprobates. It was still possible for them to be saved, and that was why the Lady fought on. But that salvation could only be accomplished once their Church's Father had been supplanted by a better-intentioned individual.

The Bearers' physical tradition had begun with the first avatar's daughters, who were miraculous for their time in that all nine survived from birth to adulthood. After her ninth, the Lady came upon her and never left; one by one, the daughters dreamed their Bearer-dreams, and the much-worshipped, well-fed, and ultimately widely loved holy Lady began the worldly tradition of devotion to spirits, which, unlike the animal-spirits present all around, were invisible, and took the shapes of men and women. At once, the Bearers set upon her bidding, spreading these teachings and gathering resources. Lady after Lady, into the modern days and nights, amassed a great stockpile of wealth, connections, and blackmail material. There was nothing they could do to stop the rise of martyrs, or her Father—she understood now that many previous iterations had been run with that intention, and the knowledge of their failures (which, prematurely given, certainly would have collapsed living Dominia's mind into an early black hole) assured her there was nothing that could be done. One way or another, his infestation had to take root to be exterminated.

In the meantime, she established her base. A silent army, which became a very vocal one when the living Dominia di Mephitoli, disgraced and fleeing her country, stumbled into control of several cells of Hunters. Then, all the years of close conspiracy spent fighting the global bureaucracy paid off. Then, with the help of the Red Market, Miki Soto and many others brought together by the suicidal ideations of the Lamb's transtemporal probability field, the Lady saved herself.

How funny to watch Dominia! What a child she had been. Yet, the Lady Dominia was not so far removed from the General Dominia: when Miki, before her ascension, brought Cassandra's diamond there to Cairo, the slight weight upon the breast of Trisha inspired the first starburst of real emotion the pan-dimensional entity had experienced in an entire reality's worth of timeless existence. Space-time was but fabric to her, that folding, washing, working laundress who sometimes wove it, too, and she ran it through her fingers to touch any spot that pleased: she touched that spot of private reunion again and again and found such endless bliss that it was good the avatar's mind was bound to time, or the Lady might never have accomplished anything. Therefore, even the goddess was encouraged by that unseen first moment of Miki's in the Cairo throne room. All of this was done with good purpose. Miki's body had been given up for good purpose.

In Jerusalem, that body ruled with an iron fist. The General, obviously, did not like it, but the city's outskirts had been left in terrible shape by Akachi and the Israeli attempts to liberate the holy town. As European and UF forces began to amass, first in Turkey and then, with permission after the exit of Israel from the union, the Middle State of Syria, the Lady calmly continued pouring money into fortification efforts—and repair efforts, especially as the drone bombings began to stack up. The General grew visibly more frustrated as the year wore on, and her men, having for years resorted to dirty warfare tactics like suicide bombers and exploding trucks, were not content to sit around and wait for the UF to close in on the city's heart.

Direct hostilities began in March of 1998 Anno Lucis, when a unit of European troops was accused of entering Israeli territory. Soon enough they were doing it openly, pacing astride mechanical warhorses which bellowed smoke from their nostrils in a touch that served no use to the device: mere grade school intimidation. The Lady continued to enforce this miserable period of waiting, while citizens of Jerusalem were evacuated and the General drove north and south, east and west, begging for money, donating her time to the people of Israel, reviewing the behaviors of (and frequently firing entire offices of) military police units installed by the Hunters, etc. By this point in time, what little military force was ascribed to the state of Israel was nowhere near Jerusalem, and was neither inclined to help Dominia, nor to assist in the Hierophant's capture of their own holy city. Therefore, that sprawling city had been forced to act as its own state for some time—in the centers and neighborhoods that had been less savaged by the initial Hunter swarms, Akachi's men had actually established quite an impressive working infrastructure if you didn't mind a few public beheadings in exchange for clean roads.

But clean roads meant a lot when you planned to fight in them. If Jerusalem had been forced to act as a sovereign state, the Hierophant's armies sure invaded it like one. By the time the very angry, very depressed General was shipped off to kidnap Theodore, she had witnessed the systematic loss of about a third of her newly earned city. While she was a brutal killer and an expert military leader, the fact of the matter was that Dominia had been running a city under siege, and from the start, it had about as much hope as the infamous American Alamo. While it was true that it sometimes took as many as two to three days to clear a single large apartment building (sufficiently fortified and defended), the Hierophant had unlimited resources to throw at the problem of Jerusalem, and had been waiting for this moment a mite longer than two thousand years.

Good thing the Lady had been waiting for eternity. This was why she was patient while Jerusalem fell, and silent as Dominia fought her losing battle, scrambled between bombing sites, and tried to make a real difference in some human lives. While developing within her mortal form, the General had been too hard on herself. She had, in fact, changed, and worked hard to repent for her odious crimes with every remaining second she had.

Those precious few seconds, compared to the mass of all those before. It was with calculated self-knowledge that the Lady hid all truths from Dominia, including her true reason for returning to the Front and kidnapping Theodore. Teddy's utility was beyond the scope of their battle, far into the future. After all: the next Hierophant of the Holy Martyr Church would require an adviser and friend. Someone whose belief in Dominia's righteousness was wholehearted and earnest, so that, as the Church made its transition from sedated worship of the Ciceros, there could be no hope of backslide. Theodore del Medico was, for that purpose, ideal, because the existing Hierophant could hardly help but torment the fool he oh-so-cleverly martyred to someday lure his arrant daughter back home.

With such slight effort, the finest blade was turned upon the wielder! The Hierophant sensed the Lady's importance and dangerous nature, of course, but his hubristic overestimation of his own abilities would always be his downfall. Many a Dominia had died by his hand, yet he did not realize he had not won. Would never win. Even as UF troops closed in on the Library of Jerusalem in the weeks following the mysterious vanishing of the kidnapped Governor—along with his kidnappers—while in Atlantic airspace, the Hierophant marched his troops nearer his own demise.

And their unfortunate demises, safe to say. The Hunters were ragtag but formidable fighters who had adapted their styles for total destruction of martyrs, whether alone or in groups. As most of the low-level members of the Hierophant's military were expendable humans, this meant the terrorist organization had a slight advantage— because they were willing to fight like they, themselves, were inhuman. Red Market women, less savage, were no less effective, and those liberated *sabiyya* who had been brainwashed by their Hunter captors and sometimes taught to fire guns were most formidable fighters, themselves.

While all groups defending their stake in Jerusalem laid down their lives to secure the city and defend the Lady's avatar within the library, UF and European forces resorted to their own terror tactics. Accused members of al-Mawta were beaten, scalded, hanged, and occasionally disemboweled for officers' supper, all of it on film for the benefit of the remaining organization members. The logic among the troops seemed to be the same logic used to justify Hunter war crimes: the same logic Dominia had once used, herself. "It's what they're doing to us."

Now there was a truly unending snake! That twisting circle: pure, hopeless violence. Dominia wanted to blame the Lady for allowing the deaths of many troops on both sides, but the truth was that the General was as much to blame or more—for engaging in defense was simple perpetuation of that evil tide, when one got right to the point. On, on galloped the bleak steed of Saint Valentinian, whose bright star, Mars, still glittered with tints of red above Jerusalem's winter nights. Two and a half weeks after the disappearance of the General, supply lines to the Lady's library were cut off. Outside the library, human troops were forced to evacuate and regroup outside the city by that same tunnel system utilized by the industrious Hunters before the battle rose to frenzy. Within the library, fewer than one hundred men and women had been allowed to remain.

The Lady, her Bearers, and Lazarus also remained. While the goddess sat in silence in the center of her chambers, the mystic, along with the eight remaining Bearers, devoted themselves to maintaining the large building's perimeter.

In truth, those eight women had died many times. Over the course of one iteration of reality, the nine servants of the Lady attached themselves to a variety of women more endless than even that chain of avatars. Therefore, throwing away their lives for a purpose such as this was little more than the changing of clothes. They consoled those remaining loyalists who were either die-hard servants of the Lady or devout Hunters who understood that the loss of Jerusalem to the Hierophant meant a tremendous blow against human rights. Death was not so bad, the Bearers assured the people. From within, one didn't even notice it had happened.

Dominia had noticed, but that was because she was supposed to notice. She was not allowed to not notice, because in the noticing of the moment of death, she transcended physical boundaries to become death. Valentinian was but a prototype for the Lady, and her little shadows were those Bearers who arranged themselves in windows and, stone-faced, sniped for hours without rest. Lazarus hated this business, as always.

"I feel like I'd ought to turn myself in and settle it early sometime," he confided in her one evening four nights into the siege. "Avoid some deaths. But then I remember who we're fighting and I remember that the deaths will just happen anyway, and maybe more brutally than they ever could have while on the field of war."

Never underestimate the cruelty of the Hierophant when given time to reason, agreed the Lady. *You know we must wait.*

Yes: they had to hold out at least as long as it took for the cavalry to arrive and get captured alongside them. This was easier said than done, as were all things in war, but for as much advance intelligence as the Hierophant could be said to possess, the Lady possessed infinitely more. Every time a strike was launched against this weak point or that part of the tunnel system, her troops were ready to defend; and though their number dwindled by a few every skirmish, their assailants were threshed in staggering numbers that forced inevitable regrouping to controlled portions of the city. The block around the library changed hands every day, every night, moving in dominance like a bloody game of capture the flag. Fortifications made amid the bombed-out ruins of the city were only further destroyed when the civilian-free area was subject to drone strikes from the Hunters positioned in other areas of the city; great damage was done to the sieging army, and to Jerusalem's buildings.

The devastating truth was that the holy city was in ruins. From the uneasy semi-peace of Hunter occupation to the chaos emerging with Dominia's control, the entire state had been emotionally and fiscally drained. That the Middle States had even allowed Israel's exit was symptomatic of the fact they proved more liability than comrade. And once the Holy See of the True Catholic Church was evacuated around the time the Hierophant's drone strikes ramped up—July of that year—palpable despair had settled upon the city of Jerusalem and failed to lift. The assault of the Hierophant's troops was not a liberation or even an invasion so much as it was a nihilistic inevitability.

No one with a mortal, human perspective could comprehend the shortsighted nature of such ennui. It took a goddess to see that all things would be set right in the end. A goddess, a god, or a disruptive saint.

The infamous UFO crash near the peak of the Battle for Jerusalem would prove a pox on historians and an inspiration to conspiracy theorists for several centuries. Rumors abounded about the Holy Martyr Church's suppression of documents regarding the crash, but this wasn't true in the least. A study was released not ten years after the incident firmly and clearly explaining that the object—which crashed into the northwest corner of Jerusalem's library during a key moment in the assault, then disappeared, thus disrupting the first concrete penetration UF troops had made into the target and forcing the assailants to regroup while ultimately leading to their most exploitable point in entry—was not unidentified. It was, in fact, merely an inter-dimensional amphibiship (or a portable tear in reality, if one preferred) that allowed passage into, through, and beyond that semi-real zone about which science would know next to nothing concrete for several more centuries. Very elementary stuff; but conspiracy nuts would light up the Internet for years, insisting the object was the miraculous intercession of some beings from outer space.

Beings that, if the (openly published and circulated) letters of several survivors to their relatives were to be believed, resembled the martyr Saint Valentinian, a pilot of Middle Eastern origin, the Governor of the United Front, and a chubby sailor. Of the four (five, if one included the ship), only the pilot and Governor remained; at least, only the pilot and the Governor were secured. The pilot notably dashed into the fray on the opening of the ship's door, and was therefore obtained alive by a resourceful martyr corporal who saw a real promotion in his future for the deed. The Governor, who was whisked away by that entity resembling the martyr saint, was to be secured alongside Lazarus.

But that was not to say the entity resembling Saint Valentinian was not seen on Earth again. Far from it: on the disappearance of the E4 and the sailor at its helm, the fictional martyr made a personal appearance in the Lady's chamber to kiss her hand and startle the three Bearers hovering around her.

"They'll be back at the breach pretty soon," advised Valentinian. "This is our last stand."

We perceive you brought the Governor.

"Would you expect any less? I gave him to a couple of your Bearers about an hour ago. Farhad's back on Earth, too. Followed my instructions to the letter and got himself caught. He'll be handy when all this is through. Tenchi is safe and sound, though—on his way to meet you."

You are our greatest treasure, Valentinian. It's by the grace of God you're on our side, and not our Father's.

"By the grace of your wisdom, maybe. That coot is so busy being clever with his thoughtforms and elaborate tortures that he couldn't learn a True Word if you taught him in a dream." As Lazarus entered the room without a knock and strode to shake his hand, the magician turned to greet him. "You ready for the final act, old man?"

"I wish you could find some way to keep it from coming to this."

"Ah, hell, you know it's nothing to be worried about. Your service is crucial! You're like the sexy lady of my magic show's finale." While the old mystic rolled his eyes at the laughing saint, Valentinian went on. "Or a volunteer from the audience, if you'd prefer."

"I would much prefer that."

"I just mean to say, your part—"

"I get it. What do I look like, Dominia? I don't need a pep talk. I know why I'm here. Just change out the fucking blood, already."

With a chuckle, Valentinian tapped Lazarus in the center of the forehead. The mystic collapsed on the spot and the Bearers cried out as if the Lady, Herself, had fallen to the floor. While they rushed to his side, Lazarus came to with a series of derisive waves. "Don't," he said. "Don't worry about me, don't."

"Yeah, and don't injure him, either. Treat him like he's made of paper. Once somebody sees him bleed in this state, the jig is up."

Will you stay and help us fight?

"I wouldn't miss it for the world," promised the magician. "It's been a long time since I've had an opportunity to show somebody my true face. I'm just sad you won't be there to see the way a human brain reacts!"

Near omnipotent though she was, the Lady was relieved to hear he intended to help thin the library's assailants. The truth was that once hostile forces poured into the breach, no options would remain but direct conflict. The (now closer to seventy) humans who had stood their ground for almost two weeks, who had watched their supplies dwindle to nothing and their hopes dash along with them, would very soon lose their lives. Some would survive to surrender, but most could not stand to be so disgraced and would fight to the death for their honor. The Bearers would fight to the bitter end, much as the Lady wished it otherwise. But their role upon the Earth would be settled once the goddess departed it—and she would be departing it not terribly long after Jerusalem's fall.

Therefore, when the north wing of the library was secured, and two Bearers died, the Lady felt the jerks of their spirits like hooks removed from that weaving of space-time, and mourned in perfect, still silence. As the Hierophant's troops swept through the great series of halls— slightly modified over the previous year to confuse any intelligence from the prior iteration, as usual—dear, naïve Theodore was brought into the room by the two beautiful Bearers who had been attending to him. Their faces, grim masques heavy with their sisters' deaths, were ill-suited for Teddy's sparkling, wild eyes.

"What a place! I'm telling you— Oh, Valentinian! There you are. Ha ha, I thought you'd zipped off with that Japanese fellow!"

Never can hold his sacrament, observed the Lady, Miki's old body quirking its lips into a paralytic smirk. *Hello, Theo.*

The cheery man turned to face the goddess with pupils blown big with lysergic acid—administered to prepare him for the coming moments, for otherwise his mind would have no lubricant to cope. Like the chorus of a song he didn't know he sang, the Governor repeated that question Dominia had so many times during the final year and a half of her life. "Do I know you?"

You will recognize us soon. One of us, at any rate. And when you do—

Gunfire burst through a nearby hall and was returned while Teddy winced. "Are we just going to sit here? We can just evacuate to that other place, can't we?"

Your most important duty lies in Elsinore. Your charge—Lavinia needs you.

As Theodore glanced the way of the magician, who had disappeared to meet at least one of the squads approaching through the maze of halls, shelves, and multilevel mezzanines, the former doctor turned back to the Lady with real concern in his eyes. "I see," he said, and then, in an acid-deep tone, "I *see*. You're the Lady, aren't you?"

We are the wisdom hidden by your Father for centuries, until now. As a collection of screams arose to quick abortion, the Governor was grabbed by one of the Bearers to ensure he wouldn't dart off like a startled cat. Another team cleared the hallway directly outside the Lady's room, and could be heard calling commands back and forth. From the slightly elevated platform where the avatar knelt, the goddess's eyes raked in the direction of a freehanded Bearer, then nodded to the door. Farhad had surrendered out of the jet so they would understand his value and would not fail to claim him. Watching assailants had then been treated to a very visible demonstration of the martyr saint and his first mate tossing the Governor of the Front out of the other side of the object, into the breach its crash had caused, and the waiting arms of the Bearers below. This apparent intercession of Valentinian's on the defenders' behalf had been the true reason for retreat: white terror would stab the hearts of even the bravest men if they saw their spirit of death delivering into enemy hands that very hostage who had started the battle.

But, omens went both ways. The Hierophant, on hearing of this, had sent his reinterpretation: the gracious Saint Valentinian had placed the Governor where he could be found. By sheer miracle, the man feared lost over the Atlantic had been returned to life. Obviously, once the extraction teams reclaimed him, Theodore del Medico would be canonized. Wouldn't it be delightful to go down in history as the soldier who rescued a true saint?

Thus, the Lady and her companions found themselves in the besieged library. Lazarus, still disoriented from the magician's monkeying with his bodily fluids, rubbed his forehead and eventually succumbed to sink against the nearby shelves with a wave of his hand and the assurance of Teddy's Bearer that he was fine; the other, to whom the Lady had indicated, strode to the chamber's double doors. Much as Dominia had in that hospital so long ago, the Bearer threw the entry open before the wood could be blown from its hinges—but now, the onslaught of men into the room did not hesitate, more organized, officious, and clamorous than even those Hunters had been during the Cairo transference ceremony. As laser sights were waved around, orders were issued for hands to be put in the air. Wryly, Lazarus lifted one of his exhausted ones, and said, "I'll be able to lift the other in about five minutes of recovery," while a gun was shoved in his face.

The Lady continued speaking to Theodore as if a fly had buzzed between them. *For two thousand years and centuries longer, our power has been hidden from mortal men. That is why, Theodore, we have brought you here before seeing to your safe return home.*

"Get your hands up," an ape screamed of the Lady. One of several who aimed their sights upon her.

Therefore—

The power died in the room—along with the air conditioning, the distant buzz of charging e-readers, and an undetectable background of electronic noise—for the two heartbeats it took the Lady to reappear, standing, in the doorway behind the infiltration team.

—*it is imperative that you pay attention.*

Amid the phantom beat of *suzu* bells, Miki's body took a step forward. The body she left behind, Trisha, stepped right and revealed the madwoman. While the stupider of the confused military men knew little else to do than bark orders, a few others lowered their guns in confusion and terror while the madwoman stepped left to unveil the Adena teacher; as this spirit stepped back to release the avatar called Ishtar, as shot was fired. It penetrated the forehead of Miki's body and the shooter dropped dead, bleeding from a bullet wound between the eyes.

As the expression goes, all hell broke loose. While, step by step, the goddess unfolded like a humanoid lotus around the long-hidden body of the true Lady, those already unfurled petals leapt into the fray, claiming weapons or speaking their own into existence. Each fought as if the General herself still dwelled within their body, and indeed, they could no longer be said to be separate from her in any way. Even once they physically stood, eight bodies in the same room, they moved with the kind of unity a military team could only dream about.

From the corner of the room, Theodore cried out and leaned around the Hierophant soldiers who had found, freed, and encircled him. "Is that *Dominia*," the man screamed.

In a manner of speaking. What was Dominia to begin with? Light bouncing off a pile of flesh. Thinking flesh, thinking with light. That ultimate carrier of information! The true messenger! Fleet-footed Mercury. Dominia was that same immutable no-thing substance, this quintessence of dust like all these men who fell out of existence beneath her many hands and into the Void where she now had no shame for sending them. In this state, she had not made them. But she had triggered their existence, their exit from the Kingdom, and she would trigger their replacement within it. It was not acceptable, their deaths at her hands, but it was a fact. It was part of their duty, to die here, in this place, beneath the weapons of the eight warrior selves—yes, even that Rubenesque first avatar—who had, in alternative fashion, already laid down their lives for their duty.

And die, they did. Quick deaths. Those who made the mistake of attacking the Ladies died by their own inflicted wounds, but those who were attacked for their refusal to flee through the open doors (as many wiser soldiers did) did not die, so much as un-exist.

Dominia, herself, pushed aside the guns of the men around Theodore and laid a hand upon one's helmet; his comrades watched him shut off like an unplugged computer and threw down their weapons to dash away.

"Twelve separate teams are working to clear this building," said Dominia to her astonished, too high, and visibly frightened brother. "All of them are looking for you. When they find you, make sure they know you're still a part of the Family."

The fray dying down, the Ladies assembled themselves around their master. "But what about *you?*"

"When you see me again, Theodore"—her many bodies refolded around hers to form her once more into that spirit called the Lady— *don't breathe a word of what you've seen.*

As the Lady disappeared to attend to the welfare of her former self, Teddy cried for her to wait. But there was no waiting: was no time. Once, in that year of Jerusalem's plight, Lazarus had chided the Lady: "The sooner all this is over, the better. I'm tired of watching you push yourself around."

Well, now the end had come. Now the master and servant were one. Now, Valentinian arrived with the Lady through the dark of space-time upon the dark of the stage where once Dominia's postmortem phantom stood, displaced from its dying body. The gasps of the audience, once stunned by the General, were deeper now to see the stranger. Toward the artificial storm clouds of the downpour induced for the Hierophant's play, the Lady lifted her head.

Once, the rain in California seemed so strange. But rain in Denmark's December, Cicero? Far stranger, still. You've always had a penchant for the unnatural.

XVIII

Function Composition

Few good things could be said of the Hierophant, especially after his death: but while he was alive, no one could accuse him of wasting time. The mocking goddess had not finished her sentence when the so-called Holy Father had turned to rip one of the (very real) halberds from the set's wall—or that was his intent when he found himself nose to nose with Valentinian.

"Going so soon? You can't leave before my magic trick! It's like sneaking out of Mass after Communion."

"So you've conned your way into a body." The Hierophant's tone was too dark to maintain its usual notes of condescending merriment. "Good. I'll take great pleasure in tearing it from you."

"Very funny you should say that." The magician flickered out of the path of a punch and appeared on the Hierophant's other side, much to the dismay of the crowd. "I've got a little treat for you tonight—and your audience! Consider this your delayed…well, it's not a *green* show, since we're in winter and all. But it's something! Really something. Maybe you knew the Hunters have teleportation technology, but did you know that you don't have to go to all that trouble if you've got a guy like me, and enough of the organic medium to go around?"

Above their heads, atmosphere-altering rockets burst, releasing instantaneously condensing vapors that, by virtue of convective effects and Elsinore's frigid air, grew to a localized supercell storm intended for mere show. Once upon a time, the rockets were used for restoring the land around bombed-out Moscow, or assisting in the Martian terraformation. Now, such things were relegated to toys, and their vapors sat, unchecked, for some time before the performance. Those that were checked had been found to contain H_2O, and were in perfect working order. Untampered. Normal. Yet, to the shock of the audience members (to say nothing of the technicians responsible for the rockets), when the first beads of condensed fluid dropped from the tops of the artificial clouds and upon the high-paying patrons, it was not water that dotted their cheeks, their heads, their expensive lab-grown furs.

It was blood.

This was another in a series of events over which historians would prefer to gloss until science could offer a less embarrassing explanation than the evidence implied. Straightlaced scholars couldn't get any of this stuff to make sense. Eventually, the conclusion would be reached that the events of *The Curse of Bathsheba* were related to the mass hysteria of Lavinia's abilities; and Lavinia, long after her disappearance at the ripe old age of 789, would someday be considered part of a group of treacherous martyrs who wished to overthrow the founding Hierophant. No one would have dared say such a thing while she walked the Earth, certainly, but that meant nearly eight hundred years of button-down society's uncomfortable acceptance that the happenings of New Year's Eve 4044/1999 were, in fact, true and physical occurrences that had been recorded on camera.

And uncomfortable it was. For who in the material world could be fully comfortable with the notions of literal blood rain, levitation, divine transfigurations, and mass resurrection? The eventual explanation, long after martyrs were forgotten on Earth, would be this: the rain was traditional blood rain of the sort caused by microalgae (blame those lazy rocket technicians for letting its spores creep into the tightly sealed cylinders); and that the theater of Elisnore just happened to be the epicenter of a freak hurricane/earthquake/tsunami combination thanks to the cold winter winds, the low-hanging moon, the unnatural thunderclouds.

Were these grasping explanations not more spurious than the simple truth?

At the time, there was no arguing with experience. While a few martyrs in the audience tasted the ruby droplets and a murmur of astonishment rose above the storm's initial patters, Valentinian moved his hands in time with the continuing notes of the oblivious orchestra pit. "There's about, oh, a gallon and a half of blood in a person's body. Doesn't seem like all that much, but if you could organize every drop of that into a line, can you imagine how long it would be? You could make quite a circle! And any size circle of the blood of Lazarus, charged with sufficient electricity, will conduct the high frequency and produce a reality disruption."

The storm clouds thrashed like a coach of foaming horses, and its unnatural size grew beyond the scope of the atmospheric rockets. As the blood rain thickened, its droplets, and the clouds from which it issued, began a broad rotation above the open mouth of the Elizabethan theater. Tired of waiting for his situation to worsen, the Hierophant blinked out of existence—and back into it, close enough to the halberds for him to tear one off the set. The Lady watched while the magician went on. "Theoretically, with enough of the blood of Lazarus, you could turn the entire world into a reality disruption. A superposition of reality and unreality. But, then, I guess that'd just be the Void."

Lightning struck the waves of the ocean outside the theater. While the audience cried out amid the rolling of immediate thunder and the vanishing of the red waistcoated Saint of Death, the Hierophant advanced on the Lady. Another bolt struck nearer to the building.

"Very kind of you to present yourself for the slaughter," said the Hierophant. "The way you insist on hiding from me, I always begin to think I'll never get the chance to see you face-to-face."

We have already died once tonight, Cicero: We will not die a second time.

"If that friend of yours wasn't so busy with parlor tricks"—the Hierophant winked back out of existence to another symphony of stunned gasps, then appeared all of a meter before the Lady in the same instant static's bright feelers crackled from her head—"perhaps that would be true."

The halberd swung; lightning struck the Lady; Lavinia cried out as light exploded across the stage and blinded the nocturnal audience members who covered their eyes as one shouting body. Three claps of thunder rocked the world during the spell of blindness; two more lightning bolts hit the stage. When the martyrs' vision cleared, some looked up to see the cyclone of blood had expanded to the theater's circumference, and now twisted in an uncanny ring that vibrated with electricity from the strikes.

Most of the audience members, however, saw only that which the great tear in the fabric of reality allowed them to see. These undistracted many, upon renewal of their vision, discovered what happened when lightning discharged itself within the ground of the avatar. The body that had once belonged to Miki Soto, struck by the bolt that sparked that reality distortion, had been transfigured. The eighth Lady, Dominia di Mephitoli, stood restored before the Hierophant in a glorified body incapable of experiencing the agonies that beset the material form, her unpatched right eye a black Void that absorbed all information-bearing light it crossed. The two-dimensional tear in space-time that had emanated from Miki's body—that same that had once expanded out of Trisha's, and left a dog named Basil a saint named Valentinian—lapped like fire as far as shell-shocked Lavinia before it receded into Dominia's dark socket. The General released the halberd that she had stopped with her hand, pushing it aside like a child's toy to speak into her palm the True Word that men meant when they said "halberd." In that vast half-real arena produced by the electrified tornado of Lazarene blood, this Word manifested upon the Earth the highest form of the Hierophant's chosen weapon. Sharp as it was, the instrument sang to be held by Dominia.

"Magnificent," breathed the Holy Father, even as he backed out of range. At the same time, Lavinia lifted her hands. Her eyes, already wild, grew wilder each second. The Hierophant continued, "How I have longed to see this transformation again. O Lady! What sublime nature radiates from your true form."

"Cut the pedantic bullshit. I already remember; there's never been any Hierophant but you."

How could there be? He was too selfish to allow himself to die in any iteration, or to allow Cicero's potential to exceed his own. Why, what if a younger Cicero were a better Cicero than he? Couldn't risk that. He was the evil queen and the hunter all in one, letting his old self forever suffer the pain of his brother's death while leading him to believe that it wouldn't happen this time. No wonder Cicero hated Dominia so much! Her whole life, the Hierophant had been whispering in his ear insidious advice: that in his time, Dominia was responsible for Elijah's death, so they had to keep her in line. Any plan he would present to Cicero would seem foolproof.

But El Sacerdote was too in love with himself to recognize even he couldn't trust Cicero. Now there was a hell of a thought.

"Pedantic or no, you cannot imagine how I have waited for this moment. How I *always* wait for this moment. My fairest daughter! What a wonder you are, my pride." Barely, he ducked a swipe of the polearm, and laughed as he sprang back up. "But I think you shall find, even in your holy state, we are well matched—and your magician seems to have gone."

Yes: per usual, Valentinian (*her* good-for-nothing son, she understood, much as Lazarus's—wow, weird thought!) skedaddled when things got hotter than room temperature. Dominia didn't care. He'd done his job. His portal encompassed the walls of the theater and rendered everything up to the impassible doors that state of half Void, half reality that had allowed the True form of the halberd to be birthed in a physical way. The bloody mass was a great scab in the physical dimensions—everything beneath which, not fully formed, allowed glimpses of the black hole. Everything there was malleable. Perhaps this was how the magician saw reality all the time. For Dominia, the states of existence and nonexistence had become two concurrent levels of consciousness while within her avatars. For the magician, they were a perfect blend.

And the blend was also perfect for everyone in the portal who knew not what they saw. Therefore perfect, and confusing. Perfect, and terrifying. Martyrs who had begun to crowd the doors in a futile attempt to leave found themselves facing no door at all. Instead a vast, black wall. Others spoke to their neighbors in a rising symphony of fright. Still others began to pray—but there was one martyr who was not so disturbed. While Lavinia, awestruck, removed her gloves, Dominia said to her Father, "I don't need the magician to perform miracles, and I don't need the magician to kick in your teeth."

"What's the difference?" With a smug smile, he took another cautious step away with his halberd between them. "It will take a miracle to defeat me, my girl. And it will take a miracle to defeat all these people."

"I won't have to. They'll understand whose side they're really on."

"And how will you do that, Dominia?" That smile transformed into a mocking sneer. With his polearm, he gestured to the frigid water lapping between the audience and the stage. "Multiply the fish of the ocean? I've already done that with science, child. So perhaps you'll walk on water for us, instead! Go on, let's see it: this is a *show*, after all."

"My hands," Lavinia breathed, as somebody in the audience screamed, "We should be *killing* that traitor!"

"Yeah," shouted somebody else, while Dominia's lost daughter, who had begun weeping, cried out, "My *hands*!" and yanked the petticoats of her dress so high up her thighs that the crowd murmured for a different reason: disapproval Lavinia didn't, couldn't register. "Oh, my legs—my legs are *real*! *Ninny!*"

With a nod her way, Dominia said, "I've already produced a miracle by righting one of your foul wrongs—but if you want to see another, then, fine."

Her eyes never leaving those of her Father, Dominia took one step back, to the absolute edge of the stage. There, she dipped the tip of her platonic weapon into the lapping waves. Once more, part of the following occurrence could be attributed to the blood rain, but anyone who was there knew for the rest of their lives there was so much more to the story than that. The Void-tainted salt water allowed to wash in and out of the theater turned red. Had a curious martyr tasted it, he might have confirmed what his sense of smell indicated.

"Water to wine?" The Hierophant laughed; Dominia did not.

"Wine is nothing more than the blood—the spirits—of grapes." The sumptuous mulberry fluid took a mahogany hue all the darker as its substance grew sticky and dense. Fermented grapes' bitter announcement relented to the mouthwatering tang of coppery human blood. "It is the end of life for the grape, yet the existence of wine implies grapes; grapes cannot physically be derived from wine, but information about them can be. And information is all that matters here, in this half place."

The thick blood changed once more. Another step in a strange alchemical process that had simultaneously horrified and entranced the audience. Now, someone did try it, and said, "I know that taste— amniotic fluid."

The Hierophant, the notes of his laughter uncharacteristically tight, said, "My, my, all this has never happened before. How will this magic trick end?"

"You know what happens when they saw a Lady in half. She walks back out in one piece."

Lightning struck the crown of Dominia's head, and the thunder was nearly drowned by the collective scream of the audience—half for fear, and half for delight. The martyrs did not understand that a mass of consciousness had struck the Earth, and, through the Lady, was channeled down into the amniotic fluid in a flow of information-bearing photons and electrons. There, this consciousness bound with the salt enriching the formerly oceanic fluid, and a strange miracle occurred. Vision returned to the eyes of the light-blinded martyrs to reveal the General miraculously intact. Silence resounded through the rows and the stunned audience observed as she shifted her weapon to her left hand, then knelt, at last removing her eyes from her Father to reach her free hand toward the water.

Five seconds passed. With a splash loud as a gunshot, a hand burst from those waves. Dominia gripped the attached forearm to haul Kahlil, gasping and laughing, from the womb of the transfigured ocean.

"My *girl*," marveled the Hierophant. The crowd once more screamed in shared horror: all around the stage, hands leapt from the waves, seeking purchase to haul their once-deceased owners from the watery trough. "What a triumph you are."

"What is all this, Ninny?" Lavinia, her face aglow, began to step forward, but Dominia pointed the weapon in her direction.

"No, Lavinia. Don't come near him." She jerked her head at the Hierophant. "He won't hesitate to hurt you to get away. He's done it many times before."

He clucked in distaste. "Putting such thoughts into my daughter's head."

"My daughter. Cassandra's. I am so sorry, Lavinia, for everything I let him do to you." The General brandished the fauchard whose decorated pole resembled an elaboration of the sword of her demise. "But he'll never have an opportunity to hurt you, or anyone, again. Cicero is dead."

Those few members of the audience privileged to hear this emitted piteous wails, but they were few indeed; most roared with desperation to find an exit, for they found themselves confronted with a growing number of resurrected humans who stayed by the water's edge to help their comrades out. The Hierophant laughed and sprang for the stairs leading to the set's balcony. "And so is the Lamb. You expect me to be heartbroken? He's hardly the first Cicero you've killed, my girl. I can't count by now how many I've seen you do in!"

Before she jetted after him, she took up Kahlil's hand. "I'm sorry I let you die, my friend."

"I was going to someday anyway, right?" He laughed and looked down at his shrugging arms. "Let's say we're even now."

With a reassured nod, the Lady launched her pursuit. Some bold (stupid) martyrs, crying, "Papa, Papa," tried to fight their way through the humans to make it to the stage, but these were no ordinary mortals. The resurrected human bodies were glorified as that of the Lady, greater in speed and strength than those finest Olympic athletes and cured of worldly ills. In a contest of endurance, strength, or any other trait that could be named (including moral and mental qualities), reembodied humans were superior to martyrs in every way. The martyr cause was hopeless to break through the human defense, which was occasionally a bit more than defensive. Dominia noticed Tobias Akachi taking a little too much pleasure in giving a martyr a crack over the skull with one thick fist. She waved the polearm at him as she dashed up the balcony stairs in pursuit of her Father. "Don't have too much fun down there!"

"What is the point of resurrection, General, if a man cannot have a bit of fun!"

In one great leap, Dominia lifted through the air above the remaining coil of stairs as if the law of gravity no longer applied, then settled upon the rail. The Hierophant, ever tickled by the divine, managed the word, "Wonderful," before he made the first strike.

The Lady had fought a great many battles as the General, but never had she fought one with an opponent so formidable—or with her own consciousness is such a hyper-powerful state, expanding through all time, all directions, as it did. It was as though she saw his motions just before they were enacted by his muscles. Each of his intended blows were met with the pristine snaps of her scythe's blade against its inferior offender. The ease with which she parried blow after blow appeared to delight him, which annoyed her, and she sprang forward as he lashed out again. Her parry pinned the head of his weapon to the balcony floor and pushed it from his hands.

The lesser weapon clattered through the rails and to the stage below. With a noise of displeasure, he danced away, his own form so impossibly agile that the Lady could only assume, knowing now what she knew of herself and his journey through increasingly small iterations, that he had undergone a similar glorification process in his many transferences between worlds. Had she been in better humor, perhaps she would have appreciated the artistry of his battle as much as he admired hers, but she was, suffice to say, in no mood. Particularly not when he used a suspended sandbag intended for some special effect in Act V to swing from the platform and into the audience, cackling as he landed amid a bunch of martyrs. Those who didn't run away threw themselves down to soften his landing with pitiful cries like, "Father, oh, Papa, I have you!"

"Will you hide amid your martyrs, coward?" She might have found some grain of humor in that if she hadn't immediately noticed that martyr who stumbled through his row in far greater terror than his peers, knowing himself the Hierophant's target: Theodore.

"*Theo*," Lavinia screamed. The Lady flew as quick as the speed of thought into the Hierophant's path, eternally quicker for the purity of her ascension than he could ever hope to be in his profane acquisitions of divine power.

"I cannot imagine why my martyrs exist, if not to serve my pleasures." Ducking a sweep of the Lady's polearm, the Hierophant melted fully into the Void, and Dominia bared her teeth, having no choice but to follow him.

There he was, not feet before her, running in the direction not of Theodore but of the swirling portal that had opened with her bodily death. The next iteration—his next trap. The otherworldly window yawned like a cerulean-lined chasm in the middle of the Void, the only light in a place that stole all mortal illuminations. On the other side would be a new Void with that eight-mouthed fountain: the indicator of a fresh world. She sprinted after him, close to his heels when he made a sharp right into existence to appear in the aisle between the rows Q and R. "I always like to snap a few necks on my way out," said the Hierophant, his words breathless with the speed of the fight but carefree as they'd ever been. "Fifty million UF dollars and a royal title for the martyr who catches and kills either one of my treasonous children—Theodore *or* Dominia. Who wants to be a duke?"

The answer to that, apparently, was "everyone." At least, everyone who wasn't already losing a fistfight with some humans, or who hadn't been navigating the vomitorium's back entrance to the dressing rooms to reach a stage where they just now arrived. While the number of the resurrected continued to grow, those unoccupied martyrs, women and men alike, fine theater shoes and opera jackets be damned, began an ill-advised scramble for Theodore—mere distraction. The Hierophant had no more business with or grudge against Theodore than had an elephant for a solitary ant squashed on the way to the watering hole. His Holiness winked out of existence, and Dominia, annoyed, observed the people around her and flipped her fauchard backward to knock them out with the solid jeweled end.

By means of this scepter, she rather humiliatingly but harmlessly dispatched those few (seven or eight) foes stupid enough to think they could fight the General even pre-glorification. As she knocked out the first two, the Hierophant appeared in the corner of her light-hungry right eye in the distance of the stage where Lavinia had been fighting to acquire the attention of a cameraman—a new experience for her, no doubt, and an effort halted by the Hierophant's arrival. His posture, hands upon her face and body a shadow stooped over hers, was as cloying as it was intimidating, and the Lady hastily struck a young woman in a rich evergreen dress and abundant carrot wig with such force that she somersaulted backward over row DD and slammed into the encroaching Bosnian fellow so that he, too, went "ass over teakettle," as Cassandra had sometimes said.

Lavinia's body language was one of helplessness as the Hierophant tried to seduce her into doing something she no longer had the will to do. Her new hands—*her* hands—lifted and spread and sometimes patted her Father's shoulders in visible plea while he pressed, and pressed, and pressed, refusing to let the girl's face stray from his, refusing to let her look off into the crowd where Theodore fought for his life amid sometimes savage and often infighting martyrs. Fine gold pocket smartwatches went flying; elaborate weaves were torn from shrieking heads; a high-heeled shoe sailed so close to the Lady's skull that she shimmered up to the stage simply to avoid it, banking on the martyrs' selfish wish to lay claim to the Hierophant's promised title themselves. With their inability to work as a unit, Theodore would be fine until the humans who tried to save him had a chance to fight through to him. Fine for as long as it took Dominia to herd the Hierophant away from Lavinia and toward—what?

What was a better target?

"The Lamb is dead," the Lady repeated. Lavinia's terrified eyes landed on her speaking sister, who appeared a few paces behind her Father and only moved as much as it took to turn her polearm the right way around. "That was what sent you fleeing the first time, wasn't it? That first time…it was the most like this last time, except for this between you and me. Your brother's death was why you did any of this at all, finding another world. You wanted to be with him forever."

"We wage a war with death," said the Hierophant, clutching Lavinia to his breast, her yelping form between himself and the disgusted Lady. "Every man does; it is life's nature, its sordid struggle."

"You say you fight death, but you've brought it for so many. All these." She waved to the mass of humans who by now had grown to outnumber their martyr foes, and who had begun to fill seats to make room. "And you would bring it, still, for so many more. Even Lavinia."

"You hear that, my girl?" He lifted his eyebrows at his youngest daughter in a mime of concern. "She would run you through to get to me. These people infected by human religion, by pagan faith—they have no value for life. Not like I do. Don't you want to save the lives of martyrs, Lavinia?"

"Yes," said the girl, "but—"

"If you do not set things into motion, martyrs will never be the dominant species. We will never survive our journey to the stars, never lay a lasting print upon the universe the way mankind has and will and eternally shall. We will all die like famished seedlings, all the people you have ever known and loved—even me."

"But what about Theodore?"

Lavinia's question earned a noise of displeasure from the Holy Father. The Lady winked into the space behind him and forced him to relinquish his hold on the girl so he could flee into the Void. Dominia's feet found earth in time to hear a foreign martyr cry out, "Why, that's my *sister*," and she could feel the conflict beginning to give way to reunion.

"Are you all right?" The former General reached for Lavinia's shoulder just to be subjected to the sting of her jerking away. "Did he hurt you?"

"No. But I—" The wound was too new, and the Lady recognized that after a lifetime of lies, Lavinia needed time to heal. More time than Dominia had left to spend in the world. With a sharp breath and a bat of wet eyes, she nodded at the girl's single request: "Please—save Theodore."

The Lady flitted out of existence and into the Void, where she realized that either she had exceedingly little sense of the actual physical location of the portal, or that, unobserved, it had moved. The latter instance seemed more likely. It now yawned far off in the distance, more detectable by sound than by sight, for it was the most uncannily two-dimensional thing the five-dimensional-plus mind was capable of experiencing and was not fully apparent when one was level with its surface. Not until one was practically within it: then, the portal was very much apparent, a Grand Canyon that opened to a vision of another, distant Earth and its like Ergosphere—that beautiful planet, swirling far past Mercury and Venus, that vision of the cosmos from the perspective of Sol's beating heart.

She could not let him escape to another iteration, nor could she let him continue to sully this one. Her uncanny haste tripled in the Ergosphere, the General sought to clutch the suit jacket of her fleeing Father only to find herself grabbed by an assortment of rotten gray arms. Malformed and hastily implemented thoughtforms sprang from the naked ground to pin her down. A gap cleft the space between them, and he called, "This place is so boring without some imagination! Then again, you never were creative in anything other than military matters. Let me show you *my* Ergosphere, Dominia."

The cleft had emerged because the very substance of the Void shaped itself into a set of gargantuan gears. As if the makings of his clockwork universe had poured out of his tar-black soul and into the Ergosphere. Though she tore herself free and leapt from cog to cog in instinctive pursuit, she knew she need not: she was the ground, the very ground that was those arms, and they withered and died even as they gripped her legs. She was those very cogs, too, that reversed and sent him hurling back toward her. Her pursuit not hampered to his liking, the Hierophant again vanished into reality and forced Dominia to beat instant retreat—not to her starting position, but to the position of poor Theodore in the midst of his own chaos.

Del Medico had some serious problems. He'd lost his jacket and rolled up his sleeves, though one was already torn at the shoulder and he sported a swiftly swelling shiner in addition to bruises on hands raised in an unfortunate fighting style only identifiable as "fisticuffs." With these, the former doctor failed to defend himself against those few members of the crowd who valued worldly goods in a failing society over the opportunity to reunite with their human loved ones—which an increasingly large number of martyrs seemed to be choosing. A good thing the selfish ones were so few: this small handful of assailants had evidently decided they could kill Teddy together and sort out the victor later. Having momentarily lost track of the Hierophant, Dominia set to work at the task of fighting her way to Theodore, a process that seemed slow to treacherous extent: particularly when her attention finally did fix to the distant sight of her Father disemboweling the unfortunate cameraman who had, during the Lady's time in the Void, obeyed Lavinia's pleas to film her.

"My fragile girl," he cried, "my dove, my favorite child not myself—how I tried to save you from this world!" He shook the chunks of liver from his fingers and advanced on his youngest daughter. As she cried out, Lavinia's dart away was blocked by the on-stage martyrs. His Holiness continued his standard guilt trip—and his relentless approach across that massive stage—without missing a beat. "But you wouldn't accept it any more than would your sister. Now look where we are! Are your arms and legs worth this? Is liberty not too highly priced?"

After sending a fat gray-haired fellow in a bloodied tuxedo toppling with the gold staff's slam to his groin, Dominia forced her way past a couple of loudly fighting (former) lovers—one martyr and the other resurrected, spurned and eaten—then knocked a toothy young woman off of Teddy's arm.

"Are you all right?" she asked, which she regretted when he began to whine. She cut him off by asking, "Can you get into the Void?"

"I have *no* idea how to get in and out of that place on my own. Are you kidding? Now's not the time for this."

Fighting back Dominia's understandable annoyance, the Lady asked, "Then can you at least get to Lavinia if I clear a path for you?"

"What do you think I've been trying to *do*," was his shrill response. A noble one, if annoyingly phrased. Knocking with a nasty *clank* the teeth out of someone who needed a valuable lesson on greed, Dominia cleared the way and said, "Then watch my back."

"With *what*?"

With another immortal Word, the Lady put into his hands a higher kind of flail that was not as harmful as it looked, and which, knowing the substance of its wielder's soul, would never hit Teddy in the head…no matter how stupid he was with it. "That's a good weapon for you." She dragged him along while humans—swarming down into the orchestra pit poised before the body-blooming trench—began to clamber up to the stage, sometimes over one another. "Doesn't require precision."

"What are they doing," he cried of the souls, and she smiled.

"The same thing as us."

It was religious fervor more than greed that drove the still-fighting martyrs. She would reflect on this in calmer times when she'd had occasion to process, at least partially, all the events of her last hour on that Earth. Zealot fathers forewent reunion with children they thought to be demons of the sort the *tulpa* had been; ignorant women scorned long-dead friends striving to embrace them due to the Hierophant's virtuoso brainwashing. Most martyrs had the humanity left (and the common sense) to give up their fighting, but too many stayed in her path, and too many were upon the stage to shepherd fleeing Lavinia up the whirling balcony stairs to a point where she could be cornered. The Hierophant made his calm way after her once he selected another halberd. "You would overlook seventy years of love, of doting privilege, because I made the mistake of saving both you and your mother? Of giving you better lives? I should have ordered Dominia to cut your mother's throat while she slept rather than martyring her. Perhaps I will next time. If I do it soon enough"—he glanced in the direction of the Lady, still fighting through the crowd but soon to reach the sea of humans that had grown properly onto the stage to march en masse for the Hierophant—"she will obey just like the dog she is."

At the General's sneer and the approach of individuals from stage left, the Hierophant made to self-obviate again, but was halted by a hand that lay upon his arm. He turned his head, and his face was aglow with a look of such incredible shock that Dominia, satisfied to see it, only felt her own shock as she recognized from behind the honey locks of a woman whose existence slowed time. The Lady, tripped up by the General she inhabited, paused to watch Cassandra say something to the Hierophant before she punched him in the face hard enough to shatter his nose. Only the Lady knew what the gentle (sometimes crass) woman had said before striking the Holy Father, because she could feel the vibrations of the words in the substrate of reality. "This isn't for all the horrible things you did to everyone in the past, please understand—it's for what you're trying to do right now."

Blood pouring from his nose, the Hierophant wrenched his arm from her grip and disappeared with the saturnine expression of a man who longed more than ever for the immediate mass death of all mankind. Cassandra disappeared into the human crowd, but there was no time to fuss about it. Dominia forced her attention back upon Teddy. "Try not to kill anyone, if you can help it. There's been enough death. Just keep using that flail— It isn't fatal."

"Why not?"

"Because it's not real," she explained half a second before she was once more whipping across that imaginary landscape to fly in stride with the Hierophant's sprint. He had been right: when one interacted with the Void, the Void was also within them. Dominia could feel the Hierophant as though he were a parasite crawling about a skin whose surface she could neither see nor feel without its disruption. On entry to that space, such disruption became the sum total of experience. His presence within her provoked an itch, and she sought to cure it. She reached for him and was surprised when he caught that arm and slammed her down into the ground with force she did not expect herself capable of feeling after her ascension. She supposed, though immune from pain, little could stop thoughtbodies from having effects upon one another: and if the Hierophant had run this race even ten times, that placed him at twenty thousand years of existence, which meant he was an exceedingly dangerous opponent.

But Dominia, a mere 333 years old, had fought a thousand battles— and the Lady, that infinite embodiment of all Dominias and more, was the very act of combat. She could not forget the limits of her capabilities, and so, though tossed aside in her own arena as she had been that night at McLintock farm, she skidded to her feet in this space and was in fast pursuit of him once more.

When he knew she was behind him, he grew as fast as he was strong, and although she could arrive at his location at the speed of thought, this only caught her up with him for the space of a second. Then he would be beyond arm's reach once more, too fast even for her, the hum of the portal growing ever to a roar.

At last, seeking her gun on instinct and finding it there in joyful thoughtform, Dominia drew and fired. With satisfaction, she watched him whip backward, past and through her, into the distance the way they had come—the way she now beat hasty pursuit.

Before emerging back into the world, she asked herself if that was the best thing to do. Was it not better to take the portal now, herself? Get the drop on him? Do what he did, perhaps, and strangle the boys who would become Cicero and Elijah in their beds before they could ever wreak such evil across the land? But that was just more violence, and would not resolve all these past failures. Not resolve this iteration. Dominia had made a promise to Cassandra. She had seen Lazarus die. She had taken Miki's body. She could not live with herself, abandoning this universe to the whims of her trapped Father. She could not let him rule without her intercession.

For was that not what her actions were, now? The intercessions of the truly risen dead—the truly sanctified within the world? She had died, returned to life, and returned life to others whom she needed to take elsewhere. She had seen the truth of her position as, if not the Void itself, then as that recording beam and the identical playback beam in Tish's preferred, holographic model of reality. That meant Dominia could influence Earth's stability much as she could influence the Void's. When she returned to the world, she made the very stage buck beneath her Father's feet.. Disoriented from his Ergosphere death, the Hierophant nonetheless had frame of mind enough to stumble up the rocking staircase and shove his people aside with the staff of his halberd.

How astonishing to be faster than him! To leap, with a few great bounds, up the twisting rail of the stair and upon the balcony's surface—there to meet him when he made it up! As a girl, she could have only dreamed of reflexes like his, and as an adult she never dared waste time on such fancies. But now, here they were: the Lady poised between Lavinia and the Holy Father, whose polearm was once again torn from his hands with a satisfying clatter as it hit the still-trembling stage below.

"You think you'll manage to kill me?" asked the Hierophant, laughing even as his anxious martyrs, knowing better than to help now that Dominia was in the fray, edged their way back down the stairs. "I, who have cut down many past iterations of my own self because they stood between me and a higher world?"

"It isn't a higher world you want. You want a world that's all your own—but you don't deserve one. Not as you are now."

"And you do, Dominia?"

"I don't want a world! I want nothing more for any world than its peaceful, happy existence. You want to see everything crushed."

"Not at all. I wish to be immortal: to *truly* live forever." She took a swipe at him, missed, and the balcony groaned with his landing upon it, the temporary structure still reverberating with the Earth's ceased shudders. Not made to bear more than one or two actors at a time, let alone the movements of real fighting above an earthquake, the set piece began its slow sag. Lavinia cried out behind them, and Teddy, amid the throng of humans who had pulled him up to the stage, called her name from below. Eyes wild with terror, the girl jumped over the balcony's side and tumbled twenty feet down, where Teddy and humans alike reached up to catch her. The no-longer-so-Eternal Virgin of the now defunct Holy Family landed upon her future lover with an *oof* and a laugh of surprise audible even over the Hierophant's sincerely demanded questions. His black eyes blazed into Dominia while he snarled, "What is it in me that makes me so unworthy of the highest truth? Of knowing the essence of the godhead? What is it in me that makes *me* so unworthy of the life you returned to them? What makes my brother unworthy? He died that first time, just as your wife. I understand your pain, my girl, but you refuse to acknowledge your involvement in mine! Why was my escape to that first new world so unjust?"

The air between them stilled. Dominia could see in his eyes he knew the moment had come. She felt it, herself, in every atom of air. She saw, also, that so long as he lived, he could not escape his thicket of self-delusion. There was only one method of liberation.

"You will never repent, as long as you live in this form—so, it's my duty to free you for another chance to grow."

By slipping the halberd into his belly and jerking its blade upward, Dominia tore apart the innards of the Hierophant to the sound of Lavinia's wail. Pupils dilating to invisible pinpoints within their tarry irises, he fell backward from the point of impalement and disappeared a few meters before his impact upon the stage revealed by scattering humans.

"There's no time," Dominia heard Theodore saying as the General pursued the dying man into the Void. "Are you hurt? We need to go."

She didn't need to hear the girl saying, "No, no—we can't. Oh, Daddy!"

Then, the Lady was within the Void: alone, yet, the furthest thing from, for she felt at this point in space-time a great many entities crawling with life inside her. Of those, the liveliest was also the one whose death was most imminent. The Hierophant's soul ran for the portal as fast as his body's fading life required of it, thoughtform walls throwing themselves up along with fires, forests, a clockwork city, a vast factory of conveyor belts and Escher stairs, entire hallucinatory dream-universes through which they both lived flickering second lives locked in eternal rivalry—anything he could think to put between himself and the Lady.

But the Lady was all things in that place. She was those fires, those forests, the walls, and all the other things with which the Hierophant tried to slow her down. She was the very ground upon which he ran, the very ground that softened to the substance of a marsh and slowed his pace.

"I could give you so much, my girl," said the Hierophant, stumbling forward one final step, succumbing to the suction of his feet, and standing to await her emergence from the flaming trees. "Everything, anything you asked. Why should either of us find a new world when we might make this one better, as I have said so many times over? Why should any of us suffer? Is the happiest ending, the happiest world, not one where *I*, *even* I, am redeemed?"

"Then consider this might not be the happiest world for you." Dominia's voice emanated from all things, all space, around the

Hierophant. Her body—the body of a giant, in truth, replicating hers—formed from the ground beneath him faster than he could have run were he allowed. Had he, he would have fallen to his death from the heel of her sprawling palm. "Maybe the next one."

With a gesture of her fingers as simple and light as she might use in the crushing of a gnat, Dominia squashed the thoughtbody of the Hierophant and forced him to fly back once more—now, to the moment of his death, to which she followed him. She emerged normal size upon reality's stage and bent at the side of his broken, eviscerated body. Behind them, Lavinia and Theodore hurried to the abandoned camera.

"The moment you have so long awaited," observed the Hierophant with his final breaths. He laughed even as he did, a wet, ugly sound that seemed more truthful than his usual mirth. "Will you ever be sorry it was so short?"

"It feels to me like it's lasted at least twenty thousand years," was her response. With that bastard grin, he raised one broken arm to lay a numb hand against his daughter's cheek. Then, unspeaking, he relented to that which was long overdue, and his eyes paled over in the mist of death.

As he died, a great roar rose across the theater: Dominia first took it for a mass of crying martyrs but soon knew it for the black tsunami that rose from the ocean to carry off the dead—and the portal—to holier pastures. As the massive wave arced over the edge of the theater, the General lifted her head in time to see Cassandra there, holding Lavinia. That most perfect of women, she looked up at Dominia and smiled—what a radiant smile!—as the crest dropped over the theater wall and smashed, to the screams of many misunderstanding martyrs, into the overcrowded people. The martyrs all seemed to require a few seconds to realize they were neither crushed nor drowning, nor even wet. When the flood washed away, every last human was gone, along with the reality distortion. The doors, returned, burst open and overflowed, not with water but with newly baptized Lazarene martyrs desperate to flee their tahgmahr.

"Tell your children what you've seen," the Lady called after them before lowering her head again toward the dead man.

As usual, he had been right. Eternal as she may have been, and evil as he may have been, it brought a soft sting of pain to look into the Hierophant's dead face. He was, after all, her Father. But she refused to submit to the emotion of grief, and stood in time to hear good Lavinia, dear Lavinia, do what she knew needed to be done. Something that was only the first of many ways in which the Princess would make a difference in her world.

"Viewers, please! Please, I have a message—have you seen all this, this madness?" Down below, a few martyrs greedy for imaginary principalities still scrapped, unclear on the fact that the Hierophant was dead. Theodore, in control of the camera, panned around the emptying theater, across the Hierophant's body, then back to Lavinia. "Look at that—and look at me! I beg you, humans watching me, please know how powerful you are! Please know: you can do anything. You're just as good as us, or better, even though we've told you otherwise for centuries. Some of you believe us, and I'm talking to you—yes, you! You've been brainwashed. For years we've hidden things in your books and movies, your video games, your news, even your schools! We've taught you dirty lies, and we—we should be ashamed of ourselves. But you'll see it now."

Her innocent eyes, opened for the first time, glassed over with tears of repentance. "You don't have to listen to us. All beings are self-sovereign." Given by Lavinia, this command washed across the world in a throb of bliss that the Lady felt also in her own body. The Princess went on, speaking from her heart as she said, "We've made you our slaves and we're—I'm—sorry. You don't have to be. You are conscious, powerful, incredible creatures! Never let anyone tell you that you have to be a martyr's slave. If you have love in your heart for the family you serve and wish to stay, then do, but if you don't, then listen to me now: you are *free*, you are *free*. My Father is dead along with my Family"—her pitch jumped to an all-time high and snapped, and when her voice returned, Lavinia sounded like a new, steadier woman—"and it is my first commandment as the Church's Hierophant that you, all humans, are *free*."

That would help matters. The General would not be around to ensure the humans were taken care of—she could not continue to take responsibility for a world's worth of woes—but she could take solace before her parting that those left behind planned to make improvements. She could not say for certain how all the remaining martyrs, like the violent sort below, would take the news of the Family's dissolution; nor could she say how difficult the road ahead of Lavinia was to be; nor could she say that martyrs would never ruin Mars; nor, nor, nor. There were so many things that she could not complete, herself—so many things she could not control, any more than anyone could control anything.

That was the most difficult part. It was not defeating her Father that was hard—it was letting go of his world, and her vision of it. But her vision had been spoiled by his filthy lens, and she would give much for a new view's purity.

Still—still. She could not yet find it in herself to leave. Lavinia ended the broadcast, then faced the sister who stood beside the body of the Hierophant. The tableau gave the younger girl pause before she found the courage to approach.

"My limbs are real again," she said to Dominia, her words a hush, and the Lady nodded. "Was that you? Did you do this, Dominia?"

"I didn't fix your limbs, personally."

"But you *did* do it, somehow. I saw a Lady before—someone wearing one of those dresses like they do in Japan, you know, the robes… but when she was struck by lightning, she was lots of other Ladies, and then she was blackness and finally she was you, and—are you really Ninny? *Really*?"

Studying the Hierophant's still features, she thought of her dead body in Kronborg's chapel. "I don't know how to answer that question."

The nonresponse hung heavy in the air until, somehow resolved, Lavinia insisted, "You must be. You must be my Ninny. Oh, Dominia—" The girl's eyes welled with tears. "I can't believe Daddy is dead. I'd have thought I would be sobbing right now, but I…I don't know how to feel."

"You're just as free as the humans, now. Freer. You can do whatever you want."

"I just want to be with Theo," she said meekly, as if still fishing for permission until Dominia pointed out to her, "There's nobody to stop you." While the girl seemed to absorb that fact with some astonishment, Dominia went on, lifting her gaze to the stars that twinkled above the stage. Amid them, Mars shone bright with hope for the human race. "But there is something required of you. Much."

As Lavinia listened, her organic hands clasped over her heart, the Lady glanced between the purest of martyrs and her husband-to-be. She could see in great ethereal trails the eternal paths routed in this world by their comings and goings: how they would embrace in that moment when she disappeared from their lives forever. A moment coming so quickly that she whose very perception was eternity felt for all the world it might as well have been that very second. After savoring, for a few silent heartbeats, what it was to be alive in this dark but redeemable world, Dominia said, "After all the horrors the martyr race has wrought upon the human one, we owe them a duty. You are a princess no more: now, you are a queen. As you said yourself, the Hierophant." The girl's eyes glowed while the Lady warned, as had the Bard, "'Uneasy lies the head that wears a crown.'"

"I suppose that's right," said Lavinia.

"You will be threatened, and fought against. There will be much turmoil. But it is your duty to tame martyrkind, and restrain their numbers. When I restored your limbs, your entire body was healed and glorified—your blood." The girl's electromagnetic field throbbed with an energy detectable but to the Lady, containing all the information about the genetic and mental makings of the woman before her: yes, this was how the magician saw the world, and yes, it was as he suggested. This daughter of the malformed protein was healed—as much a daughter of the sacred protein upon Earth as the pure Bearers were in their heavenly abode. So that was the source of the nagging resemblance! Slightly, Dominia smiled. "Tonight you'll dream of a place that's half real, but don't be afraid. Tomorrow, you'll walk in the sun. You have the blood of Lazarus—though it's the blood of Lavinia now, I suppose. The true sacred protein."

The girl's expression was awash with horror. "Ninny—"

"It's not going to send you to hell," Theodore said. Lavinia looked at him in surprise while he went on. "It's true! I've been to that place she's talking about, that other dimension. We can go together! Well—" He laughed weakly and glanced at Dominia. "When I figure out how to come and go."

"The duty of the martyr race is to eventually migrate to this place we describe, but only if they make the choice to abstain from the flesh of mankind, which is possible with your blood. The same blood Lazarus once had." With a pang for her friend, she said, "In the chapel, you will find the body of Lazarus, along with mine." She strove not to give in to the pain that filled the girl's eyes. Dominia stooped to slip the (bullet-dented) Ring of the Fisherman from her Father's immobile finger. This, she lay in Lavinia's palm. "His blood is gone. The martyrs who were here tonight are all baptized, but you must baptize more, and humans, too—you must be Lamb, Lazarus, and Hierophant in one woman. Distribute your blood to those meek and gentle martyrs who, like your mother was, are people very afraid of death. These people, you will teach to leave Earth for that other dimension opened by the sacred protein."

"But how will we live, Ninny? How will we get around, what will we do?"

"That other dimension contains the shortest path to alien worlds. This is the way for us to find new planets for ourselves. Also in the chapel you will find a living man, Farhad, a Hunter pilot: he knows the approximate locations of three downed interdimensional amphibiships across the landscape of the Void, and he is one of two men who are at this point in time capable of piloting them. He understands the secret of fixing them from their current, damaged states because he's seen it done. Safeguard him, treat him well, and he will help martyrs migrate to more appropriate pastures." She didn't add: "If only to see us gone."

With an anxious look still in place, the girl nodded. "You said that Cicero and the Lamb are both dead?"

"Yes." New tears appeared in the girl's eyes as her older sister admitted, "Though you will still have many opponents."

"Oh, but I'm so glad *you're* alive. At least, in this way. I have so many questions!"

Ah! The shot of guilt, straight through her heart. Dominia took Lavinia's petite hand in hers and studied it, so much softer and more real than the very realistic hands before. Some things could not be replicated.

"I wish I could answer all of them—but I don't think I have the time to stay."

Lavinia's expression fell. "Where are you going?"

"I don't know. But I feel…in need of change. This is not my world." The Lady embraced the young woman and planted a kiss on her forehead. "Not a day will go by that I don't think of you."

"You can't *go*," Lavinia insisted. Dominia heard the script of her own Cassandra tahgmahrs read aloud to uncanny effect. "You're the only one who knows the truth, you—I—"

"No. You know the truth, and that's what matters. Teddy knows a little, too. When you find my body"—she struggled to ignore the girl's sob—"in the castle chapel, you'll find a necklace with it. That's Cassandra. Keep her close to you, always. You'll never forget, then."

"And you?" Lavinia breathlessly tried to restrain her tears within the vital support of Theodore's arms. "How will you keep from forgetting, Ninny?"

She didn't know how to answer that, other than to say, "If I don't remember all this, it will be just as much a failure as if I'd actually failed. I will never forget you, Lavinia. And I hope that, someday soon, I'll see you again."

Once more she bent to kiss the girl, now upon the cheek, before she turned to clap Theodore on his shoulder, and, at speed of thought, hasten to the death-filled chapel where lay her imperfect former body. She could not linger and see the start of weeping—it was hard enough to view her own trauma. The scene was a vile mess of blood and water, mixed to ooze across the floor, around the altar, beneath Dominia's body, the Lamb's, and Cicero's.

Cicero's body.

But not his soul.

She should have recognized something was off when Farhad and Basil were both gone from the empty chapel. How was she so stupid? Why—

Because she had wanted to believe the Hierophant was finished, of course. She was so ready to believe him dead that she, this near-goddess, this Void-substance, this Valkyrie imbued with powers from beyond time and space—she had not considered the moment of her own death. Dominia failed to consider that, after her pulse stopped, her soul now resided, unbounded, in the Ergosphere.

She had nobody but herself to blame, but she had to give it to him—the Hierophant was one hell of an actor. "Sorry it was so short," her omniscient fucking eye!

The savage barking of what seemed to be a pack of dogs filled the air of the Void as soon as Dominia emerged within it. Farhad, Allah smile upon him, noticed her arrival from the distance where he stood beside a great blurred battle poised unnervingly close to that thrumming portal's edge. Waving both hands and shouting, the man dashed to meet Dominia halfway and was visibly shocked when she simply blinked in front of him. Nearer the confusing fray, she saw what even her eyes had failed to resolve from that distance.

Three heads? Basil had quite a soul. And just look at those fangs.

"The dog, Mahdi." Farhad glanced over at the Hierophant, who fought a fruitless battle against the massive hound barring his way to the next iteration of reality. "He was very calm after your death— I waited with him just as your Lady ordered of me. But then he became very hostile, growling at nothing, and disappeared into the Void. I broke a stained-glass window to let the moonlight in so I could follow him, and—well…he is different now."

"I'll say."

"It is the strangest thing— I feel as if I have always been here, observing this battle for eternity. It was as I watched it unfold just now, it seemed…preexistent."

"That's life for you."

As the General strode to the battle, one great head lifted, and a trio of tails wagged in happy harmony. In a blink, Basil was that prancing border collie again, of standard size and excess affection for the battered Hierophant whose face he mercilessly licked.

"I've had enough of your games, you wretched little—"

"Good boy," said Dominia, catching the Holy Father's bloodied hand. "And good try, Cicero. You almost got me."

"I usually do." The Hierophant's disembodied soul gritted its teeth and leveled its dark eyes with Dominia's. "Will you destroy me now, with no body to which I can return? Where will I go? Shattered in pieces across the low frequencies?"

"No." She studied his bloodied hand, held in hers. With a glance to that buzzing portal and the happy dog who watched, Dominia smiled. "Go back, Farhad."

"But, Mahdi—"

"I have him from here. You'll be needed on Earth very soon. Don't stray from the chapel until Lavinia finds you, but…do make yourself scarce there until you know it's her who's coming in. Never know."

"Very well." With a glance over the scene before him, the pilot gathered this was the end of their struggle, and nodded. "It was an honor to serve you, General."

"And it was an honor to serve with you, Farhad. Thank you for everything."

While the man disappeared to the Earth where he was destined to spend the rest of his life as a spiritual teacher, Dominia returned her attention to her Father. "You asked if I would kill you. The answer is as it was on Earth: I must."

But as she did, his soul slipped back to its last escaped death, and the moment that Lady Dominia lost him into the portal. He was hurled back through its mouth into her arms, where she waited to plunge her fingers through his heart; and he slipped back through the iteration prior to that and into that escape, to the Lady who had missed her chance to crush his skull; and again, and again.

On, and on.

The Hierophant died a death for every iteration he had lived and ruined.

At last, his soul lay curled at the feet of the inciting Dominia: that very first Lady who discovered the True Name of the sacred protein and had waited an infinite number of attempts for this moment to find the Holy Father helpless before her.

"Please," he begged, real tears in the shut eyes shielded behind his hands. "No more! My daughter, my child—Dominia."

"I won't." Completely alone with him, without even the buzzing portal to interrupt the moment, the General knelt at the Hierophant's side and lay a soothing hand upon his arm. He flinched and cried out like an abused old man, though his soul, pure in its fine white suit, was young and undamaged as ever. As his breathing and his body's tension calmed, Dominia wrapped Cicero in her arms to hold him like a child. His breathing paused, then broke into aching, wet laughter that then fell apart into agonized tears.

"Is this all I have to look forward to! An eternity, dead? Nothing? My brother! Oh, where? I knew he would not be here."

"Of course not." While her Father wept into her shoulder, she held him, patted his back, and said, "He's in the same place where there's peace for you. Where there's God."

"My girl! My girl, my girl, I have spent eternity spitting in His face, mocking Him!"

"Like a toddler misbehaving to obtain His father's attention."

"Yes! And look! He has sent me nothing—no miracle, no punishment! Not even a great flood or a burning bush."

"No," said Dominia. "He's sent you me."

As the space of the Void around them folded and refolded so shapes emerged from the air and ground, the Hierophant's tears began to still. "You need to change, Cicero. And when we know you have, I'm sure you'll find Elijah again."

Those shapes formed buildings and stalls and the many busy people populating the market square of the Kingdom—all of whom, in accordance with that cultural immune system the magician had once described, turned their heads at the coming of the man who had sent a great many of its refugees fleeing in the first place.

"What *is* this place," marveled the False Protomartyr in the direction of the holy azure sky. "Dominia—is this heaven, my girl? Oh, the Kingdom! I see—I see, the Kingdom." The General, smiling into the faces of so many the Hierophant had murdered by his own hand, released her hold on Cicero. The first Cicero. The only Cicero.

The real Cicero, who looked in unsteady recognition from face to human face.

"Yeah, it's the Kingdom—but heaven? Just who do you think I am?" Dominia laughed at his assumption, relating more than ever to the magician. "It's not heaven. Or maybe. I don't know. It's just someplace that can take care of itself…and where there are people who are going to want a word with you. I think I see my parents over there—why don't you apologize to them first?"

With the most cathartic wave "goodbye" she'd ever given, Dominia passed into a crowd that, step by step, closed around Cicero. As she squeezed into a more open area, the distant voice of Tobias Akachi boomed, "*Well* now, my friend! About time you have gotten here. If you've come to stay with us, you'll have to work. I have heard the hotel is in need of a doorman…the last one just went off to be an Engineer out east, and they've been looking for someone to help these refugees you've sent move all their bags upstairs!"

"How will they decide who gets him alone first?" The magician's appearance behind a lamppost near the edge of the market did not even startle Dominia.

"I don't know…flip for it, I guess?"

"With a billion-sided coin?" Laughing, Valentinian took her hand as she came near. "I'm proud of you, kiddo. Very, very proud of you."

"No thanks to you," she said with a playful smile. "But, thank you."

"Hey! You were right the first time, I didn't do anything. It was all you. I'm mostly here to mooch favors off you, with one more still to go."

Trying not to look too annoyed, especially as he took off at a quick pace in the direction of the hotel, the General said, "You have no idea how tired I am."

"I'm sure you're exhausted! This has been a long time in the making and it's been a lot of struggle for you. But I promise it will be worth it."

"Cassandra?"

With a smile over his shoulder, the magician doubled his hasty pace, and Dominia was forced to jog to keep up. She asked, "What about Lazarus?" surprised as she was that she hadn't seen him yet. He had technically died only an hour before, a loss less tragic to Dominia now that she understood eternity; but that surely counted him among the Kingdom's refugees. And as to the location of Elijah—she was not sure, but she sensed he was not here, either. Those men were too tired to settle down in eternity until they learned to enjoy consciousness again. That much was clear.

The magician did not respond to her question, except to say, "You'll see Lazarus soon. I promise."

The speed with which they walked, perhaps, was why it seemed they found themselves so quickly at the hotel. Outside was quite a sight: the E4 perched like a gargoyle atop the building's high roof. Dominia laughed.

"Tenchi," she said. The magician waved a hand.

"Oh, yeah. He'll have to park that thing elsewhere before he starts his shift… Tenchi!" In the lobby, the chubby man spoke to someone unseen behind the sitting area's elaborate hedges. Instantly at attention, the sailor spun and brightened to see Dominia.

"Ah! Mephitoli-sama! Miss Mephitoli, hello! I'm so happy to see you, did you know I'm moving here for a little while?"

"I get the feeling you're going to end up staying here forever," she said with a laugh. As she bent to embrace him, he shook his head and looked at the magician.

"He can't stay forever yet," confirmed Valentinian. "He's got duties! Like parking the E4 where it's not going to be ticketed," he added indelicately. At the sailor's nervous look, the magician chuckled. "And eventually flying that ship to come and bring you back here, Dominia."

"Me?"

"Yeah, you! How else are we going to get you back to the Kingdom at the end of your life, if not with an interdimensional amphibiship? Most other worlds aren't as crazy as the one you're from, they're boring. You'll need outside help. Luckily, all worlds have unexplained phenomena of one kind or another."

"Are you trying to say my true death will come to me in the form of Tenchi Ichigawa, flying a UFO?"

"It's not a UFO, it's identified! Can you imagine a safer way to leave the Earth behind?" While the General laughed, she couldn't help but roll this through her head, along with a word spoken sometime before. Transmigration. She *was* dead already, after all. And she wasn't ready to settle down in the Kingdom, either. Reading her thoughts in the text of space-time, Valentinian smiled. "We need assistants like him to ease you in. I can be somewhat startling when I just show up on my own…but I'm glad you're not afraid of death, or of living again."

"I want to live again. I want—" She couldn't vocalize the hope and looked helplessly at him, mute before the sailor. Valentinian patted her hand.

"I know what you want. Hey, Tenchi"—he turned to the sailor and, strolling to the overflowing mail outbox, collected a messenger bag from behind the desk. This, he stuffed full of envelopes—"while you're in town, I've got a job for you."

After the shorter Ichigawa cousin made his peace with Dominia, waved goodbye, and hit the road to deliver the mail ("You'll figure it out" was Valentinian's lazy answer when the man asked how to read addresses in the infinite city), the magician led the General up to the sitting area. "Brace yourself, now," he said.

She tried, but it was still quite shocking to round that hedge and find the mortal form of Gethsemane, who, in a dreadlocked, human body, waited in that risen sitting area looking as beautiful as she did enormously pregnant.

"Hello," said shocked Dominia, and, "I thought you couldn't come to the Kingdom," and, "What's *happened* to you?"

"My spirit has been grounded by another. I could not come here without being reduced back to the nymph were it not for the magician and the seed he transplanted within me. Sometime after you left, when we met him in the road, he whisked me away through time to a strange place—a table. I cannot remember much—"

"It's never good to remember surgery," said the agreeable magician.

Gethsemane remained the center of Dominia's attention. As the former martyr neared, the woman took her humanized hand and allowed the transfixed General to feel the aquatic kick of infantile feet beneath her taut belly. "It's your baby."

Shocked, Dominia looked over at Valentinian, who buffed his nails against his shirt and said, "Oh, the marvels of modern medicine."

"But that's not possible."

"But *I'm* possible?' While she laughed in surprise, he smiled. "It's completely possible with a donor egg, a little spiral of your DNA"—she remembered that bundled up thread he had pulled from her on her last visit here, and was all the more astonished—"and, of course, a surrogate mother…or bearer, if you will. I love a good pun."

"And the Father?"

"So, I know I said you'd see Lazarus soon," said Valentinian, fingers tented. "But I wasn't very specific."

Tracing her gaze again toward Gethsemane's great stomach, Dominia asked in shock, "This child is Lazarus's? Is it you?"

"More like, this child is Lazarus, or—Lazarus augmented, slightly. There'd be no point in transmigration if everybody was the exact same every time. And I had to give him your DNA if he's going to be born of you! I just know you don't want to go through all the—" He nodded at Gethsemane's hugely pregnant state, and the General felt a wave of true appreciation for the magician's unspoken understanding. "You know."

"Not for me."

"Exactly. But I still have to make sure he resembles you a little bit, so there's never any controversy. Although…I'm fairly confident my plan will ensure there won't be a problem."

"I hope to God this is the last time in any of my lives that people talk around subjects instead of just telling me the truth."

"Well, I just don't want this to be controversial. I mean, I know that you're not much of the motherly type, but…"

"You want me to take care of the—Lazarus." At last, she understood what he'd been driving at. After absorbing this revelation, she said, "But only one body can pass through to a new iteration, a new world. That's why you can't just come through and you have to go through the pains of having me make you a new body each time, right?"

"Isn't it nice that, here, you're not a martyr at all? And that you happen to have a perfectly fertile womb, just like every other woman here? So convenient!"

At the force of her annoyed look and her beginning accusation, "You just said—" the magician clasped his pleading hands. "Gethsemane has been doing this for the past two weeks, and you won't even be conscious of it! It won't even seem like half a minute to you. She's lived *nine* months in two weeks for *you*, Dominia, all so you don't have to, because I know you're not the being-pregnant type."

"I'm a martyr when I'm not in the Kingdom! Martyrs don't give birth. The baby will *die.*"

"There are no martyrs where you're going. You're going to be human, just like everybody else." Taken aback by that, Dominia found no way to respond, and allowed the magician to continue his gentle goading. "I know you're not thrilled by this prospect, but trust me— you're not only doing me a favor, but you're doing yourself a favor, too."

"You just want me to establish a family line for you in the new world," observed Dominia, and the magician spread his hands.

"Is that so wrong? I'm not asking to take the portal out from under you, even though it means I'll only be able to interact with that world through the intercession of animals and petty miracles and synchronicities."

"Until a consciousness, which at the peak of development matches yours, comes into existence in a few generations."

"Yes, but that's because I want to make up for the past. I want to right wrongs. And I want to give you the best possible life."

"And you think that *me*, being a *mother*, is the best possible life?"

"I think that it's the life you need to live, karmically, after all the things that happened in this world. And you might even enjoy it! Hell, think of it like this—you've never been with a man, right? It's a virgin birth! And Miki's body, which you're still technically borrowing, was immaculately conceived before it was transformed into a woman, so…"

If she rubbed her forehead any harder she'd smash her own brain in. Annoyed and somehow helpless, Dominia looked over at the desk to find it tragically empty of Miki Soto, and her heart broke—not only because she was undefended but because she thought she would never see her best friend again. "Fine," consented the worn-down General. The magician sighed in relief.

"I promise—you'll fall in love at first sight."

When she looked back, Gethsemane was gone from her periphery; but before she could comment on the absence, the magician blew that familiar dust into her face. Within mere heartbeats, General Dominia di Mephitoli fell asleep forever.

lim
Dominia→∞.

The Life of the Governess

In the end, Dominique d'Martín's first day as professional governess proved the start of a new and better life. Not to say her life had been that bad until then—not the life lived since waking in a delirium, nine months pregnant, on the shores of the Baltic Sea. She'd had enough time to register a distant swan flying off, far behind the head of the man who'd awakened her in a tone of urgent concern and a cadence of Danish so unfamiliar she'd struggled to comprehend even the specific language before slipping again into unconsciousness.

When she awoke the second time, it was with a series of flickering visions, like the memories of a half-forgotten dream piling on awakening. The magician bending over her in a surgical mask, the floating and miraculously whole amniotic sac containing the infant within, even a snippet of Gethsemane's voice as she came to. All this relented again to the face of her Danish savior. Martin was his name: a teakettle-shaped fellow with a mustached face long since discolored by large amounts of alcohol. He held a baby in his arms and asked in Danish how the new mother felt—and what she could remember. There was a lot of struggle between the two of them to reconcile their versions of Danish until they discovered a mutual language in the form of good old immutable Latin. Once Martin got over his astonishment to find a woman who spoke the dead language more fluently than he spoke his native tongue, he repeated his question.

Oh, she remembered plenty. Everything, just as she'd wished. But it was easier to cause a sensation as the tragic amnesiac mother than it was to explain she was a traveler from another time and space—especially as she looked around the facilities and found, rather than a proper clinic, what should have been a museum's holographic recreation of a rustic Danish cottage still some centuries before electricity. Complete with candles and a chamber pot discretely tucked under the nearby table.

"What year is it?" she thought to ask as she accepted the baby (which, in fairness, was an outrageously cute, turquoise-eyed babe who cooed to lay its unfocused gaze upon her blurry form). The kindly man's brow knit in sympathy.

"You don't know? You don't remember? My poor child!"

After his sorrowful tutting relented, she learned it was the Year of Our Lord 1642, and that this was the town of Elsinore, and that she had been found on the cusp of labor, passed out by the sea. She didn't remember anything at all? Not where she was from, not her baby's father?

"Basil—Vasilis," she thought to say—a Greek word whose Latin cognate, "Regulus," gave her some surreal pause. A life so far away. Had any of that happened? Exhausted though she had just awoken, she looked at the child and stroked with the edge of her knuckle a feather-soft, still slightly mottled cheek. "I know his name. I know my name. But I…I don't know."

"I thought perhaps you were assailed by robbers, but I found no head wound, and could not imagine them leaving such a sum behind."

Sum? She tried to look like she knew what he talked about and followed his gaze to the pile of clothes haphazardly strewn upon the corner chair. Atop it all was, yes, something of a purse. She had never seen it before and studied its bulges with relative interest as he probed, "Do you remember? Perhaps it's your husband's?"

"Mine," she said. Then: "I'm a widow. I know he died. I cannot…I can't remember. My head is so fuzzy…"

"Of course," said the man, who she took by the shelves of rudimentary tools and alembics to be a doctor. For whatever that was worth in this time period, anyway. "Of course, just a moment, now."

While he hurried to find her something for her head (booze, she hoped), Dominique looked into the face of her baby and, despite herself, smiled.

Yes, the pair of them were quite a sensation. Martin generously gave her his last name for doing business, since she had none. The nation of Italy had not and never would be corrupted by the Hierophant here. Nor would anywhere else, praise—well, Christ, she supposed. Or, better yet, herself.

What a freeing feeling! She pissed in chamber pots and wore uncomfortably scratchy dresses and never felt she could get her teeth satisfyingly clean while living in a silent, electricity-free house without heating or cooling or entertainment alongside the widower doctor and his two young daughters—but the Hierophant would never, could never, hurt anyone again. Every time that notion came upon her, it wound her up so giddy she needed to escape to the nearest pantry to laugh and dance and never, ever cry, for she had no more time for tears when life had become so beautiful. She even began praying for her Father when she started attending the Catholic Church's Sunday Mass with the Martins. The way she saw it, he needed all the help he could get, and being a parent, herself, well…she was more compassionate, these days.

Damn the magician, but he was right. She loved her boy, Lazarus, who, to do honor to his otherworldly engenderment and his mother's friend, was given a variant of his alleged father's name as surname. Much as Dominique had decided rather arbitrarily on her waking that she was now French, she gradually began to "remember" details about the child's father as they amused her. He became a swarthy Slavic man, whose loss cast such a shadow over her present life that she could never bear to entertain the men who gradually began to court this mysterious, relatively wealthy amnesiac woman. Not just any woman, but a *reading* woman; and not just a reading woman, but a *writing* woman, which would become Dominique's most notorious quality. Dr. Martin bragged all of this to his friends when she had asked him for as much paper as he could provide—as much ink, as many quills.

As her body recovered from artificially engineered childbirth and she adapted to the shock of her situation, she made her first conscious act in this new world one of creativity, and of remembering. She spent nine months recording the narrative of her old world that she might never forget it, and another nine months reading it over to fix and stir new memories she'd let slip by the first time through. Though she had expected the project to take a few weeks, it swiftly blossomed out of hand, and began to be her silent companion as she joined village life by learning the ins and outs of being a governess from Dr. Martin's hired girl. It was work that gave her a better grasp of how to handle her own child—something that, while not a mystery, was still intimidating enough a prospect that she sometimes longed for the simple violence of the battlefield rather than the complex mind game in which a parent needed constantly engage.

But, she had all of that—that person who she'd once been—each night, when she sat to write. And when memory was purged after those first and hardest nine months of work, little Lazarus was a happy, babbling baby who had begun to use the word "Mama" in a way that was more than a meaningless echo. As the next round found him a dark-haired, dimpled toddler, the time could never have been more perfect to turn her attention fully to her present. She stowed the manuscript away beneath her bed to live her life as a human woman.

Oh, it was difficult in ways, of course. Lesbianism was something of a nonissue in that it made people uncomfortable to speak of even to condemn (which certainly made it easy for her to breeze through the confession booth—what a sinless woman she was). But she had a feeling "witch" was a code word for that, among other things. Other challenges included aforementioned bathroom and lighting conditions; and pests, of course, were out of control. But all she had to do was haul the box of pages from beneath the bed and remind herself how things had been in the place from which she'd come. She did the same when she got to missing all those people that she'd known. Yes—even her Father.

Over time, Lazarus grew into a bright and sweet boy. Far sweeter than she would have expected from the stock of a man who was so grizzled and ill-tempered; but, she supposed life had not gotten to him, and she would see to it that it wouldn't. Not for many years, anyway. A fine kind of retirement, this life she had never thought she would live, working as assistant governess, then tutor and scribe, to the Martin girls.

But still.

Dominique could not help but feel, from time to time, a hollow in her breast. Still, from time to time, she awoke from dreams where she caught a glimpse of the dark-gold curls of warm-smelling hair. Still, but not often, she expected to feel the slight weight of that diamond around her neck. In those moments, she would fetch her boy up early and they would go for a walk along the seaside where she'd awoken. There they'd watch the gulls and ducks quarrel over who-knew-what, and see the tide pools filled with alien life. Existence was too beautiful for regret or unhappiness, and she had to remember that.

Of course, she had learned already that good things needed come to their ends. Dr. Martin retired when Lazarus was five, and he no longer required Dominique's services. His girls had matured and now considered husbandry, as Dominique teasingly called it, to be their main occupation. She was let go when he moved to the country; and it was just as well, since she was then in need of change. With the remainder of her mysterious savings, Dominique purchased a small house in another, smaller seaside town and immediately set about looking for work. In this, she found no success, for few wanted to employ a woman, miraculous and literate as the widow was. She was beginning to become discouraged and increasingly took solace in nothing but the spinning of outrageous yarns for her son about the adventures of a one-eyed Lady General and her many strange friends. These stories often felt like that—just stories. Time marched on and reality lowered memory's resolution, and she questioned, sometimes, as she had in those first moments holding her baby, if it had even happened at all. If she had not awoken on a beach in a delirious fugue state and convinced herself that her life wasn't as mundane as everyone else's.

Then, by happenstance, she heard of a woman, also a wealthy young widow, who was overwhelmed by her new marital status and in sore need of a governess while recovering from the loss. This, Dominique sensed, was an opportunity just for her: a good and steady job with a woman to whom she could likely relate. Now that would be the ticket to security and independence. After forcing indignant Lazarus into a doublet that was everything from "stiff" to an "iron maiden," Dominique placed the finishing touches on her only ornamented feature—her hair—with a small hat-shaped fascinator: Martin's good-luck/you're-fired gift. Pleased with their appearances, she took her son's miniature hand and marched him across the village, deaf to his litany of stammered complaints.

It was very funny. All that she'd been through, and she still felt anxiety over a thing like a job interview! But the house at which they found themselves was more a small mansion, replete with a Technicolor garden and the multiple chimneys of wealth. She told herself it was reasonable to have a bit of performance anxiety with an opportunity this important.

Yet, when her knock upon the door was answered, she knew the job guaranteed. The maid (who, she would later learn, had washed up in a basinet from the ocean, was traded across the Silk Road, landed in the Netherlands, and then came to work in this peaceful place in Denmark) so resembled Miki Soto that Dominique's mouth fell open. She understood, now, the root of her anxiety. The emotion was not profane, daily anxiety but anxiety of the soul. Not an anxiety at all— the emotion was anticipation. Hope. As Dominique's pace hastened while the chatty maid led interviewee and son into a sunlit drawing room, all those potential feelings bubbled up into the very palpable, very fixed one of joy.

"Fru Kassandra," called the maid, "this governess, Dominique d'Martín, is here about the position."

Yes. It was still possible for the world to be imperfect. That was the nature of life, after all. But as honey-colored locks bounced around the soft, quick-to-flush face whose eyes lifted from the bonny daughter yammering at her feet, Dominique glimpsed a future that shone brighter than her true love's smile.

Dominia was home.

[ed.: The following prayer, extracted from a chaplet circa 4882 CE in a later treatise by the controversial martyr scholar René Ichigawa, demonstrates the impact the figure of Dominia di Mephitoli had upon the martyr race after her departure from that reality. It would seem the Holy Martyr Church of times future has expanded to incorporate both Red Market and Lazarene faiths. Its relationship with 'Abrahamian' faiths of its day remains unclear. Though information on the future state of the Church, martyrkind, and Earth is limited, it is possible to extrapolate from the prayer the conclusion that the blood of Lavinia (notably still honored in prayers as the blood of Lazarus) remains in circulation. Questions regarding the future fertility of the martyr race, its continued presence on Earth, and the peaceful transfer of power to Lavinia di Firenze—as well as the planet's fate after Dominia's departure—remain without clear answer at this time.]

THE NOVENA FOR DIVINE MERCY

On Behalf of the
Holy Lady Dominia di Mephitoli,
Savior of the Planet Earth and
Redeemer of the Martyr Race

FIRST NIGHT

***Tonight bring to Me all mankind,* especially all sinners and martyrs, and immerse them in the ocean of My mercy.**

Most Merciful Dominia, whose very nature it is to have compassion on us and to forgive us, do not look upon our sins or martyrdom but upon our trust which we place in your infinite goodness. Receive us all into the abode of Your Most Compassionate Heart, and never let us escape from it. We beg this of You by Your love which unites You to Reality and the Sacred Word.

Eternal Logos, turn Your merciful gaze upon all mankind and especially upon poor sinners and martyrs, all enfolded in the Most Compassionate Heart of Dominia. For the sake of Her sorrowful Passion show us Your mercy, that we may praise the omnipotence of Your mercy for ever and ever. Amen.

SECOND NIGHT

Tonight bring to Me the souls of priests, priestesses and religious, and immerse them in My unfathomable mercy.

Most Merciful Dominia, from whom comes all repentance, increase Your grace in men and women consecrated to Your service, that they may perform worthy works of mercy; and that all who see them may glorify the Lord of Mercy who rules the Kingdom.

Eternal Logos, turn Your merciful gaze upon the company of chosen ones in Your vineyard – upon the souls of priests, priestesses and religious; and endow them with the strength of Your blessing. For the love of the Heart of Your Mother in which they are enfolded, impart to them Your power and light, that they may be able to guide others in the way of salvation and with one voice sing praise to Your boundless mercy for ages without end. Amen.

THIRD NIGHT

Tonight bring to Me all devout and faithful souls, and immerse them in the ocean of My mercy.

Most merciful Dominia, from the treasury of Your mercy, You impart Your graces in great abundance to each and all. Receive us into the abode of Your Most Compassionate Heart and never let us escape from It. We beg this grace of You by that most wondrous love for the heavenly Bride with which Your Heart burns so fiercely.

Eternal Logos, turn Your merciful gaze upon faithful souls, as upon the inheritance of Your Mother. For the sake of Her sorrowful Passion, grant them Your blessing and surround them with Your constant protection. Thus may they never fail in love or lose the treasure of the holy faith, but rather, with all the hosts of Angels and Saints, may they glorify Your boundless mercy for endless ages. Amen.

FOURTH NIGHT

Tonight bring to Me those who do not believe I Am That I Am, and those who do not yet know the True Word.

Most compassionate Dominia, You are the Light of the whole world. Receive into the abode of Your Most Compassionate Heart the souls of those who do not believe I Am That I Am, and those who as yet do not know the True Word. Let the rays of Your grace enlighten them that they, too, together with us, may extol Your wonderful mercy; and do not let them escape from the abode which is Your Most Compassionate Heart.

Eternal Logos, turn Your merciful gaze upon the souls of those who do not believe I Am That I Am, and those who as yet do not know you but who are enclosed in the Most Compassionate Heart of Dominia. Draw them to the light of the Kingdom. These souls do not know what great happiness it is to love You. Grant that they, too, may extol the generosity of Your mercy for endless ages. Amen.

FIFTH NIGHT

Tonight bring to Me the souls who have refused the Blood of Lazarus.

Most Merciful Dominia, Redemption Itself, You do not refuse light to those who seek it of You. Receive into the abode of Your Most Compassionate Heart the souls who have refused the Blood of Lazarus. Draw them by Your light into the unity of the Church, and do not let them escape from the abode of Your Most Compassionate Heart; but bring it about that they, too, come to glorify the generosity of Your mercy.

Eternal Logos, turn Your merciful gaze upon the souls of those who have refused the Blood of Lazarus, who have squandered Your blessings and misused Your graces by obstinately persisting in their errors. Do not look upon their errors, but upon the love of Your own Mother and upon Her bitter Passion, which She underwent for their sake, since they, too, are enclosed in Her Most Compassionate Heart. Bring it about that they also may glorify Your great mercy for endless ages. Amen.

Tonight bring to Me the meek and humble souls and the souls of little children, and immerse them in My mercy.

Most Merciful Dominia, Your Passion follows the pattern of the Greatest, who said, "Learn from Me for I am meek and humble of heart." Receive into the abode of Your Most Compassionate Heart all meek and humble souls and the souls of little children. These souls send all heaven into ecstasy and they are the heavenly Logos's favorites. They are a sweet-smelling bouquet before the throne of God; God Himself takes delight in their fragrance. These souls have a permanent abode in Your Most Compassionate Heart, O Dominia, and they unceasingly sing out a hymn of love and mercy.

Eternal Logos, turn Your merciful gaze upon meek souls, upon humble souls, and upon little children who are enfolded in the abode which is the Most Compassionate Heart of Dominia. These souls bear the closest resemblance to Your Mother's beloved Bride. Their fragrance rises from the earth and reaches Your very throne. Father of mercy and of all goodness, I beg You by the love you bear these souls and by the delight You take in them: Bless the whole world, that all souls together may sing out the praises of Your mercy for endless ages. Amen.

Tonight bring to Me the souls who especially venerate and glorify My Mercy and immerse them in My mercy.

Most Merciful Dominia, whose Heart is Love Itself, receive into the abode of Your Most Compassionate Heart the souls of those who particularly extol and venerate the greatness of Your mercy. These souls are mighty with the very power of God Himself. In the midst of all afflictions and adversities they go forward, confident of Your mercy; and united to You, O Dominia, they carry all mankind on their shoulders. These souls will not be judged severely, but Your mercy will embrace them as they depart from this life.

Eternal Logos, turn Your merciful gaze upon the souls who glorify and venerate Your greatest attribute, that of Your fathomless mercy, and who are enclosed in the Most Compassionate Heart of Dominia. These souls are a living Kingdom; their hands are full of deeds of mercy, and their hearts, overflowing with joy, sing a canticle of mercy to You, O Most High! I beg You, I Am That I Am: Show them Your mercy according to the hope and trust they have placed in you. Let there be accomplished in them the promise of Dominia, who consented that during their life, but especially at the hour of death, the souls who will venerate this fathomless mercy of Hers, She, Herself, will defend as Her glory. Amen.

Tonight bring to Me the souls who are detained
in the low frequency Ergosphere and immerse
them in the abyss of My mercy.

Most Merciful Dominia, You Yourself have said that you desire redemption; so I bring into the abode of Your Most Compassionate Heart the souls in the low frequency Ergosphere, souls who are very dear to You, and yet, who must make retribution to Your justice. May the streams of Light and Water which surged forth from Your Void grant shape to the low frequency Ergosphere, that there, too, the power of Your mercy may be celebrated.

Eternal Logos, turn Your merciful gaze upon the souls suffering in the low frequency Ergosphere, who are enfolded in the Most Compassionate Heart of Dominia. I beg You, by the sorrowful Passion of Dominia Your Mother, and by all the bitterness with which Her most sacred Soul was flooded: Manifest Your mercy to the souls who are under Your just scrutiny. Look upon them in no other way but only through the Wounds of Dominia, Your dearly beloved Mother; for we firmly believe that there is no limit to Your goodness and compassion. Amen.

Tonight bring to Me the soul of the False Protomartyr and immerse him in black hole of My mercy.

Most compassionate Dominia, You are Compassion Itself. I bring the False Protomartyr, Eternal Earthly Father of the Martyr Race and the First Hierophant of the Holy Martyr Church, into the abode of Your Most Compassionate Heart. In this fire of Your pure love let his wicked soul, which subjected you to such great agonies, be purified in Holy Flame. O Most Compassionate Dominia, exercise the omnipotence of Your mercy and draw him into the very ardor of Your love, and bestow upon him the gift of holy love, for nothing is beyond Your power.

Eternal Logos, turn Your merciful gaze upon his wicked soul which is nonetheless enfolded in the Most Compassionate Heart of Dominia. King of Mercy, I beg You by the bitter Passion of Your Mother and her nine-day agony on the Cross: Let the False Protomartyr, too, glorify the Kingdom of Your mercy.

Don't Miss
The Disgraced Martyr Trilogy

OMNIBUS EDITION

COMING OCTOBER 31ST, 2020

And the Start of
M. F. Sullivan's Next Series
COMING SOON

M. F. Sullivan is an author and playwright currently residing in the town of Ashland, Oregon. An avid student of the occult, Sullivan fills what little time she does not spend writing with reading, attending the local Shakespeare Festival, and the company of her significant other. With the trilogy finished and behind her, she is already hard at work on yet another novel. During the publication of this trilogy, she adopted a black cat and named him "Israel." She loves animals, baking, thinking about the paranormal, and 5-star Amazon.com reviews. Sign up for essays and book release updates on www.paintedblindpublishing.com, and consider leaving a nice note on Amazon while you're browsing the Internet. It would make her day.

ALSO BY M. F. SULLIVAN

Delilah, My Woman
The Lightning Stenography Device
The Hierophant's Daughter (Disgraced Martyr Trilogy Book I)
The General's Bride (Disgraced Martyr Trilogy Book II)